And The Bride Wore Plaid

"More than anything in the world, I want to kiss you. Right now. May I?"

Kat blinked. "A kiss?"

Without giving her time to react beyond a simple gasp, he lowered his mouth to hers and kissed her, expecting shocked surprise.

But instead, despite her flushed cheeks, she met his gaze directly and said in a rather breathless voice, "Bloody hell, not again."

He pulled back so that he could see fully into the maid's face. "I beg your pardon, but did you say, 'Bloody hell, not again'?"

"Aye," she said, her gaze even with his. Her lips were swollen slightly, her chest still moving rapidly up and down.

"What do you mean 'again'?" he demanded.

She merely sighed. "Every time Strathmore has a guest, I get mauled. I am damned tired of it."

Devon's lips twitched. The maid's breath might be sweet, but her language was not. "If you don't wish to be mauled, then perhaps you should try to be a little less tempting."

By Karen Hawkins

AND THE BRIDE WORE PLAID
HOW TO TREAT A LADY
CONFESSIONS OF A SCOUNDREL
AN AFFAIR TO REMEMBER
THE SEDUCTION OF SARA
A BELATED BRIDE
THE ABDUCTION OF JULIA

ATTENTION: ORGANIZATIONS AND CORPORATIONS
Most Avon Books paperbacks are available at special quantity discounts for bulk purchases for sales promotions, premiums, or fund-raising. For information, please call or write:

Special Markets Department, HarperCollins Publishers, Inc., 10 East 53rd Street, New York, N.Y. 10022–5299.
Telephone: (212) 207–7528. Fax: (212) 207–7222.

KAREN HAWKINS

And The Bride Wore Plaid

AVON BOOKS
An Imprint of HarperCollinsPublishers

This is a work of fiction. Names, characters, places, and incidents are products of the author's imagination or are used fictitiously and are not to be construed as real. Any resemblance to actual events, locales, organizations, or persons, living or dead, is entirely coincidental.

AVON BOOKS
An Imprint of HarperCollins*Publishers*
10 East 53rd Street
New York, New York 10022-5299

Copyright © 2004 by Karen Hawkins
Party Crashers copyright © 2004 by Stephanie Bond Hauck; *And the Bride Wore Plaid* copyright © 2004 by Karen Hawkins; *I'm No Angel* copyright © 2004 by Patti Berg; *A Perfect Bride* copyright © 2004 by Sandra Kleinschmit
ISBN: 0-06-051408-6
www.avonromance.com

All rights reserved. No part of this book may be used or reproduced in any manner whatsoever without written permission, except in the case of brief quotations embodied in critical articles and reviews. For information address Avon Books, an Imprint of HarperCollins Publishers.

First Avon Books paperback printing: June 2004

Avon Trademark Reg. U.S. Pat. Off. and in Other Countries, Marca Registrada, Hecho en U.S.A.
HarperCollins® is a registered trademark of HarperCollins Publishers Inc.

Printed in the U.S.A.

10 9 8 7 6 5 4 3 2

If you purchased this book without a cover, you should be aware that this book is stolen property. It was reported as "unsold and destroyed" to the publisher, and neither the author nor the publisher has received any payment for this "stripped book."

Chapter 1

I pity people who think to fool their fellow man. Take poor Mary Gillenwather. She stuffed the front of her gown with paper in an effort to appear better endowed. We all knew she'd done it, but no one said a word; you simply cannot work that sort of thing into a genteel conversation. But it wasn't necessary after all. Last night, at the Pooles' dinner party, she sneezed and dropped an entire issue of the Morning Post *into her soup.*

Lady Mountjoy to her friend
Miss Clarissa Fullerton,
while sipping chocolate at Betty's Tea House

*I*t was raining. Not a soft, whispering rain, the kind that mists the world into a greener, lusher place, but a harsh, heavy deluge that sopped the earth and saturated the very air with unending grayness. Water pooled, collected, swirled, swelled, and then burst into fields, raged through ditches, and rampaged across roads.

It was in this heavy, unending torrent that the

lumbering carriage finally reached its destination late at night. The driver and footmen were exhausted, the horses straining heavily as they pulled the mud-coated ornate wheels through the muck and mire that had once been a road.

Ten minutes later, around the curve of a hill, appeared a looming stone castle that stretched up into the blackness of night. The coachman didn't even bother to wipe the rain from his face as he halted the carriage at the door. Too wet to do more than tilt his hat brim to empty it of whatever water had collected, he squinted at the dark edifice that loomed in front of them. "Gor," he said softly, awe overwhelming the tiredness of his voice.

Beside him on the seat was Paul the footman, a relatively new arrival to Mr. Devon St. John's rather considerable staff. Paul was inclined to agree with John the coachman. "Dark, it is. It fair makes me shiver in me boots. Are ye sure we've come to the right place?"

"Mr. St. John said to go to Kilkairn Castle and to Kilkairn Castle we've come." The coachman shook his head disgustedly. "Though to tell ye the truth, I think Mr. St. John has bumped his noggin."

"Why do ye think that?"

"Just look at the facts. First he leaves his own brother's weddin' afore it even begins and then he orders us to bring him here, drivin' through godforsaken rain fer days on end. And when we do get to this lumbering pile of stone, there's nary a light on!" He sourly regarded the bleak building in front of them. "Looks deserted and hainted by ghosties, if I ain't mistaken."

Paul stood, stealing yet another glance at the dark edifice before them. While he wasn't a great believer in ghosties, the castle definitely left him with an uneasy, spine-tingling sensation that was as unnerving as the constant pour of rain.

Biting back a sigh, Paul made his way down from the seat, landing in a huge puddle of muck that sank his wet boots up to his ankles. "The drive's a rank mess."

"I only hopes they've a barn, though I daresay it is as leaky as a sieve, judging from the looks of things. Didn't they knowed we was comin'?"

"They was tol'. I posted the letter for Mr. St. John meself." Paul tugged his hat lower, though it was so wet it no longer protected him from anything the elements had to offer. He hoped the owner of the castle was not as ramshackle as his edifice and had a place prepared for them all.

Holding this warming thought in place, the footman trudged back to open the door for his master, stopping to collect a lantern from a side hook. It took a while to get the blasted lamp lit.

He carried the lantern to the door and hung it on a hook there, the golden pool of light greatly diminished by the weather. He tugged on the door handle, opened it, and then let down the steps.

Inside the plush carriage sprawled a long, elegant figure dressed in a well-fitted coat and breeches, sparkling top boots, and a perfectly starched and folded cravat, set with a blue sapphire. The jewel echoed the master's blue eyes in an uncanny manner. There was no mistaking a St. John—black hair and blue eyes, a square, determined chin, and a sharp wit marked them all.

At the moment, though, Paul couldn't make out his master's face in the shadows, which left him momentarily anxious. Though it was rare that Mr. St. John took an irritation, he could be cold and cutting when occasion called for it. Paul cleared his throat. "Mr. St. John, we have arrived at Kilkairn Castle."

The figure inside stirred, stretching lazily. "It's about time. I fear I had fallen into a stupor when—good God!" Mr. Devon St. John's blue eyes widened as he looked at Paul. "You're drowned!"

"Just a bit wet, sir."

"That is an understatement if I've ever heard one. Go ahead and say it— it's wretched, horrid, awful, godforsaken rain and you wonder why we're arriving so late at night."

Paul hesitated, then nodded. "Aye, sir. All that and more."

"Indeed," the master said. "The reason I pushed us so hard was because I mistakenly thought we'd be able to outrun the family curse."

"Curse, sir?"

"The St. John talisman ring. It's a curse if there ever was one. It seems that whoever holds the bloody thing is doomed to wed."

Paul had heard of the St. John talisman ring, and it

sounded horrid indeed. "Do ye hold the ring, sir?"

"Unknowingly, I've held it since before we left England. My brother Chase hid it in the blasted carriage. He must have known I'd flee before the wedding, the bastard. I didn't discover it until we were well on our way."

Paul shook his head. "Then ye're doomed."

St. John smiled, a peculiarly sweet smile, one that made Paul stand a little straighter despite his tiredness and the wetness that trickled down his back. "Like hell I'm doomed. I was not made for marriage. Not now, not ever. I'm afraid the fates will have to wait a few weeks to deliver their verdict."

"Weeks, sir?"

"Until I can get this blasted ring into my oldest brother's hands. Marcus is the last of us to remain unwed other than myself."

"God help him then, sir. Marriage is a horrible thing indeed." Paul shuddered, thinking of all the near misses he'd had. "I don't envy you, sir."

The master's blue gaze twinkled. "I don't envy myself, Paul. At least not on this occasion."

Not a single one of Paul's previous employers had bothered to remember his name, so he was impressed that Mr. St. John had bothered to do so. Not that his new master was overly familiar in any way; he wasn't. He might stand for an occasional exchange of quips, but he brooked no nonsense when it came to disrespect, thievery, or slovenly behavior.

It was that special combination of familiarity and

stern but fair grace that made Paul and all the other servants loyal unto death for Mr. Devon St. John. It was well known throughout the servant circles in London that there was no more plum spot to work. Had Mr. St. John's last footman not succumbed to an unfortunate stomach complaint that had turned fatal, Paul would not now be in such a wondrous position. Even with the rain, he could scarcely believe his luck.

Smiling, Paul opened the door wider. "The rain has let up, so ye shouldn't get too wet."

"Thank God." St. John placed his hat over his black hair, grimacing as he stepped into the thick mud. "Tipton will be appalled when he beholds my lovely new boots."

Tipton was Mr. St. John's valet, and a more starched, outraged person Paul had yet to meet. "Indeed, sir. Wouldn't surprise me a bit if the sight of yer boots don't put him to tears." Paul grabbed the lantern and held it aloft to light the way as they proceeded to the large wooden doors.

"I am sure Tipton will not hesitate to tell me what he thinks of the mud upon my boots. He has a tongue in his head that could scorch your soul if you were so silly as to bare it."

They reached the portico and stepped beneath the overhang, the rain dripping steadily behind them. St. John stood on the covered steps and frowned up at the stone castle. "Bloody hell, the place looks deserted. Is no one up?"

Paul set aside the lantern and went to the large knocker. "Per'aps they thought ye'd be delayed 'cause of the rain. I'll knock and see if we can't rouse someone." He grasped the knocker firmly and rapped. After several more raps, each progressively harder, a light finally appeared between the cracks of the large oak doors.

After what seemed an eternity, the door creaked open to reveal a rather scrawny-looking woman wearing a coat hastily donned over a night rail, large unlaced boots sticking out from beneath the hem. An assortment of keys hanging about her neck on a cord proclaimed her the housekeeper.

She stood in the opening, a brace of candles in one hand, her thick, gray braid flopped over one shoulder, squinting at the two men as if they were gargoyles come to life. "What do ye want?" she asked in a thick Scottish brogue.

"Is this Kilkairn Castle?" Paul asked in a haughty voice that made Devon smile.

"Indeed 'tis. And who might ye be?"

The footman drew himself up to his most impressive height and announced, "Mr. Devon St. John to see Viscount Strathmore."

The housekeeper's gaze traveled from Paul to Devon. After a grudging moment, she stepped out of the doorway and motioned for them to follow her. "I don't know any St. Johns, but ye're welcome to step inside a bit whilst we sort it out." She set about lighting the lamps in the hallway, muttering as she went. "Where is that blasted butler? Never where he should be, that's where."

James, one of the St. John underfootmen, came with the luggage. Devon watched as James stacked the valises beside the door, bowed, then left. Really, it had been a simple plan—all Devon had wished to do was leave England for a few weeks. A few simple weeks, and all would be well.

But fate was not cooperating. First the rain, then he'd found that blasted ring hidden among the carriage blankets on the seat, and now no one was awake to greet him at Kilkairn Castle. What was supposed to be a haven was rapidly becoming something quite different.

Devon met the minatory stare of the housekeeper and managed a smile. She sniffed and turned away. Devon had to hide a grimace of his own as he gave the castle a quick appraisal. They were not in a foyer, but a great hall of some sort. Heavy timbers hung overhead, while stone made up the outer wall. In contrast, the inner walls were heavily plastered and hung with battle antiquities, augmented by a scattering of standing sets of armor.

But what stood out the most was the fact that the whole room was thick with dust, a faint musty odor permeating the air. Two mismatched chairs stood by the fireplace, one sporting a broken arm. One of the tables by the entryway had a dirty glass left on it, the scent of soured wine evident even from where Devon stood. And the rugs were ashy in color as if it had been years since they'd been cleaned.

James brought the last of the baggage, bowed, and then left.

"Whot's this?" the housekeeper demanded, her affronted gaze on the pile of valises.

"I wrote to Viscount Strathmore," Devon said

coolly, deciding he was too tired to deal with impertinent servants. "He is expecting me. I assume you have a place for my servants and horses?"

The housekeeper's sullen expression did little to assure him. Devon stifled a sigh and turned to Paul. "Return to that inn we passed down the road. Have you money enough left for room and board for yourself and the others?"

"Yes, sir. Of course."

Devon nodded. He was not a man who was miserly with his blunt. When the time came to spend it, he spent it and regretted not a penny. "Thank you, Paul. Return in the morning, then."

"Yes, sir. At ten?"

Devon's brows rose. "I said in the morning. My morning will not begin until well after noon."

Paul managed a reluctant smile. "Yes, sir."

"And Paul . . ."

"Sir?"

"See to it that everyone gets a hot meal and all the ale they can hold. We made excellent time, and I am most grateful."

Paul brightened. "Yes, sir." He bowed, sent a sharp glance at the sulking housekeeper, and then left, the door closing behind him with an ominous thunk.

Devon shrugged out of his wet coat. Thank God he was only staying for three weeks before continuing on to see to some business for Marcus. "May I ask when Lord Strathmore is expected?"

"Expected? Why, he's here now."

Devon couldn't help glancing back at the shambling state of affairs in the main room. From what he remembered of Malcolm Macdonald from their school days, this disorganization was a bit of a surprise. What had caused Kilkairn Castle to be in such a state of disarray?

The housekeeper harrumphed, the keys about her neck jangling. "I wisht Davies was here."

"Davies?"

"The butler."

"Ah."

The housekeeper made a face. "The wretch is off a-sleepin' somewheres, if I know him."

Devon immediately had an image of an elderly individual reeking of gin.

"I suppose ye'll be wantin' a room to sleep in."

"Please," Devon said, removing his gloves and laying them, with his wet coat, on the table in the entryway, ignoring the thick layer of dust that was sure to cling to the fine wool. "And some food, if it is not too much trouble."

The housekeeper shook her head. "There's nary a crumb to be had till breakfast. Cook locks up the larder each night."

Wonderful. Devon began to think, with something akin to envy, of his servants holed up in that dry, snug inn. "Just a bed, then. My valet will be arriving shortly in another coach."

"Och dearie! Ye brought a valet? Whotever for? This isn't Edinburgh, ye know." The housekeeper scratched her chin. "Ye'll be needin' a room, won't ye? Blast Davies fer dodgin' his duties."

Devon swallowed a sigh. "I'm certain you know better than he which rooms are ready and which aren't."

That appeared to mollify her some, for she nodded. " 'Tis unlikely the gold chamber is ready, though it might do in a pinch. Mayhap the green one isn't too bad off. I suppose we can put yer man—"

"I wrote Strathmore last week," Devon broke in, a little frustrated. "He should have received my letter stating the date of my arrival and—"

"Don't ye fash' 'bout His Lordship. I'm sure he forgot aboot it, whot with—" The housekeeper clamped her mouth closed, as if swallowing something unpleasant. Devon waited, but she just looked away. That was interesting. What was happening at Kilkairn Castle? Devon wondered if perhaps he'd made an error in coming to Scotland after all.

The woman sighed. "Come with me, if ye please. Let's find ye somewhere to sleep." She picked up one of the lamps and began walking up the stairs, not once glancing over her shoulder to see if Devon followed or not. "No one ever said whist to me aboot a visitor, and I've too much to do to go guessin' as whot needs to be done and whot doesn't. I suppose we'll make a go fer the green chamber first and see if 'tis clean enough. I'd put ye in the gold chamber, but the sheets haven't been turned in I don't know how long and . . ." She rambled on and on, only pausing for a quick breath now and again.

Devon followed her up the stairs, realizing with each step just how tired he was. His back ached from traveling so far, his shoulders were stiff, and his temper was wearing thinner by the second.

They reached the landing and walked down what seemed an interminable length of dark, dank hallway before the housekeeper stopped. She held the lamp high and opened a large oak door. Thick, dusty air crept around them. Devon looked about the large chamber and noted that not only was the fire unlit, but a swath of cobwebs stretched in every corner. Worse, there was a damp spot beside the window, the rug black where water had seeped.

The housekeeper caught the direction of his gaze and waved a dismissive hand. "Whist! Tis naught, that leak. Ye should see the one in the dining hall. It fair gushes when there's a good rain." The housekeeper moved forward to finger the linen on the bed. "Seems to me 'twas three months or so ago when last we changed this bed, so it can't be too bad."

Months? Devon raised his brow.

Before he could form a reply, she sighed. "It won't do, for ye might catch yer death of the ague. I daresay the linens could do with an airing."

To say the least. Devon struggled to control his impatience. "Are there no other bedchambers?"

"This is a large castle, make no mistake," she said proudly. "There are ten guest chambers on this floor alone."

"Good! Surely one of them is made up."

"Och, I wouldn't go so far as to say that. Indeed, 'tis a sad truth to admit, but as Her Ladyship prefers to stay in Edinburgh, we've no reason to upkeep every room."

Devon had to clamp his mouth over a curse. "It's late. I'm tired. There has to be one room, at least." He took the lamp from the housekeeper and began walking down the hallway, throwing open doors and peering inside. "I'm not picky, I just want something dry and—" He paused inside a doorway. Unlike the other rooms, it didn't smell musty.

Best of all, an especially large bed draped with thick blue velvet curtains and piled high with white lacy pillows filled the center of the room. While there was no fire, logs were already in place, ready to be lit. The air, too, was refreshingly clean and spicy, smelling of lavender and something else.

"Perfect," he said. And it was.

The housekeeper appeared at his side. She took the lamp, grasped his arm, and firmly led him out of the room. "Perfect or no, ye canno' stay here."

Devon planted his heels in the doorway. "What's wrong with this room?"

"Nothing but—"

"Are the linens clean?"

"I changed them meself just yesterday, but—"

"Any leaks in the floor, walls, or ceiling?"

"No, but—"

"I'll take this one." He reclaimed the lamp and held it over his head to better illuminate the room. "Yes, this will do nicely."

"Yes, but the room is—" She bit her lip, faltering at his stubborn expression. "I suppose one night won't hurt. I can always get another room ready on the morrow."

"Of course you can," he said, though he had no intention of giving up what he suspected was the only decent room in the entire castle.

She eyed him sullenly, then walked past him, pausing at the candelabra that decorated the nightstand. "If ye promise not to move anything, I'll let ye stay here." She lit the candles. "That door leads to the suite for the mistress of the house, though Lady Strathmore prefers the new part of the castle and has never slept there. This room was built to be the maid's room, which is why 'tis so small."

"I don't mind that it is small." Devon wondered why it was so clean while the others were not. "Small rooms are easier to heat."

The housekeeper nodded. "Ye're right aboot that. And it doesn't smoke, neither. Lord Strathmore had the fireplace rebricked to keep it from wheezing."

"Wonderful," Devon said. He smiled his most winning smile. "Thank you for your assistance. I am so dreadfully tired that I would have fallen flat on my face had I been forced to wait for that Davies fellow to appear."

Her expression softened as if she'd just conjured the room on her own. "Then off to bed wid ye, my good sir. As soon as yer man comes, I'll send him up. And in the mornin', when Lord Strathmore awakens, I'll tell him ye're here." She curtsied, and then left, closing the door behind her.

Devon was all too glad to finally be alone. He lit the fire and, to his immense satisfaction, the wood took instantly, blazing a toasty warmth.

Bone-weary, he kicked off his boots and pushed them under the bed. Then he shrugged out of his coat, untied his cravat, and tossed them into the far corner of the room. Tilton would collect them in the morning and see that they were washed. Yawning, Devon removed his waistcoat. Just as he pulled it from his arm, a faint plink sounded and something silver fell from his pocket and rolled across the floor.

Devon followed the small circlet, catching it just as it headed for a wide crack in the hearth that led to God knew where. "Oh no, you don't," he muttered, picking up the ring and tossing it into the candle dish on the night table. Heaven knew he didn't want the blasted thing, but the ancient ring was an heirloom of sorts, and if he lost it, his brothers would kill him. Worse, they'd do it one at a time just to make certain it hurt.

He glanced at the St. John talisman ring, a feeling of unease tightening about his throat. Blast his brother Chase for hiding the damned thing in his carriage. Devon had thought that if he was nowhere to be found, then Chase would be forced to trick their oldest brother, Marcus, into taking the ring.

Devon, of course, didn't believe in curses. It was all nonsense. Just a fairy tale his mother had woven to entertain her six busy children.

But still . . . Devon paused, glancing out of the corner of his eye at the ring, a pinch of disquiet nipping at him. So far, the legend had proven itself true. Three of Devon's brothers had fallen victim to the ring already; Chase, Anthony, and Brandon were all three married. "Good for them," Devon told the ring. "But not for me."

Some men were made for the wedded state. But not Devon. Sometimes, late at night, on the few occasions he happened to be alone, a horrid thought would creep in. One he never spoke aloud. He was almost thirty years old and so far, the grand passion had missed him. Completely. Oh he'd fallen in love numerous times, but he had never been in *love*, the kind of passion his parents had had, the kind that might last forever . . . or at least longer than two months, which seemed to be the maximum length of time he was able to stay interested in a woman no matter how beautiful, how witty, how acceptable she might be.

Every time Devon thought he'd found the perfect woman, the second he won her and held her in his arms, he found himself looking over her shoulder for another challenge. It disturbed him sometimes, far more than he cared to admit.

Which was why the ring rattled him. What if he succumbed to the ring and got married, only to wake up a month later to the heart-chilling realization that he'd made a horrid mistake.

Thus it was, on the trip to Kilkairn, Devon had formed a plan designed to protect himself; he would eschew the company of women—all women. At least until he could return to London and deliver the ring into Marcus's unsuspecting hands.

Devon removed the last of his clothing and tossed them along with his waistcoat into the farthest corner with the rest. Then, naked and warmed by the fire, he fell into the bed, pulling the covers up over him. The pillows were plump and lace-edged, the sheets soft and cool against his skin. He turned his head and took a deep breath of the feminine scent of lavender, thinking how nice it would be to twine his legs with the smooth, rounded legs of a wo—He caught himself. No, damn it. Not until he got rid of that blasted talisman ring.

Pushing the thoughts away, he snuggled deeper and closed his eyes.

But sleep eluded him. Tired as he was, the thought of being without a woman, any woman at all, for several weeks, depressed him. He loved women. He loved their smiles, their fascination with ribbons and bows and jewels, the way they'd get irked over something trivial, yet had large enough hearts that they could forgive the grossest indiscretion with just a few well-chosen words. He loved the scents they used, the sound of their laughter. He loved the feel of their soft skin, the taste of their rosebud mouths. He loved the giggles and the sighs and the ease with which they showed their feelings. He loved them all.

Only . . . it wasn't real love. It couldn't be. But it was the only kind of love Devon was able to feel—exciting, thrilling, and lamentably brief.

He thought of the way his younger brother, Chase, had looked at his soon-to-be wife, Harriet, at their wedding. There had been something intense and almost magical about it. Devon had asked Chase how he'd known Harriet was the one, and he'd answered, "Because life without her would be worse than death."

"Drama," Devon said disgustedly, even as a flicker of jealousy touched him. Drama or no, it seemed as if Harriet and Chase had indeed found something special, something lasting. Something forever.

But that was not for Devon. The backs of his knees

itched with a sudden yearning to burst into a full out-and-out run, away from the thought of being leg-shackled to a woman who would eventually come to bore him. Once the magic of discovery was over, there simply wasn't enough feeling left to sustain a relationship of any kind. Perhaps that was an ugly truth Chase had yet to discover.

Tiredness pricked at Devon's lids, and he pulled the curtains more tightly closed about the bed, hoping the pitch blackness would lure him to sleep.

Perhaps he didn't need to give up *all* women. Perhaps he could avoid only the ones who might be a threat to his heart.

Hm. Now that was a far more worthy plan. All he would have to do was define exactly what qualities were common among the women he tended to develop feelings for, brief as they might be, and avoid prolonged contact with those types of women. In his mind, he made a list of his past conquests and began comparing traits.

Half an hour later, Devon had to admit that he had a certain inclination toward petite, very feminine types of women. Women of birth who knew the benefits of guile.

Devon decided he wouldn't have too much difficulty staying away from vixens of that particular cut. He would instead amuse himself with only ineligible, hoydenish women.

There. That should take care of that blasted talisman ring. Life was not too difficult after all. His eyes slowly slid closed and he fell weightless into a deep, deep sleep.

Chapter 2

Devon St. John is no better than any other man. It's true, I suppose, that he is quite handsome. And everyone knows his family is both wealthy and well connected. I suppose it is also accurate that there is something charming about a man who knows his own value and is so very willing to appreciate yours. And God knows I'm not immune to that smile of his; it quite melts me where I stand. But other than that . . . oh blast it! I suppose he is better than other men.

Miss Clarissa Fullerton to her sister-in-law,
Viscountess Mooreland,
while watching the waltz at Almack's

orning dawned, and with it a fresh, stiff breeze that rippled the grassy moors and chased the rain clouds to distant regions far beyond Kilkairn. Sunlight shone through the narrow windows of Devon's room. Full of golden mischief, a beam slipped through the single crack in the curtain to tickle his nose.

Devon rubbed his face with both hands. He yawned, then blinked into the sliver of light, slowly becoming aware of where he was. The standing ruins of Kilkairn Castle. He was suddenly glad for the shroud of bed curtains that kept out most of the sunlight. It would have been dismal indeed to have to face the wrack and ruin of his surroundings before breakfast. The door banged open, and footsteps sounded as someone entered his room.

Ah, Tipton! Thank goodness. The valet had a knack for making things pleasant. By now he would have everything hung and ready for the new day.

Devon lifted on one elbow and raised the edge of the curtain. But it wasn't Tipton at all. A woman stood with her back to him, a housemaid from the look of her rather nondescript clothing.

She threw open the wardrobe, the door banging against the wall. Just as he began to ask her what she needed, she sighed aloud and ran a hand through her hair, moving ever so slightly into the sunlight. Her hair gleamed brightly, red and gold threads vying for the light.

Devon was caught by the sight, the color almost mesmerizing. He wondered if her hair was as soft as it appeared, so thick and curling, as if it had a life of its own. She bent over to drag a bandbox out of the bottom of the wardrobe. She yanked off the top and then began digging through a tangled waggle of ribbon, muttering as she did so.

Devon raised his brows. From his vantage point on the bed, he was now at eye level with her rump. That was enough for the moment, for this particular rump was outlined very prettily by the thin, home-spun material of the maid's gown. It was almost as if she were tempting him.

The red-gold hair . . . that lush rump. Was this what the arse of pure temptation looked like? It was certainly well rounded, he decided, cupping his hands at the approximate size of her cheeks. Lush. Sensual. Generous. Fleshy enough to make even his sleepy body stir to life. His manhood tightened in anticipation.

His curious gaze dropped lower. Her rump, in addition to being full and curved, was attached to a very long pair of legs. An instant image began to form in his mind—of the maid's firm, well-fleshed body against his own, of holding that rump while those long legs clutched at his waist. Beneath the covers, his manhood hardened even more.

A warm smile crossed Devon's face. This was something indeed! He'd gone to bed with the desire to pursue only the most ineligible women available, and then had awakened to find the perfect candidate within arm's length—a simple housemaid with hair the color of fire and a rounded, curvaceous body. She was so unlike the sophisticated, petite women he'd pursued in the past that she could well be his salvation. He'd be so busy entertaining her in his bed that he'd have no thoughts of love or anything else, for that matter.

He eyed her with new appreciation, suddenly anxious to get through the awkward first moments. She was deliciously different from his usual flirts. Not only was she a good head taller, but she was also wider of shoulders and hips. Quite a magnificent specimen, if he said so himself. Better yet, he'd never bedded a woman with quite that shade of red-gold hair. All told, it would be a daring, exciting new experience.

"St. George's dragon," the woman muttered, her voice rich and husky, like the smoky roil of fog across a morning moor. She kicked the bandbox as if utterly disgusted before turning toward the door, her profile presented against the deep cherry wardrobe.

Devon was given a glimpse of a straight nose, full, sexy lips; and long lashes shadowing eyes of an indeterminate color. Well! This was looking better all the time.

Grinning, he pushed back the curtains. "Good morning, love."

At the first rustle of the velvet, the woman whirled to face him. "Who are you?" Her brows snapped lower as she seemed to regain her breath. "And who let you in here?"

She didn't have the rich brogue he'd expected. Indeed, her tone would not be amiss in London. But what really caught his attention was her eyes—a deep and verdant green, they sparkled angrily.

Devon took the time to collect himself. "I am a friend of Strathmore's."

She returned his look with a flat one of her own, completely unimpressed. "Does he know you are here?"

Devon shrugged. "I sent him a letter, though it seems he kept the information to himself. No one seemed to know I was to arrive."

"And who are you?"

"Devon St. John." He waited to see if there was some flicker of acknowledgment in her gaze, but none came. Good. Curse or no curse, he'd be damned if he'd trade on the family name in an effort to win a chit to his bed. He'd never had to do so before, and he wasn't about to start now.

He gathered the pillows and piled them behind him so that he could lean back and still see the woman's expression.

She eyed him cautiously, but made no move to dash for the door. "Who let you in?" she repeated.

"The housekeeper, I believe. Short woman, rather thin." He held out his hand. "About this tall, with big feet and a thick, gray braid."

"That would be her," the maid said grimly. "I wonder why the devil she didn't show you into one of the guest chambers."

"None were ready."

"That is not surprising. Still, she had no right to give you this chamber." She met his gaze and said stiffly, "It is mine."

The housekeeper had said that it was the room of a lady's maid, which would explain the green-eyed woman's rather polished tones. "So this bed is yours, is it?" He smiled his most winsome smile. "I love the scent of lavender." And would have loved it even more if he had been inhaling the sweet scent from her bare skin and not just her pillows and sheets.

"How pleasant," she said in a tone that implied the information was anything but. "I'm certain someone has by now prepared a room for you. It is time you left."

The maid was as hospitable in manner as the housekeeper from the previous night. The help at Kilkairn Castle were poorly trained. They were, in fact, the worst Devon had ever experienced, with the exception of his brother Brandon's coachman, a not-quite-reformed thief.

Still, it behooved Devon to jolly the maid along, especially if he wished to visit her bed with her in it. He let his gaze travel across her, touching on the fullness of her breasts, the round curve of her hips. Rich like an oversoft mattress, her body beckoned him to while away a few pleasant hours. He imagined what she'd be like between the sheets and had to shift to get comfortable again. He didn't know if it was the faint air of challenge that clung to her very generous curves or the curves themselves, but he was quite ready to sample her bounty.

He stretched a bit, letting the sheet slip a touch lower. As soon as her eyes traveled over his chest, to his lap, he said, "This is a wonderful bed. The mattress is firm, the sheets sweet-smelling. Perhaps I should just stay here."

Her gaze jerked back to his face, and she plopped her hands on her hips. "Nay, you will not."

There it was, the faintest hint of a Scottish brogue. Apparently when my lady's maid was irked, her accent began to show. Devon hid a smile and shrugged. "We'll see."

"We won't see anything. You will leave now."

He looked down at his lap, barely hidden from sight by the thin sheet. "Now?"

Her gaze followed his to where his obvious reaction was visible against the folds. Her cheeks heated, a lush pink color beneath the creamy white. "Nay," she said hastily, "not now. But as soon as I've left. Then you can put on your clothes and be on your way."

He was not going to leave without at least a kiss— or something more—to give him the strength to fight off whatever enticements the blasted talisman ring had in store. He glanced down at the bandbox she'd been peering into. "What are you looking for?"

"A ch—" She snapped her lips closed, glaring at him as if he'd committed a sin of some sort. "None of your business." She bent down and plunked the lid back on the bandbox. Then she picked it up and returned it to the stuffed wardrobe, slamming the doors closed. "I'll leave you to dress and then I'll return and finish what I was doing."

"Don't leave yet." He patted the bed beside him, watching her from beneath his lashes. "Stay and talk a bit."

One brow raised in skeptical disbelief. "Talk?" Her gaze dropped pointedly to his lap. "That's not what you appear to be wanting."

He choked on an unexpected laugh. She was a brazen one with a wit to match. It was a pity he had so little time, for it would have been wonderful to luxuriate in that deliciously decadent body of hers. As it was, he was forced to immediate action.

Devon met her gaze directly. "I wish I had more time to spend here at Kilkairn."

"You aren't staying long?"

He ignored the satisfaction that threaded her voice. "I've business to attend to for my brother, so I must leave in three weeks. Which is a great, sad pity." He peered at her from beneath his lashes and waited.

She shifted from one foot to the other, curiosity rampant in her gaze. After a moment, she asked in a rush, as if the words were forced from her, "Why is it a pity?"

"Because if it were not for that wretched fact, I would stay here and spend days, weeks, slowly seducing you, teasing and tormenting away your frowns until you had nothing left but ecstatic gasps and contented sighs."

If she'd colored before, it was nothing compared to the blaze of pink that heated her cheeks now.

Devon leaned forward. "More than anything in the world, I want to kiss you. Right now. May I?"

She blinked, and he realized that her lashes were so long that they tangled at the corners. "A kiss?"

It wasn't an invitation exactly. But it would do. In one smooth movement, he slid to the edge of the bed, swung his feet to the floor, grasped the woman's arm, and pulled her into his almost-bare lap. It was unfortunate that the sheet had tangled about his hips or there would have been naught but her skirts separating them.

Without giving her time to react beyond a simple gasp, he lowered his mouth to hers and kissed her.

He kissed her deeply, thoroughly, his mouth opening over hers, his tongue pressing between her lips. He tasted, teased, poured every ounce of his longing and desire into that one touch.

She stiffened, but didn't move, neither welcoming nor fighting off his embrace, though he could feel her heat thundering beneath his hands as he held her close. Could taste the wanton desire that answered his own.

A soft moan sounded in her throat, and Devon deepened the embrace. But even as he did so, she went limp in his arms, her face turning away from his as she gasped for breath.

It was an unbelievably sensual moment, the feel of her in his arms, her taste on his lips, her heart beating so fiercely that his own raged in response.

Devon held her tight and didn't move. After a long moment of fighting off the heavy wave of desire that made his loins ache and his throat tighten with need, he caught his breath enough to lift his head and look down into her face.

He expected shocked surprise. Or perhaps a pretense of outraged virtue, all of which he was prepared to kiss away.

But instead, despite her flushed cheeks, she met his gaze directly enough and said in a rather breathless voice, "Bloody hell, not again." To his further astonishment, she seemed to school her expression into one of supreme disinterest.

Of all the hundreds—nay, thousands—of kisses he'd delivered, none had met with a reaction anywhere close to this—disinterest tinged with boredom. Nor was he used to seeing a tedious expression on the faces of the women he gifted with his expertise. Bemusement, yes. Wonderment, yes. Even awed excitement. But boredom?

He pulled back a little more so that he could see fully into the maid's face. "I beg your pardon, but did you say 'Bloody hell, not again'?"

"Aye," she said, her gaze even with his. Her cheeks were flushed, her lips swollen slightly, her chest still moving rapidly up and down—those few things assured him that she was a pretender.

But still, it was intriguing that she could manage such a disinterested look and tone. "What do you mean 'again'?" he demanded.

She struggled to sit upright, but when he refused to loosen his hold, she merely sighed, her breath sweet, brushed with cinnamon. "Every time Strathmore has a guest, I get mauled. I am damned tired of it."

Devon's lips twitched. The maid's breath might be sweet, but her language was not. "If you don't wish to be mauled, then perhaps you should try to be a little less tempting."

"Tempting? Me?" Kat Macdonald blinked into the blue, blue eyes of her captor, fighting a losing battle to appear unaffected. Her mind whirled around the fact that the handsomest man she'd ever beheld had swept her into his lap and bestowed an expert, passionate kiss on her astounded lips. Then she'd had to fight the fact that her body had immediately softened, her heartbeat had tripled, her chest had tightened with an unfamiliar emotion.

It had been all she could do to appear bored,

though she'd managed. It was the best way to depress unwanted attentions, something Kat excelled at. Something she was far too familiar with, as it was. But in a way, that was her own fault. She'd sold her reputation for something that had seemed far more important, only to discover that she'd been wrong, dead wrong. Now she was forced to deal with the repercussions of that decision, one made so hastily eight years ago.

He lifted a finger and traced the curve of her cheek, the touch bemusingly gentle. "You are a lush, tempting woman, my dear. And well you know it."

Kat's defenses trembled just the slightest bit. Bloody hell, how was she to fight her own treacherous body while the bounder—Devon something or another—tossed compliments at her with just enough sincerity to leave her breathless to hear more?

Of course, it was all practiced nonsense, she told herself firmly. She was anything but tempting. She looked well enough when she put some effort into it, but she was large and ungainly, and it was way too early in the morning for her to look anything other than pale. Her eyes were still heavy with sleep, and she'd washed her hair last night and it had dried in a most unruly, puffy way that she absolutely detested. One side was definitely fuller than the other, and it disturbed her no end. Even worse, she was wearing one of her work gowns of plain gray wool, one that was far too tight about the shoulders and too loose about the waist. Thus, she was able to meet his gaze and say firmly, "I am not tempting."

"I'd call you tempting and more," Devon said with refreshing promptness. "Your eyes shimmer rich and green. Your hair is the color of the morning sky just as the sun touches it, red and gold at the same time. And the rest of you—" His gaze traveled over her until her cheeks burned. "The rest of you is—"

"That's enough of that," she said hastily. "You're full of moonlight and shadows, you are."

"I don't know anything about moonlight and shadows. I only know you are a gorgeous, lush armful."

"In this?" She looked down at her faded gown with incredulity. "You'd call this gorgeous or lush?"

His gaze touched on her gown, lingering on her breasts. "Oh yes. If you want to go unnoticed, you'll have to bind those breasts of yours."

She choked.

He grinned. "And add some padding of some sort in some other areas."

"I don't know what you're talking about, but please let me up—"

"I was talking about padding. Perhaps if you bundled yourself about the hips until you looked plumper, then you wouldn't have to deal with louts such as myself attempting to kiss you at every turn."

She caught the humor sparkling in his eyes, and it disarmed her a bit more.

"Furthermore," he continued as if he'd never paused, "you will need to hide those eyes of yours and perhaps wear a turban, if you want men like me to stop noticing you."

"Hmph. I'll remember that the next time I run into

you or any other of Strathmore's lecherous cronies. Now, if you'll let me go, I have things to do."

His eyes twinkled. "And if I refuse?"

"Then I will have to deal with you myself."

"Oh ho! A woman of spirit. I like that."

"Oh ho," she returned sharply, "a man who does not value his appendages."

That comment was meant to wither him on the vine. Instead he chuckled, the sound rich and deep. "Sweet, I value my appendage, although it should be *your* job to admire it."

"I have no wish for such a job, thank you very much."

"Oh, but if you did, it would then be my job to wield that appendage in such a way as to rouse that admiration to a vocal level." Devon leaned forward and murmured in her ear, "You have a delicious moan, my sweet. I heard it when we kissed."

Her cheeks burned. "The only vocal rousing you're going to get from me is a scream for help."

A bit of the humor left his gaze, and he said with apparent seriousness, "I would give my life trying to earn that moan yet again. Would you deny me that?"

In all her years of avoiding the clutching hands of her half brother's friends, never had any attempted to woo her with words. Not a single one. The tactic surprised her, and very few things did. "Please let me go. It is very improper of me to sit in your lap." Improper, but comfortable for all that.

He pursed his lips. "I'm not sure I can. Not without a toll."

"A toll? To gain release from my own bed?"

His eyes glinted suddenly, a smile on his sensual mouth that left her heart trembling in her throat. His hands, so warm before, now seemed even warmer, almost hot through the material of her gown. "My sweet," he said, "you aren't in bed, but in my lap. Were you in bed, I'd demand much more than a kiss for your freedom."

She frowned. "That is not fair." And it wasn't, not in any way.

"Life is rarely fair," he retorted.

Kat couldn't very well argue with him there. Life had already proven that. Blast it, it wasn't fair if he was going to use logic. "I already gave you one kiss," she pointed out reasonably.

"You didn't kiss me—I kissed you."

"That's all you'll get from me."

"Really?" His lids lowered, and he regarded her with a sleepy, sexy look that quite stole her thoughts. "What a pity, for I enjoyed that kiss. More than I should have. Without a doubt, it was the most intriguing, most delicious kiss I've ever received."

Despite Kat's determination to appear unmoved, a tiny flicker of pride tickled through her. From the stranger's manner and appearance, she was certain he was quite used to being kissed . . . in fact, there had been something of a master kisser in his manner and ability. And yet *he'd* been impressed with *her* efforts. She hadn't even tried to impress him, either. She wondered what he'd think if she *did* try. He would be completely astounded and—

Kat blinked. St. George's Dragon, but if she continued on this line of thought, she'd talk herself into kissing him again. And all without him saying another word!

Her gaze narrowed on the stranger and she noted that he was watching her expressions intently, a pleased smile on his lips as if he knew exactly where her thoughts were taking her. *I'm playing right into his hands, blast it!*

"Enough of this. I will give you until the count of three to free me."

Amusement laced his blue eyes. "Or?"

"Or I will be forced to hurt you."

He chuckled, the sound rumbling in his chest. "Really? And how will you—"

"One."

"Oh come now. All I want is a kiss. You've already given me one, what can be the harm in—"

"Two."

He shook his head. "I vow, but you are a stubborn thing. Far more stubborn even than my sis—"

"Three." She lifted her foot and swung it back, hard. There was a solid thunk as the heel of her boot hit his bare shin. His arms loosened instantly. Kat was on her feet and across the floor before her captor finished a rather colorful string of invectives.

Once she reached the door, she wasted no time hurrying out and slamming it behind her. Then she continued on her way down the steps, through the great hall, and out the door, where she hurried on to the stables.

She didn't think Mr. Devon St. John would follow— he'd have to stop long enough to find some clothes.

But still, her heart was pounding as if he were hard on her heels. And perhaps, in a way, he was.

Kat found the stables thankfully quiet. She hurried by the nearly empty stalls, the scent of hay and oats mingling in the cool air. She went straight to the tack room, where she locked the door and then stood with her back against it, fighting for breath and the return of her usual calm thinking.

In all the times she'd fended off the groping hands of Kilkairn guests, never had Kat allowed anyone to touch her, much less hold her in his arms and kiss her. This man had merely caught her by surprise with his soft words and smiling eyes. But now she'd be cautious around him; very cautious indeed.

Certainly Kat had never *enjoyed* the attentions of any of Malcolm's other miscreant friends, yet this time she had to admit that she'd felt a definite trill of excitement. In fact, she'd felt many things while in Devon St. John's arms, and none of them was safe.

That thought firmly in mind, she waited only until her breath returned to normal before leaving the tack room and finding her horse. Then she mounted and left, riding through the forest and hills as if the hounds of hell were indeed following her.

Chapter 3

I am not here to argue, sir. I am here to inform you of my wishes and to see to it that you consent in all matters forthwith.

Viscountess Mooreland to her mirror,
practicing for an upcoming "conversation"
with His Lordship regarding
his wasteful gambling habits

The chit had kicked him. Hard. Devon's temper went from amused interest to astonished outrage in the space of a few seconds, his irritation complete when she swept from the room in seemingly righteous indignation, slamming the door behind her.

All told, it was a new, and unpleasant, experience. Women rarely refused his requests for a dalliance and never bothered to kick him before leaving the room.

Damn it, what was wrong with the woman? A simple "No, thank you" would have sufficed. Although . . . He rubbed his shin and winced. Perhaps he'd been too determined to keep the damned effect of that blasted talisman ring at bay by holding the chit in his lap. Truly, he had meant no harm. It was just the realization that she was so absolutely perfect for his plans—and right there, at arm's length—that had made him reluctant to heed her request for release.

Of course, most women he knew wouldn't have complained had he kept them in his lap for much longer than a few miserly minutes. Had he offered, many would have stayed and even suggested additional amusements to accompany such a luxuriously naughty position. But apparently London misses were something less particular than Scottish misses. Perhaps some small part of that was due to his position in London society . . .

An insidious idea crept into his mind and latched about his thoughts. What if all the women who had bedded him had done so merely because they had known who he was, that he was a St. John?

He glanced down at his ready "appendage," as the chit had called it, and relief swept through him. His name might have been the reason some women had tumbled into his bed, but it wasn't the reason so many of them clamored, cajoled, and begged to return.

Feeling a bit more himself, Devon rose and began to dress. He didn't have Tilton's way of decreasing wrinkles, but Devon managed quite well. His cravat was sadly crushed, of course, but here in the wilderness, who would know? He tied it as best he could and then pinned it in place with a sapphire pin. He'd just bent over to fish his boots from under the bed when he caught sight of the St. John talisman ring where it still rested in the candle dish on the night table. His gaze narrowed, and he reached out and touched the slender metal band.

The ring was warm beneath his fingertips, and surprisingly smooth despite the runes carved on the side. For some reason, the feel of the silky metal reminded him of the maid. She was every bit as prickly on the inside, and then just as surprisingly soft to the touch.

He traced the curve of the band, his mind lingering on the memory. Suddenly he caught himself, stepping hastily back from the table and ramming his hands into his pockets. Bloody hell, if he wasn't careful, he'd be bedded and wedded before the day was out.

Not to the saucy maid, of course—not only was she completely unsuitable, but she had also apparently developed an unreasonable dislike for his presence, as indicated by the bruise on his shin. He realized that she'd bruised far more than his shin; his pride was injured as well.

He shrugged into his waistcoat. Devon knew there had to be other unsuitable women to dally with, though he doubted any of the others possessed the creamy skin, red-gold hair, or pure audacity of the one he'd let escape.

Damn. He turned his back on the ring and pulled his boots from beneath the bed, grimacing at the mud on the once shiny leather. Sighing, he crossed to a window and opened it, pausing as he leaned out to dust his boots onto the gardens below. The scent of the flowers and herbs rose to meet him. For all the mismanagement inside Kilkairn Castle, the gardens were glorious. The green of the grass reminded him of the eyes of the wench who'd kicked him.

Damn. I'm doing it again. Apparently he had a weakness for women with green eyes and pointed shoes. He closed the window, then held up his boots to the light. They were now mudless, but covered in some sort of gray grime. Tipton would not be pleased.

Devon swiped them with the hand towel on the night table, stomped his feet into the boots, and shrugged into his coat. The sooner he lured the serving maid into his bed, the sooner he could relax and stop worrying he might meet a paragon of feminine virtues—the exact type of woman one might feel compelled to marry.

A woman he might not be able to refuse.

Fate might be conspiring against him, but she had not beaten him yet. Devon whistled softly to himself as he stepped out of the cozy confines of the room into the hallway, pausing a moment to get his bearings.

If he had thought Kilkairn Castle disreputable during his brief view of it the night before, it was even more forlorn in the bright sunlight. At first glance, the wide stone-lined hallway benefited from a brace of large, high-set windows, the tall ceiling arching gracefully over a set of elaborate iron chandeliers. But closer inspection revealed the layering of dust that piled in the corners of the hall, and the thick bracket of cobwebs that stretched from cornice to chandelier bracket. He followed a particularly long cobweb where it stretched down to the corner of the rug that ran the center of the hallway. In all probability, the runner had once been a rich red, though now it was an indiscriminate brown.

All told, it was a strange state of affairs considering that while at Eton, Malcolm had been so fastidious about his possessions that he'd taken a ribbing from his classmates on more than one occasion. It had taken the force of Malcolm's hot fists and ready temper to silence most of the naysayers.

Since then, of course, Malcolm had married, a supposedly "blessed state" that seemed to have the effect of immediately turning a sane, logical man into a quivering, starry-eyed impostor. Devon had seen just such a transformation occur in no fewer than three of his own brothers.

Thank God he was prepared to fight off the talisman ring's curse. He was a man who favored a more lively way of life. His needs were simple—enjoyment of life, an occasional flagon of brandy, and the warm company of a large number of the fair sex.

His stomach rumbled and he sighed, then made his way down the stairs. He wondered if there was to be breakfast or if he would have to procure his own. Considering the state of the castle, he would not be surprised to discover that there was ham for breakfast, but first he'd have to catch the pig, strangle it with his bare hands, and dress it himself.

The unmistakable clank of a serving dish sounded at the very bottom of the great stairs and alleviated his fears. Devon followed the sound, his stomach growling louder as the wafting scent of bacon reached his nostrils.

He didn't even pause on reaching the room, but entered forthwith. Only two occupants were inside. One was a bent-over, hunkered old man dressed in a footman's livery who stood beside a sideboard filled with steaming platters. He didn't even look around when Devon entered, but continued to move a water pitcher slowly toward an empty water glass.

Across the room sat the other occupant, a slender, well-dressed man with an expressive face and deep auburn hair. A rather small, solitary figure at the huge gleaming table, he occupied an ornate chair, a plate before him.

The man was just lifting a bite of egg to his mouth when his gaze fell on Devon. The man's eyes widened, and he dropped his fork. "Damn me, but I'll be drawn and quartered!"

"So you shall, Strathmore," Devon said. "An event I've predicted on more than one occasion."

Malcolm grinned from ear to ear as he jumped up from the table. "Devon St. John! How are you, you pox-ridden, swiving, crimped-ear dog!"

Devon took the hand Malcolm thrust toward him. "God save us all, but it is Malcolm Macdonald, scourge of Scotland and bane of Britain. Hide your money and your women!"

Malcolm laughed. "Och, laddie! You haven't changed a bit! When did you arrive? I didn't expect to see you till after this rain quit us."

"Last night, rather late. Didn't anyone inform you?"

"No one has informed me of a bloody thing! Who was up to greet you?"

"The housekeeper. Your butler was apparently unavailable."

"Davies," Malcolm said with a disgusted snort. "He's never where he should be. Still, I'm surprised one of the footmen didn't mention it." Malcolm looked at the humped-back old man who stood by the buffet and said loudly, "Damn it, Ketron! Why didn't you tell me St. John had arrived?"

The old man didn't look up but continued with his task, his blue-veined hands trembling as he lifted the pitcher to pour water into the glass. Large droplets splattered everywhere, sizzling on the ham plate.

"By St. Brennan's boat, I am surrounded by imbeciles and deaf mutes!" Malcolm sighed, then shrugged as if to move past his irritation, a pained smile touching his mouth. "There's naught for it now. Accept my apologies, St. John. I shall have to force you to drink a bottle or two of my best port as a way to offer solace for my shortcomings as a host."

"I accept," Devon said without hesitation.

"Thank you. You always were a generous man." Malcolm glared at the elderly retainer. "As I'm sure you've noticed, things are in a wee bit of disarray."

That was an understatement. Devon cleared his throat and said politely, "I'm sure it's not as bad as all that."

"Yes, it is. These servants are horrid. They were m'father's, most of them. The only ones who would stay. Except that one." Malcolm nodded toward the ancient footman who was now slowly wiping up the spilled water using the corner of his coat. "That one was a wedding gift from Fiona's mother. The harridan swore she was doing us a great service and claimed that he was indispensable to her household. At the time I thought she was being too generous, but now I am not so certain."

"A parson's gift, hm?"

"Aye. I think the real reason she sent him here was to cause us the greatest inconvenience she could. Devon, honestly, the man cannot hear a word."

Devon chuckled. "How inconsiderate."

"Aye. But enough of my misfortunes." Malcolm gestured to the table. "Come and eat!" He waited for Devon to sit before he took a chair. Then he said in a very loud voice, "Ketron, bring another plate!"

The old man didn't so much as blink, but continued, ever so slowly, to wipe yet another bead of water off the sideboard.

Malcolm closed his eyes, a deep crease appearing on his forehead. After a moment, he opened his eyes. "Perhaps I should just get it for you."

"Oh no—"

"Nonsense," Malcolm said, standing up with the air of a man who has suffered long and sees no end in sight. He made his way to the buffet, where he startled the butler by reaching past him to get a plate and then piled it high with a spoonful of every dish available.

Devon blinked at the amount of food that was eventually set before him. "I am overwhelmed." He supposed he could get used to the drafty halls, damp beds, and cobweb-strewn corners if his sojourn at

Kilkairn Castle promised food like this. "I don't believe I've seen a more lovely sight."

Malcolm resumed his seat and beamed affably. "Breakfast is my favorite meal of the day. Fiona has the ordering of dinner, so I have to—" He broke off at Devon's expression. "Never mind that. Just eat and enjoy." He glanced over at the elderly footman and then said in a loud voice that was a hair from a yell, "Ketron, could you inform Lady Strathmore we have a guest?"

The footman turned from the sideboard and put his hand to his ear. "Eh?"

Malcolm muttered under his breath and then repeated his request, even more loudly.

"Aye, my lord," the old man said. He straightened his shoulders, then lifted his foot. He shuffled more than walked, and it took him forever just to reach the door.

The second he passed through, Malcolm pulled his plate closer and reclaimed his fork. "So, how are those brothers of yours?"

"Chase just wed. Brandon returned just a few months ago from his honeymoon, and Anthony and Anna are talking about having even more children."

"Chase just wed? And Brandon as well? Saints, but it sounds as if the whole lot of you have gone daft." Malcolm eyed Devon up and down. "You don't have that bloody ring, do you?"

Devon nodded once.

"Blast! I knew it."

"Why does it matter?"

Malcolm drew back a little, his eyes wide. "Because it means that your goose is cooked, my friend."

"It means no such thing," Devon said much more firmly than he meant to.

A crack of laughter met this. "How do you plan on escaping?"

"By staying busy." Devon shifted in his chair, his shin hitting the leg of the table right where his morning visitor had kicked him. He winced.

Malcolm's brows lowered with concern. "The table has odd-placed legs."

"It isn't that. I merely struck a previous injury. A bruise caused by a rather spirited mare."

"A mare?"

"Yes. One with very intriguing green eyes." It was somewhat odd, but every time Devon thought about the sassy maid, he smiled.

Malcolm grinned in return. "Oh ho! An armful, was she?"

"And then some." Devon rubbed his shin once more. "She wears pointed boots, too. Apparently she took something I said in an unfavorable light and delivered a kick worthy of my new gelding."

"What did you say to cause such a reaction?"

"Nothing that I can think of. I merely told her she had to pay a toll to leave my room. A kiss. Inexplicably, she took offense."

"Och, you found a spirited one!" Malcolm spread some marmalade on a piece of toasted bread. "Where did you meet this maid? At a tavern along the way?"

"No. It was here. In the blue room."

Malcolm's laughter froze on his lips, something flickering in his gaze. He looked down at his toast, a strange expression on his face. "Did you . . . did you say the blue room?"

"Yes," Devon said cautiously. "Why?"

Malcolm shook himself, as if waking from a deep sleep. "Och, nothing. A thought, 'tis all. How did you come to be in the blue room?"

Reassured, Devon reached for the salt. "It was the only one clean enough to inhabit. When I awoke this morning, the maid was there and claimed the room to be hers. So, in return for vacating the premises, I asked for a kiss."

Malcolm started to take a bite of his toast, but then apparently thought better of it and returned it to the side of his plate. "What did this, ah, lass say to your price of a kiss?"

Devon grinned. "She didn't say anything while I was kissing her."

A faint flush crept up Malcolm's neck. "She *let* you kiss her?"

"Yes. Then I decided I wanted another kiss, and that was what caused our little disagreement."

"But she let you kiss her once," Malcolm repeated as if unable to believe his ears.

Devon frowned at his host, a sense of unease prickling along the back of his neck. "Why? Is she maid to your wife?"

"Maid to—oh no!" Malcolm apparently found that comment amusing for he snorted a laugh, then said, "She's no one's maid, is Kat. Tell me more about this encounter."

So the chit's name was Kat. Most likely a short version of Katherine. Devon shrugged at Malcolm's interested gaze. "There's not much more to tell."

"What do you think of this lass? Do you think she is pretty?"

"Pretty" wasn't quite the word for it. In comparison to the woman's true attributes, "pretty" was a pallid, winter shadow. " 'Lush' is a better word. She was well rounded with red gold hair and green eyes and—" He broke off, uncertain how much to reveal. "She was quite a noticeable woman." Which was understating the truth by a wide mark. Still, it never behooved one to bare all of one's secrets. For all Devon knew, Malcolm might have an interest in the maid himself. Devon regarded his friend for a long moment. "Why do you ask?"

Malcolm waved an expansive hand. "No particular reason. Did the two of you speak for long?"

"For several minutes. She was quite sharp-witted." And had a body that had begged for further exploration. "I take it you know this woman."

Malcolm's lips twitched. "Oh yes. I know her. That's why I'm surprised that all she did was kick your shins. It's amazing she didn't blacken your lights, too."

"She's a feisty one, I'll admit that. At one point she threatened to, ah, remove a certain 'appendage.' One I'm very fond of and have no wish to go without."

Malcolm burst into laughter. "She didn't!"

"Yes, she did. I tried to talk her into admiring my appendage at a closer distance rather than threatening to remove it, but she refused—" Devon frowned. "Good God, what is wrong?"

Gulping great gusts of air, Malcolm rocked back in his chair, his face red as he struggled to contain his laughter. "D—don't tell me any more, please! Let me—have to—catch my breath!"

It was too much. Malcolm had always been a laughing soul; it was one of the things Devon liked best about him. But for some reason, this time Devon had the feeling that Malcolm was actually laughing *at* him and not *with* him.

So it was that he said in a rather frosty voice, "I beg your pardon, but while it was certainly an amusing moment, it wasn't that funny."

Malcolm wiped his eyes, chuckling. "Ah, laddie! If only you knew!"

Devon threw his napkin on the table. "Knew what?"

"Th-that—by the saints, I c-can't talk." Malcolm fell into yet another paroxysm of laughter.

Devon was forced to wait while his host composed himself. It took several moments and three or four gulps of tepid ale before Malcolm finally gasped a calmer breath.

The Scotsman wiped his eyes and said, "Here's the whist of it: the woman you were kissing in your chambers this morning was none other than Miss Katherine Anne Macdonald."

Devon stilled. Surely Malcolm didn't mean . . . "Katherine Anne *Macdonald*?"

"Aye. My half sister."

"That tall Amazon is your sister?" Devon repeated, too bemused to do more. Bloody hell. And Devon had thought she was "safe."

Malcolm read his look of chagrin as something altogether different. "Aye, 'tis a sad thing my father had such a short one for his male child and then sprung a giantess for his daughter, but so 'tis, her mother being a wee bit on the English side."

"That explains her lack of accent."

"Lack? You mean it explains why she has one to begin with."

Devon smiled. "That, too."

"She's a wild one, is Kat. My parents' marriage was not pleasant. After one particular fight, my father stormed out and didn't come back for three months. Seems he found a seamstress in a nearby town, an impecunious English woman who made her way doing fancy stitch. She was tall with green eyes and red gold hair and was rumored to be a lady of some birth, though that was never substantiated. Kat is the spitting image of her."

Devon's spirits began to climb once again. So Kat Macdonald was the result of an illicit affair. Perhaps she was yet a good candidate for a dalliance after all. As long, of course, as Malcolm didn't mind. Devon didn't know what Malcolm's feelings about his half sister were, but judging from the mirth he'd thus far displayed . . . well, things weren't as grim as Devon had thought. "Tell me about this half sister of yours . . . Katherine."

"You'll call her Kat lest you are fond of bruised

shins. She dislikes the name Katherine and has never used it."

Kat it was, then. "Did you grow up with her?"

"In the same house? Lord no. My mother couldn't stand the sight of her. My father asked and asked to have her live here, but my mother was not a forgiving sort of woman. Eventually he quit asking and instead had a snug little cottage built in the woods near here for Kat and her mum. Kat lives there now."

Devon lifted his brow. "But she has a room here, in the castle."

"Indeed she does. She oft comes for dinner and stays the night. I had the room made up for her after I came into the title. My mother had a fit, but I thought it was only right."

"Your mother sounds like quite an opinionated woman."

Malcolm made a face. "You don't know the half of it. At first she flatly refused to have anything to do with Kat, even though it was painfully obvious that the girl needed some guidance. Eventually, I was able to talk sense into my mother."

"After your father died, I'm sure some of her hard feelings must have dissolved."

"In a strange way, it only made it worse. I think Mother blamed Kat's mum for the problems in the marriage even though they were in existence long before she came along."

"How awkward."

"For me, it was difficult." Malcolm's expression sobered. "For Kat, it was painful. But I brought my mother round eventually. I told her that if she wished to continue living in the Strathmore Dower House in Edinburgh, she'd make Kat welcome and present her to society."

"So Kat is a society miss."

Something flickered across Malcolm's face, but was quickly suppressed. "Hardly. Kat didn't . . ." The Scotsman hesitated, then shrugged. "She didn't take."

There was something more to that story, Devon was sure of it. Still, it seemed equally obvious that Malcolm did not want to tell him.

Of course, it was entirely possible that Kat had not been accepted based on the circumstances of her birth. That and she was far too bold, too bright to be welcomed into the tepidness offered by society. Small, prim-mouthed beauties were lauded by the *ton*, not tall, strong women who possessed enough red gold loveliness to make even a soggy morning appear fresh and intriguing.

Devon found himself nodding. "I imagine she didn't take at all."

Malcolm opened his mouth as if to say something, but then his gaze locked with Devon's. After a charged moment, the Scotsman apparently changed his mind, for all he said was, "Aye. I'm just surprised she was so lighthearted with you this morning."

"Lighthearted? I would hardly call her that."

"She let you kiss her and didn't remove your appendage. That is lighthearted where Kat Macdonald is concerned."

The words intrigued Devon all the more. It had

been a bitter pill to discover that his perfect flirt was the half sister of his host. But the fact that she was illegitimate, had apparently been shunned by society, and now lived tucked away in a cottage in the woods not far from the castle, seemed to make her the perfect object for a flirtation once again.

All Devon knew was that he needed a diversion to protect him until he removed to Edinburgh. Someone passionate enough, and challenging enough, that he would not be tempted to fall victim to an eligible woman, one with strong familial connections and a name in society . . . *If* there were any other eligible women about. So far, the castle seemed unusually free of feminine charms.

Hm. Devon wondered if he was to be blessed with peace, after all. "Malcolm, I hope I did not come at a poor time. I'd hate to bother you when you've other guests about."

Malcolm looked up from his plate with apparent surprise. "Other guests?" He glanced about them, Devon's gaze following. While the dining room didn't suffer from the obvious neglect that tainted the rest of the castle, it was still far from perfectly tended. The rugs could do with a beating and two dusty cobwebs hung in opposite corners.

"We used to entertain weekly," Malcolm said. "But not as often now that—" He gestured towards the cobwebs. "Now only a few of Fiona's closer friends come to visit, though rarely overnight. I only wish Fiona's sister, Murien, wouldn't come so often. She's a—"

The door opened and the aged footman returned,

face flushed as he huffed and puffed. The footman come to a wheezing halt beside Malcolm and cleared his throat. As this rather noisy and elaborate process seemed to steal all the man's available air, he didn't speak for quite some time.

Malcolm gave an explosive sigh. "For the love of St. Brennan! Just tell us what Her Ladyship said!"

The footman looked disapprovingly at Malcolm and wheezed out a rather breathless "Yes, my lord. Her Ladyship says she will not be joining you for breakfast."

Malcolm frowned. "That's it?"

The aged footman's color faded to a more pasty tone, his breathing easing somewhat. "I believe so, my lord."

"You *believe*? In other words, you don't *remember*?"

The old man's wrinkled lips pursed thoughtfully. "I think . . . I'm fairly certain Her Ladyship didn't say anything else."

Malcolm threw his napkin on the table, disgust in his voice. "You are *fairly* certain? You *believe* she didn't have anything more to say?"

The footman nodded, seeming rather pleased with himself. "I usually forget something if I'm told more than one thing, but this time, I remembered it all." His smile faded. "I think."

"Thank you, Ketron," Malcolm said tiredly. "I'll see Lady Strathmore myself as soon as I'm through here."

"Yes, my lord." Still looking pleased, the elderly man turned slowly, then shuffled out of the room.

The second the door closed, Malcolm flashed a look at Devon. "Do you see what I'm saddled with? Do you see?"

Devon chuckled. "You need new servants."

"I had new servants. Well-trained servants. Excellent servants. But they all left because Fiona—" He broke off, his face red. "I suppose there is no hiding that things are not as they should be. We were doing well, Fiona and I. But then, six months ago, we had an argument about Kat, of all things."

"Kat?" Devon raised his brows.

"I dislike Fiona's sister, Murien, and I made a disparaging comment. I didn't mean it, though if you ever meet Murien, you'll know why I said what I did. She's a beautiful woman on the outside, but she has ambition beyond what is acceptable."

Devon would take care that he didn't meet Murien. She sounded exactly like the sort of woman he wanted to avoid.

Malcolm shook his head. "So Fiona took offense and said that at least her sister hadn't ruined herself like Kat had by running off with a—" He stopped and his face pinkened. "Never mind. You don't need to hear our family problems."

Ah ha! Devon was intrigued and wished to hear more, though all he said was, "All families have problems." And they did. For example, his family had a horrid curse of a ring to contend with. Which was why, in a way, it was fortuitous to confirm his suspicions that lovely, impulsive, passionate Kat Macdonald was a ruined woman. Ruined women could not demand marriage if a dalliance became something more. Of course, Devon had no intention of going anywhere he wasn't invited; he wasn't a man to take anything that wasn't freely offered. But the passion behind Kat's kiss made him believe that there was the potential for that something more.

He stole a glance at Malcolm. His friend's usually joyful expression was somber now. He sat silently staring at his half-finished plate, his shoulders slumped. He caught Devon's gaze and managed a painful smile. "I apologize for my wife's absence."

That, Devon decided, *is why I will never marry*. It suddenly seemed silly to be uneasy about the talisman ring. Magic it might be, but Devon had his own protection against such tomfoolery. Just seeing the expression on Malcolm's face as he contemplated his troubled marriage added yet another line of impenetrable bricks to an already thick wall around Devon's reluctant heart.

"Blasted female," Malcolm said with a sigh. He raked a hand through his hair, a quiver of emotion flashing over his mobile face.

Devon thought of all the times from years past that he and Malcolm had laughed at those men who seemed in the clutches of the deadly disease of matrimony. Now it seemed that Malcolm had himself become a victim. It was a damned shame.

Malcolm's smile stretched awkwardly over his cheeks. "I know what you're thinking and—"

"You have no idea what I'm thinking. None at all." Devon pulled his plate of now-cold food forward. The food might be cold, but Devon's thoughts were just heating up. "Let us eat and talk of more cheerful things."

But in the back of his mind, a plan was forming. A plan that had to do with the reclusive, ruined-to-society Kat Macdonald. A plan that would guarantee that whatever muslin-dressed pitfalls fate might throw in front of him, Devon would be ready to meet them all.

He smiled at his friend. "Tell me about your stables. I brought that gelding with me, the one I wrote to you about."

"Did you? I cannot wait to see it. Kat's mad about horses, too. She has almost two dozen of them, eating their heads off in her stables."

Devon filed that bit of information away and made another comment about horses. Soon the conversation turned toward matters of sport and the hunt and didn't falter once. But even while discussing the seeming dearth of fox this season, Devon was planning how he would find the location of a certain cottage nestled deep in the woods beside Kilkairn Castle.

Chapter 4

*I-I have something to say to you, sir, a-and I hope
that you will ... what I mean is that, I-I am not
here to argue with you precisely—nor at all because
arguing is not what I had in mind but—I mean, I
want to discuss something—but—oh blast it all!
Never mind! Just pass the stupid mint sauce and
let's talk some more about the weather.*

Viscountess Mooreland to Viscount Mooreland,
while having a rare, private moment at dinner
before attending the theater

To one side of Kilkairn lay a winding river, a
slash of silver ribbon across the deep jewel-
green fields that surrounded the castle. The river
provided a source of fresh, sparkling water as well as
negated the need to fence the entire north side of the
property.

To the other side of the castle lay a deep, dark
woods filled with huge craggy oaks and thick green
moss that carpeted large awkward boulders and the
rich black loam of the forest floor.

Some of the villagers said Kilkairn Wood was enchanted, a rumor given credence when Kat Macdonald moved into the abandoned cottage. Long ago it had housed her mother, a woman said to have bewitched the last lord of the castle.

To the villagers, the wood was reported to be enchanted and enchanted it remained.

"Blasted, ill-mannered, arrogant Englishman!" Kat told her horse, her tones ringing over the clopping of Merriweather's hooves on the packed earthen pathway. "I vow, but I am done with Malcolm and his houseguests."

She'd have to eschew all visits. At least this last visitor hadn't been as bad as Fitzhugh who tried to squeeze her knee beneath the breakfast table even after she'd darkened his lights once already. "Men. Always taking more than you want to give them."

Merriweather tossed her mane as if to agree that such behavior was beyond the acceptable.

Kat patted the mare's neck. "That's exactly what I think, too." She relaxed a little in the saddle, her nerves still a-jangle from this morning's contretemps with the handsome stranger. She wouldn't think about it any more. It was too fine a morning to let go to waste.

The lazy sun flickered through the leaves overhead as they meandered ever deeper into the forest, dappling the mare's reddish sides with touches of amber and streaks of gold. Kat lifted her face up to where towering trees laced branches over the path, wide boughs of green leaves soon encompassing them completely.

The air was even cooler here, in the deep woods. Kat loved being among the trees and away from the hard words and groping hands of Kilkairn. Calmness began to sift into her soul, though one part of her mind continued to dwell on this morning's confrontation.

Normally, though she resented such treatment, she didn't let such things bother her. But this time things had been different. For one, she'd actually allowed the stranger to kiss her, and for two, the truth be told, she didn't think she'd ever seen a handsomer man. Well, perhaps once. But that one time should have taught her to beware such men.

She thought wistfully of the prettily turned compliments that St. John had spoken, all with a disturbing glint of sincerity in his gaze.

It had been that glint that had given her pause. Most of Malcolm's guests knew her past history and came with the intention of luring her farther down the path of lost virtue. They used empty, quickly blurted suggestions and grasping hands, neither of which had any effect on her except to raise her ire.

St. John, in contrast, had seemed to genuinely admire her.

She glanced down at herself now. Not only was she taller than most women, but she had an abundance of flesh that she greatly disliked. When she'd first been introduced to Edinburgh society, she'd quickly learned that the women who garnered all the attention were smallish, slender, and delicately made.

"I felt like an ungainly, ill-dressed bull in a china shop," she told Merriweather. Her brother, Malcolm, had done what he could. He had not stinted on her clothing or anything else. He'd purchased the best the modistes had to offer. The problem was that fashion itself pandered to the slender and delicate and left healthy, normal women like Kat looking and feeling uncomfortable and less than attractive.

She smoothed a hand over her gown. Of plain worsted, it was not at all fashionable. Instead, she'd had it cut to fit her form, with a waistline at her waist and not tied directly beneath her breasts, a style that made her chest and hips appear twice their normal size. Really, did the fashion mongers think that all women were like Fiona, as tiny and delicate as a doll?

Kat snorted. "They need to look around. Most women are like me, a little too wide here and a little too wide there to be able to wear such nonsense."

Merriweather pranced a bit.

Kat chuckled. "My thoughts exactly." She was fortunate that she'd left society's frivolous expectations behind and now had complete freedom to be and wear what she wanted. She took a deep breath, the cool, fresh air sending a grin all the way to her feet.

They rounded a sharp turn in the pathway and came out into a clearing. The trees and foliage had been cut back, then kept at bay with a meticulous hand so that the sun shone freely here, bright and warm, bathing all in a golden light.

The cottage, if one could call a twelve room structure thusly, sat in the heart of the forest. It was a tall, two-story house with a steep roof and large, square windows. The building was of hand-thrown brick, covered with mud wattle, the walls a foot thick to protect the inhabitants from the extreme weather that graced this portion of the country.

But despite a severity of design, the house was ringed with welcome. The thickly thatched roof was braided into an intricate, cheery design. Every window sported a window box filled with lavender and St. John's wort, while a bright red door beckoned one to enter. Most days, the shutters were thrown wide and singing could be heard, often a set of deep baritones, though more likely than not, Kat's own fine feminine alto.

Kat loved the place with a fierce passion. Not because of its beauty, though that was part of it. But because it was hers. Every last blooming inch. A fact she made known to any who dared say nay about her or her chosen way of life. For some reason, for as long as she could remember, there had always been people telling her what to do, how to look, which way to act, and who to be. But not here. Here she was just Kat.

She smiled in satisfaction. "It's a lovely place, isn't it, Merriweather?"

The horse jangled her bridle bells in agreement.

It was a sad truth of life that those who were born on the wrong side of the sheets spent the rest of their lives in a state of "almost." Almost an accepted part of the community. Almost a member of a real family. Almost, but never quite anything.

So it had been for Kat until she discovered her "gift," as Malcolm called it. Then things had changed forever.

She'd found her gift by chance. She'd been searching for something useful to do with her time. One day, while sitting in church and admiring the beautiful colors that filled the windows, she began to wonder if perhaps . . . just perhaps, she could find a pastime more significant than embroidery or watercolors, neither of which was bold enough to hold Kat's interest. What she needed was a pastime that would produce something glorious and beautiful. Something like the stained glass windows that cast such gorgeous shadows of red and blue and gold across the floor of the church.

The thought took hold and grew. She began to make inquiries, and to her delight, she found that one of the groomsmen in Malcolm's stable—a large, ruddy giant of a man by the name of Simon—had once apprenticed doing glasswork. Soon Kat was visiting that very glass shop and learning the craft herself. Though it took time, Kat had a natural instinct for color and design, and she found that she loved every painstaking minute.

The glasswork quickly became more than a pastime. It became a goal. With it, she would carve her own niche in the world.

The cottage had been a natural choice. Kat had grown up there, and though it needed some work after sitting empty after her mother's death, it was basically sturdy. Though Malcolm had protested loud and long, Kat had moved into the cottage a scant month later, taking Simon with her. His sister, Annie, came along soon after that.

Kat guided Merriweather across the clearing to

the barn. Sensing a carrot was waiting, the mare kicked up her feet and attempted to trot.

Kat laughed. "Easy now! You'll get your carrot in good time."

A large, red-haired man came out of the barn door, a plank of wood resting easily on his shoulder. He paused when he saw Kat, his craggy face softening slightly. "There ye be! Annie has been lookin' all over fer ye."

Kat grinned at Simon as she kicked her foot out of the stirrup and stepped down. "What does she want?"

Simon lowered his brow. "I don't know, but she has some of her bosom friends with her. Last I heard, they were talkin' aboot the new guest at the castle."

Kat undid Merriweather's saddle, hefting it off the mare's back and onto the fence rail. "I met him this morning."

"Did ye now? What do ye have to say aboot him?"

Kat had an instant image of mischievous blue eyes fringed in thick black lashes, her body tingling at the memory of strong hands moving sinuously over her body. She forced a casual shrug. "I don't have much to say at all." Not to Simon, anyway.

Why *had* she been so slow to react when the stranger had kissed her? None of Malcolm's other houseguests had managed to weasel a kiss out of her. But this guest . . . Kat had to smile a little. Whatever the reason, she wasn't really sorry it had happened. It was a lovely, warm memory, and as long as it went no further, there was no harm. No harm at all.

Besides, the man had been damned good at what he was about. The thought made her grin even more.

Simon's gaze narrowed. He set the wood against the fence. "Out with it, lass. What has ye smilin' so big?"

Kat's cheeks heated. "Nothing. I was just thinking about—" Good Lord what did she say now? "Things," she finished weakly. Things like strong, well-defined hands that could cup one ever so intimately and make one's stomach tighten with need. Things like a pair of firm, warm lips that knew all too well how to send one's thoughts to places they were better not going.

"Hmph," Simon said, eyeing her up and down as she rubbed down Merriweather and then led the mare into the coolness of the barn. Simon followed along, his gaze never leaving her. "Whatever ye're thinkin' aboot, 'tis makin' yer cheeks turn red."

Kat wisely ignored him. Though he was a scant two years older than she, she thought of Simon as a father. Certainly he'd been more involved in her life than her own father had been.

"I'm fine, Simon. Just a bit heated from the ride back." Kat closed the stall door on Merriweather, and then left the barn. "Where is Annie?"

Simon followed her outside. "She's in the kitchen with Fat Mary."

Kat curled her nose.

Simon nodded morosely. "That's what I thought, too. Fat Mary does nothin' but spread rumors, night 'n' day. I don't know why Annie puts up wid it."

Kat could have told Simon that his sister was addicted to gossip. While Annie rarely passed on any information she gathered in her meticulous cullings, she enjoyed knowing more than anyone else.

Simon crossed his arms and leaned back on his heels. "I've got the lads down in the workshop, finishing off the last window for the Earl of Argyll. I tol' the lads they'd best make it something to behold. If we do a good job, there'll be more where that comes from."

Kat nodded. "The earl has a new wife. She'll be wanting to put her own mark on his household. She told me she wants to commission a window for every child they have."

"Women," Simon said, shaking his head. "They can think of more ways to spend blunt."

Kat lifted her brows. "I'm a woman."

"Aye, but ye ain't all trussed up in the need to tell everyone what to do." Simon glanced at the house for a moment, before adding in an undertone, "Take Annie. M'sister has a bad habit of bossin' a man aboot until he's ready to bundle his clothes and run for the hills."

"Just see to it that *you* don't run," Kat said, leaning over to give him a quick hug. "Or if you do, at least promise to come back after you've enjoyed a pint or ten of freedom. I can't do without you more than one day. Perhaps two, if things are slow."

Simon's smile blossomed. "I have to come back, lassie. Who else'll make the windows bearing the coat of arms fer those fancy earls and dukes?"

"Who indeed?" She kissed his cheek and turned to the house. "Tell the lads I'll be with them directly.

I just want to see what Annie bought in the village today."

"I'll tell them," Simon promised. He retrieved his plank and hoisted it over his shoulder, then winked. "I'll tell them ye're in a rare mood, too. That should get them to hoppin'."

"I don't want them hopping, just working. We've more orders to fill than there are hours in the day."

"Don't ye fash, Miss Kat. We'll come aboot. See if we don't." He gave her a reassuring nod, then left, walking toward the workshop, a long, low building set on the other side of the cottage, back against the line of trees.

She watched him go, a fond smile touching her mouth. Simon possessed a heavy sense of responsibility and a natural tendency to step in and do what most needed doing. These were just two of the many things she loved about him.

Kat turned and crossed to the back door of the cottage. If there was any chance that mud or dirt was clinging to her boots, she always entered through the kitchen. As she stopped outside the open door to scrape her feet, Kat heard voices from inside.

"I seed him meself, I did!" said a woman in a breathless voice. Kat recognized Fat Mary, a kitchen maid from Kilkairn. As round as a barrel, there was no mistaking her rough voice. "He's as beautiful as Lucifer, all black hair and blue eyes."

"Is he tall?" asked another woman. That sounded like Lucy, who came from the village to help Annie with the cooking.

"Tall he is," Fat Mary agreed with so much enthusiasm that Kat found a scowl upon her face. "He has a fine arse, too."

Arse? How on earth could Mary know that? Kat leaned closer to the open door and tried to peek around the corner.

"Och now, how do ye know aboot the man's arse?" Annie asked, her voice sharp.

God bless Annie, Kat decided with rising satisfaction. The housekeeper never stood for any nonsense.

"Why, I walked into his room to stoke the fire and there he was, lying on the counterpane, sound asleep and as bare-arsed as the day he was borned."

Kat took a hasty step forward, then caught herself. St. John had arrived in the middle of the night, and Kat herself had been there when he'd awakened, so it was highly unlikely Mary knew anything more than the man's fully clothed appearance. Mary was lying; she had to be. But Kat knew that bursting into the room, ringing with indignation, would only draw undue attention to herself.

In the time Kat had known her, Fat Mary had launched and sailed several hot air balloons' worth of gossip. None of them landing anywhere near the truth. But if Fat Mary started such a rumor about Malcolm's new guest, every single maid in the countryside soon would be making excuses to visit Kilkairn in an effort to glimpse the handsome stranger. For some reason, Kat found that very annoying.

Lifting her chin, she walked into the kitchen and looked directly at Fat Mary. "I was at the castle this very morning, and you did not light the fires in any of the bedchambers."

Fat Mary flushed. She was a large, fleshy woman with pale, stringy hair and watery gray eyes. "I did the guest chamber!"

"Oh?"

"Yes. That's when I seed him, whilst I was lighting the fire."

Kat lifted her brows. "Which chamber did you say St. John was sleeping in?"

"Which—" Mary shifted uneasily. "I don't remember, exactly—perhaps 'twas the green one."

Lucy frowned. "But ye tol' me on the way here that he was in the gold room and—"

"Ha!" Annie plopped her fists on her narrow hips as she glared at Mary. "Ye were fashin' us, weren't ye? Tellin' us fibs aboot one o' Lord Strathmore's guests. Ye ought to be ashamed o' yerself."

"I'm not tellin' fibs," Fat Mary said, though her gaze shot to the door and back as if she were considering running for her life. "I seed him, I did. And his arse, too!"

"I don't know who you 'seed' or whose arse, but it wasn't St. John's," Kat said. "He was in the blue room because none of the others were ready."

"There!" Annie eyed Mary with disgust. "Isn't it time ye returned to Kilkairn? I daresay they've more dirty pots fer ye to scrub."

Mary stiffened, her plump shoulders rising almost to her ears. "I was just tellin' ye what I seed, was all."

"What you *wished* you'd seed," Annie amended. Though a good head shorter than any other woman in the room, she managed to maintain control of every conversation, simply through sheer force of her character. Even now, her hair tucked beneath a cap, her whip-cord thin body covered with a gray gown, and solid, plain shoes on her feet, she was plainly in command. "Off with ye. Mary, ye know where ye're wanted . . . and where ye're not. I'll have yer cart brought around. Lucy, thank ye fer the jelly. Tell yer mum we're grateful."

Kat watched while Annie bustled her guests out to their cart and waved them on their way. Then, wiping her hands on her apron, Annie returned and pulled out a wooden bowl and a sack of potatoes and began peeling them.

Kat found another knife and joined in. "I'm sorry your visit turned out so unpleasantly."

"Och, don't think on it. Fat Mary is as Fat Mary is. By this time tomorrow, neither of us will remember who was mad aboot what." Annie finished off a peeling with an expert twist of her wrist.

"She's a braggart, all right," Kat agreed.

"Indeed. Actin' as if she was the only one who saw him in the castle." Annie turned to Kat and eyed her up and down. "Well?"

"Well what?" Kat asked uneasily. She kept her gaze on the potato she was peeling so she wouldn't have to meet Annie's gaze.

"What do *you* have to say aboot the stranger at the castle?"

"I know his name is St. John." And that he had a mouth made for kissing. Kat cut the potato with more force than was necessary, the knife thunking soundly on the cutting board.

Annie eyed the flashing knife with some misgiving. "Indeed?"

"Aye. If I remember what Malcolm told me a while ago, I believe they met whilst the two were down at Eton." Or so she thought.

"Indeed?" Annie said. "Is that all ye know?"

"Aye," Kat said.

"Hm. I suppose I'll have to wait until my cousin Jane gets a look at him. She's ever had an eye for a handsome man."

Kat didn't like that at all. Jane was the upstairs maid at Kilkairn, and a more lascivious woman was difficult to find.

In fact, Kat was quite certain that Jane had bedded most, if not all, of Malcolm's guests. "I daresay St. John isn't the sort of man Jane would like to dally with."

Annie looked astounded. "He was breathin', wasn't he?"

"Aye, but—"

"Then Jane would enjoy dallyin' with him. She's not particular, is our Jane."

Kat cut another potato in two, this time slicing it so thoroughly that she buried the tip of the knife in the table top. "Oh! I'm sorry."

Annie's hand closed over Kat's. "Just leave the knife there. I'll take care of the rest of these."

"Are you certain? I can at least—"

"I'm certain. Besides, aren't the lads waitin' on ye?"

They would be, of course. Since housework had never held any appeal, Kat readily washed her hands in a bucket and dried them on a towel Annie kept nearby. "You're right. We have to finish the windows by the end of this week or we'll be good and behind."

"There is no 'good and behind.' There's only 'behind.' Get to work, Miss Kat." Annie flashed a smile, her angular, usually morose face lighting. "I'd never let the lads alone for a minute. You canno' tell what they'll be into."

Kat agreed, smiling in return. The men they'd gathered as glassworkers were a singular lot, all of them strong on personality. Simon had collected most of them, scrutinizing them carefully. Kat paid more than a fair wage, and she rewarded quality work, which meant the best of the best were drawn to her cottage.

Waving good-bye to Annie, Kat left. She lifted her face to the sun as she walked across the clearing to the workshop where the pleasant sound of hammering and male voices made her smile. All in all, it was a good thing she wouldn't be going to Kilkairn Castle any more this week. She'd spent far too much time mulling over the handsome Englishman as it was, and all for no more than a little kiss. Heaven only knew what state she'd be in if he'd done more. So to preserve her own peace, she'd stay away from Kilkairn. At least until St. John was on his bonny way.

The carriage swept into the drive and pulled up in front of Kilkairn Castle much as it had done the night before. Paul leaned forward and caught a glimpse of a solitary figure standing on the front portico.

"Mr. St. John's biting at the bit, ain't he?" John the coachman said.

"So it appears." Paul jumped down the second the coach came to a halt. He hadn't been entirely certain he'd find the master up and about. It was only eleven, after all. But there he was, pacing the front portico, hat in hand, dressed for riding.

As soon as Paul approached, St. John smiled. "There you are! How was the inn?"

"Adequate, sir." Barely. But it was better than staying at the castle.

"Excellent. I find Kilkairn just as satisfying."

A smile hovered over St. John's mouth, and Paul found himself responding. "I'm surprised ye're up so early, sir."

"What? Me? Why, I love mornings!" Devon waved a hand. "Just smell the fresh air. Taste the crisp coolness of the dawn."

Paul didn't point out that dawn had been hours ago. "Indeed, sir. I hadn't noticed."

"You'd better wake up, Paul. Such glorious mornings do not come often." St. John's eyes twinkled. "Almost never, where I am concerned."

Paul grinned. "No, sir. Did you wish us to take you somewhere today?"

"Actually, yes. But I'm not sure where."

"Sir?"

"I want to find a house located in the woods. A smallish house, from what I understand."

"A small house? Ye want one to let?"

"No, no, no! This house belongs to someone, and I wish to pay a visit."

Things suddenly became clear to Paul. He was beginning to smell a petticoat. "Sir, who might this house belong to?"

"Miss Katherine Macdonald."

From the look on the master's face, this was obviously a promising errand of a romantic nature. "If Miss Macdonald lives hereabouts, I daresay someone in the stable will know how to get there."

"Excellent idea! Furthermore, I believe I should ride there myself. All I need are the directions."

"Of course, sir. Shall I have the gelding saddled?"

"Yes. I daresay Thunder could use a stretch." Devon had paid a small fortune for the horse, and had never regretted it. Especially today when he could ride up to Kat's cottage astride a horse worthy of carrying a knight.

Paul bowed, then went on his way. In a relatively short time, he returned with directions, leading Thunder to the steps. The animal was huge, all gleaming black muscle and streaming mane and tail. Devon pulled on his gloves. Miss Katherine's head was bound to be turned.

Moments later, Devon galloped across the green fields of Kilkairn toward the forest. He was spurred forward by the memory of Kat's lush body in his lap.

Devon considered briefly the information Malcolm had let fall. There was an unspoken code of gentlemen that averred that one did not attempt to seduce the sisters of one's best friends. Malcolm must have decided that any flirtation of Devon's was nothing more than that—a flirtation, begun and ended with a kiss. Of course, Malcolm also knew that Devon would never go beyond the line of the acceptable, not without the permission and encouragement of the lady in question. What stung was that for some reason, Malcolm seemed to think his sister was immune to Devon's particular charms—that Kat would want nothing more from Devon than a kiss.

But Devon was not so sure; Kat seemed to possess a very passionate nature. Whatever the truth, it would certainly take more than a kiss to ease his lustful thoughts of Kat Macdonald, and to satisfy the curiosity and heat he'd seen burning in her eyes.

But the real beauty of it all was that the more time Devon spent with Malcolm's ineligible sister, the less chance there was that Devon might fall victim to the talisman ring's magical powers.

With Kat and her ruined reputation, Devon was completely safe, no matter how far their flirtation went. More proof that he was smarter by far than any ring ever made. Smiling to himself, he urged Thunder farther into the woods, certain he was on his way to dislodge an evil fate.

Chapter 5

It's really quite easy. As soon as you see the fires of wrath in their eyes and know your time has come, you begin the seduction. A brush of your hand across theirs when they reach for the crème pot. A heated glance. A lingering appreciation for how they look . . . smell . . . taste. Just try it, sir. I've been married fourteen years, and not once has she managed to ring a peal over my head without stammering and blushing like a school girl.

Viscount Mooreland to his uncle,
the Earl of Stempleton,
whilst viewing the horses for sale at Tattersall's

$\mathcal{D}$evon had always believed that one's greatest strength was also one's greatest weakness. Such was his case, anyway. From the time he'd been a child, he had never been known for his lack of persistence.

Once, when he had attained the ripe age of five, his parents had left for a brief visit to London. Devon had begged to go with them, but had been refused.

Looking back now, he could see that perhaps his parents had desired some time alone. Even though they employed a squadron of governesses and tutors, six children had to have been a drain on their marital reserves.

But at the time, all Devon had known was that he was being left behind. Thus he'd waited until the trunks for the upcoming journey were sitting in the front hall and he'd opened the largest one, removed one of his mother's voluminous gowns and stuffed it beneath the settee in the front sitting room, and then paid his brother Chase a shilling to close the trunk and lock him in.

Moments later an unsuspecting footman had carried the trunk to the waiting coach and strapped it on the back. Neither Devon nor Chase had thought of such mundane things as food or air. Within thirty minutes of rumbling out of the long drive, Devon had begun to realize the shortfalls of his plan.

He became increasingly hot, the air stifling and then thin, and all the while he was aware of a horrid need to relieve himself.

By the time the first hour had passed, he'd begun to panic and tried to gain the attention of the coachman, but the noise of the creaking, swaying coach and the clopping of the horses concealed the thumping of his small fists on the trunk lid. No one heard him.

It was a good thing the trip to London was a mere three hours, though by the time Devon was discovered, he was ill from the heat and the confinement. It took almost two days before he could get out of bed.

Of course, he'd been thankful for his convalescence as it prevented him from receiving the switching that should have been his. As his father would later say when the incident was brought up, "Devon's determination will be both the making and the breaking of him. God only knows which."

Now here he was, not in London, but in a clearing in the forest, looking at what had to be Kat Macdonald's cottage, and that same determination that had caused him to ride in a trunk all the way to London was urging him forward.

The sun shone on the house and lit the clearing until he almost expected the door to fly open and little men in matching tunics to come tumbling out, turning buttercups into gold, or making mushrooms into sweet cakes, or some such nonsense.

"Either that or seven beautiful maidens," Devon said to himself, trying to remember the fairy tales his mother had so delighted in telling. Something about seven pairs of shoes and dancing . . . He frowned. Whatever the tale, he'd forgotten most of it. Not that it mattered. It was all childhood nonsense anyway.

Devon urged Thunder across the clearing. The gelding frisked and frolicked, prancing as if afraid of the splotches of sun that trembled across the ground in unison with the breeze. They were only about halfway to the cottage when Devon realized they had an audience.

A group of men stood outside a long, low building. The group was small, but the men were not. They were all huge. "Giants," Devon muttered. "One. Two. Three—good God. Seven giants."

He pulled Thunder to a halt. He wasn't afraid of the giants. The tall ones always fell the hardest. Still, it wouldn't do to be rude.

He led Thunder up to them and dismounted. "Good day," he called. "I am looking for—"

Kat stood in the doorway behind the men, dressed in the same drab gown as before. It hung gloriously on her curves, molding itself to her slants and slopes. The sunlight dappled her hair gold, muting the red and making her shine like a new guinea. Standing with the men, she looked petite.

"What are you doing here?" she asked, one hand propped on her hip.

It was hardly the welcome he wished. "I came to ask you a question." He glanced at the men, offering a smile to offset their glares. "In private," he added.

They didn't move. Neither did Devon.

"I don't wish for a word in private with y—" Her gaze wandered past him to Thunder, her eyes widening. "What a lovely horse!"

Devon hid a smile. Malcolm had been right; Kat loved horses. "Thunder is a lovely animal. And he knows it, too."

One of the men—a red-haired, burly sort with disapproving eyes and a grim expression—said, "Miss Kat, we've work to do."

"Aye, Simon," she said, though she continued to walk toward Thunder. "How long have you had him?"

"I purchased him a year ago."

She reached them and placed a hand on Thunder's neck. The horse pretended to shy. She laughed and grabbed the bridle, holding him still while she patted his side. "He's a high-strung one, isn't he?"

"Miss Kat!" Another of the men chimed in, a large, brown-haired man with a beard and thick brows. "We've glass to do and time's a-wastin'." He glared at Devon the whole time he was speaking.

"Glass?" Devon said quietly so that only Kat could hear him.

She started to answer, then hesitated. "It doesn't matter. A business concern, no more." She turned to the brown-haired man. "I wish to speak to Mr. St. John. Go ahead and begin on the next brace of cuts."

The men eyed him sullenly, apparently blaming him for Kat's answer. Devon took the opportunity to eye them all back. It was a strange assortment. Some were brown-haired, some red; some had freckles, some didn't. Except for their size and the glares on their faces, they were as different as the day was long.

Devon wondered if they were going to allow Kat to stay and speak with him. Hm. How did one deal with seven giants? He didn't recall a single one of his mother's fairy tales that gave instructions. If only he had some magic beans. The thought made him grin, a fact that did not sit well with the giant conclave one bit.

"Miss Kat," snapped the redheaded one. It was quickly becoming apparent he was the leader. "I don't think ye should be standin' aboot, talkin' to a stranger."

"Simon, for the love of—what could happen? We're here, in the middle of the clearing. If the man is foolish enough to attempt to molest me, I'll black his eyes and send him on his way."

Devon had to bite back a smile for the calm way she spoke. He didn't know of another woman who would have made such a statement in such an unemotional manner.

"Simon," Kat said. "Take the lads back inside; I'll be in shortly."

"We've two more windows to make," he answered, though his gaze never left Devon.

"I realize that," she answered, a note of steel in her voice. "Which is why you all need to get back to work. I cannot do the cuts until you've got the glass ready."

Whatever that meant, it must have been true, for the men began to shift uneasily. Finally Simon flexed his shoulders and nodded once. "Very well. If ye need us, ye've but to call." He cast a last, cold glance at Devon and then turned to the others. "Back inside, lads. The sooner we get the glass ready, the sooner Miss Kat can get it cut."

As soon as they shuffled back into the building, Devon glanced down at Kat. "Your servants?"

"No. Apprentices. Except Simon." She gave Thunder one last pat, then stepped away, her gaze meeting his. "Why are you here, Sassenach?"

"Sassenach?"

"Englishman."

He wasn't sure he liked the way she said that. "You're English, too. At least half."

Her mouth tightened, her green eyes accusing. "You've been talking to Malcolm."

Devon nodded.

A faint line of color touched Kat's face, and she turned away, facing the building. "I suppose I shouldn't be surprised."

Devon eyed a large wood curl in Kat's red-gold hair. He reached out to untangle the sliver of wood, but Kat yanked away.

She eyed him suspiciously. "What are you doing?"

He smiled and reached again, only this time more slowly. She held still, though her body was so stiff he could almost feel the tension seeping from her.

Apparently, when she wasn't surprised, Kat Macdonald was a bit shy of touch. He wondered if that was a result of the incident that left her "ruined" in the eyes of society, or because of Malcolm's other guests continually groping her when they came to visit.

He plucked the wood curl from her hair, then showed it to her. "What *have* you been doing?"

She took the sliver of wood and tossed it to the ground. "Helping Hamish with the frames."

"Frames?"

"Malcolm didn't tell you everything, then. I am not a lady, St. John. I make my own way, I do." Her firm chin lifted and she said with simple pride, "We are glassmakers, the lads and I. The best there is."

"If you're a glassmaker, why is there a wood shaving in your hair?"

"Because glass must be fit in a frame. And the right frame is as important as finding the right colors for the picture."

"You and the 'lads' do this by yourselves?"

"Aye. And we've more work than we can fill."

His gaze roved over her, from the pride in her eyes, to the strength of her body, to the broad grace of her hands. She was a conundrum, this woman, a strange mixture of strength and . . . was it vulnerability? Or pride? Something sweet and delicate rested deep in her eyes, and he was determined to discover what it was.

Despite Devon's determination to merely establish a dalliance with Kat, he had to admit that he was somewhat fascinated. Not too much, of course. He was no wet-eared halfling to think interest was love. It wasn't, of course. But it did promise to make the flirtation something special, which was fine by Devon. It had been a long time since a woman—any woman—had truly intrigued him.

Devon reflected that of all the women he knew, with the exception of a housekeeper, laundress, or maid or two, none had had professions of their own. Truly, everything about Kat Macdonald was larger than life—her size, her blazing color, even the gentle rasp of her husky voice—all were *more* in some way. More than he expected, and far more than a proper lady should be.

The thought was rather exciting. "Do you know what I think?"

Though her expression didn't change, he felt her withdraw, as if in expectation of a blow. Devon placed a finger beneath her chin and tilted her face to his. "I think you're an exceptional, astounding woman, and I want to know more of you."

Kat discovered that it was possible to stop breathing

even while panting. And she was panting. There was a fey magic about the stranger, something that made her body quiver the second he was within range.

If she looked back in her memory, there was only one other time she'd been so affected by a man. The memory tightened about her throat and halted her voice.

"Furthermore," Devon St. John continued, his voice low and smooth, "I wonder why you are the way you are." His gaze wandered over her, from her head to her feet, a question in his blue gaze. "Who are you, Katherine Anne Macdonald?"

She stiffened. "I am who I am. And I would prefer it if you did not call me by that name."

"Katherine? Why not?" His eyes twinkled. "It's your real name, isn't it?"

"Yes. But my mother never used it unless she was angry, so I prefer Kat. Or for you, Miss Macdonald."

He laughed. "Miss Macdonald it is. But only if you'll call me Devon." His gaze darkened the slightest bit. "I want to hear my name on your lips."

Kat had to rub her arms to stop the goose bumps that traveled up her skin at the silken tone of his voice. It took all of her composure to answer in a steady voice. "I hope you aren't counting on such. I will never say your name."

He leaned forward, his eyes so rich a blue that she couldn't look away. "Is that a wager?"

"No, Mr. St. John. It is a fact."

The man smiled then, a faint curve to his well formed mouth that drew the gaze and sent heated thoughts through her mind. "Miss Macdonald, may

I say that I look forward to the challenge of our continued friendship."

Friendship . . . was that what this was? Kat was held by the thought. It had been a long time since she'd thought of having a friend—any friend, even a dangerous one like Devon St. John. And he was dangerous. She stole a glance at him from beneath her lashes.

Kat was used to seeing rather robust men appear pallid beside the likes of her lads, especially Alistair and Simon, who had to dip their heads to enter the lower barn door. But this man carried himself with such masculine ease that she caught herself looking at his legs, his hips, his hands . . . wondering what he would be like in bed. She already knew his kisses were hot and lethal, a fact that only made her wonder the more about the rest of him.

Kat's cheeks heated. Bless her, but she was worse than Annie's cousin, Jane.

Well, perhaps not *that* bad, but bad enough. "I am exactly what you see, St. John. Can you say the same?"

"I think so," he answered, nodding thoughtfully. "I have never been one to dissemble."

Before she could stop herself, she snorted in disbelief.

His brow jerked lower. "I am serious. I do not lie."

"Never?"

"Never."

"Have you ever told a woman she had beautiful eyes for no other reason than to tempt her into your arms?"

He opened his mouth. Then closed it. After a long moment, he puffed out a sigh. "Up until now, I hadn't thought of that as a lie."

"No? What would you call it?"

"A hard-won compliment."

Her own lips twitched, but she swallowed the smile before it could blossom. "That is the problem with men like you. You lie so much and so oft that you no longer know the truth. Now if you'll excuse me, St. John, I've work to do."

She turned to go, but his hand was about her wrist before she could take a step.

"I came for a reason, Miss Macdonald. I came to ask you if you'd do me the honor of taking a ride with me."

"A ride?" She tried to pretend that the feel of his strong hand about her wrist wasn't making her stomach heat in a most disturbing way.

"A ride," he repeated. He gave her a rueful, lop-sided smile. "That's all. One simple ride. I'm here alone, you know. And I've no place to go for three weeks. Surely you can spare a few hours of your time for something as innocuous as a ride."

For one blessed mad moment, Kat thought of agreeing. She could almost see the two of them, riding across the fields, laughing and talking. But then reality returned and she remembered another time, another man, also pleading for nothing more than "a few hours." At the time, she'd wondered what harm could occur in a few hours. Now she knew.

She pulled her wrist free. "No thank you, Mr. St. John. You'll have to find someone else to pass the time with. I'm not available." With that, pride stiffening her weakened will, she turned on her heel and quickly made her way into the shop.

Malcolm climbed the stairs to his wife's bedchamber, his boots landing heavily on the grayish runner. He tried to ignore the small puffs of dust that swirled with each footfall and the dusty slickness of the railing beneath his hand, just as he tried to ignore the cobwebs that hung unattended from the branched chandeliers displayed overhead, and the faint musty odor that was slowly permeating his once orderly household.

Though he'd been unable to explain the entire situation to Devon, the truth was that Malcolm and his wife were not arguing. Oh no, it had progressed far beyond that. They were now at war. What had begun as a difference of opinion had escalated into something far worse.

It was a simple matter, really. He wanted children; his wife did not. Worse, he wanted to stay here, at Kilkairn, and enjoy life at the castle, while she was determined to drag him to Edinburgh.

Normally, Malcolm had nothing against Edinburgh. He rather enjoyed a taste of town life on occasion. But after Fiona had denied his request for a child and refused to stay at Kilkairn for more than two weeks at a stretch, he'd dug in his heels and refused to go anywhere. Better yet, he'd refused to allow her to travel, as well.

He'd thought to wear her down, make her agree to his wishes—once she had his son, she could travel all she wished, and with his blessing. It seemed a fair enough request, but she'd been far from agreeable. What was worse was that he'd underestimated one small facet of his lovely wife's character—her overgrown sense of pride. It was equal to his own, if not larger and far more entrenched.

In response to his ultimatums, she'd done what she could to make Kilkairn Castle the uncomfortable mess it was today, irritating the capable servants until they left and neglecting to oversee the ones that stayed. Malcolm had uneasy dreams of Fiona dancing through the castle, tossing dust in the air. Then, once she tired of that game, resting in his favorite chair by the fire to knit cobwebs of every shape, size, and color.

Malcolm paused outside a wide oak door and straightened his shoulders. "Do not give an inch," he muttered to himself. His father would have never put up with such nonsense, and neither would Malcolm. Still, it was difficult to maintain his pride because he loved Fiona . . . didn't he?

A cold grip of uncertainty held him in place. As always, it was the one question he couldn't answer. What if his love for his wife only lasted as long as his father's love had lasted for his mother? Malcolm remembered his mother's pain each time his father strayed.

It was a long moment before he lifted his hand and knocked on the door and then entered.

The room was decorated in delicate blue and white, Fiona's favorite colors. A large bed sat in the center of one wall, an ornate dressing table across the room, near the large fireplace.

His bride sat at the dressing table, a lace gown tossed over her shoulders, her hair streaming down her back as her maid brushed out the long curls.

Fiona's gaze met Malcolm's in the mirror and a stubborn flush rose in her cheeks as she looked away.

Malcolm flicked a glance toward the maid. "Marie, I wish to speak with Lady Strathmore privately."

Marie's gaunt face reddened and she gripped the back of Fiona's chair in a protective manner. "I was just brushing Her Ladyship's hair and—"

"That will be all, Marie," Malcolm said firmly.

The maid sniffed and then looked at Fiona. "Madam?"

Fiona sighed. "You may go, Marie."

"*Oui,* but—" Marie glanced at Malcolm as if to ascertain his trustworthiness.

That irked him. By the saints, he was the man of this house, and he wouldn't stand for such impertinence. He spun on his heel and went to the door and held it open.

Head high as if she were on her way to the guillotine, Marie slowly went to the door. The second she crossed the threshold, Malcolm kicked the door closed behind her.

Fiona jumped. "Malcolm!"

"Sorry. My foot slipped. I meant to plant it in her arse."

Fiona's cheeks pinkened. "There is no need to be crude."

"I disagree." He met her gaze in the reflection of the mirror. "I came to speak with you about this morning. You, madam, are out of hand."

Fiona adjusted the cut-crystal decanters on the dresser. "I am no such thing."

"I sent you a request to join me and a guest for breakfast. You refused to attend."

She picked up the brush and began brushing her hair. "I was not yet up."

"Then send word that you had to dress! I asked you to attend us and you should have."

Her chin lifted. "You know how I prize my mornings."

Mornings. The thought echoed in his mind. At one time, he'd loved mornings. Mornings when he'd come into this very room and climb into Fiona's bed to find her warm and soft, snuggled deep beneath the blankets. A pain tweaked his heart. "It has been some time since I was allowed to share mornings with you."

Her cheeks turned a deep pink, though her gaze met his steadily. "You know the cost of returning to my bed."

Malcolm paused. A part of him wished to end this ridiculous standoff. To return to the warmth of their previous relationship. But he could not bend. "And you know the cost of returning to Edinburgh. I will have a son, madam."

Fiona pulled the brush through a long strand of hair. It was thick and as brown as the forest floor, with threads of gold glimmering in the silken mass. "As before, we are at an impasse."

Malcolm rubbed his neck where an ache was beginning to form. "Look, Fiona, I didn't come here to argue. I came to ask that you be polite to St. John."

"Oh!" She tossed the brush to her dresser where it clattered to a stop among a mass of crystal bottles. "When have I ever been rude to any of your guests?"

"Never. It's just that I happen to think that perhaps St. John is interested in Kat."

"They all are, at first. But you know what will happen. St. John will take one look at Kat and she'll set her fist in his eye for his impertinence. And then he'll want nothing more to do with her. Her attraction never seems to last past the first meeting."

"This seems different."

Fiona's delicate brows rose. "Oh?"

"They met this morning, and if I'm not mistaken, Devon is quite interested."

"But Kat is—" Fiona bit off the rest of the sentence.

Malcolm's gaze narrowed. "She's what?"

Her cheeks glowed. "Nothing."

"My sister may be a tad unusual, but she is right as rain. Give a man a chance to get to know her, and he'll come up to snuff. See if he doesn't."

"I've nothing against your sister, you know that. It's just that a man like St. John would be more comfortable with someone like . . . oh, Murien."

"*Your* sister?" Malcolm almost stuttered.

Fiona flounced in her seat. "You have *never* liked Murien!"

"That's not true—"

"Oh, just admit it!"

He paused, fighting to control the tight ball of anger that burned in his stomach. "I've never been fond of Murien and well you know it, though that has nothing to do with us."

Fiona met his gaze a moment. "Except that it is yet another way in which we differ. I vow, but I am sick unto death of our squabbles. If only there was a way to—" She paused, a light coming into her eyes. "Malcolm."

"Aye?" he answered, a faint quiver of alarm dancing up his neck. "What is it?"

The look she turned on him was almost blinding in its luminance. "I know what we need to do to end this argument between us!"

"What?"

"You and I will make a wager. I shall invite Murien here and we shall see whose sister is more to Mr. St. John's liking."

Malcolm frowned. Murien here? Under his roof? "I don't think I could stand it."

"There is nothing wrong with her!"

He shrugged. "If you say so."

"At least *my* sister knows how to dress."

"You have me there. Kat has never been one to toss her good sense after fashion."

"No," Fiona snapped, "just her virtue."

Malcolm's jaw tightened until it ached. "My sister may have made some mistakes in her youth, but you have to admit that she lives circumspectly now."

"Circumspect? You call living with seven men in the middle of a forest—"

"They are her apprentices. I have explained that time and again."

"Of course," Fiona said tightly. "Do we have a wager then? My sister against yours."

Malcolm considered this. He was so dispirited by

their disagreements. Perhaps this would be a way to regain at least a little of his peace. "Done," Malcolm said. "And the wager?"

"If I win, you will cease pestering me to have a child and we will spend every season for the next five years in Edinburgh."

"The whole season?" he sputtered. "For *five* years?"

"All of it. And you will spare no expense."

"That's a steep wager."

"Afraid you'll lose?"

He ground his teeth. "No, I am not afraid to lose. I know Kat, and there are things about her that you wouldn't understand. Things that make me certain she'll win hands down over your whey-faced sister."

"Oh!" Fiona stood in a faint rustle of silk. "Don't you dare speak ill of my sister! At least Murien has manners. Kat goes about in clothes covered in wood curls and smelling of burned metal."

Malcolm jammed his hands into his pockets to keep from reaching for her. "*Enough*! My wager, madam wife, is to be allowed back in your bed until you bear the fruits of that endeavor. I shall have my son. One way or another."

Fiona's hand tightened about the back of her chair, tears threatening. "I know what happens to marriages once a child is born. My own father—"

"I am not your father. I would never leave you."

"He didn't leave, either. Not physically. Once he had his heir, he was just more interested in other things."

Malcolm raked a hand through his hair. "Fiona, I will not—"

She took a step forward, her gaze almost pleading. "Malcolm, can you promise me that your feelings for me won't change? Not even when we have a child?"

He opened his mouth to say the word, but then it happened. Could he care for a woman forever? She saw it in his eyes, a flicker of his uncertainty, dark and fearful. Fiona's heart sank and it took all her pride to keep her head upright. She'd been right to deny him. Right to worry that his feelings for her were not immune to change.

She steeled her heart once again. He was angry with her decision not to have children. But she could stand his anger better than his absence. One day she might agree to have a child, just not now. Not while she was still desperately in love with her own husband.

Malcolm shook his head. "Madam, I await your answer. Do you agree to our wager?"

She hoped her lips didn't tremble as she resumed her seat and reclaimed her brush. "Yes, I agree. And I hope with all my heart that I win."

His jaw hardened. "We are settled then. I won't burden you with my company any longer." He spun on his heel and left, slamming the door behind him.

Fiona scarcely waited for his footsteps to fade before she dropped the brush, jumped up and threw herself across her bed, where she cried until she could cry no more.

Chapter 6

A man will vow to his dying day that he hates being chased by a woman. But let him meet one who will not chase him, one who barely knows he is alive, one who acts not only disinterested, but disgusted as well, and he will do everything in his power to fix her interest.

Earl of Stempleton to his neighbor Mr. Poole,
while sharing a glass of port after dinner
at His Lordship's London house

*A*fter riding Thunder another two hours, over hill and through valley, Devon returned to Kilkairn. His disposition had not improved on the ride. That was twice now he'd been rebuffed by Kat Macdonald, and it was twice too many.

Not that he was giving up. Bloody hell no. If anyone deserved to be brought down a peg, it was that golden-haired waif who thought herself better than the world. Devon now had *two* reasons to visit the glen in the woods. One, to escape the threat of the ring, and two, to teach a certain high-handed miss a much needed lesson.

Devon strode into Kilkairn, his mind on the problem ahead. What could he do? If only—

"Devon!"

He paused to see Malcolm standing in the doorway to a room off the great hall, a brandy glass in his hand. "Malcolm! How was your day? I took a ride—"

"Come and have a drink with me," Malcolm said, lifting his glass and gesturing. "Finest batch of brandy I've ever had. And there's plenty where this came from."

A glass of brandy would be welcome, Devon decided. He followed Malcolm into the room, finding a snug library of sorts, lit by a large, warming fire. It bore only a few signs of the slovenly care that infested the rest of the castle.

Malcolm went to a sideboard and splashed a generous amount into a fresh glass, then touched up his own drink. "There you go."

Devon took the drink and then made his way to the brace of leather chairs that sat by the crackling flames.

Malcolm joined him, stretching his legs before him. He eyed Devon a moment, then said, "Where have you been today?"

Devon thought about prevaricating, but something about Malcolm's expression made him pause. "I went riding. And I found your sister's cottage in the woods."

Malcolm's eyes brightened. "Did you indeed?"

"Indeed." Devon shrugged. "She was very busy, and I didn't get to speak with her much." It would be different next time; Devon would see to that.

"Busy?"

"Yes," Devon said in what he hoped was a firm voice. He really didn't want to continue this topic of conversation. "I rode about the lands some. You have a magnificent property here."

"It's nice," Malcolm said absently. "While you were visiting the cottage, did you get a chance to see some of Kat's work?"

"The stained glass? No. I'm surprised you didn't mention it at breakfast this morning."

"I should have, but I was rather taken aback that she'd allowed you to kiss her."

"Had I known she was your sister—"

"Pssh. It wouldn't have made any difference."

Devon met Malcolm's gaze. After a moment, Devon grinned. "You are right, of course."

Malcolm chuckled. "I know I am right. Kat's a lovely woman but she's stubborn as they come. Frankly, there's no way in hell you or anyone else will ever get more than a startled kiss out of her."

Devon paused in taking a drink. "No?"

"No," Malcolm said firmly. "She's a strong-willed lass, is Kat. She'll have nothing to do with a man who doesn't appreciate her for what she's worth. And most men wouldn't prize her Independence. Most men would stupidly want a woman who was more like Fiona . . . or that sister of hers, Murien Spalding."

"I don't believe I've met Miss Spalding."

"Count your blessings," Malcolm said darkly. He glanced at the open door, then leaned closer to say in an undertone, "She's a bloody witch, make no doubt. Oh, she looks well enough. Like Fiona, she exudes helpless fluttery womanliness. But unlike Fiona, Murien's heart is made of marble, her soul so chilled, the devil fears to take her to join him lest she freeze the flames of hell."

Devon chuckled. "Bloody hell, she can't be as bad as all that."

"Wait and see. Her grandest wish is to marry and marry well." Malcolm eyed him for a moment. "You might be safe, for you've no title. But then there is that blasted St. John fortune . . ."

"That sounds dire indeed."

"Aye." Malcolm shook his head. "I wouldn't be surprised if Fiona invites her to come. Best you avoid her like the plague, that's my advice."

And good advice it seemed. The thought of the talisman ring still resting in the candle dish on his night table made Devon shift uneasily.

"Meanwhile," Malcolm continued as if unaware he'd just caused Devon concern, "you might be able to help me with a small problem I have myself."

"Oh?"

"Yes. 'Tis about Kat, too. And since you seem to know her—"

"Barely."

"Enough," Malcolm continued, undeterred. "I thought you might have some insight to the problem."

"Which is?"

"It's become clear to me that Kat will never marry. Or so she says."

Good for Kat, Devon thought, silently toasting her with his brandy.

"But I can't help but think I should bring her to the notice of some potential suitors, just to be certain she's not rushing into a life of being a stained glass master and nothing else."

"Is she happy?"

"Doing her stained glass? Lord, yes. Do you want to see some of her work?"

Devon nodded before he could catch himself. He couldn't help but wonder what sort of work Kat did as it might give him another connection to her.

Malcolm brightened and jumped up. "She's magical, she is. Just look." He set his glass on a small table, then went to the farthest window and pulled back the drapery. There at the top was a round window, hidden by the uppermost foot of curtain.

Devon rose and went to stand beside Malcolm. It was exquisite. Even with his lack of knowledge, he knew it was quality work.

The glass formed a picture of a large stag on a bluff, antlers pointed toward the sun as he stood proudly surveying the rolling grasses and forest below him. There was something about the combination of colors, the line of the bluff, and the stag's proud head that drew the eye and kept it. "It's beautiful."

"She's a master of the craft. There are twenty-six such windows at Kilkairn; old arrow awls used to fire on attackers in the early years of the castle."

"Ah, the charm of an older residence."

"Indeed. They used to have wood shutters over them and let in far too much cold before Kat began replacing them. I'll have to show them all to you one day." Malcolm dropped the curtain, and he and Devon returned to their chairs.

Devon absently took a drink of brandy. Kat Macdonald was a complex woman, and he was only beginning to realize how much. "Do you think your sister is happy living in the woods?"

"No one is happy alone."

"She's not alone."

Malcolm's face creased into a sudden smile. "Och, you met her merry lads."

"Merry? They looked as if they wished to kill me." The next time Devon went to the cottage, he'd arm himself with a cudgel, just in case.

"Well, they're merry when you're not about. I've seen them myself and they don't mind me in the least. 'Tis to strangers that they're so forbidding."

"I suppose they're better protection than a pack of wild dogs."

"Aye. That they are." Malcolm took a drink of his brandy. "You know, if I was to mount a campaign to win over Kat, the first thing I'd do is gain the approval of her lads. Though she rules them with a velvet glove, they are a strong-willed lot and make no bones about telling her what they think."

Devon looked into his own brandy, the light of the fire reflected in the amber depths. There was something in what Malcolm was saying. Not that Devon wished to "win" Kat over. That sounded far too much like wooing and not enough like seducing.

"And then," Malcolm continued, as if unaware that anyone else was in the room, "then I'd work on Annie."

"Annie?"

"Kat's housekeeper." Malcolm glanced about the library, a wistful look on his face. "I tried to steal her away, for she's a stern hand on the household and keeps it neat as a pin, but she's loyal unto death to Kat."

"You tried to steal your sister's housekeeper?"

"I was desperate. I still am." Malcolm gestured to their brandy glasses. "You see these? I had to wash them myself. There wasn't a servant to be found anywhere."

Devon grinned. "I daresay it was good for you."

"Perhaps, but I'll be damned if I'll see to my own laundry." Malcolm scowled into his drink. "Devon, never marry a dainty-looking woman, for they're anything but. They'll ruin your peace of mind, empty your house of its comforts, and then complain they've naught to do and wish to return to town."

"Fortunately for all concerned, I don't plan on getting married. Ever."

"We'll see what the talisman ring has to say about that."

"I don't care what it has to say. I'm not getting married and that's that."

"Hm. Well, speaking of rings, I don't think Kat is at all fond of jewelry. If I was to get her a gift, 'twould be something for her glasswork, or for her house."

Devon set down his drink. "Malcolm, if you're

thinking I'm about to engage a campaign to win your sister, you're wrong."

Malcolm's eyes widened a ridiculous amount. "By the saints, what gave you that idea?"

"You did. You and your 'if I wanted to win Kat over' ideas."

"Well, you're far and away from the truth, my laddie. Know why?"

"Why?"

"Because you haven't a chance in hell of garnering her interest. You, my lad, are the exact type of man she is least likely to take up with."

Devon didn't know whether he'd been insulted or not. "What does that mean?"

"Only that she's run up against libertines before and she—"

"I am not a libertine."

"Rakehell, then. Or do you prefer rogue?" Malcolm asked politely, laughter in his gaze.

Despite his irritation, Devon found himself smiling a little at this. As soon as he relaxed, he realized, reluctantly, that there might be something to what Malcolm said. Devon sighed. "She's had a bad experience, eh?"

All of the laughter left Malcolm's face. "The worst. I think it hurt her even more than she let anyone see. Which is why she's turned her back on all men. Especially those with a silver tongue like yourself." Malcolm sighed. "There's only one thing that will remedy that."

"What?" Devon asked before he could stop himself.

Malcolm's gaze darkened. "The truth. She needs

someone who will never lie to her, no matter the cost."

The quiet words sifted through the silence. Devon looked at the glass he held in his hand, the edges smooth against his fingers. "I hope she finds him."

Malcolm opened his mouth as if to reply, but then shut it. "So do I."

"I don't mean to pry, but it seems as if your sister is doomed to spinsterhood."

Malcolm sighed. "I know. I have worried that—" He bit his lips, his shoulders slumping. "It doesn't matter what I think. Or you, for that matter. Kat is even more stubborn than you, and there aren't many who can make that claim. A pity you are the type of man Kat avoids the most. Otherwise . . . but no, I don't think you have a chance. She won't like you at all."

Devon slowly lowered the glass from his lips where he'd been about to take a sip. From the time he'd been old enough to marry, he'd been used to people trying to fix his interest with their sisters, cousins, family friends. This was the first time someone had told him that his sister, or even half sister, would not like him. Whatever else he was, Devon was always likable.

He opened his mouth to say something more when Malcolm unexpectedly asked about Thunder, mentioning that he'd seen the horse from the window earlier in the day.

The conversation never returned to Kat and her self-imposed banishment to the cottage in the forest. But Devon's mind remained firmly fixed on the woman, even more so than before. No one told him he couldn't do something—even his own brothers knew better than that. And Malcolm's words, as off-hand as they'd seemed, had set up Devon's back a bit. Could he win another kiss from Kat Macdonald, one earned without surprise? Without guile? The thought was intriguing.

Across from him, Malcolm hid a smile behind his glass. Devon's answers were becoming increasingly vague, a clear sign his mind was already dwelling on Kat. Which was good because Malcolm feared that once Devon saw Murien Spalding, he might forget about Kat. Lovely as Kat was, Murien was exquisite.

Which was why Malcolm was determined that Devon spend as much time in Kat's company as possible. Murien might be beautiful, but she was no match for either Kat's force of personality or her intelligence. The problem was that most men felt with their eyes first, and their brain last.

If his wager with Fiona worked, then Malcolm would have all he desired—his wife back at his side, a son, and Kat happily married. As for his feelings for Fiona. . . . Malcolm frowned. Surely he was not so fickle as his own father. The love Malcolm felt for Fiona was so vivid, so much a part of him, that if he lost it, he thought perhaps a part of him would go with it.

Was that what his father had felt, too? A heavy weight seemed to press on Malcolm's chest, and it was with difficulty that he turned his attention back to Devon. His friend would make a fine brother-in-law. A fine one, indeed.

Other men might hesitate to put their sisters into the notice of a man who bluntly stated that he had no intentions of marrying, but Malcolm had three things in his favor. First, he knew that for all of Devon's philandering ways, he was a man of integrity. All of the St. Johns were, whether they realized it or not.

Second, there was the talisman ring. Those who didn't know any better might scoff all they wanted, but Malcolm believed. And when all was said and done, so would Devon.

And last, if by some miracle Devon was successful in breaking through Kat's rock-steady defenses, her brother Malcolm would be there to make sure the right thing was done. Friend or no, if Devon compromised Kat Macdonald, he would marry her, whether or not she or he wished it.

All told, it was a good, solid plan, and only Fiona and her be-damned sister could ruin things. Keeping his thoughts to himself, Malcolm got up to pour more brandy in his and Devon's glasses. It wasn't time to celebrate. Not yet. But judging from the thoughtful look on Devon's face, things were getting off to a fine start.

The next day, as afternoon approached, a coach and six rumbled up to the front door. As usual, the door was not answered on the first knock. But eventually the housekeeper came and let in the sole occupant, then sent a note to my lady's room, informing her of her visitor.

Moments later, a flurry of footsteps sounded on the landing. "Murien!" Fiona flew down the steps to the main hall, her dressing gown floating around her, a froth of pink and lace. Her slippered feet barely touched the worn runner. "You came!" She threw her arms about her sister. "And so quickly! I am so glad to see you!"

Murien grimaced. "Fiona, my hair!" She disentangled herself and then glanced at the dusty mirror beside the front door. What she surely saw had to have pleased her, for there was not a more beautiful woman in all of Scotland. Delicate blond hair swept back in a mass of shiny curls from a face of such perfection that no portrait painter had ever managed to quite capture it. Her skin shimmered white even in the dull light that shone through the dust-ridden windows, her figure perfect in the white pelisse and blue gown with matching bonnet.

Fiona clasped her hands together. "I am sorry! I was just so excessively glad to see you that I didn't think. Your hair still looks lovely." And it did. Every blond curl was in place, a ribbon artfully tied about the whole.

Murien patted an especially fat curl that hung to one of her shoulders. "It turned out better than I'd hoped, though I'm not sure why I bothered. There is no one in the whole of Scotland worth such effort."

"Oh!" Fiona gave an excited hop. "That's exactly why I asked you to visit!"

"Yes, well, I can only stay one night. I am on my way to Duart to stay with the Macleans."

"Can't stay? But—" Fiona bit back a sigh. "I really wanted you to stay at least a week. I *need* you to stay at least a week."

"Don't look so dispirited! We still have a good portion of the day together." Murien stripped off her gloves and looked around for the butler, the expression in her green eyes hardening. All she found was an elderly footman who stood half asleep on his feet.

Murien walked up to him. "You, whatever your name, pray put these in a *clean* place. And I hope you've washed your hands sometime in the last few days. The last time I left my gloves here, they looked as if someone had stored them up the chimney."

The old man blinked a few times, as if confused by her instructions. But after a moment, he bowed and took the gloves with but one finger and thumb. "Yes, miss."

Fiona barely waited for him to turn away before she took Murien's hand in hers. "Perhaps once I explain things, you will change your mind and stay for a while."

"As much as I enjoy chatting with you, I simply cannot remain out here in the middle of nowhere without getting a headache. It's the quiet, I think. It won't let me sleep."

"Yes, but—" Fiona bit her lip. How was Murien to ensnare Devon St. John if she wouldn't stay at Kilkairn? That was if Murien could be persuaded to make the effort at all.

The truth was, though Fiona had been brazenly confident in front of Malcolm, she wasn't sure she could count on her sister's cooperation in this venture. Murien was notoriously sure of her own worth and had turned down every offer of marriage that had been made to her. From beneath her lashes, Fiona regarded her sister for a covert moment. There really wasn't a more beautiful woman in all of Scotland. And Murien knew it, too; her confidence radiated from her like a beacon.

Filled with pride, Fiona hugged her sister yet again. "Come up to my room. I'll have tea brought and I'll explain why I asked you to visit." Talking rapidly, Fiona led the way upstairs.

Moments later, they were seated before the fire in Fiona's chambers. She poured some tea for her sister and handed her the cup. "How you are, Murien? Are you well?"

Murien's brows rose. "Don't I look well?"

Fiona sensed a rebuke and she instantly flushed. "Of course you look well! You look lovely—radiant, in fact. You always do, you know. Even when we were children, you would—"

"Fiona." Murien frowned over the edge of her cup, then placed it back in the saucer. "What do you want? Your note said it was dire. Have you decided to leave Malcolm?"

Fiona blinked. Leave Malcolm? Where had Murien gotten such a crazed notion? Had Malcolm said something? Panic flooded her. "Of course I'm not going to leave Malcolm. Why would I do such a thing?"

"Come, Fiona. Don't pretend you haven't thought about it. The two of you haven't ever gotten along as you should. He treats you abominably."

This was distressing indeed. Malcolm had treated her poorly? Had he? Fiona looked down at her teacup. "I don't think you understand how Malcolm and I care for one another. We've just had some . . . disagreements. That's all."

Murien looked unimpressed. "He's a monster to try and keep you locked up here, at Kilkairn. It's a wonder he doesn't make us climb up your hair just to visit you. It's my opinion that your marriage is already over."

Fiona gave a watery giggle, tears clouding her eyes. Good God, did Murien see what she, Fiona, did not? Had she and Malcolm grown so apart that they were doomed? Her throat tightened. Worse yet, was that what Malcolm thought, as well?

The thought pained her, a splinter shoved into the tenderest morsel of her soul. All she had was hope . . . hope that somehow, someway, Malcolm's feelings for her would return to the fervid passion he'd once had. Back when they'd been courting. Perhaps if they returned to an atmosphere not unlike that when they'd first met—surrounded by gay, happy people; brilliant amusements; and the constant thrill of a filled social calendar. It was a thin hope, but all she had.

Murien gave a graceful shrug. "Don't look so crestfallen; I daresay everyone knows how it is."

"Do you mean to say that a lot of people are discussing this?"

"I suppose so. Not to me, of course. No one would dare. But I hardly think it a secret that you and Malcolm do not see eye to eye on anything. It is certainly the first thing I notice whenever I come to visit."

The words had a strange effect on Fiona's heart, hollowing it out and making it thud painfully against her ribs. She managed a belated laugh. "Murien, you are so silly! Malcolm and I are fine. I just wrote you because . . . Well, I have a favor to ask."

"Favor?" Murien's pretty mouth turned down. "Really, Fiona, I hope this is not about money. I only have what Father left in trust and it's hardly enough as it—"

"No, no!" Fiona said hastily. "It has nothing to do with money. Murien, did you find anyone to interest you in Edinburgh?"

"Hardly. Provincials, every one."

Thank heavens! Just to be certain, Fiona said artlessly, "What of Lord Davies? He has been to Paris, and I'm certain he's the most sophisticated gentleman I've ever seen."

Murien sent her a fulminating glance, a frown on her pouting lips. "That shows how little you go in public. Once you've been to London, as have I, you will know there is little in the way of eligible men to be found in Scotland."

"You prefer Englishmen?"

"I prefer well-titled, wealthy, handsome, sophisticated men," Murien said, dissatisfaction radiating from her. "There are none to be found in this backward country. If I had the funds to stay in London, I would take the place by storm. I just know I would."

This was good news indeed. Had it not been for that depressing thought that perhaps her marriage was in dire straits, Fiona would have been ecstatic. As it was, she barely managed a smile. "That is precisely why I invited you to visit. Malcolm has an old friend from Eton visiting him, and I thought the man would be just the thing for you."

"A friend of Malcolm's?" There was just the tiniest hint of a sneer to Murien's voice.

Fiona stiffened. "Malcolm has many intelligent, well-bred friends. Why, he is personal friends with the Earl of Argyll, and I know not how many times the Earl of Carlysle has invited us to visit his country estate outside of Sterling."

"Really, Fiona, there is no need to be so argumentative."

"Yes, well, I think Mr. St. John is excessively well bred and—" Something gripped her arm. Fiona looked down and realized that it was Murien's hand. "Ow!"

Murien didn't loosen her hold. "Did you say *St. John*?"

Fiona nodded, pulling on her arm.

"Black hair? Blue eyes?"

"I don't know, as I haven't yet seen him. Murien, my arm—"

Murien released her, eyes ablaze. "But which St. John? Marcus? Never say 'tis the marquis!"

"No, it's Devon St. John."

"Devon. That is almost as good! He has no title, but—" Murien leaned closer, oblivious to the fact that the lace of her sleeve was now trailing in her tea plate. "Fiona, do you *know* who the St. Johns are?"

"No. I mean, Malcolm hinted that they were important, but I've never really heard—"

"They are the wealthiest family in all of England—all the world, perhaps!" Murien stood and began to pace about the room, the lace of her blue gown trailing the carpet behind her. Her green eyes gleamed.

"And to think that Devon St. John is here, of all places. I cannot believe—" She whirled back to Fiona. "For how long? How long will he be here?"

"I don't know. He hasn't really said. I just thought that you might—"

"You don't know?"

"A week, I think. Perhaps two—"

"I need more time." Murien came to kneel by Fiona's side, gripping her arm once again. "You *must* make him stay."

"How?"

"Oh for the love of—must I think of everything? Plan something in his honor—a hunt or a ball—and he will be forced to stay until it is done."

"Without asking his permission? Wouldn't that be rude?"

Murien grimaced. "Don't you *wish* to see me wed to one of the wealthiest men in the country?"

"Of course, but—"

"Don't you *wish* to see me wed to one of the handsomest men in the country?"

"Yes, but—"

"Then you must do this for me." Murien stood, swiftly walking to the mantel to inspect herself in the mirror that hung there. She rubbed her cheeks to give them more color. "This is fate, Fiona. I know it. He will be here for weeks, with nothing else to do. I cannot fail under such circumstances."

With all her heart, Fiona hoped Murien would succeed. If Murien was right about Fiona's marriage already being over, she had to win the wager. She simply *had* to.

Murien clasped her hands together, her eyes narrowed in thought. "Devon St. John at my sister's house. And with no competition to contend with."

"Well, there is some competition. A little, anyway."

Murien whirled on her, her eyes blazing, her face contorted in sudden fury.

Fiona drew back, saying hastily, "It's only Kat."

"What? Malcolm's half sister?" Murien laughed. "Good God, I thought you were serious."

"Well, I am in a way. You see . . ." Fiona hung her head. "Murien, this is more important than you know."

"Why?"

"Because Malcolm and I made a wager."

"A wager? On me?"

"I hope you don't mind, but he was so smug, saying that Mr. St. John had shown a decided interest in Kat and positively *gloating* about it, so I . . . well, I made a wager that you were more St. John's type and that you could attract his interest much quicker than his sister."

Murien merely smiled. "I hope you wagered something of great import."

"I did," Fiona said. She wet her lips nervously. "Murien, if I lose, I fear my marriage will indeed be over." It hurt, just saying the words aloud.

Murien frowned. "You aren't going to cry, are you?"

Fiona blinked back the tears. "No! No, of course not."

"Good. I hate it when you cry. But you needn't worry. If I have anything to do with it, I will not only attract Mr. St. John's interest, but I will secure it." She held up her hand and looked at it as if admiring a ring. "By this time next month, Mr. Devon St. John will be mine."

Fiona gave a sigh of relief. Once she and Malcolm settled this one argument, their relationship could go back to the way it had been when they'd first gotten married. She knew that once she got to Edinburgh, she would be merry again, and then so would Malcolm. "Thank you, Murien! I knew I could count on you."

Murien smoothed her hands over the front of her dress, pressing her breasts up, her eyes gleaming softly. "Indeed you may, Fiona. You will win this wager. Devon St. John won't know what has befallen him."

Chapter 7

I love you. I really, really love you. Like the stars in the sky, like the water in the oceans. You, my dear, are everything to me and there will never be another.

Mr. Poole to Lady Lucinda Sutherlund,
while stealing a kiss beneath the stars
on the veranda at the Sutherlund rout

"Ye're sure ye're feeling well?"

Kat turned from where she'd been supervising the loading of the cart. They'd finished the earl's final window late last night and had spent the morning grinding off the uneven edges and cleaning the glass until it gleamed. Now all the windows were safely packed in frames and were ready for delivery. "I'm fine, Simon. I'm fine now. And I was fine five minutes ago when you asked me then."

He reddened. "Sorry aboot that, Miss Kat. I was just wonderin'—" He clamped his mouth closed. "Never mind."

She waved good-bye to Alistair and Donald, who dutifully waved back. Alistair was, as usual, grinning from ear to ear, while Donald, ever the sooth-sayer of doom, was muttering about the bad roads ahead and how his left knee told him they were in for a fierce storm.

Kat waited until they were well down the path before she turned to Simon. "I'm ready now. You may begin."

"Begin what?"

"Whatever it is that has been worrying you all day. Out with it before you explode."

"Nothing's worrying me, Miss Kat. I was jus' wonderin'—" He scratched his neck. "'Tis not my place to say anything, but from what I've heard aboot the Sassenach, you'd best have a care."

"Have a care about what? I've only spoken to him once." That Simon knew about. Kat didn't see the need to inform him of the other time as it would just raise unnecessary questions. Questions she wasn't sure she could answer.

"I know, missus. But he seemed a wee bit deter-mined to take you for a ride when he was here a few days ago. I'd thought he'd be back by now." Simon's eyes narrowed. "I don't trust him as far as I can throw him."

"Well, I said no, didn't I? So you have nothing to fear."

Simon looked at her.

"What?"

He raised his brows, his gaze fastening on her gown.

Kat flushed, her hand smoothing her skirt. "So I

wore a different gown today than I normally do. That doesn't mean anything."

"Ye've worn a nicer gown every day since he last visited. Are ye wishin' he would return?"

"No! Not at all."

Simon raised his brows again.

Kat's face heated even more. "By St. George's dragon, I'm not about to apologize for wearing something other than one of my old gray work gowns! Besides, it's not as if I came to work dressed for a ball or anything ridiculous."

Of course, it was a better quality of gown than the ones she usually wore. Of soft dove-gray cotton, it fell in fuller, more graceful folds. And the neckline, while not precisely fancy, did have a thin stitching of trim.

Kat self-consciously traced the stitching. "I wear this gown all the time."

"To church, mayhap. But not to work in. 'Tisn't practical as ye'll get soot on it and the sparks'll mark it."

There was something in what he said; Kat didn't own a work gown that didn't have at least one small hole burned in the skirts.

Simon crossed his arms over his barrel chest. "Know what I think?"

"No, but I'm sure you'll tell me."

"I think ye were hopin' the Sassenach would come a-callin'."

"I did no such thing," Kat replied hotly. Although, to be honest, there had been a moment yesterday when she thought she'd heard horse's hooves clopping on the path and her heart had pounded a bit harder than usual. She sighed to herself. Very well . . . perhaps she *had* hoped to see the Sassenach again. He'd been much in her thoughts. But she'd be damned before she admitted such a thing to Simon.

Of course, she was a little chagrined that St. John hadn't returned before now. Perhaps he wasn't as interested as he'd pretended. The thought pricked at her pride.

"Lass, ye're dreamin' if ye think this Sassenach will come a-callin'. Not that ye're not a lovely woman, fer ye are. But the Sassenach didn't look like the kind of man who'd take the time to act like a proper gent—" Simon's gaze moved past her, his brows lowering until they met over his nose. "Bloody hell!"

Kat turned, though she already knew what she'd see. And there he was—Devon St. John, riding across the clearing. He was hatless, the sun gleaming off his black hair, limning the bridge of his nose and touching the plane of each cheekbone. Dressed in a blue riding coat with buff breeches, he looked far too handsome to be in the woods.

There! She'd been right to wear one of her better gowns. She cleared her throat. "Simon?"

"Aye, lass?" It was a testament to how upset he was that Simon's voice was more of a rumble than actual words.

"Why don't you take the rest of the lads and begin cleaning the workshop. I'll be there in a trice."

Simon glowered. "I don't like leavin' ye with His Namby-Pamby Lordship. Ye need a chaperone."

"Out here? In the middle of the clearing? What's

he going to do? Throw me to the ground and have his way with me in front of all of you and the house staff?"

"I wouldna put it past him, the bounder."

"Simon, you've gone daft, you have. Now off with you. I'll be there to help shortly."

"But—"

"Please."

Simon sighed. "Very well," he mumbled. He slowly turned on his heel, glaring at Devon as he went.

Devon pulled Thunder to a halt as Simon walked by. It didn't take a man of unusual discernment to read the message on Simon's craggy face. Devon hoped that the fact that he returned the look without flinching sent a message back.

He reached Kat and dismounted. She looked especially lovely today, her hair a little tousled by the wind, her gown hugging those luxuriant curves.

It made all his efforts worthwhile. He thought he discerned the slightest bit of excitement in her green gaze, a hint of warm welcome that was quite different from the calm dismissal she'd last given him. Good. Though he'd wanted nothing more than to storm back to the clearing after their last meeting, he'd decided that Miss Kat needed some time to decide what she wanted. He'd hoped that being alone in the woods with her work—doing the same thing she always did, talking to the same people she always talked to—would make her yearn for something out of the ordinary. Something special. Like an Englishman with a ready smile.

He smiled down at her now, bowing a little. "Good morning." Last night he and Malcolm had whiled away the evening playing billiards and drinking brandy. As soon as night fell, Devon excused himself and went to his room, where he began to formulate a plan, all the while feeling the onerous presence of the talisman ring. With the information he'd garnered from Malcolm, added to his own innate knowledge of women, and the little he knew about Katherine Anne Macdonald, Devon was fairly sure that by the end of the week, if he was not in her bed, he'd be close to it. She was a hot piece, and all he had to do was break through some of the barriers she'd erected around her heart.

Not too many, of course, for he had no intention of becoming the focal point of that heart. All he wanted was the pleasure of her body, a brief taste of her spirit. Her heart she could save for whomever she came to love, as long as it wasn't Devon.

But first, before he did anything, he had to win her trust. After that, he would woo her with a thoroughness that would leave them both panting and pleased. Malcolm had said Kat needed the truth and Devon was ready.

He bowed, glancing up at her through his lashes.

Her cheeks flushed pink beneath the cream, though her gaze did not waver. "Perhaps we should skip the civilities and go right to the reason you are here."

Devon had to smile. "I came to ask you once again if you would come for a ride with me."

"No."

"Poor Thunder. He would have enjoyed having such a lovely rider."

Her mouth formed a no, but it never came out of her mouth. Instead her gaze went over his shoulder to where the horse was tied, the sun gleaming on the gelding's pure, strong lines.

After a long moment, she turned her gaze back to Devon. He was amused, as well as chagrined, to see that some of the admiration that had sparkled in her gaze when she'd looked at the horse had disappeared when she focused on him.

Devon had to bite back a sigh. Kat was so different from the women he usually met; like Malcolm's sister-in-law, for example. Murien Spalding was everything Malcolm had warned of—she was small and feminine and exuded a helpless charm—exactly the sort of woman Devon knew he should avoid, though it had been difficult. Murien seemed determined to waylay him every chance she got, which made Kat's reluctance all the more appealing.

Kat looked at him now. "If I ride *your* horse, what will *you* ride?"

He shrugged. "I daresay you have any number of animals in your stable that could hold me."

"None are as fine as Thunder."

"No, but I will be justly compensated by your lovely company." He knew he'd made a mistake the second the words were out of his mouth. Kat Macdonald didn't want flowery phrases and empty words. She wanted . . . He almost frowned. What *did* she want?

Her expression had shuttered, and he could see

that she was already pulling away. There was nothing for it but the truth. "Miss Macdonald—Kat, please. I am a stranger in Scotland. And while I am thankful for your brother's hospitality, it is rather tense in the castle."

Her expression softened just the tiniest bit. "Fiona and Malcolm are still at it?"

"Oh yes. So far I haven't had the opportunity to witness them do anything other than snip at each other, though I'm sure they were a charming couple when they first wed."

She tilted her head to one side, curiosity making her eyes appear lighter. "You don't sound as if you approve."

"Of what? Marriage?"

She nodded.

"I don't believe in it. At least not for me."

A faint smile touched her lips, the first one today. For some reason, Devon felt as if the sun shone a trifle brighter just because of that tiny upturn of her generous lips.

"So you aren't a marrying man." Her eyes were bright with amusement. "I'm surprised you admit that."

So was he, though it was the truth. Had he made such a statement to a society miss in London, one with a matrimonial gleam in her eye, he would have been labeled crass and unfeeling. But Kat merely nodded. "I don't think I believe in it, either. Not anymore."

A faint hint of sadness touched her smile. Devon knew she was remembering her past, and he was hard-pressed not to ask her about it. He certainly didn't know her well enough to ask such personal questions, but somehow he knew that if he did, she would answer. There was no pretense or artifice about Kat. There was . . . just Kat herself.

Thunder whickered in indignation at being made to stand, and he pawed the ground impatiently.

Kat chuckled. "You had better go. He doesn't look happy."

"He can stay where he is until I've had my answer. Will you ride with me?"

She turned her head to give Thunder a final, lingering glance. Devon knew the instant she made up her mind, for her shoulders straightened.

"Very well. I will ride with you. But it cannot be for long. I've work to do."

"I know that. We'll make it an hour, no more."

She raised her brows.

"Half an hour then. Later this afternoon?"

"No. Best make it tomorrow."

He'd hoped for today, but if he wanted to breach the walls Kat had built, he'd have to let her set their pace. So instead, he took her hand and turned it over in his. "Shall we say morning? At ten?"

"Fine."

He uncurled her fingers and pressed a kiss to her palm. Her skin was warm and firm beneath his, her fingers roughened. He ran his thumb over hers and smiled into her eyes. "You work far too hard."

She pulled her hand back, her face shuttering once again. "Work is good for the soul, Mr. St. John. Perhaps one day you'll try it and see."

"I may not have cut firewood for a living, but I've done my fair share of work."

"Indeed?"

"I'm solely responsible for various aspects of the St. John holdings. More than any of my brothers other than Marcus, I have safeguarded the family fortune and helped it grow."

"That's not work."

He thought of the countless meetings he'd sat through, some lasting days, of the hard-won negotiations, of the endless hours he'd spent traveling to their holdings. "Tell me, Miss Certainty, have you tried it?"

She pursed her lips. "No. I suppose I shouldn't speak, then."

"No," he agreed. "Any more than I should make assumptions about your glasswork." He hesitated a moment, then added, "Perhaps one day you can show me the glass shop. I wish to see how it all works."

She shot him an uncertain look. "No one has ever asked me that."

"Well, I'm curious. Especially after your brother showed me some of your efforts."

"I could spit on a glass and tell Malcolm it was a lantern shield and he'd think it was the best thing he'd ever seen."

Devon smiled. "That's what brothers are for."

She nodded, her lips curving into a returning smile. For a moment, a simple sort of harmony seemed to build between them. Perhaps it was the cool breeze that kept tugging her dress and fanning the fringes of her hair. Or perhaps it was gradual realization that they were not quite as different as they thought. Whatever it was, Devon found himself lingering, wanting to stay a little longer. And a little longer yet.

Kat scuffed her toe on the ground. "How many brothers do you have, St. John?"

"Four. And a sister."

Her eyes widened. "That many?"

"My father said we were his army, and indeed our house was often like an army camp."

She looked at him wistfully, but didn't say anything.

"You and Malcolm seem unusually close."

"He's been a good brother to me."

"And I'm sure you've been a good sister."

"I try," she said softly, "though he does so much—" She bit her lip.

"I daresay you do more than you realize."

A horse could be heard coming down the path. Devon recognized Malcolm the same instant Kat did.

"Blast it," Devon said with a sigh. "Your brother has an uncanny way of showing up when he's least wanted."

"It's a trait he's had his whole life," she replied in a grim voice.

Devon pulled Thunder closer. "I shall see you tomorrow then?"

"At ten," she agreed.

"Excellent." He took her hand and placed one last kiss on the back of it.

Kat had to fight a shiver as his lips brushed her

skin. Her entire body seemed to tighten whenever he was about, and when he touched her, she had to clench her teeth against a tremor that traced her spine.

"Till tomorrow, Miss Macdonald." With that, he left her and remounted Thunder.

Kat watched him go, a dashing figure on the black horse. A horse that tomorrow she would be riding. And oh, what a horse. She eyed it greedily, almost giving a little hop of excitement. Only the knowledge that Simon was most likely standing in the window, watching, made her hold it back. She wasn't really excited about seeing Devon St. John, she told herself; all she wanted to do was ride that beautiful horse.

Still, she could not deny that it would be pleasant to have someone with whom to while away a little time now that the earl's windows were done. There were more orders to fill; there always were. But none so urgent.

Malcolm had pulled up to speak to St. John, and she stood there a moment, watching them and feeling strangely bereft.

All she had for company were the lads and Annie and Malcolm, whenever Fiona could spare him from the castle. While they were all good people, Kat sometimes wished for more. Something was vaguely disquieting about the way things had settled in her daily existence. Kat thought that perhaps a conversation or two with Mr. Devon St. John might help her discover what that was.

Of course, she'd make good and certain those conversations were held in broad daylight. She'd also make certain St. John's hands stayed closer to his person than to hers. Not that she was worried; she had experience in such matters, and St. John already had one bruise to prove it.

Malcolm and St. John said their good-byes, and Malcolm turned his horse toward Kat. He hopped down from the large bay and gave her a broad smile.

"What's that all about?" she asked, instantly suspicious.

"What?" he said, blinking innocently, though his grin dimmed not one whit.

"That smile. I don't trust it. You never smile like that."

Malcolm did a little jig, pumping his arms in a ridiculous way. "There," he said, coming to a stop, panting hard, though the smile still lit his eyes. "I never dance, either, but I am today."

She had to laugh; she felt a little giddy herself. For a mad moment, she wondered if this was all from St. John's presence. But then she realized how silly that was. "So, Malcolm, what has you in such a good mood? Did you and Fiona solve your differences?" Kat immediately wished she hadn't mentioned Fiona, as some of the light left Malcolm's face.

"Not yet." A set look touched his mouth. "But hopefully soon."

"I hope so, too." And she did. She knew how much he cared for his wife. Though Fiona didn't seem capable of seeing it, it was painfully obvious to everyone else.

"Did you get the windows off to the earl?"

"Aye. You just missed them."

"Excellent." Malcolm rubbed his hands together. "I have a favor to ask you, Kat. A big one."

"What?"

"I need you to entertain St. John a wee bit—" He held up his hand when she opened her mouth to deny him. "Only during the days. No more."

"Why?"

"Because Murien arrived at the castle earlier this week."

Kat pressed her lips together. "Murien has her sights on St. John."

Malcolm nodded. "And you know what she is. She won't stop until she has him."

"Surely he can avoid her if he wishes—"

"He might, but then there is that blasted talisman ring." Malcolm shook his head solemnly.

Kat caught him looking at her from beneath his lashes. "What talisman ring?"

"Didn't he tell you?"

"No."

"Och now, why hasn't he done so? I suppose he's a mite embarrassed." Malcolm sighed heavily. "Poor Devon. His family is cursed with a ring that seems to cause marriage."

"Marriage?"

"That's what happened to three of his brothers. And they each had the ring in their possession when it happened, too. Devon fled London, hoping to escape the ring, but he found it in his carriage after he'd left, and so here he is, stuck with the blasted thing."

"Malcolm . . . surely you don't believe in this ring?"

He shrugged. "Perhaps."

"I don't."

He eyed her shrewdly. "Not at all?"

"Not even a little."

"Good!" He reached into his pocket and withdrew a small object. "Since you don't believe in it, you won't mind trying it on."

Kat blinked down at the small circle that lay in the palm of his hand. Silver with tiny runes etched in the surface, it appeared innocuous. "Does St. John know you have that?"

Malcolm looked slightly shame-faced. "Perhaps."

"Perhaps? Och, Malcolm! He's your guest."

"Whist, Kat! I am going to put it back. I was just curious." He held the circlet up to the light. "You must admit 'tis pretty."

It *was* pretty, glistening in the sun. As Kat looked at the ring, the urge to touch it began to simmer through her.

She shook her head. "I want nothing to do with it."

"Damn, Kat! Must you be so stubborn?"

"Yes," she answered implacably.

A sigh burst from his lips. "You are the most irritating woman I know, with the exception of Fiona."

"Thank you. I'll treasure those words."

"I only borrowed the ring; I did not steal it, so you can stop glaring at me."

"Why would you do such a thing?"

"Because I was curious to see it. Don't you fash, I'll have it returned to his room before he knows what's toward. Meanwhile, hold out your hand and let's see if the ring fits."

"Fits?" Her brow lowered. What was he doing? "Why would you want to see if it fits?"

"Because I'm curious, is why." Malcolm reached out and grabbed her hand. Before Kat could say another word, he'd slipped the ring over her finger.

For an instant, she felt nothing. Not even the tang of cold metal against her skin. "It's noth—" She caught her breath. A slow, almost insistent heat was beginning to radiate from her finger.

"What is it?" Malcolm asked, leaning forward, his gaze fastened on her face. "What do you feel?"

"I feel . . ." Bloody hell, what *did* she feel? Her entire hand was warm, her arm tingled, and now her breasts were beginning to shimmer with heat.

Malcolm blinked. "Kat, love. Are you well? Your face—" He gripped her arms. "Kat?"

She gasped. Heat arced from her breasts to her stomach and then lower. Somehow, she saw St. John. Saw his face above hers . . . felt his hands on her body . . . felt his hips against hers . . . She clenched her teeth against the onslaught of emotion and feeling. It was as if every thought she'd ever had, every feeling, was suddenly thrown into her heart at once. It was almost too much to bear.

Her entire body trembled and ached, and it took every ounce of her strength to grasp the ring and yank it from her finger. The second it broke free, she sagged, her breath wrung from her lips.

"My God, Kat!" Malcolm's arm was the only

thing that kept her from falling down. He took the ring from her lax fingers. "Are you well? What happened? Is it your heart? Good God, Kat, talk to me!"

"I—I'm fine," she said, her voice trembling. "I just didn't have any breakfast and I—" She couldn't finish the falsehood. She took a shuddering breath and pushed his arm free of her shoulders, moving back, away from him, away from the ring. "I'm fine now. Really I am."

His face was pale. "Are you certain? Perhaps you should go into the cottage and lie down a bit."

"No, no. I'm fine. I just got a wee bit dizzy was all." Her entire body ached, her heart still raced.

Malcolm looked at the ring a long moment, a queer expression on his face. Then he slid it into his pocket as carefully as if it had been made of crystal. "I will return it."

"Yes." She pressed her hand to her forehead, trying to still the turmoil in her mind. What had just happened? She'd never felt such a reaction, such heat, and certainly never from a mere ring. It almost felt as if . . . Her cheeks colored. No. Surely not.

Malcolm untied his mount from the railing and led it forward. "I'm sorry, Kat. If I'd realized . . ." He paused, a dawning look spreading across his face. "Kat! If the ring gave you such a strong reaction, then you must be—"

"The wrong woman for Mr. St. John," she said, far more steadily than she felt.

Malcolm shook his head. "No, no! If the ring—"

"Malcolm, think a moment. If the ring finds St.

John's future wife, then it would have to be someone other than me. I am not going to marry. I've told you that time and again."

"Yes, but—"

"No buts. I have no need for a husband. I like my freedom and my solitude. Besides, what man would let me have my lads and the glasswork? I can no more leave that behind than you can stop caring about Fiona."

He grimaced. "Don't—"

" 'Tis true and you know it."

Malcolm sighed. "I had hoped that you and St. John—"

"Well, we're not. Besides, he's no more a marrying man than I'm a wedding woman." She smiled at her thin joke.

Malcolm pulled the ring from his pocket and looked at it. "I suppose you are right. It didn't seem to have a *good* effect on you, anyway. Are . . . are you certain you're well?" Concern tightened his expression. "You looked as if you were in pain."

It hadn't been pain, but pleasure. Pure, unadulterated pleasure. Kat managed a smile she was far from feeling. "I'm fine."

He eyed her a moment more, then tucked the ring back into his waistcoat pocket. "I hate to ask this, because you're still a little pale . . ."

"What?"

"Remember to keep St. John about this week. For his sake, if not mine."

A feeling not unlike panic nipped at her. "St. John is not in need of a nursemaid."

"You don't know Murien well enough, then. She's unscrupulous, that one, and I don't trust her."

"St. John can take care of himself."

"How can you say that? He's used to the frail misses of London. Murien would devour him with her tea and crumpets, and he'd never know what had happened."

"You're exaggerating."

"Kat, I would not put it past Murien to try and trick St. John into her net. I think she'd even claim ruin, if she had to."

Kat paused. The rules regarding a woman's reputation were murky and gray at best, which made them all the easier to break. In truth, since St. John's family was so high and mighty, all Murien would have to do was trick Devon into being alone with her and arranging for someone to "discover" them. All told, in a castle the size of Kilkairn, it was an easy enough feat. Especially if Fiona was to assist Murien.

Kat sighed. "If she cried foul, even if he'd done nothing, it's possible he'd be forced to marry her."

Malcolm nodded. "And a bloody, sad shame it would be, too, for I cannot imagine two worse matched people in all of the earth."

Kat had to admit Malcolm had a point. Her gaze dropped to his waistcoat where the ring was now safely tucked away.

There was so much she didn't understand. Why had that ring affected her so? Why did her body warm every time St. John was about?

Kat had never considered herself a particularly

sensual woman. But somehow, every moment she spent with St. John seemed to prove her wrong.

She had to find out more, discover what the ring was and what it meant. And she needed to know who Devon St. John really was.

"Very well," she heard herself say. "He's coming to ride tomorrow. I will see if he'll stay for a wee bit of lunch, too."

Malcolm's face cleared. "Thank you, Kat! You won't be sorry."

Kat wasn't so sure. All she knew was that she'd never feared anything the way she feared the St. John talisman ring. Except, perhaps, Devon St. John himself.

Chapter 8

I love you. I really, really love you. Like the stars in the sky, like the water in the oceans. You, my dear, are everything to me and there will never be another.

Mr. Poole to Miss Elizabeth Standon,
while stealing a kiss behind the shrubbery
of Standon House in Mayfair

"There he is!" Fiona exclaimed.

Murien rushed to the window and almost pushed Fiona aside in her determination to garner a look. "It's about time! He's been gone an hour."

"Aye."

A flash of satisfaction crossed Murien's face as she watched Devon. "He's magnificent. We shall make quite a pair, he with his dark looks and me with my fair ones."

Fiona smiled. "He is most presentable."

"Presentable? He's more than presentable." Murien began smoothing her gown. "How do I look?"

Fiona admired Murien's choice of gowns. It was

cream over white, the heavy, cream-colored lace draped over a white silk undergown. Small pale blue and pink flowers were woven into the lace, their tiny, pale green leaves adding faint touches of color.

The overall effect was one of fairylike delicacy, something Murien's own pink and gold coloring supported. And indeed, if one didn't look too closely into her eyes, Murien looked fresh and innocent and achingly beautiful.

Murien patted her hair. She'd pinned it up in a simple knot that emphasized the graceful length of her neck and the delicate turn of her shoulders. Fiona didn't think Murien had ever looked so perfect.

They could only hope it was enough. For some reason, Devon St. John hadn't been as enthusiastic about Murien as they'd hoped. Oh, he was pleasant enough, complimenting Murien on her beauty and paying her every attention. But he made the same efforts for Fiona, often including her in conversations that Murien obviously wished her out of. It was all rather confusing. Did he like Murien? Or was he merely being polite?

The sound of footsteps echoed down the hall.

"Quickly!" Murien said, hurrying to sit by the fire. She picked up her discarded embroidery frame and adjusted her skirts. "He'll be here any moment!"

Fiona took her place across from Murien, and together they waited. The footsteps walked closer . . . louder and louder. They paused outside the door, and then began to fade away.

"Blast it," Murien whispered. "I thought that footman of yours was going to direct him in here!"

Fiona stood. "Just wait. I'll fetch him myself." She smoothed her own gown of pink muslin before crossing to the door and opening it.

It wasn't Devon who was walking away, but Malcolm. He turned on hearing the door open, pausing with one foot on the lowest step. He'd had a smile on his face, but when he saw her, it faded from sight.

Her heart ached. At one time, he'd lit up every time she walked into the room. She swallowed her disappointment and made a quick curtsy. "My lord."

He nodded, his handsome face grave. "Lady wife." His gaze flickered past her to the door. "How goes your campaign?"

"Better than yours, I dare say. Which you would know if you had breakfast at a decent hour. Neither you nor our guest was there."

A faint hint of smugness crossed his face. "St. John and I agreed to eat earlier than usual so that we might have a morning ride. Then he went to visit Kat."

"You should have told me about that," Fiona said, wincing a little at the petulancy she heard in her own voice.

Malcolm smiled, that bright flash of teeth and a crinkling of eyes that always made her want to smile back.

He was a handsome man. He wasn't tall, but then she liked that, for large people overwhelmed her. He was quicksilver and charm, a lethal combination where Fiona was concerned.

She realized she missed him, missed their morning breakfasts together, missed his visits to her room . . . Tears threatened to well.

To hide her distress, she said, "Murien and I were waiting on St. John. I just saw him in the courtyard."

"I fear you are going to lose this wager before you even begin it. He seems quite taken with Kat."

Fiona stiffened. "Indeed, I am not. In fact—"

Footsteps sounded once again, this time slower and more shuffling. The elderly footman led Devon up the stairs. He bowed on seeing Fiona. "I was told you were expecting me."

She smiled and placed her hand on his arm. "Indeed I was. Pray come in. Murien and I wanted to ask your opinion on something." With that, she drew St. John to the drawing room door.

From where he stood on the landing, Malcolm could see Murien standing by the fireplace, her expression one of artful innocence. Damn it, but she looked beautiful . . . beyond beautiful, even. He thought of Kat this morning, in her plain gown and slightly mussed hair, and he grimaced. He was going to have to do something about that. And soon.

Malcolm's heart sank when he caught sight of Devon's admiring expression as he faced Murien. Bloody hell, there was no justice in this world.

Just before Devon went through the door, he paused and sent Malcolm a quizzical glance. "Are you coming?"

"No, no! Perhaps we can meet in an hour for a game of billiards?"

"Of course. I hope you are prepared to lose again."

With a grin, Devon followed Fiona the rest of the way into the room.

As Fiona moved to shut the door, her gaze met Malcolm's. For an instant, a tense silence bound them. Malcolm had never wanted anything more than to throw caution and his pride to the winds and reclaim her for himself. What would she do if he marched up to her and threw her over his shoulder, then took her to their room and locked them both away for a week?

The urge was almost overwhelming. But first he'd have to make a promise he didn't know if he could keep. He let the words die on his tongue. Fiona's gaze faltered and dropped. Her shoulders slumped and she turned away and then pushed the heavy door closed.

Grumbling to himself, Malcolm turned and made his way up the stairs, hoping against hope that Devon was made of sterner stuff than most men.

The next morning, Devon flipped one end of his cravat over the other, then twisted them in an intricate knot. It took almost fifteen minutes, but when he finished, his cravat was tied in a fabulous creation known as "the mathematical."

His valet, Tilton, watched a respectful distance away, preserving the utmost silence. As Devon finished, he cast an amused glanced at the valet. "You can speak, you know. I don't need silence just to tie a cravat."

Tilton sniffed. "They say Beau Brummell required absolute silence and that the slightest noise would cause him to go into a fit."

"Brummell was a fool. A well-dressed fool, but a fool nonetheless." Devon made the final adjustment to his cravat. "There. How's that?"

"Superb, sir. Simply superb." Tilton regarded the cravat a moment more, and then, nodding faintly, he picked up the coat he'd just brushed. "A pity you got so dusty yesterday morning."

"I was riding. That happens to my riding coat when I use it."

"You've been riding before, but never have I seen so much dirt."

"That's because I rode in the woods and not in a genteel park with tended pathways."

Tilton curled his nose. "How shabby of Lord Strathmore not to have a park for your amusement."

"I shall tell him you think so."

"Pray do. Otherwise I shall be forced to share my opinion with the upper footman in the hopes that he might tell the second housemaid, who is, I have been informed, sleeping with His Lordship's valet. I would hate for Lord Strathmore to hear my opinion in such a hodgepodge manner."

"Consider it done," Devon said, waving a hand.

Tilton paused. "Would you indeed, sir?"

"Of course. One should never ask a servant to do what one is not willing to do oneself. I may want you to spread some gossip for me one day."

The valet sniffed, his thin nostrils flaring. "I suppose next you will be offering to iron your own waistcoats. What a delight for me."

Devon raised his brows. "I wouldn't take it that far."

"Then I'm to understand that in return for my extra services, you are only going to claim such duties as carrying gossip and, if pressed, an occasional note for a tryst, and not such duties as laundry, pressing the creases from your shirts, or polishing your boots?"

"I have to leave something for you to do. Otherwise I might realize I don't need you, and you could lose your position."

"Don't tempt me, my lord," Tilton said. "The Duke of Claridge has been asking for my services for years now."

"That old clod-digger? You'd be miserable. He doesn't dress, he merely rolls into his clothing. Besides, I have it on good authority that his funds are tied up on the 'change and he pays his servants in a very clutch-fisted manner."

"Then Viscount Addinton. He cuts a good figure."

"When he isn't drunk. If that's the turn you wish to take, I wish you well." Devon knew Tilton would never leave his service; the valet had far too high an opinion of himself to work for anyone with less style. Besides, Devon paid handsomely and Tilton had little to complain about.

Devon glanced about the room Tilton had just moved them into. The valet had arrived the day after Devon and had wrought a miracle in one of the less damp chambers. Gone was the dust, grime, and gloomy air. The sheets and coverlet were fresh and crisp and even the rug was a brighter color than the others in the castle.

Truly, Tilton was worth his weight in gold. Devon

picked up his gloves and tucked them into a pocket. "I'm off to ride with Miss Kat."

"Cat, sir?"

"Miss Katherine Macdonald. Kat."

"Ah. That would be His Lordship's half sister."

Devon cut him a glance. "You've heard about her?"

"Indeed, sir. I've heard all about Miss Macdonald *and* Miss Spalding."

Devon cast a glance at where the ring had been on the night table. He frowned. "Tilton, I thought I put the ring in the candle dish. Did you move it?"

Tilton's gaze followed his. The ring was no longer in the candle dish, but beside it. "No, sir. I did not move it."

Devon crossed to the table and picked up the ring. "Perhaps I just forgot. Take this and put it somewhere safer."

"Of course, sir." Tilton took the ring and placed it in a box with Devon's cravat pins. "There. It's fortunate you do not believe in the power of the ring, for I have it on the best authority that you have come to Kilkairn to meet your future bride."

"Just what have you heard?"

"Only that speculation is rife over who you will choose, Miss Macdonald or Miss Spalding. Wagering is heavily favoring Miss Spalding."

Devon frowned. "I favor neither. I've no wish to get married." Which was why he was on his way out of the castle now. It was a good thing he had Kat to while the day away with, for he could not be certain he'd escape Murien's spell otherwise.

"Sir, I am well aware of your feelings toward matrimony. And so I informed the other staff, but I fear I come into the servants' hall too late to have any influence."

For some reason, it irked him that the servants were speculating on his future. "Old gossips, the lot of them."

"They are quite antiquated, sir. I feel as if I've stepped into a world filled with gout and a disturbing fascination for flatulence." Tilton cast a glance about the green room. It was still a long way from meeting Tilton's standards. "I shall attempt to organize your room a bit more today, although I have little hopes of actually causing an improvement."

"You've already wrought miracles," Devon said. Though there really wasn't much to be done about the smoking chimney or the stained walls.

Devon glanced at his pocket watch, then started. He'd be late if he didn't leave soon. Now all he had to do was get out of the castle without being forced to pay homage yet again to Fiona's sister. "Don't expect me to return until after dark."

"What a long ride. I do hope your horse will be able to maintain such a pace."

"I hope *I* can maintain such a pace," Devon said. He grinned at the valet and then left the room, hat tucked beneath one arm.

He ran lightly down the stairs and had just reached the front entryway when a door opened off the great hall. Fiona stood in the opening. "There you are, Mr. St. John!" she said in a breathless tone.

Devon stifled a feeling of impatience. "Good morning, Lady Strathmore."

"I'm so glad I caught you. Murien and I were just sitting here talking about how pleasant it would be if you visited."

"I am on my way out, so I can only stay a few moments." And that was all. He followed her into the room, bowing to Murien when he entered.

Murien was standing beside the pianoforte, holding some sheet music, looking as beautiful and radiant as she had the day before. Devon knew what the music sheets portended; she wished to play for him as evidence of her correct upbringing. All women were raised the same, and it was a damned shame.

"There you are," Murien said in warm voice, smiling at him.

"Here I am."

"You're dressed for riding."

"Indeed."

She laughed softly. "I am sorry. I didn't mean to state the obvious. Where are you riding today?"

"The woods." He wondered if Kat's laugh was as seductive as Murien's; he'd seen her smile, but had never heard her laugh. He resolved to fix that situation today.

"How lovely!" Murien said. "I daresay it will be nice and cool in the forest." And with that, she took her place at the pianoforte, leaving her sister to entertain him.

Devon had to give Murien credit, she knew what she was about. She didn't press him for his attention, but merely indicated that she was there and was a pleasant and beautiful companion. Which was why he had no intentions of spending more than a minute's worth of time with her, not while the talisman ring was still in his possession.

Devon wasted no more time making his escape. If he waited until Murien began to play, he'd be stuck there for the next hour. As quickly as he could, he made his excuses and left.

As he walked out of the castle, his step grew lighter, his mouth began to widen in a real smile. Just to be certain that he did not develop an unnecessary passion for Murien, he'd spend the rest of the day trying to wheedle kisses from Scotland's most ineligible woman.

It was a perfect plan. His grin widened, and it was with a lift to his spirits that he finally rode out of Kilkairn and into the woods surrounding it.

Simon leaned in the window. "Miss Kat?"

Kat looked up from where she sat at a desk in the front room of the cottage, poring over the account books. "Aye?"

"Do ye wish to see the new shipment of glass?"

"Of course! I'll be there shortly."

Simon nodded and pulled his head out of the window.

Kat looked down at the account books. She'd been trying to stay busy so that she wouldn't think too much about St. John and his devastating smile. Though she hated working on the accounts, it was an absorbing business and should have kept her mind busy and off things better not thought about.

It hadn't worked. Instead she'd spent a good hour alternately staring out the window and drawing little horses representing her upcoming ride with St. John.

Sighing heavily, she put away the quill and closed the books. It was nice having something to look forward to other than work. Not that she didn't enjoy the glassmaking. But there was something special in being pursued.

It really wasn't that she'd been totally without masculine attention. Malcolm had enough of his Edinburgh friends to visit that she'd had numerous occasions to slap hands and kick shins. Like Mr. St. John's. But none of them had really *pursued* her, taken the time to get to know her, asked her questions, even something as simple as offering to take her for a ride . . .

She sighed and rose, making her way to the front door. St. John's offer to go riding had been so unexpected, so . . . pleasant. And while she knew she should have said no, she also knew that she would have regretted saying the word. Some of it, she suspected, had to do with Mr. St. John's blue eyes. They had a way of looking at one as if he understood everything there was to understand, a curiously empathetic look for one so obviously spoiled by life.

"Hmph," she told the air as she stepped outside, "he's probably still in his room, sitting on his bed, waiting for his valet to come and dress him."

"Whot's that?" Douglas asked, looking up from the wagon bed. He was Simon's right-hand man, and as suspicious as they came.

Her face flushed. "Nothing. I was just talking to myself."

Simon nodded. "Bad habit, that."

"Indeed it is," she agreed. "Fortunately I only do it when faced with extreme circumstances." Before he could ask anything more, she said, "Did the new glass make the journey?"

Simon brightened. "Indeed it did, Miss Kat. Donald got us a right good price for it, too." He unlashed the canvas and lifted it, standing back to say with great satisfaction, "I'll wager you've never seen a prettier blue than that."

She leaned over the edge of the cart and ran her finger down the large sheet of glass. It was a deep, rich blue. Simon was right—it was beautiful. But she had seen a blue just this color—in the eyes of the man who had held her in his arms not a week hence. "It's a lovely color."

Douglas grunted. "'Tis fair. Would like to see more green glass, but that is neither here nor there."

"We need more green if we're to complete this new order," Kat said.

"Aye, and we need to find it fast," Douglas agreed. "'Tis coming on a rain and the roads will suffer. Miss Spalding's man said the way to Sterling is washed out."

Kat tried to look uninterested. "I'd heard that Miss Spalding was in residence at Kilkairn."

"Arrived earlier this week. I don't think she was going to stay at first, for she didn't unload her trunks. Daresay all of the servants at Kilkairn were glad to see that. But then she changed her mind and had the entire place in an uproar, directing this trunk here and that one there. She even made Janie wash the sheets on her bed, she did, claiming they were dusty."

"They probably were," Kat said absently.

Simon drew the tarp back over the glass. "Miss Spalding has been trouble since she put on her first petticoats. I hope ye stay clear of her. There's no reason to stir her up; 'twould be like jamming a stick in a beehive. You're bound to get stung."

"Of course I'll stay out of her way. I have no reason to so much as talk to her to begin with." If that was the type of woman Devon St. John admired, then he was welcome to her. Murien was beautiful, there was no doubt about that, but she wasn't particularly pleasant. At least, not to Kat. There had always been a certain superior air to the woman, as if she knew her beauty and valued it more than anyone else.

"Should we put the glass away?" Simon asked, drawing on his leather gloves.

"Aye," Kat agreed.

"Very well, Miss Kat." He and the others climbed into the seats and hawed the wagon in the direction of the workshop.

Kat entered the house and caught sight of the clock that hung over the mantel.

Good heavens! Where had the morning gone? St. John would be here soon and here she was, still wearing her work clothing. She gathered the account books and ran up the stairs in her work boots. She halted on the fourth step when she realized that

Annie stood on the middlemost step, disapproval in her clear gray eyes.

"Fie on ye, Miss Kat!" the housekeeper said, sending her a stern frown. "Ye'll tear the runner wid those shoes of yers."

"Sorry," Kat mumbled, slowing down and walking more or less sedately up the final few steps. It was difficult to walk up the stairs in such a mundane manner when seconds ago she was flying up them, but she managed to take three or four more-or-less properly feminine steps until Annie was out of sight.

The second Annie could no longer see her, Kat kicked off the offending shoes, hiked her skirts, and dashed the rest of the way to her room, skidding on her stocking feet as she rounded the door.

An emerald-green habit lay on her bed, spread out in luminous glory. Kat had to pause before she touched it, just to admire it once again.

" 'Tis a lovely color fer ye, mistress," Annie said from where she'd followed Kat into the room. "Deep green and severely tailored. Ye'll look pretty as a picture, ye will."

Kat's face heated. "Thank you." It was the only article she'd kept out of the generous wardrobe Malcolm had ordered. Mainly because she so loved to ride. On a horse, flying down a path, she felt light and thin and pretty.

"Ye'd best hurry," Annie admonished. "Or His Lordship will be here afore ye're ready."

"He's not a lord."

"Och, he looked like one. Lord Handsome is what he should be called. Now come and dress."

Later, Kat stared at herself in the mirror. Annie had been right—the habit fit perfectly. And the plain, almost severe style suited her, too. The coat was simple, following the nice line of her shoulders, angling down to her waist and ending there, at her waistband. The sleeves were long and narrow while the skirts were full, but not too much, so that they could be adjusted on her side saddle.

The only levity in the entire ensemble was a starched white cravat that filled the gap at her neck, and a fluttering white scarf that draped over her shoulder. The splashes of white served a purpose for they emphasized the full curves of her breasts. Kat frowned at that. She had more than her fair share of curves, a fact that made clothing difficult to fit.

Kat turned to Annie. "Well? What do you think?"

Annie sighed again, her grin belying her exasperation. "I think the same thing I thought two minutes ago. Ye look like an angel. If ye don't believe me, ask the lads. They'll tell ye what they think, will ye or nil ye."

That was true. "Thank you, Annie." After placing a quick kiss on the housekeeper's cheek, Kat snatched up her hat and dashed down the stairs and across the clearing to the workshop.

She stopped outside the wide door, pausing to gather her nerve. Inside was the warm murmur of masculine voices as the men worked, joked, and teased one another.

Kat fingered the stiff material of her riding habit.

Perhaps she shouldn't ask them what they thought. It was just that she wasn't certain it was the type of clothing to appeal to a man. Perhaps she should wear her black habit instead. It wasn't as fitted, but was of a more modern design.

She took a deep breath and then stepped through the wide open doors. "I've a question," she announced, waiting until every eye was upon her. Then she held out her arms to either side. "What do you think?"

With the exception of the crackle of the fire in the large pit, silence reigned.

Finally, Simon set down the lathe he'd been using to smooth a rough board. He rubbed a thick finger alongside his nose, staring at her intently. "Och now, lassie. Ye look perfectly well."

Donald nodded quickly. "Aye. And, ah, your hair looks well, too." He darted a nervous glance at Will, who was firing up the bellows for the soldering. Donald jerked his head toward Kat.

Will frowned, his heavy jowls quivering. He was a massive man, more than six feet tall, his arms bulging with muscles from his work at the forge. He blinked hazily at Donald, who was still motioning toward Kat. "What?"

" 'Tis Kat," Donald said with a meaningful jerk of his head. "She wants to know what we think."

"Of what?" Will said, plainly bewildered.

"Her *hair*."

Will turned to look at Kat, squinting thoughtfully. "Hm . . . weeel, it don't look a mite different than the last time I seen it." His brow lowered. "Least I don't think it looks any diff—"

"*Will!*" Simon hissed, glowering.

Will reluctantly smoothed his dirty hands on his smock. "Och now, I dinna know what ye want me to do!" He turned a bewildered eye on Kat. "Miss Kat, ye look loverly, whatever ye done wid yer hair."

Kat sighed. "I didn't do anything with my hair."

"Ah ha!" Will turned an indignant eye on Simon and Donald. "She didn't do nothin' to her hair!"

"I heard her," Donald hissed. He stared at Kat as if perplexed. "What did ye do then?"

Simon nodded, crossing his arms and studying Kat as if she was a puzzle to be solved. "If I know one thing about women, 'tis that they do love to ask ye what ye think of their new locks or new trappin's."

Alistair rubbed his chin, rasping his blond whiskers. "Mayhap 'tis her boots."

Seven pairs of eyes fastened on Kat's boots.

She dropped her arms to her sides. "Oh for the love of—It's not my hair and it's not my boots, either." Encountering yet more looks of bewilderment, she finally sighed and said, "It's the riding habit. Do you like my riding habit?"

Neal sent a covert glance around the room, then offered, " 'Tis a new one, then? How loverly."

She stomped her foot. "No! 'Tis my old one, but I had it brushed and pressed."

To a man, they appeared relieved.

" 'Tis brushed! O' course!" Simon said.

Donald beamed. "That was me next guess."

"Whist, now," Will said, sending a stern glance at Donald. "Ye weren't a-goin' to say nary a thing aboot her habit and ye know it."

"I was, too," Donald protested, his face flushing. "Was goin' to say that if 'twasn't her hair, and 'twasn't her boots, then it had to be her riding habit. Whot else could it be?"

"Donald has a point, he does," Neal said, nodding wisely.

"Whist now, all of ye," Hamish said in his quiet way. "Miss Kat looks loverly in her habit, she does. And that's all she needs to hear from us."

The others nodded their agreement.

Simon appeared relieved the moment had passed. "There ye are, Miss Kat. We all agree ye looks wondrous."

Kat had to smile. Over the last few years, these men had become her family, and she loved them dearly. It was wonderful how they each added to Kat's life and livelihood. After years of practice, Simon was better than she was at glazing, his touch delicate and smooth. Both Donald and Hamish had a way with soldering that made her shake her head in wonder. Alistair could get the most cuts out of a pane of glass. Neal was a marvel at etching, while Douglas's ability to trace and replicate a design was almost uncanny. He had but to see a picture to reproduce it. And Will's exquisite woodworking skills made suitable frames that blended the beauty of the glass with the more functional aspects of the windows and doors Kat's patrons demanded.

But for all the talents of her apprentices, none had

her eye for design and not one understood the use of color, though she'd tried time and again to explain it to them. It was the combination of all their skills that made the glasswork so unusual, so exquisite.

A noise arose outside, and Simon crossed to the window. He frowned. "There's that Sassenach again. Does he have nothin' better to do than come here?"

"He came to see me. We are going riding."

The warm glow of approval evaporated as quickly as it had come. "Riding?" Donald said. "With a Sassenach?"

"With one of Malcolm's guests," Kat said a bit defensively. "Besides, I get to ride his gelding."

"'Tis a bonny horse," Simon said, "but I hope ye'll have a care. I don't trust any of Lord Macdonald's guests, particularly not the Sassenach ones."

Kat placed the hat on her head, tilting it to a jaunty angle, then she went to the door. "I will take care, Simon. You have my word on it."

"Like ye'll remember oncet ye're cavorting with the Sassenach," Simon said sourly.

"I promise not to let the 'cavorting' go to my head." She grinned at the lads. "I will be back soon, and then we'll begin working on the designs for the windows for that London church. I've an idea for a panel that will leave them all breathless."

With that, she waved a good-bye and then almost danced out the door, closing it behind her.

Chapter 9

Most men are trustworthy providing you trust them only after they've proven themselves worthy.

Miss Elizabeth Standon
to a rather distraught Lady Lucinda Sutherland
upon discovering Mr. Poole's duplicity

*E*very eye focused on the closed door.

Simon raked a hand through his hair, wondering what he should do now. He didn't trust the Sassenach, or any man. Not around Miss Kat.

Donald pursed his lips. "Is it just me, or is Miss Kat actin' a wee bit strange?"

Neal nodded. "I was thinkin' the same, I was."

"And I," Hamish agreed.

The others murmured an agreement.

Simon cocked a brow at Donald. "I think she's actin' mighty strange. And it all has to do wid that St. John fellow."

"It canno' be another," Donald said.

"Have ye spoken to him?" Neal asked.

Donald shook his head. "Nay, but Annie has,

though what good that does, I canno' tell ye. She said he was a bonny Sassenach. Went on about his blue eyes till I was near to castin' up me lunch."

"Sassenach." Simon spat the word.

The others nodded glumly.

Silence filled the workroom. It was one thing for Miss Kat to have a beau. God knew she was a taking lass and needed a strong hand. But for it to be a Sassenach; that was another matter all together. He'd bear watching all the more closely.

Simon flexed his shoulders. "I'll say this: if anythin' untoward seems to be happenin', then we'll take a look at this man. Perhaps we'll invite him to a meetin'."

Donald brightened. "That's a right good idea. But . . . what if we do no' like him?"

Neal rubbed his nose. "Then we'll make certain Miss Kat knows aboot it. What she does then, well . . . that's up t' her."

The others nodded, muttering agreement.

Feeling better by the minute, Simon stood, smacking his fist in his hand. "Good then. When the time comes, I'll see if we can convince His Lordliness to join us fer a brief spate o' conversation."

"But—" Hamish's blond brows were drawn low. "What if he won't come to see us? He is a man of wealth and position, and we are just apprentices."

Simon considered this for a moment. Then he shook his head. "Don't ye fash that he might refuse; I can be mighty persuasive. 'Deed I can."

A slow grin traveled about the room. Neal picked

up the hammer he'd lain down when Kat had entered the room. " 'Tis done then. If things seem to be gettin' out of hand, Simon will collect the Sassenach and we'll test him fer Miss Kat, whether he wants to or not."

Devon wasn't quite sure what his expectations for the ride were . . . and later he'd tell himself that perhaps it was better he didn't have any except to escape Murien's cloying presence. Yet the day turned into one of surprises, most of which involved Kat.

His first surprise had been on arriving. Kat had looked tantalizingly beautiful, even more so than she had before. Perhaps it was the green habit, for it clung to her curves as if painted. Or perhaps it was that her hair was now pinned up, away from her face so that the loveliness of her features was even more evident. Whatever it was, there was something about Kat Macdonald that appealed to him. While Murien might be lovely in the conventional sense, something about Kat whispered of tangled sheets, damp skin, and other deliciously earthy matters.

Even after mulling it through, he could not distinguish what it was about her that made his thoughts instantly turn lascivious. It was not her manner, for she was neither brazen nor suggestive. It was more the curve of her cheek, the plumpness of her lips, the fullness of her hips. They all told Devon that if he was ever fortunate enough to win his way into her highly protected bed, it would be an experience he would never forget.

Which brought about the second surprise of the

day—from the moment he saw Kat walking across the clearing toward him, his body reacted. But that was not the end of it. For the rest of the day, all he had to do was rest his gaze on her hips as she rode before him, and his manhood would stiffen instantly.

Never had Devon felt such lust for a woman. But perhaps that was a good thing, for it greatly dimmed his memory of Murien until he scarcely thought of her. He soon found that thinking of another woman around Kat Macdonald was an impossibility; she was so vibrant, so uninhibited, so different from any woman he'd ever met.

The third surprise of the day was less spectacular, but even more perplexing. For all the attraction he felt for Kat, it appeared that it was completely one-sided. He was the one sneaking glances, trying to catch her eye, and feeling bereft when she didn't notice. She was totally caught up in experiencing Thunder, a fact that Devon found somewhat insulting.

In fact, Kat was so engrossed in the blasted horse that they rode for almost twenty minutes without speaking a word. Devon's pride was pricked. He wasn't used to being slighted. And while a part of him acknowledged that it was unintentional and he was probably due his fair share—for God knew he'd danced with numerous young ladies only to promptly forget their names—it didn't make the experience any less irksome.

Finally, Devon decided he'd had enough. He urged his mount forward a bit until Kat saw him. She blinked as if surprised, and then smiled, her teeth white between her lips.

Devon's ire evaporated instantly as she pulled up.

She glowed with enthusiasm. "What a lovely horse! Where did you get him?"

"Italy. My brother deals with a trader from there who dabbles in breeding. When the trader couldn't pay, he offered to send the horse to close the debt."

She bent over to rub Thunder's neck. "Your brother is to be commended! I don't know what the trader owed him, but Thunder was worth every guinea."

Looking at Kat's face, Devon realized that he would have paid twice the amount had the smile been for him and not his horse.

Devon wondered if Murien could even ride, and if she did, how she would compare to the effortless way Kat rode Thunder. No woman he knew had such a confident seat, and certainly none of them could have handled Thunder with such ease.

She sighed happily. "It has been so long since I had an opportunity to ride like this. I'm afraid I'm being rude, leaving you behind."

"Nonsense," he said, forgetting his ill feeling from a moment before. "Trusty and I were doing well on our own." He had to admit that she'd given him a pretty animal in exchange for Thunder. They were no match in stride, of course, but the bay had a neat mouth and a steady pace. "This is a good animal."

"Trusty is one of my favorites, though I fear riding your mount has spoiled me for all my horses. I shall have to sell them now."

He grinned. "How many do you own?"

"More than I should," she confessed ruefully,

tucking a stray strand of hair behind one ear. "I felt rather decadent when I first began buying them, but I can afford them, so why shouldn't I?"

"Why shouldn't you, indeed."

"Besides, having to keep them in grain helps me to get out of bed when the lads do. It's a marvelous incentive."

Devon chuckled. He'd never met a woman who paid her own way in the world. Not once. Previous to meeting Kat Macdonald, he'd always thought a woman who dabbled in trade would be brutally harsh and unfeminine. Instead he was finding that it added a pleasant aura of confidence.

She sent him a curious glance, her skin smooth as silk beneath the flicker of sun that broke through the trees. "How many horses do you own?"

He didn't know for certain, so he shrugged and said, "Far more than I can ever ride."

"Me, too. I am forced ask the lads to exercise the horses whenever they can."

"The lads?" A smile quirked his lips. "Is that what you call them?"

"Aye," she said. "That's what they are."

"Even Simon?"

"He's the oldest lad." An answering smile curved her mouth. "And as such, he is in charge of a great deal."

"Including your virtue."

The smile left her mouth. "No one is in charge of my virtue but me."

"I think Simon would disagree with you. He glares at me every time I see him."

"That's just his way."

"Hm," he said, unconvinced. He knew a challenge when he saw one and, having a sister himself, recognized a protective stance for what it was. "Well, if you ever decide you need someone to watch over your virtue, he would be an excellent choice." Devon looked around. They were on a wide path that seemed a great deal used. "Where are we going?"

"This is the road to the village. There's a path off to the right that leads to a stream. We can water the horses there, if you wish."

"Excellent," he said. He followed her onto a narrower path, and soon the rush of moving water could be heard. Once there, he dismounted and tied Trusty to a low branch, then went to where Kat was gathering her skirts and preparing to dismount. He reached out a hand.

Kat shook her head. "Thank you, but I don't need any help." She got on and off a horse at least four or five times a day, and it would be very irksome indeed if she couldn't do it without help.

"Too bad," he said, holding out his arms. "For I insist."

She paused, uncertain what to do. But even as she hesitated, he stepped forward. His warm hands encircled her waist, and he set her on her feet as easily as if she wasn't an ungainly size.

He didn't release her, though, but stood smiling at her. His hands were warm through her habit, his mouth only a few inches above hers. If she wished to kiss him, all she'd have to do was raise ever so slightly on her toes and . . . To her chagrin, her body softened in response. With his devilish smile and black hair, he was an incredibly attractive man, far more so than most of the visitors who tried to trick her into their beds.

But this stranger with the quick smile and flashing eyes hadn't attempted to hold her against her will. In fact, she was quite certain that were she to move now, his hands would drop from her waist and he would make no more effort to touch her. It was that knowledge that kept her still, enjoying the almost forgotten feel of a man's hands on her body. A feeling she'd tried her best to leave behind.

St. John smiled, a dimple flashing in one of his cheeks. "Know what I'm thinking?"

"What?"

"That you smell as good as you look. Of warm summer days and hot scones with butter."

This man seemed made up of words; some soft, some urgent, some funny, but all of them seductive. For the first time since she'd agreed to ride with him, a genuine stirring of alarm rose in Kat's chest. Blast it. She should have never agreed to help Malcolm keep Devon away from the castle.

As if he could see her distress, he reached up to smooth the hair from her forehead, the touch gentle, his eyes darkening. "I'm thinking something else, too."

"That you are hungry and should leave and hurry home?" she asked hopefully.

He chuckled. "No. Although the word 'appetite' did flicker through my mind."

Her cheeks burned. "That's quite enough, Mr. St. John."

"Do you mean that?"

Kat wet her lips. If she was honest with herself, she'd admit she rather liked the feel of his hands on her waist.

As if he read her thoughts, he asked, "What is wrong with me holding you?"

She thought about this for a moment. Why couldn't she just enjoy a man's hands on her waist? She forced herself to relax the tiniest bit. "I suppose there is nothing wrong with it. I am just used to others telling me what is and isn't proper."

"Society is a capricious mistress."

"She is vicious," Kat said, remembering a time when she'd felt the full brunt of disapproval.

His hands tightened slightly and he pulled her closer, his face only inches from hers, his gaze intent. "Listen to me. When you and I are alone, there is no society. No Kilkairn. No Simon. Just Devon and Kat. Do you think you can remember that?"

There was sincerity in his gaze and something more. Kat bit her lip. "Mr. St. John, I have to ask you a question."

He raised his brows.

"What are your intentions?"

He looked at her for a long moment, his blue eyes searching. "For today?"

She nodded.

"For today, I plan on kissing you again, which is a

realistic goal, I think. There is nothing wrong with a kiss between newly formed friends."

"Friends?"

"Like us. Then, after today . . ." He shrugged, his eyes gleaming with humor. "That is up to you, though I must admit I hope that a kiss might eventually lead to other things."

Kat blinked. "Well. You are certainly honest."

"I didn't think you'd accept anything less."

She wouldn't, of course. She just wasn't used to having the truth tossed at her in such a bald way. In her experience, the truth was something elusive and hidden, something one had to ferret out on one's own.

Perhaps there was more to Mr. Devon St. John than the other wastrels who had visited her brother. And he was right about one thing—there wasn't anything wrong with a kiss between new friends. He'd already stated that he'd allow her to decide how far that kiss would go.

Besides—she stole a glance up at him through her lashes—perhaps another kiss would assuage her curiosity about Devon and break the tug of longing his presence sent through her. Even now, she was achingly aware of his hands on her hips, of his chest just inches from hers. "I suppose one kiss won't hurt."

"Excellent," he said gravely. "We'll get to that in a moment. Now, relax and just enjoy being held. Isn't this pleasant?"

It was more than pleasant. It was warm and increasingly sensual. She caught his gaze and managed a smile. "You are right; it does feel well."

"So I think. Kat, you are beautiful, intelligent, and quick-witted. All of which make me want to hold you even more. If there is something wrong with that, you have to tell me."

When he said it like that, it made her want to wrap her arms about his neck and kiss him in earnest. The feeling startled her, and she cleared her throat. "St. John, what if I say I want to be released?"

He dropped his arms and stepped away immediately, leaving Kat feeling strangely bereft.

"See?" he said quietly. "That is all it takes. One word and I'll stop."

She nodded. He meant the gesture to comfort her fears, but it only raised more.

"So," he said, moving back into place, his thumbs tracing small circles on her back. "May I tell you what I am thinking at the very moment?"

Good Lord, a man who *liked* to talk while holding you in his arms. It was . . . frustrating. Kat wanted the kiss he'd promised, and being so close to him was making it hard to even think. Perhaps if she pretended to listen, then she could get her kiss more quickly. "Yes? What are you thinking?"

"I'm thinking of all the reasons a dalliance with a tall woman can be beneficial. For one, neither of us has to bend so far." He lifted a hand and drew his fingers down the side of her face.

The soft, simple touch sent a shiver through her, as did the almost somber tone of his words. "I—I have never been glad I was tall," Kat said breathlessly.

"You should be. You have amazing legs." His hand returned to her waist, and he was once again holding her before him.

She looked down at her skirts. "How would you know? You can't even see them."

He wagged his brows. "Couldn't I? When you were riding Thunder, your skirts outlined them. Along with other things."

Her cheeks heated. "Oh."

"You have legs that could capture a man and never let him go."

Heavens. He was certainly bold. And handsome. And yet . . . there was something almost wistful about him. As if he was searching for something.

She managed a small smile. "Fortunately for us both, I don't intend to use my legs to capture a man."

"No?"

"No." She took a deep breath, aware of the slow build of heat that surged between them. "Mr. St. John, I—"

"Devon."

The name crept into her thoughts and wrapped about her brain as if never to leave. She closed her eyes for a moment but refused to say anything more. She didn't think she could. The moment lengthened, stirring restless feelings she'd thought she'd forgotten.

She shook herself mentally. *It is just a feeling, and sometimes feelings are not real.* Thank God she was immune to men who bandied soft words and warm hands. Men who declared their love on Monday, only to realize by Tuesday that they'd made a mistake. Yet here she was, with a man who promised nothing more, yearning for his kiss. She put her hands over St. John's and pulled them off her waist, then moved out of reach. She crossed her arms over her, as if warding off a chill.

For some reason, that tiny moment caught at her, lodged in her chest like a weight. She searched desperately for a safe topic of conversation. "How was Malcolm? Did you see him this morning?"

St. John smiled as if he knew what she was doing, but he turned and gathered the horses and led them to the water. "He was fine. A little distracted, perhaps. But that's all."

She followed him to the edge of the stream. "I suppose he and Fiona have been fighting again." Kat knelt by the bank and picked up a smooth rock.

Devon turned to look at her. "There is a lot of tension at the castle."

"Aye. Whatever their argument is about, it is very desperate because neither will budge an inch."

Devon's brows lowered. "I've arrived in the midst of a domestic dispute."

"That is Malcolm's entire marriage." Stormy, violent, and flush with passion. There were indeed times Kat yearned for peace. She hefted the rock in her palm. "I don't think I believe in marriage anymore."

"Nor I." He caught her gaze and shrugged. "Not for me, anyhow. My brothers, however, seem to be rather fond of the arrangement. My sister, as well."

"Only one sister? Poor woman."

He grinned, his eyes crinkling in the most disarming manner. "Don't pity her. Sara more than held her own. When I was eight, I hid a snail in her bed. I waited and waited for her to scream, but she didn't do anything at all. Two nights later, I found an entire army of ants in mine. She'd poured sugar in the sheets, and it took me weeks to get rid of them."

Kat chuckled. "Served you right."

"Indeed it did, though at the grand age of eight, I felt sorely misused."

"Poor man." She dropped the rock and stood. "Would you like to ride into town?"

"What's there?"

"Nothing really. But it's a beautiful ride."

He looked directly at her. "It's beautiful here."

"Yes, but—you'll want to eat soon."

"You're right." He turned to Thunder and unbuckled the bag that hung across the horse's back. "Which is why I brought a luncheon."

She laughed then, the sound low and musical. "A man of resources." Devon found himself chuckling with her as he pulled out the picnic lunch.

They sat beneath a tree and ate. Devon tried to keep the conversation light, talking of this and that adventure with his brothers and sister, but it was difficult. Every time Kat opened her lips to take bite of the flaky pasties that he'd filched from the kitchen at Kilkairn, Devon's mind would burst into flames of heated, sultry imagination. He barely ate himself, but simply watched Kat.

He welcomed the building heat. It was what he'd

counted on to save him from the ring. With every breath, every word, Kat was proving herself to be the woman to keep the ring from working its magic.

Still, she needed some gentle wooing. Though she didn't flinch from his touch, he felt both her hesitation and her yearning, and something in him wanted to change that, to soothe her fears away. So he talked, and better yet, he listened, learning from her every word.

Soon the conversation turned to glasswork. He was amazed at the process and the length of time it all took. He wondered what other skills she possessed. Looking at her pouty mouth, he decided there were one or two that, if she didn't already know, he'd take great delight in teaching to her.

The shadows grew and lengthened, and before either knew it, the sun was slowly descending. Kat started. "St. George's dragon, it's late." She jumped up, brushing leaves from her skirts.

"Must you go?"

"Aye. The lads will be wondering what has become of me and we've an order to fill before—" She colored. "You don't want to hear this."

Devon realized with surprise that he did want to hear it. "Please go on."

"No," she said, smiling ruefully. "We really should go. The lads will be out looking for me if I don't return soon. They tend to expect the worst."

He could see that she was determined, so he rose to his feet as well and began putting away the remnants of their lunch.

As he went to help her onto Thunder, her clear

green eyes met his, measuring and seeking. He knew she was thinking of the promised kiss. He wasn't sure if she was looking for reassurance of some sort or was just curious. He smiled, and took her hand in his.

The touch of her fingers sent a wave of awareness over him. She gathered her skirts, preparing to mount the horse and he wondered again exactly what horrid happenstance had turned her from society, so scared that she hid deep in the woods like a princess asleep, waiting for a prince.

Well, he was no prince. Not even close to one. And charming companion or no, he had no plans for staying at Kilkairn longer than the short time he'd intended. But if nothing else, perhaps he could at least give her something to make the next two weeks memorable. Perhaps he could even get her to lower her defenses, show her that trusting was not always painful.

With that thought in mind, before Devon lifted Kat into the saddle, he tilted her face to his and kissed her.

Devon couldn't remember all the women he'd kissed. Still, it was novel to kiss someone whose mouth was so tantalizingly close to his. He didn't have to bend down at all.

But what really sealed the kiss as one of the best he'd ever had was Kat's reaction. She held nothing back, but threw herself into the embrace with her heart and soul.

Her arms crept about his neck, her body molded to

his, and her mouth opened, her tongue running over the edge of his teeth and setting his body aflame.

How long he kissed her, he didn't know. But every stroke of her tongue, every movement of her hips, threatened to send him over the edge. He finally broke the embrace, his breathing harsh, his mind numbed at a flood of demanding lust.

She met his gaze, her own breath quick between her lips. "That was . . . memorable."

He laughed. "Yes, it was. Memorable indeed."

She gave him a smile that was touchingly sweet, then turned and let him assist her into the saddle. He wondered at that smile the entire way back to the cottage.

The truth was, Kat Macdonald fascinated him. She offered an uncomplicated friendship tinged with a taste of passion so wild that he found himself unable to stop thinking about her. Of course, he was certain that once he sampled her passion, she would fade from his mind like all the others. But in the meantime, she offered a unique and fresh challenge, one perfectly suited to his rather jaded palate. One designed to protect him from the treachery of the talisman ring.

When they reached the clearing the lads came pouring out of the workshop. Simon was foremost. He planted himself before Devon. "Where have ye been?"

"Riding," Devon said calmly, though he was irked to be questioned in such a fashion. He pointed to Thunder and then to Trusty. "On horses."

Simon's face reddened. "I knew ye were on horses, ye bas—"

"*Simon.*" Kat sent him a warning glance from beneath her lashes.

The huge Scotsman pressed his lips together and said nothing more, though if glares could melt a man, then Devon would be a puddle.

One of the other lads growled, "We've been worried about ye, Miss Kat."

"Why?" she asked coolly, dismounting from Thunder without any help at all. "Because you believe I'm not capable of taking care of myself?"

Silence ensued as well as some uneasy shuffling. More than one uncomfortable glance was exchanged.

Devon had to pretend a sneeze just to hide his amusement. Kat's cool glance and calm demeanor had cut a swath through the rowdy men and reduced them all to abashed youths.

Simon cleared his throat. "Miss Kat, ye know we weren't sayin' that ye *couldn't* take care of yerself. Just that we worried about how the Sassenach might—well, ye know."

"No, I don't know," she answered. "You were worried about how the Sassenach might *what*?"

Simon rubbed his neck, clearly miserable. "Och, lassie. Don't ye look like that. Ye know what I mean."

She crossed her arms. "Simon, I am disappointed in you. How can you think such rubbish?"

Simon scuffed his toe on the ground, his face so red, Devon thought the man likely to burst into flames. "Miss Kat, I didn't mean to suggest—it's just that the man's a Sassenach, and ye were gone fer so long—then Hamish suggested that perhaps the Sassenach had—"

"*I* suggested?" one of the largest lads said. " 'Twasn't me."

Simon gave a dismissive wave of his hand. " 'Twas Neal then."

"No," returned one of the other lads in a huge rumbling voice.

Simon gave an exasperated sigh. "I don't know which of ye said it, but one of ye did!"

No one volunteered a word.

Kat gave an impatient gesture. "It doesn't matter. Simon, you owe Mr. St. John an apology."

"I owe him a *what*?" Simon shook his head as if to shake something clear from his ears.

"You owe Mr. St. John an apology." Kat's green gaze narrowed. "You owe me one, as well."

"What fer?"

"For having such indecent thoughts."

"Ye can't apologize fer yer thoughts," Simon protested.

Devon had to agree with the man there. Certainly had Devon been forced to do penance for every indecent thought he'd had while being with Kat, he'd have to spend a fortnight in a confessional talking nonstop.

Simon sighed, then mumbled an apology, though he glared the entire time. Devon nodded curtly. Simon had best get used to Devon's presence, for this would not be his last appearance at the little clearing in the woods.

Devon turned to Kat. "Thank you for a lovely day."

She shrugged, though her color was a bit high. "Thank you for a pleasant ride. And for allowing me to use your mount." She reached up to stroke Thunder's neck. "He's a lovely animal."

And she was a lovely person, both inside and out—a fact Devon was just beginning to realize and appreciate. He took her hand and pressed a kiss to the back of it, her fingers trembling against his lips. Ignoring Simon's muttered curse, Devon kept Kat's hand in his as he smiled at her. "Tomorrow?"

"No. I must work."

"The next day then?"

She pulled ever so slightly on her fingers and he released her. "The next day," she agreed.

With a final smile, he mounted Thunder. A short time later, Devon was riding toward Kilkairn, dreading his upcoming dinner with the warring Malcolm and Fiona, and the wily Murien. Perhaps he could slip in unnoticed.

With that in mind, he took the back stairs. As he rounded the corner to his room, he came to a halt.

"Mr. St. John!" Murien appeared from the shadows.

That gave him pause; her room was not on this level. He glanced around uneasily, then bowed. "Miss Spalding. Forgive my clothing. I just returned from my ride."

"How delightful for you." She smiled at him, the picture of a lovely, gracious, well-bred lady of fashion. "I daresay Miss Macdonald has worn you out. She is quite a . . . robust woman."

Though Murien's expression didn't change at all,

Devon felt the contempt beneath her voice. His mouth tightened. "She is a *lovely* woman," he corrected softly. Dangerously.

Murien knew a threat when she heard one. Her heart contracted at the realization. Yet her pride would not let it go. "Did you have a good ride?"

He looked at her for a long moment, then said in a deliberate tone, "Yes. I had a delightful time."

Murien's jaw ached where she clenched it. She was not used to doing all the pursuing. He *should* have made a comment about being sorry he had not been home, that he wished he'd spent more time with her. That he'd thought of her, at least once.

This was not going well. How could she captivate him if he was gone all the time?

Frustrated and uncertain of how to proceed, she toyed with her handkerchief, a gesture she'd adopted after a lovesick swain mentioned that it drew his gaze to her graceful hands. "Mr. St. John, you aren't from here . . . I don't mean to pry, but Strathmore's sister is—" She broke off as if embarrassed to go on.

"What?" St. John prompted her.

"You should ask Malcolm what happened in Edinburgh. I'm certain he'll tell you even though it was quite embarrassing at the time."

St. John leaned a shoulder against the wall, a smile on his handsome face. "Is that what you think I should do? Collect information from Malcolm about his sister?"

Murien nodded, adding in a gentle undertone, as

if loath to say more, "I am not one to gossip, and heaven knows I don't blame poor Miss Macdonald. But if your attention is being engaged, then you have the right to know all." She watched him from beneath her lashes, hoping he'd deny that his attention was anywhere near engaged.

But all he did was cross his arms, his coat stretching over his shoulders, a lock of dark hair falling over his brow. She wet her lips. He was quite attractive, her equal in looks. They would make a brilliant couple, feted for their beauty, admired for their culture and breeding, and envied for their fortune. Well, it was his fortune now, but it could be hers if she played her cards correctly.

Resolution grew in Murien's breast. She was not going to let Devon St. John get away. He was the perfect man for her, the one she'd been waiting for. "Mr. St. John, I wondered if perhaps tomorrow you might like to ride out with me and—"

"Do you ride?" he asked, surprised as if she'd admitted to vaulting off roofs as a hobby.

"Why yes. Of course I ride."

"Ah. But do you ride *well*?"

What was this? She frowned. "Of course I do."

His gaze narrowed, and she found herself fascinated with the way his lashes tangled at the corners of his eyes. It was unusual, black lashes and those blue, blue eyes.

"When *was* the last time you rode a horse?"

She wasn't quite sure. All she remembered was that she had received several compliments and two impulsive proposals of marriage before she'd even mounted the nasty animal someone had saddled for her. "I think it was two years ago. Perhaps three."

He laughed then, the sound startling her. She lifted her chin. "I fail to see what is funny."

"Don't worry, sweetheart," he said, shoving himself from the wall and walking past her to his room. "I wasn't laughing at you, but at myself. For being afraid of a silly legend. Apparently the St. John talisman ring can be beat, after all."

With that cryptic comment, he went into his room, shutting the door and leaving her all alone in the hallway.

Chapter 10

I was lying in bed, unable to sleep, when a truth was revealed to me. Mama, men are boils on the backside of the earth. If I had my way, I'd take a knife and lance them all.

The once gentle Lady Lucinda,
to her astonished mama, the Countess of Bradford,
when that gracious lady came to see why
her daughter did not appear at breakfast

"*H*e is never here."

Fiona pressed her fingers to her forehead where a raging headache threatened. "Murien, you have only been here a week or so. How can you—"

Murien whirled to face her. "Don't be a fool, Fiona! How can I make him fall in love with me if he won't even stay within arm's reach? He has been riding with Malcolm's sister three days in a row now. I *never* see him."

Murien had a point and Fiona knew it. But her head ached too much for her to do anything but nod dumbly. Something was going dreadfully wrong with her plan; not only was St. John unaffected by Murien, but Malcolm, even though he was winning the wager, was becoming colder by the day.

It was as if the closer he came to winning, the angrier he became.

Her lips trembled and she hastily took a sip of tea to stave off the tears. Murien hated to see people cry.

Murien sank into the chair opposite Fiona's in a cloud of pale blue muslin, a petulant expression on her face. "We have to think of some way to keep St. John here, at the castle. At least for an evening or two. I just know that if I could spend more time with him, he'd begin to see how well we would suit."

Fiona sighed. "I don't know what to say. St. John comes home every night, but goes straight to bed or closets himself with Malcolm in the billiards room. He's only been to dinner twice in the time he has been here."

Of course, part of that could be her fault. She had to admit that the cook was horrid—part of Fiona's original plan to force Malcolm to remove from Kilkairn. How Malcolm managed to get such breakfasts out of the man was beyond Fiona's ken. She imagined that the cook, like all of the other men in the household, was siding with Malcolm.

Murien's mouth thinned. "My brother-in-law does not wish me well."

"Nonsense. He merely enjoys St. John's company and likes a good game of billiards."

"Oh Fiona, stop it. Malcolm does not care for me;

he never has. That's fine with me for I don't care for him, either. How you could marry such a—"

"*Don't.*" Fiona wasn't sure who was more surprised at the icy tone of her voice.

Murien recovered first. She leaned back in her chair, a placating smile on her lips that did not quite reach her eyes. "I was just teasing, sister. There is no need to get in an uproar."

Fiona tilted her head in acknowledgment, mainly because she didn't trust herself to speak again. Heavens, what had caused that reaction?

"This is all so very perplexing." Murien placed her elbow on the arm of her chair and rested her chin in her hand. Her brow pulled down as she considered her options. "I wish there was some way we could expose Kat Macdonald for what she really is, gauche and unformed."

"Actually, she would have a very pretty figure if it was not for today's fashions," Fiona said absently. "They do not suit a woman with such curves."

"Curves? I wouldn't call them that. But it scarcely matters for the woman has no name, is practically two stone heavier than she ought to be, and has ruined whatever reputation she possessed. There is simply no reason for St. John to be dallying with her unless she is rewarding him in some way."

Fiona's cheeks heated. "Murien! Do not even suggest such a thing. I know Kat Macdonald and she's nothing like that."

Murien curled her nose. "Kat Macdonald hasn't

the least call to think herself worthy of St. John. She has no real beauty to speak of."

Fiona didn't understand it, either. Not that she harbored ill will for Malcolm's half sister, for Kat had been very kind to Fiona when she'd first come to Kilkairn.

But Fiona had to admit that there were far more reasons that St. John would avoid a woman like Kat rather than wish to be with her, unless of course . . . Fiona sat up straighter. "Murien, do you believe St. John might have developed a true tendre for Kat?"

"Lud no," Murien said, her lip curled. "He is just amusing himself at her expense. It is painfully obvious he is running from that blasted ring. He even said something to me about it. I didn't really understand it at the time, but now that I think about it, it makes perfect sense."

"Oh? When did you speak to him—"

"It doesn't matter. I think he is afraid of being forced to marry. And with Kat . . . how could she claim that she was ruined when she has already been so? She's safe for him. Perfectly safe."

"You don't think he's going to marry her?"

"No! He's not a foolish man." Murien's impatience was clear to see. "If only he would spend more time here." Murien leaned back in her chair, her gaze hard. "What we need is a reason to keep him here while proving how horridly unsuited Malcolm's sister is, even for a flirt."

Fiona tried to will her tired brain to think, but it was nearly impossible. She pressed her finger to her forehead. "Perhaps I should have a dinner party. A large one. Then we could invite Kat and he might see—"

"Fiona! That's it! But not a dinner party." A slow smile curved Murien's mouth. "A ball. An honest-to-goodness ball. Oh, I can picture it now. All of Edinburgh will be here and we'll dazzle them with Kilkairn Castle!"

Fiona looked around the room. Though it was one of the cleaner rooms in the castle, the rugs were still dusty and the mantel hadn't been wiped in weeks. She'd thought of seeing to it that the house staff did a better job, but that would only pander to Malcolm's comfort. Besides, why should she make such an effort to make Kilkairn a lovely place when Malcolm refused to allow her to live elsewhere for even part of the year?

She shook her head. "Murien, it would take weeks to get Kilkairn ready for a large ball. I don't know how—"

"Then have a small one and hire help from the village. I don't care. I just know that you have hit upon the perfect plan to show Miss Katherine Macdonald that she does not belong in the same room as St. John. That she is outclassed by far. Meanwhile . . ." Murien tapped her fingers on the arm of her chair, a sly smile on her lips. "Meanwhile, I shall do what I can to show St. John I am indeed the one to fear— that I am the woman he is to marry."

"And how will you do that?"

"Leave that to me. You just take care of the ball. We'll show St. John the pitfalls of having a consort like Kat."

Fiona bit back a sigh, wishing Murien didn't appear quite so happy about seeing Kat in such a humiliating situation. But Fiona would do it—she'd have the ball if for no other reason than to win the wager and keep her marriage intact.

Feeling miserable, she excused herself and went to her room to indulge in a good cry.

To the chagrin of more than one person, Devon came back to the clearing twice more over the next two days. Both times, despite Murien's attempts to lure him into staying at the castle and Simon's attempts to convince Kat that there was too much work to be done, Devon succeeded in carrying Kat off on Thunder. They rode far and wide, exploring pathways and galloping over meadows. And every day they'd have lunch beneath a tree of Kat's choosing.

Devon kept the conversation light on purpose. And at the end of every ride, before they mounted up for the ride home, Devon would kiss Kat. Just once. Just enough to leave her—and him—wanting more.

It was the sort of seduction he'd never before carried out, one slowly paced and carefully planned. Every day was a tempting challenge, and Devon found that he was enjoying every minute of it.

Of course, he didn't really think he needed to protect himself from Murien anymore . . . her charms did not appeal to him, which somewhat surprised him since she truly was the exact type of woman he'd pursued over and over. Perhaps that was why Kat was so appealing; she was just . . . Kat.

It was nice, too, to get away from the castle. Fiona continually attempted to throw Murien in his way, even though he'd been plain in his desire to stay away from her. And Murien, the gold standard gleaming in her beautiful eyes, encouraged Fiona to do just that.

In the end, there was nothing for it but to avoid Kilkairn until the time came for him to leave for Edinburgh, a day he should be looking forward to, but strangely was not. In fact, he refused to allow himself to remember the exact day. Every time he began to think ahead, an uneasy feeling rose in him.

Kat, of course, could have told him exactly how many days until he was due to leave, for it was a thought that was never far from her mind. In fact, this very morning she had awakened and lay in her large bed staring up at the hangings overhead, her mind immediately humming. She went to sleep and woke up thinking about Devon St. John. Strange how some people came into your life and then left without making a mark, while others came for only a short time and made such a dent that it would take years to fill the hole. Kat knew she was beginning to care for St. John. Oh, not in a romantic way, of course, though she enjoyed his kisses. It took far more than a kiss to sway her heart. But she was beginning to value his friendship. Yes. That was what it was.

Still . . . though he made a good friend, he was only passing time, avoiding being at Kilkairn Castle, any fool could see that. Kat needed to remember that fact.

She sighed. Who was she fooling? "Thank goodness he leaves soon," she muttered. That was the only reason she'd allowed the relationship to progress as far as it had; she knew that it would all be over in a week or so and her life would settle back down to the routines she'd developed. But for the rest of her life, she'd have memories of rides through the woods, picnics beneath the trees, shared laughter, and the enjoyment of a good friend. What could be wrong with that?

A brisk knock sounded on the door and Annie entered. The petite woman was dwarfed by the huge silver tray she carried in her hands.

Annie set the tray on the night table and began arranging the dishes. A pleasant clank and clatter filled the room.

Kat pushed herself upright, tucking her hair behind her ears. "What's this? Breakfast in bed? But Annie, I am not ill!"

"Neither is the prince, but I daresay he has breakfast in bed every day."

"Yes," Kat said, "and look how fat he has gotten."

Annie waved a hand. "Ye're not fat, m'lady. Ye're rounded. 'Tis a different thing. As fer the prince, I would no' know aboot him as I try to avoid the scandal sheets whenever possible."

Kat laughed. Annie brought back every scandal sheet she could procure from her cousins in London. Kat knew because she'd read them all to Annie at one time or another. "So why did you bring me breakfast in bed?" She lifted first one cover and then another, the scent of hot bacon and ham wafting through the air.

"Whist now, Miss Kat. Can't I do something pleasant fer ye without bein' accused of false pretenses?"

Kat raised her brows. "No."

Annie sighed and took a seat on the edge of the bed, the mattress barely sagging with her weight. "Ye're talkin' nonsense. Come, lass. We can coze a bit whilst ye're eatin'."

Here it came. "Yes?" Kat said politely, cutting her ham into small bites.

"I've been thinkin', I have."

Kat took a bite.

Annie sighed and folded her hands in her lap. "See, Miss Kat, 'tis like this; whilst I know ye think ye have everything under control where the Sassenach is concerned, I have to wonder if 'tis so."

"Why is that?"

"Because there are signs ye're not so immune to him as ye think."

"Oh for the love of—Annie, I've only gone riding with him a few times. I'm not planning a hand fasting."

"Aye, 'tis a good thing, that, fer you'd not get it. From what I've heard, the Sassenach is a libertine."

"A liber—Who told you that?"

"Me cousin, Janie. She said she heard Miss Spalding say Mr. St. John's only purpose in comin' to see ye was—" Annie broke off, glancing away, her face red. "Ye know what I mean."

Kat considered this. After a moment, she said

slowly, "And if that is true? How would that change things?"

"Miss Kat!"

"Annie, he has been nothing but gentlemanly, though I'd not allow him to be else. Besides, he's leaving in a week. I've nothing to worry about."

"Are ye sure?"

"Aye. That I am."

"Oh? How will ye feel if he leaves? I worry that ye're already too attached."

Kat picked up her bread and became very busy spreading butter over it. "I am fine. Really I am. Once Devon is gone, I will have some lovely memories. Where's the harm in that?"

"Hmph. Just see to it that ye don't have a baby full of memories."

"Annie!"

"Whist now. Ye know what I mean. A man who looks like that, why, if he so much as stumbled, I'd fall flat on the floor and pray that he fell atop me."

Kat had to laugh. "You are incorrigible."

"I don't rightly know what that means, but it sounds well enough, so I'll thank ye." Annie stood. "Now eat up and I'll come in a wee bit to collect the tray."

"Thank you, Annie."

"Whist. It was nothing." The scrawny housekeeper waved a hand. "By the by, Simon is gettin' worried about you. Ye might want to set his mind at ease afore he does something silly."

"Simon is a worrier. He always has been."

"Aye, and that makes him all the more dangerous, fer he's apt to get involved if he decides things are not progressin' as he thinks they should or shouldn't."

Kat nodded. She'd have a word with Simon. Meanwhile, her mind returned to Devon. Was Annie right? Was Kat getting too attached? All she knew was that she was not going to stop seeing Devon. Not yet, anyway. She'd just let the days unfold and enjoy them all, and then worry about Devon's departure when that day arrived. She'd just have to make certain she didn't let go of her heart.

That settled, she pulled the tray closer and ate.

Devon rode into the clearing, but unlike the previous days, Kat did not come out to welcome him. But of course, he was well over an hour late thanks to Murien's machinations. She'd caught him in the stables and had quizzed him mercilessly about his horse. Devon ground his teeth.

He dismounted and tied Thunder to a rail, then tilted his head and listened. He could just make out the faint sound of voices from the workshop. Deep masculine voices and a lone, husky feminine voice.

Devon walked to the workshop, pausing outside. Was Kat angry at him for not arriving when he'd said he would?

" 'Tis a complete ruin." Kat's voice filtered outside.

"Aye," agreed one of the lads. "The fool couldn't even draw a proper bead."

Another lad added, "An' look at the bit o' a smudge that's on the bottom."

"Aye," came a voice that Devon recognized as Simon's. "A cow-handed job if I ever seen one."

"We'll have to melt the seams and take it all apart," Kat said.

Devon stepped quietly into the workshop. It took a moment for his eyes to adjust, but they eventually did. He was intrigued with what he saw.

Rows of large tables ran the center of the shop, strewn with pieces of glass of every color, as well as several large squares. To one end of the room was a fire that was banked and covered until it smoldered. Beside it was a large, flat table strewn with long sticks and covered with drips of dried metal.

He turned his head toward the side of the shop that had no windows. Against the wall stood racks of glass, each sheet stacked on end and arranged by hue. There were cobalts and sky-blues, deep greens and mints, sun yellows and rich golds, royal-purples and pale violets, and every color in between. Truly, the room bore so much color that it seemed magical.

Yet the colors were not so much what caught him as Kat herself. Gathered with her lads around her at a table, Kat stood in one of her plain gray gowns. She was looking down at a seemingly finished piece of glasswork, a large square that depicted a unicorn grazing in a grass field.

She traced a line between two colors with one finger. "I've never seen such a horrid piece of work."

Simon rubbed his chin. "Do ye think we can—" He caught sight of Devon. Simon's jaw clenched.

Kat's gaze followed Simon's. Her face reddened. "St. John."

Never had his name sounded so unwelcoming.

He had to stifle yet another surge of irritation for Murien's clinging ways. There was nothing for it but the truth. "Kat, I am sorry I am late. I was detained at the castle by a very determined committee of one."

Kat's brow cleared. "Murien."

"Aye. I tried to get away, but she made it impossible."

There was a short moment of silence, and then Kat shrugged. "We can go riding another day."

Another day? He'd be damned if he'd return to the castle without spending at least a little time with her. Besides, he wanted their kiss. For some reason, the thought of going without that simple embrace made his jaw set. Ignoring the hostile gazes of the lads, Devon clasped his hands behind him and walked to the table. "You know . . . you did promise to show me your workshop."

"Indeed I did." She gestured around them. "Here 'tis."

He looked at the glasswork before them. "Did you just make this?"

Kat looked startled. "This?"

Simon spat on the dirt floor. "We're good at our trade. Don't think we aren't."

"Easy, Simon," Kat said, unrolling her sleeves and buttoning them back around her wrists. " 'Tis time ye were all back to work. Simon and I will find a way to at least make this better, if not fix it all together."

The lads left to go about their work, except Simon, who stayed in listening range.

Devon managed a rueful smile for Kat. "I'm afraid

I don't know much about glasswork. What's wrong with this piece that it offends you so?"

"A thousand things." She tilted her head to one side, her eyes narrowed. "See the line of the solder, how 'tis thicker on one side than t'other?"

He nodded.

"That is poor workmanship. Now see here, where the corner is patched and you can tell? Again, poor workmanship."

"Your men would never turn out such work as that, would they?"

"Not if they valued their jobs, they wouldn't. Oh, we all make mistakes now and again, and I'm well aware of it. But this type of work where the metal is heavier in places than it should be leaves the window weak and prone to cracking."

"Ah. So the problem with this piece isn't the uneven metal, but the weight of what is there."

"Aye. The secret is balance. If you're heavy on one side and not the other, the window can warp. The metal's only purpose is to link the glass together and lend some form to the whole. The frame is where the real strength of the window is built."

Devon watched her glowing face, faintly envious. "You like doing this."

"I cannot imagine not doing it," she said honestly. "I love the whole process, from the design, to cutting the pieces, to applying the metals, to seeing the finished window."

He tapped the glass on the table before them. "What about fixing other people's errors?"

She laughed, the sound infectious. "Even that,

though 'tis fortunate we are not oft asked to do such a thing. Truly, had this one not kept cracking, no one but the lads and I would have ever noticed the flaws. 'Tis a lovely piece despite the errors."

Devon leaned his hip against the table, facing her so that he could see every nuance of her face. With the exception of Simon, who stood glaring not five feet away, it was as if Kat and Devon were alone, for no one else was near enough to hear. "You are very different from the women of my world."

Her face shuttered. After a moment she said, "Not so different."

"But you are. Most of the women I know think marriage their goal. But not you."

"No," she said. "Not I."

He had to smile at her flat expression. Usually he was the one with that particularly unimpressed look. "Would you give up all of this for the right man?"

She snorted, then caught herself and blushed. "I am sorry. See the hazards of working among men all day? I've no delicacy left."

Oh, but how he disagreed. Even dressed in servant's clothing and with soot streak down one cheek, she was beautiful, womanly, and ladylike. He couldn't explain how she did it, but she did. He reached out and wiped away the soot with the pad of his thumb.

He dropped his hand when the mark was gone. "I have to wonder if you snorted because you would never give up your calling for the right man?"

"The right man wouldn't ask me to give up anything." She turned her gaze on him, clean and clear, as if looking right through him. "The right man would accept me as I am, and learn to love the things I love, or at least appreciate them."

One of the lads came up to discuss the cut of a pane of glass, and Devon was left alone for a moment.

He wondered what it would be like to be loved by a woman like Kat. He suddenly realized one reason that his previous affairs seemed so unsatisfactory; those women had been pale shadows of what a woman could be; Kat was beginning to show him that.

In fact, the passion he'd shared with his past loves didn't seem nearly as exciting to him as it once had. It had been about the chase, and nothing else. No wonder none of them had lasted more than a few weeks.

He looked down at the picture of the unicorn, absently noting that though the metalwork was uneven, the animal itself was well rendered. What *would* it be like to be loved by Kat, both physically and emotionally?

Emotionally, he didn't know. But physically, he could vouch for her reactions—at least partially. He'd kissed her no fewer than six times now, each one more scorching than the last and though he'd attempted to keep the kisses sweet, chaste even, in an effort to reassure her, she'd been the one to tug them both closer to the edge. She was responsive, wildly and passionately so, a fact that warmed his blood and heated his soul.

He knew the time was approaching when he wouldn't be able to stop at just one kiss. He both looked forward to and hated the thought of that day, for it would signal the beginning of the end of their relationship. Just as it did in all his previous relationships. Because once that occurred, the chase was over.

He thought of their last kiss, the memory enough to make his body react. Devon glanced at the door, wondering how he would get Kat away from the prying eyes of her lads so that he could taste her once again.

Suddenly he realized that he had only a week and a few days before he left.

Blast and hell, what was he waiting for? It was time he moved the relationship forward, at least some. If he didn't do so soon, he'd be gone before he could discover the true extent of Kat's passion, and Devon was determined not to let that happen.

Kat's voice sounded at his shoulder. "Do you like the unicorn?"

He realized he'd been blindly staring at it. "Just trying to see all the flaws."

"Sometimes 'tis best just to focus on the beauty."

He smiled. "Miss Kat, would you do me the honor of walking me to my horse?" He held out his elbow, and after a moment's hesitation, Kat tucked her hand in his. Out of the corner of his eye, Devon caught a glimpse of Simon, who stood watching, arms crossed, a fierce scowl on his craggy face. "Kat m'love," Devon whispered. "I think we have a problem."

She looked at him, surprise in her wide green eyes. "What problem?"

"Your friend Simon does not think much of me."

"He's just a mite protective."

"Hm. I see. He also does not like me. At all."

She seemed to consider this as they strolled outside to the railing where Thunder was tied. The horse had been there so many times that he was quite comfortably reaching through one of the barn doors to nibble some hay that stuck out around a corner.

"Simon is like a member of my own family. He watches out after both Annie and me."

"Annie is your housekeeper? The little bird of a woman?"

"Aye. She's his sister, and he treats us much the same."

"Hm." They were at Thunder's side. Devon looked around. Even from here, he could make out Simon's shape in the window of the workshop.

Devon took Kat's hand and pulled her around to the other side of Thunder.

"What are you doin—"

He kissed her. But this time, he didn't do the chivalrous thing and hold back. Instead, he kissed her with every ounce of his desire. He wrapped his arms about her, held her tightly to him, pressed his length to hers as he plundered her mouth, hotly and passionately. He kissed her until he could feel the tremors in her body and her knees weakened and he had to hold her upright.

When he finally lifted his head, he looked into her eyes and said, "Kat, I want more. More of you."

Her breath rushed through her lips, her eyes were

wide and luminous. He could see she was as affected as he. He set her back on her feet. "Think about that, would you? I will return tomorrow."

Then he mounted Thunder and left, whistling all the way back to Kilkairn Castle.

Chapter 11

*A disappointment in love is one of the hardest
things for a woman to overcome. One would like to
blame the entire male gender from youngest to oldest, for it always seems that, as a group, they have a
peculiarly uniform method of failing. As if at some
point, they held a meeting and simply voted to un-
derperform en masse.*

Countess of Bradford
to her favorite sister, Mrs. Compton,
while taking the waters in Bath

Tilton held out Devon's riding coat. "Your coat,
sir."

Devon shrugged into it. "Thank you, Tilton. Did
you call to have my horse saddled?"

"Yes, sir." The valet sniffed. "Again."

Devon grinned. "I am sorry if you find my habits
so tedious."

"Indeed I do, sir. But I try not to fall asleep whilst
performing my duties. I consider it a matter of professional pride."

Devon grinned and began to answer when his gaze fell on something small and shiny on the floor. He retrieved the object. "My sapphire cravat pin. I wonder how it got on the floor?"

Tilton frowned, all levity gone. "I don't know, sir. I've kept all of your pins in—" He picked up the jewelry box from the dressing table and flipped it open. He began sorting through the pins and fobs inside, his brow lowered.

"What is it?" Devon said.

Tilton paused, looked one more time, then closed the box. "The talisman ring, sir, it's gone."

"Gone?" Devon stared at the box. Surely the ring wasn't—hadn't been—"Are you certain? Perhaps it's on the floor like the cravat pin."

Tilton shook his head. "There is nothing else on the floor."

"Then perhaps it is behind the dresser." Devon began to search, his heart sick. Bloody hell, his brothers would kill him. And he'd let them, too. If he had lost the talisman ring, he deserved a beating and worse.

"Where in the hell is it?" he asked no one in particular when a thorough search turned up nothing.

"I don't know, sir. Someone had to have come in and stolen it."

Yes, but—who? Who would bother with such a theft, leaving the assortment of other, more valuable jewels? Devon raked a hand through his hair, wondering what in the hell he was supposed to do now.

As much as he disliked having the ring in his possession, it had been Mother's favorite. The entire family cherished the thing because of that, in spite of the horrid curse it supposedly carried.

He sat on the edge of the bed and yanked on his riding boots, consumed with the need to do something. He'd speak to Malcolm, have him question the household staff. It had to be one of the servants. Who else could benefit from the thing? "I'll speak to Lord Strathmore. Perhaps he has an idea of where we might look."

"Hmph. Well, the first place they should look is inside the pockets of that lazy upstairs maid. I've seen her sleeping under the steps on a number of occasions, reeking of gin."

"I'll mention that to Malcolm," Devon said. He grabbed his riding gloves and let himself from the room. He had just reached the bottom step when he caught sight of Fiona coming out of the front room. She was walking quickly, her head down, her hands clasped before her. While he watched, she then spun on her heels and turned back the other way. She was pacing, he realized, marching back and forth, her agitation clear.

"Lady Strathmore?" Devon said, pushing aside his own anxiety.

She came to an abrupt halt, swinging around to face him. "Y-yes, Mr. St. John?"

"I seem to have mislaid something. A ring. It was in my room and now it has disappeared."

"Oh dear. Do you think one of the servants stole it?"

"I am casting no blame. But do you think you might make some inquiries for me? It is the talisman ring, and my family would be loath to lose it."

"The talisman—Oh dear! Of course I'll make inquiries."

Devon could only hope she was more thorough in her inquiries than she was in overseeing the housekeeping.

She suddenly seemed to notice his clothing. "Are you going riding? Again?"

He hesitated, not quite sure why. "I am meeting Miss Macdonald, and we are going to visit the North Wood. Malcolm says it is quite magnificent."

Fiona's eyes flashed. "Malcolm? Has *he* been giving you suggestions for your rides?"

"Why, yes. I don't know the area, and he has been most kind in determining which trails would be best."

Her lips tightened. "He has been doing that, has he? And there is Kat, ready to escort you. How convenient."

Devon raised his brows. "Miss Katherine has taken great pains to assure me it is not at all convenient. She's quite busy, and I gathered that she wasn't very excited about becoming a guide."

"Oh. Well, if that is so, then perhaps you should take Murien instead. I'm certain she'd enjoy the exercise. If you'd like, I could return to the sitting room and—" She turned as she spoke, but Devon caught her arm.

"That's not necessary, I assure you." He hesitated, feeling the need to offer something more. "Besides, I will see Miss Spalding at dinner."

Fiona's face cleared as if by magic. "Excellent! That will give you a much better chance to talk than riding about on horses."

It would be much better chaperoned, too. Lately Murien's attempts to capture Devon's attention had seemed more determined than he liked. Still, he could afford to spend an hour across the dinner table from her, and if she was polite, he might even take her to the garden, providing there was a chaperone in the vicinity. If there wasn't, then Miss Murien was going to find herself alone among the roses.

He bowed now to Fiona. "I hate to leave so quickly, but Miss Katherine will be waiting."

"Oh. Yes, well—" Fiona took a deep breath as if to gird herself. "By the way, I meant to mention it to you, but I quite forgot. I . . . well, Malcolm and I thought to have a small gathering in your honor. I sent out the invitations yesterday. I would have told you sooner, but you have not been around much."

Devon almost winced at the gentle reproof in her voice. "I sincerely hope you haven't gone to any trouble. I'm not sure how long I'll be staying and—"

"It is planned for Wednesday next."

Four days after he'd planned to leave. He really needed to make the trip to Edinburgh but . . . He supposed he could stay a few more days. It would give him a little more time with Kat. "Very well. I look forward to it."

An uncertain smile swept over her face. "Excellent. I shall see to it that the servants are made aware of your missing ring, Mr. St. John."

"Thank you. Now I must be off. Pray have a good day, Lady Strathmore."

She flickered a smile, then watched him leave. He made his way outside, halting on the steps. The day was not as fine as the others, a low scattering of clouds and a hint of a breeze promising rain.

Devon took the pathway to the stables. Just as he rounded the last corner, he paused. Kat stood in the courtyard with the largest bay he'd ever seen. She was holding an apple behind her back, and the horse was attempting to reach behind her and steal it.

As beautiful as the horse was, Kat outshone it. She looked adorably mussed as she dodged this way and that, trying to avoid the horse's velvet nose. She glowed of health and laughter.

Devon waited until he was almost even with her before he spoke. "That is the tallest horse I've ever seen."

"Shhh!" Kat twinkled up at him and gave the apple to the horse. "Lady thinks she's a tiny, delicate thing. I try not to disabuse her of those notions. If she had any idea how heavy she really is, she'd refuse to take another fence."

Devon patted the horse's velvet nose, grinning a little. "She'd wait to sprout wings, hm?"

"Or for someone to carry her. She's dreadfully spoiled."

"Surely not that badly."

"Oh yes. She is everyone's darling. Even Malcolm brings her carrots and sugar when he thinks no one is watching."

Devon had no doubt about that, though he rather thought Malcolm did not bring treats to the horse, so much as he brought treats to his sister's favorite pet. "And here I thought Trusty was your most prized horse."

"Trusty? Why would you think that?"

"Because Trusty is the mount you gave me when I allowed you to ride Thunder. When two people trade, there is an unspoken implication that the two will strive to trade something of equal value."

Her green eyes sparkled with mischief. "Oh? Are you saying that Trusty was not an equal?"

"Not compared to this horse, no."

"Well . . . of all my horses, Trusty has the sweetest temper."

"And?"

Kat pursed her lips. "She also has a lovely mane."

Devon tried not to look too long at her lush lips. "What else does Trusty have?"

"Isn't that enough?"

"Not after seeing Lady." He reached out and patted Lady's neck. "I suppose I should ask if *this* is your finest mount rather than just assuming that it might be."

She grinned. "Yes, she is. I haven't ridden her for a week because she had a strained foreleg. But it seems healed now."

"She's a beauty and will make my poor mount appear lame."

"Thunder?" Laughter shining in her eyes, Kat covered Lady's ears. "Please do not get her hopes up. She can be quite despondent if she thinks to win and then doesn't."

It was nonsensical, but it helped dissipate some of the tension he'd felt earlier, though it did nothing to alleviate his concern over the lost ring. He put away those thoughts; surely the ring would turn up. "What brings you here this morning? I thought I was to meet you at the cottage."

"I'm escaping," she said. "Simon has been most obdurate about things of late. Besides, I thought we might ride out from here, to the north. You've only just a few days left, and should it rain, you might not have another opportunity."

"Actually, I may stay a few days longer than I'd originally expected." He didn't have to wait long to see her reaction.

She gave an impulsive hop. "Wonderful!"

The natural eagerness of her voice made his heart lighten. "Lady Strathmore is planning an event of some sort," he said. "It appears that I don't have a choice in the matter but to postpone my business in Edinburgh."

"Your brother will not be happy."

"Marcus will be fine; he's rarely happy, anyway."

"Poor man! Still, I am glad you'll be staying."

"Oh?"

"Of course!" Kat's smile lightened the cloudy day. "I am selfishly hoping that means that all of us can have more rides together."

"All of us?"

"You, Thunder, Lady and I. In fact . . . would you like to ride Lady today?"

"That is very kind of you," Devon said, touched despite himself. He reached over to pat Lady's neck. "She's a lovely horse."

"Aye. You know, if she didn't already have a name, I might consider calling her St. John, but she's not in the least bit averse to being held to bridle, so . . ." She shrugged, an impudent grin on her lips.

"So this magnificent beast could have been my namesake. How lovely."

The horse nudged Kat's pocket, sending her stumbling to one side. "Easy!" she ordered. "That is for later in the day."

"Another apple?" Devon questioned.

She nodded, patting her pockets where two round bulges could be seen. "I have one for her and one for Thunder."

The horse sniffed her pocket loudly, leaving a damp imprint, and then reached up and tugged on the white scarf that hung from Kat's shoulders. Kat sighed as she rescued her scarf. "Oh for the love of—"

Devon chuckled. "We had better go before she nibbles off your clothing in an attempt to win another apple." Although . . . nibbling off Kat's clothes held some appeal. A lot of appeal, if he was truthful.

They were soon riding, down the path. They rode on for some time, the slight wind rustling the leaves, the sun soaking the world with light.

After a while Kat pulled up, and they trotted along beside each other. "How are things at the castle?"

Devon hesitated. He wanted to tell her, but wasn't sure how much to confess.

She caught his look and said, "I know how it is there. I lived there once, too, you know."

"You are right, of course. I hadn't thought of that." He sighed. "Things are tense, with Malcolm and Fiona glaring at one another when Fiona isn't crying on the settee or Malcolm storming about the house. And Murien—" He stopped and shrugged.

"I know all about her, too. You should be on your guard, I heard that—" Kat's mouth clamped shut. "You should just have a care."

He managed a wry smile. "You may not credit this, but I have been on my guard against marriage traps since I was fifteen. I have no wish to ride out a bachelor and return an engaged man, and yet I have seen it happen to friends of mine."

"You need not worry about it with me. I do not find the thought of marriage attractive."

He looked at her quizzically. "May I ask why you're so set against it?"

She shrugged, looking away. "Some people are born for that sort of thing. I find that I am not."

"People . . . you mean women."

"Like Fiona."

"And Murien," he added.

Kat sent him a sharp look. "Has Murien been trying to get her claws into you?"

"I wouldn't say that, exactly."

Kat raised her brows.

Devon laughed. "Very well, perhaps I would say that."

He looked so mischievously sexy that the thrum of attraction that Kat was battling suddenly swelled and sent a bolt of heat through her. She instantly repressed it, though her body ached as if she'd deprived it of something crucial.

"I apologize for prying," Kat said. "I shouldn't be speaking of Murien or any of your other flirts."

"If we are going to talk about my flirts, we most definitely have to talk about yours."

"I don't have any."

"Well, not now. In order for someone to find you to flirt with, they'd have to have a map to the cottage and a cudgel to get through those lads of yours."

She grinned. " 'Tis true, that. Which brings me to my problem; they just don't make men capable of reading maps."

"I read maps. But only *if* there is a treasure to be found." He pulled Lady up short. "Perhaps we should find somewhere to eat before this rain lets go."

She glanced over their heads, then nodded. She led them to a small bluff, looking out over the wind-tossed fields. Devon dismounted and tied Lady to a low shrub. Then he went to Thunder and helped Kat dismount. The feel of her in his arms sparked the heat that had been growing all day. She was so perfectly made for him, her hips at his, her face only an inch or so lower. To kiss her, all he had to do was bend down ever so little—

Somehow, in thinking about kissing her, he did. Kat responded immediately, kissed him back, her arms sliding about his neck, her body melting to his. He devoured her, his mouth seeking, demanding. His hands splayed over her back as he melded her to him. Passion exploded and flared. Devon slid his hands lower until he was cupping her backside and holding her hips firmly to his.

She moaned beneath his mouth and pressed herself against him. God, but he wanted her. Every day with her had fed his desire. Every time she laughed, he wanted to kiss her. Every time she tilted back her head to look up at a bird or at the canopy of trees overhead, he wanted to open her gown and free her lush breasts, to hold them and cup them and taste them until she sighed his name. Every time she talked about the glasswork or Malcolm or her horses, or anything that ignited her passion, he wanted to sweep her from her feet and sample that passion for himself, let it sweep them both away.

And now he held her in his arms, her body moving as restlessly as his. Devon finally broke the kiss, but he did not release her as he usually did. This time he just held her. She clutched his coat, her face buried in his neck, her scarf on the ground at their feet. Her warm breathing tickled his overly active body, but all he did was hold her a little tighter. He waited for his breathing to still, resting his cheek against her silky hair, before he said, "One day soon, we are going to have to do something about this."

She lifted her face and met his gaze. "What do you mean?"

"You know exactly what I mean."

Her cheeks colored, but she didn't deny it.

"It is building between us. Can you feel it?"

She nodded.

He lifted his fingers to brush them across the line of her cheek. "I want you," he said simply. "I want to make love to you."

"Perhaps . . . perhaps we should eat." She moved out of his arms, stopping to retrieve her lost scarf.

Devon watched her open the leather bag that held their food. She hadn't agreed, but she hadn't refused him, either. For now, he would have to at least pretend to be agreeable to that.

He laid out their lunch while Kat fed apples to the horses, talking to them in a soft voice as if they were children. Thunder and Lady loved the attention and nickered in return, searching for more apples among Kat's pockets.

Devon watched from the corner of his eye. When he caught himself envying the attention she was bestowing on the horses, he shook his head ruefully. He was so randy he was beginning to act like a lovesick swain, something he never did, even when deep in the throes of a new love.

Thank goodness none of his brothers was about or they'd tease him mercilessly. Especially Marcus who, at the age of thirty-nine, was becoming something of a tyrant.

Devon gestured toward their lunch, now spread upon a blanket. "The wind is picking up, and it is beginning to look more like rain. We should eat quickly."

She smiled, finally leaving the horses. "Aye, Captain!"

He realized that her color was still high, and he wondered what she had been thinking. "I don't believe I like being called 'Captain.'"

"Oh." Some of her smile faded.

"But you may call me 'Admiral,' if you'd like." He made a magnanimous gesture. "Or 'Admiral, sir,' if it trips off your tongue any better."

Laughter gurgled in her throat, and some of the tension left her face. "I hope you're not pulling rank on me to get the largest apple tart."

"All is fair in love and . . . tartdom."

She giggled, and Devon found himself reaching out to brush a strand of hair from her face.

She jerked back at his touch. Devon frowned. "You just had a strand of hair on your cheek." His gaze narrowed. "You don't trust easily, do you?"

Kat's face heated, and she said with a slight touch of defensiveness, "I trust people. I trust Malcolm and Donald and Annie and Simon and Neal and, oh, all sorts of people."

"Just not me."

She bit her lip, wishing she knew what she did feel. Her instincts were at war with her head, and she wasn't sure which to believe. Her head told her that Devon was a rake and just wanted a few moments of pleasure. That there was nothing but pain at the end of that road.

Meanwhile, her instincts told her that she could trust him, that he wouldn't attempt to lure away her heart. That he'd been honest—painfully so—and didn't deserve her mistrust.

The idea of sleeping with Devon wasn't, in itself, a horrible thing. In fact, judging by the way her body reacted every time he was near, a few hours of mutual pleasure might be satisfying to them both. The very thought made her breasts ache as if he'd already touched them.

But even while she acknowledged the temptation that was Devon St. John, a thought clamored in the back of her mind. He would make love to her and then leave her. He had offered no more. Could she accept such a bargain?

Truly, Kat did not know. So instead of mulling it further, she bided her time. "Perhaps we should eat first and then discuss this . . . situation."

His eyes darkened and for an instant, she thought he'd refuse. But then a smile glinted in his blue eyes. "A reprieve then. But only until we've eaten."

Chapter 12

The worst part about dealing with the opposite sex, poor souls, is that they never seem to realize that even when we tell them that they are in control, they are not. Nothing would ever get done correctly, else.

Mrs. Compton to Madame Bennoit,
at a fitting at Madame's establishment
on Bond Street

$\mathcal{K}$at was agonizingly aware of Devon throughout lunch. He, meanwhile, seemed the same as ever—talking and teasing and several times making her laugh at his nonsense. Only once did she catch him looking at her with an intense expression.

Just as they finished lunch, the clouds overhead darkened. The wind rose and the plaid blanket was puffed away while they were packing the remains of their lunch back into the saddlebag. Kat had to run to catch the blanket, laughing as she did so. The wind was quick and freeing, tugging her skirts and hair, blowing fresh and cool.

Her spirits began to lift even though a part of her still dreaded the upcoming conversation.

Devon put the blanket away, then looked up at the darkening sky. "I don't know if we're going to make it back to Kilkairn."

She followed his gaze and agreed. It was looking dark, indeed. "There is a copse of woods where we can take shelter."

He glanced at her with a lopsided grin that sent her heart spinning in place. "I suppose it would be too much to ask for a cottage like yours."

"Far too much. All there is for shelter is a shed that was once used by the toll keeper. It has only three sides and probably leaks like a sieve."

"Just my luck." He untied the horses and led Lady to Kat. "Good thing I'm an admiral. We may have to swim home."

She allowed him to help her into the saddle. He set her up without effort, then stood looking up at her, his hands still on her waist.

Kat grew uneasy under the intensity of his gaze. "What? Is my hair mussed?"

He grinned. "I was just thinking that the wind had made you look as if you'd just been thoroughly rolled in the hay, even if I've yet to touch you."

But he had touched her. In many, many ways. In the weeks since Devon had arrived, Kat felt as if he'd awakened her. Brought her back to life after a long, lonely sleep.

The question was, if she allowed the relationship to go further, could she ever be satisfied to go back to the lonely sleep again, or would it be torturous to remember what she had and could no longer have?

Her smile must have faltered, for he removed his hands and said a little harshly, "Come. It's about to pour. Where is this shelter?"

She waited for him to mount and then took the lead, directing them back down the path to where the shed was almost completely obscured by a copse of trees and brush.

Just as they reached the shed, the heavens opened and rain came down in buckets. Devon slid off Thunder as soon as they reached the shelter, then helped Kat down. She was already drenched and could barely see for the sheets of rain.

He took Lady's reins, then pushed Kat gently toward the shed and yelled that he would be there soon. Kat stumbled forward, the water obscuring her vision. She could barely decipher the outline of the shed.

The old building was small and damp, but the roof wasn't as bad as she'd thought, leaking in only two or three places.

She hugged herself, shivering a little at the cold. The breeze, which had felt so good before the rain, now seemed chilly and unwelcoming. She looked around the shed to see if perhaps there was enough wood to make a fire, then decided that if she attempted to start one, the entire place might catch aflame.

Devon appeared, wet to the bone, something tucked beneath his coat. He wiped the water from his face and glanced around. "It will do."

"It has to," she answered, offering a smile. A slight shiver wracked her as she spoke.

Devon pulled the picnic blanket from beneath his coat and handed it to her. "Here. Take off your jacket and put this over you. It's fairly dry and will keep you warmer than that wet wool."

Her teeth were beginning to chatter, so she took off the jacket and the bedraggled white scarf. After looking around, she hung them both on a stray nail. "I wish there was more furniture. Some chairs, at least."

She turned to take the blanket from Devon when she saw his gaze on her chest. She looked down and winced. The rain had soaked her white linen shirt and her chemise all the way to her skin. The cloth clung to her, revealing far more than she'd intended.

Devon thought he'd never seen a more beautiful sight. Common sense told him that Kat would have beautiful breasts, but the large, full mounds revealed by her wet shirt far exceeded even his lustful imagination.

He was awash with the desire to see them, taste them, cup them in his hands. "We must have our talk," he said, wincing a little when his voice made the words seem harsh.

She colored, almost snatching the blanket from his hands and wrapping it around her. "So talk."

He wiped water from his neck, pulling off his own wet coat and loosening his cravat. "Let's sit." He searched through the ruined remains of the shed, finding a chair with a broken bottom and a bucket that, turned upside down, could be used as a stool.

He placed the chair against the driest wall and put a board across the broken seat, then overturned the bucket and made a companion chair. "After you, m'lady."

Kat took the chair, sitting primly on the edge of her seat. Whether it was because she was anxious or because the rain had wet her hair until it was slicked back from her forehead, her eyes seemed unusually wide.

"Well," he said, sitting on the bucket bench and raking a hand through his own hair. "I don't believe I've ever had a more awkward situation. But then, I've never desired to talk about having a relationship before."

She looked at him curiously. "Never?"

"No. They pretty much all just . . . happened. Mutual consent, as it were." Most of the women he'd had relationships with hadn't expected or wanted conversation. They'd wanted jewels, admiration, and his attention, all the while thriving on the hope that once he'd sampled their charms, he'd become so enamored that he'd desire something more—like marriage.

That never happened, of course. The more they wanted, the less he wished to give.

Kat was different. She didn't ask for or expect anything his former loves had craved and demanded. And it made him want to do more for her.

It was a new and perplexing feeling. Added to that was his decision to be truthful at all costs. For the first time in his life, he was enjoying a relationship based on simple truth—he didn't feel pressured to utter platitudes and inane compliments. Nor did Kat seem to want to hear false pledges of undying love. He knew that while the truth was sometimes difficult to express, Kat wouldn't accept anything less.

He glanced at her now, noting that she was thoroughly covered, the blanket clamped about her throat and hiding her wet clothing. "Kat, I'm not very good at talking about things. I'm a man of action. But for you, I'll try."

She nodded, her eyes warm in the silvered light. "I know."

Devon slid the bucket directly beside her chair, then reached over and pulled her to him.

She stiffened.

"You're cold. The least I can do is keep you warm."

She relaxed a little, glancing up at him through eyelashes that were spiked with wetness. "If that's all you're going to do."

"Until you say otherwise, it is."

They sat there, listening to the rain, their bodies gradually growing warmer. Devon rested his cheek against her hair, the faint scent of lavender drifting through the air. He always associated that scent with Kat now. Lovely and light, it seemed just like her.

Kat sighed and moved, her shoulder rubbing against his chest. Devon's body reacted immediately. God, but she was a lovely woman. A lovely person.

The tension between them that had begun at lunch

grew with each passing moment. The longer they sat together, his arm about her, her head resting against his cheek, the more insistent the urge became.

Devon lifted a strand of her hair and pressed his mouth to the tress. Wet, it curled about his fingers, clung in a way he wished Kat would. "At least your hair likes me."

She blinked at him, a quiver of humor curling her lips. "I never said I didn't like you."

"Yes, but you haven't said you did. I take that as a bad sign."

She turned and, to his surprise, trailed her lips across his cheek. It was an innocent touch, though his reaction was anything but.

He almost gasped. "If you don't wish me to touch you, you'll have to forgo little demonstrations like that."

Her brows rose. "Just a kiss on the cheek?"

"Any kiss, anywhere. They are maddening and make me want to pull you into my lap and savor you correctly."

For an instant, heat flared in her eyes, but then her lashes slid down to hide her reaction. "I have a puzzle to solve."

The soft words lingered in the air.

"Oh?"

"If I agree to take this relationship to a more physical level, what guarantee will I have that it won't hurt when you leave?" She sighed, the sound sweet in the rain-wet air. "My mind and my body are at war over the answer."

He drew her hair over his lips, savoring the silken stroke. "Sometimes the body is more truthful and uncomplicated than the mind."

"And sometimes what seems an honest and truthful response is no more than a thoughtless reaction that would happen in a variety of other circumstances. For example, the way you might jerk away if a bee were to fly close by, or how you'd react if an ember from the fire landed near your foot."

He smiled. "Has anyone ever told you that you think too much?"

She tilted her head to one side, her wet hair now more red than gold. "No."

"Then they were only being polite."

Her lips quivered with a smile, but she ruthlessly repressed it. "I don't believe it is possible to think too much."

"Hm. Would you care to put that statement to a test?"

Her wariness grew. "What kind of test?"

"We try a kiss while you are thinking . . ." He lowered his mouth to her cheek and whispered, "And a kiss while you are not."

Her skin was not the creamy white of most debutantes, but a luminous pink. He brushed his fingertips along the line of her cheek. "Sometimes, thoughts can stop us from experiencing the moment we're in. They can block feeling, emotion, energy, even pleasure."

"All by thinking?"

"All by thinking."

"I'm surprised anyone bothers to think at all,

then," she said in a slightly acid tone, though her lashes fluttered on her cheeks.

He smiled. If he merely listened to her words, he'd quit this seduction now, before it had really begun. But though she stoutly refused to give in to his verbal blandishments, she was not immune to him physically. If he could just show her that they were meant to touch, meant to be together. Not forever of course, but for this moment. "Well? Care to test your theory?"

She shrugged. "I suppose we might as well. We can't leave until this rain quits." She leaned back against his arm. "Go ahead, kiss me."

He started to lower his mouth to hers, but then stopped. "Is this the thinking kiss or the nonthinking kiss?"

"I am not going to tell you. I don't want you using any tricks to win your point."

"Very well. But you have to be honest with me about which kiss was which."

"You'll trust me?"

"With my soul."

Her face pinkened.

He didn't give her time to think that through. He tipped her face to him and kissed her. He put into the kiss all his longings, all his desires. Everything.

She was limp in his arms when he finished. The blanket had slipped and she was panting heavily, drawing his gaze once again to her nearly visible breasts.

"Ready for the next one?"

She held out a hand. "No. I've already proven my

point. That was the thinking kiss and I was reciting the names of all the kings and queens of Scotland all the while. I never made it past the twelfth century." She pressed a hand to her throat. "Thinking most definitely does not interfere with feeling."

He had to laugh. "I think you need the next kiss, too. Just to make certain."

Her gaze dropped to his mouth, and he could see she was wavering. "Just one more kiss." He bent toward her, his lips a whisper away.

"I can't," she gasped, pulling away. "No more, please." She looked at him, her green eyes sparkling with sudden tears. "I beg of you," she whispered. "No more."

Devon loosened his hold. "Kat, I don't understand—"

She shook her head, the gesture dislodging a tear. It fell from her eye and clung to her cheek. "I—I am not a fool, you know. I can see what you're doing. You are trying to seduce me."

He pursed his lips. "Yes, I am. That is what happens when there is an attraction, such as the one we have."

"I know. I am no innocent."

He chuckled. "I would beg to differ."

"Devon, I am no innocent." This time she said the words firmly.

"Ah," he said, realizing what she meant.

A grimace of anguish passed over her face. "I have made mistakes."

"We all have, sweet," Devon said. He wanted this

woman. Wanted her more than any other woman he'd ever known.

The problem was that if he succeeded in seducing her, he might damage the part of her he admired the most—her spirit.

Devon was not selfish. Not intentionally, anyway. And he knew from the conversations they'd had that Kat was not a woman given to sadness or histrionics. That fact made the tear in her eye mean all the more.

He sighed, rubbing his neck. His desire was subsiding, but only slightly. He wanted Kat in his bed, but not at the cost of her pride. "In no way do I wish to harm you."

A bitter smile touched her lips. "I've heard that before."

"But not from me. When I tell you something, I mean it. And I expect you to do the same for me."

Kat swallowed the lump of emotion that threatened to close her throat. Devon's black hair fell over his brow, his blue eyes never left her face. He'd discarded his jacket, and his black breeches hugged his narrow hips and outlined his muscular thighs. Her gaze traveled over him to where his throat was exposed. His cravat was undone and hung loosely about his neck, his shirt untied. A faint edge of chest hair showed in the opening, and she was assailed with the desire to touch it, to thread her fingers through it and feel the crispness of the tight black curls. God, but he was beautiful. Beautiful and . . . listening to her. Asking her what she thought, what she needed.

In that instant, she knew why he was different from Stephen. Stephen had swept her off her feet with smooth words and urgent hands. And she, feeling gauche and ugly after being paraded through cold receiving room after cold receiving room, had lapped it up like a starved cat.

Devon had the same passion as Stephen, but Devon had something more. Perhaps it was patience. Perhaps it was caring. Whatever it was, it had him sitting beside her, his arm offering warmth and nothing more, his head bent attentively, his eyes on hers.

In all the times she and Stephen had met, never once did she remember him looking at her with such a serious expression, or waiting to hear what she thought about anything. She wondered that she'd never before realized that.

Funny how one's expectations at seventeen were so very small. Then, years later, those same expectations transformed into a list of required virtues so long that she sometimes feared the man she wanted to meet did not exist.

She didn't want just passion, though that was part of it. She also wanted someone to talk to, someone who would listen, someone who would laugh with her and share himself the same way she wanted to share herself.

Devon reached across the space between them and drew his finger down her cheek. The touch left a trail of delicate fire that lit a heated pathway down her neck to her breast and beyond.

"What do you want, Kat? Because whatever it is, so long as it is not marriage, I will give it to you."

She tilted her head to one side. "Why do you hate the thought of marriage so much?"

His humor faded. "Because . . ." A shadow crossed his eyes. "I have a confession to make. It is not a pretty one, and you may never again wish to speak to me."

She waited, unwilling even to speculate on what he might say.

"Kat, as much as I wish it was otherwise, I cannot seem to remain . . . enamored of a woman for more than two months."

"*Two* months?"

He winced. "It sounds bad even to my own ears, so I cannot imagine how horrid it sounds to yours. I cannot help it; I grow bored after a short time, so I know I can never marry. I will not make a promise I know I cannot keep."

Kat nodded. "That is how it should be. You are very honorable."

His lips twisted. "Kat, I will not pretend I am not attracted to you—I am and you know it. And I will not pretend I do not wish for a more physical relationship than we have now. Honestly, I would give up Thunder just to spend one hour in a bed with you and nothing between us but tangled sheets and the dampness of our own bodies."

A delicious shiver tremored through her. He was so delectable, his gaze so blue, so intense. Better yet, honesty shone through him. For an instant, she thought she could see the truth shimmering over him like a light.

He raked a hand through his wet hair again, and she saw that his hand trembled the slightest bit.

"This is foolish," he said with a rueful smile. "I am ruining my chances with you, but I refuse to be less than truthful." He took her hand. "Kat, I don't know what happened in Edinburgh, but—"

"You should know."

"No. That is not necessary—"

"It is, too." She met his gaze directly, gathering courage. "If we are to continue this . . . relationship, brief though it may be, I will not have any secrets."

He hesitated, then sighed. "If you want to tell me, then do so."

She took a breath, her hands fisting at her sides. "I have thought this through a hundred times until I think I finally understand what I was doing and why. I was not raised at the castle like Malcolm. Our father really had little to do with my mother once I was born."

"He neglected her?"

"He made sure we didn't go hungry and that we had enough to survive. But sometimes whole months would go by and we'd never see him."

"That is sad."

"It was hard for us both," she agreed, "mainly because we knew he lived such a short distance away. It was especially difficult for Mama because she was the one he really rejected. I think he was always sorry he'd met her. At least, that was the impression he left us with."

Kat spoke simply, without pain. But Devon had an idea what even that gesture had cost her. "I see," he said, unable to think of anything better to add. He wondered if he should take her in his arms, but her next words forestalled him.

"It doesn't hurt so much now. Once Father died, I got Malcolm." Her face softened. "I have never regretted that trade."

"Malcolm knew of your existence?"

"He overheard his mother telling one of the stewards that my mother and I were to be ejected from the cottage. He was only twelve, but he stepped in and demanded that we be left alone. I think he'd seen us and had guessed the truth. We have never discussed it."

Devon smiled. "Malcolm's stubbornness is as legendary as my determination."

She returned his smile, her eyes warming slightly. "Determination or stubbornness? Aren't they the same?"

"I like to use the word 'determination' when applied to myself, and 'stubbornness' when applied to others."

He was rewarded with a quiet chuckle that made his heart ache.

"It is a flaw we three share, then," she said. "Anyway, after Malcolm knew of our existence, he came almost every day. His mother tried to stop him, but he ignored her and . . . he became my brother. Whatever I needed, he has been there for me. I am ever conscious of his kindness, which makes it difficult to say him nay."

"He can be persuasive."

"Indeed. When I turned sixteen, my mother died. Malcolm wished me to live at Kilkairn. Against my better judgment, I did so."

"Thus the blue room."

"Thus the blue room," she agreed. "He offered me one of the larger rooms, but I was uncomfortable. Besides, his mother resented me enough."

"I begin to dislike Malcolm's mother."

"Och now," Kat said softly, her voice gently chiding. "I reminded her of a time between herself and her husband that she wished gone. I cannot blame her for that."

"I suppose not," he said, unconvinced. "Did you like living at Kilkairn?"

"No. For so long, I had been on the outside of the castle. I thought being on the inside would be magical. But it wasn't. I felt lost, and I think Malcolm sensed that. He decided I needed more companionship, that I should be 'launched' on society as if I belonged."

"As if?"

"I was illegitimate, and everyone knew it. I had no money other than the dowry Malcolm was willing to settle on me. And—" She shrugged. "I am not a beauty. I never have been. But Malcolm was determined that I go. He coerced his mother to sponsor me, and for once she and I were in agreement; I didn't want to go any more than she wanted to take me. But Malcolm won the day and we went."

"It sounds as if the conditions were perfect for a disaster."

"It was horrid. And it got worse before it was over. I believe Lady Strathmore was sincere in her attempts to dress me well and show me about, but I did not take."

"I am sorry."

"So am I. Every event was painful and punishing. And the clothes she chose . . . now that I know more about color and texture, I can see her mistakes and mine."

Devon shook his head. "Men have it so much easier."

"Indeed they do. By the second week of arriving in Edinburgh, I was miserable. Meanwhile, Malcolm had met Fiona and he was gone a good deal, wooing her. I was left with Lady Strathmore and that . . . that was when I met Stephen."

"A rakehell of the first water, I take it."

"Worse. A rakehell of the worst water. He was unacceptable in almost every household, a fact I thought grossly unfair."

"Ah, words of the young."

"Words of the foolish. He was glib, and he spoke to me." A faint color touched her cheeks. "I'm afraid that was all it took. I eventually thought I was in love and I agreed . . . I-I absconded with him."

"You eloped?"

"So I thought. But apparently even that was too much for Stephen. It turned out later than he never intended to marry me, but merely wished to cause a scandal so that Malcolm would be forced to buy his silence." Her cheeks were deep pink.

Devon had to swallow a bitter lump of anger for

the long-absent Stephen before he could speak. "We all make mistakes."

"Most people do not embarrass their entire family with their errors," she replied sharply. "I was foolish enough to let practiced words muddle my thinking."

"Which is why you wish to think rather than feel. You believe it will keep you from making a similar error."

"Aye." She met Devon's gaze steadily. "You should know I was with Stephen for two weeks before Malcolm caught up with us. And here is where I am supposed to assure you that I am untouched. But . . ." Her lips thinned. "I cannot say that. I thought I loved him."

"Many things are done in the name of love."

"And many things undone. I believed his assurances that he wanted to marry me and that he would do so as soon as Malcolm gave his approval. But of course Stephen never asked for Malcolm's approval. Instead he asked for a thousand pounds to return me home and to keep his silence."

Devon had never been so angry in all his life. Never. "This bloody Stephen, wherever he is, deserves to be horsewhipped." B'God, if anyone had dared treat his sister the way the nefarious Stephen had treated Kat, Devon would have beaten the bastard into a bloody pulp. And then, for emphasis, all his brothers would take their turns. "If I cannot horsewhip him, then I would at least see him drawn and quartered. That might serve to punish the bastard."

"I fear you will have to dig a hole to do that; he

died two years later. I heard that he drank himself to death, though I was never certain."

"That is still too good for him."

She waved a hand. "What is gone is gone."

The gesture softened his anger, and he was once again assailed with the desire to hold her. He took her hand in his. "Kat, you are a passionate woman. There is nothing wrong with that."

She grimaced. "As Malcolm's mother was quick to point out, I am just like my mother."

"Then your mother was a joyous, warm person."

A flicker of emotion crossed over Kat's face, followed by a deep sigh. "Thank you. At the time, facing Malcolm's anger and his mother's bitter disappointment, I felt a fool."

"You were seventeen and alone." Devon pulled her closer and kissed her nose. "Listen to me, Kat. You are not a bad person. You are not an evil person. You are not a confused person. You are a strong and beautiful woman. And there is nothing wrong with being passionate with someone you care about."

"Not everyone sees it that way."

"So, who are you are going to listen to? Me? Or Malcolm's bitter mother? And let me point out that I have never lied to you, nor have I asked you to wear fashions that do not complement your gorgeous body."

Her lips quivered, her tears fading from her eyes. "You are a wretch to make me smile while I'm perfectly happy being miserable."

"It's a gift." He cupped her chin, rubbing his thumb over the softness of her cheek. "There. Do you have anything more to confess? Something of real import?"

"That was important."

"If that was your only sin, then I feel as if perhaps I should begin making confessions of my own, for my life has not been so lily-white."

"Oh?"

"I just hope you do not wish me to confess *all* my sins of a passionate nature. I fear my voice would give out before I could cover half of them."

She fingered the top button of his waistcoat. "Have there been many?"

Before now, Devon would have answered without a twinge of guilt. After all, he had never transgressed the bounds of society. He never philandered with innocents, never compromised a lady's reputation unless she initiated the event herself, and never ever mentioned names, even when deep in his cups.

But somehow, looking down into Kat's green eyes, he felt the faintest hint of a blush on his own cheeks. In all his years, Devon didn't think he'd felt a blush more than two or three times, and all before he was fourteen. "Yes," he finally said. "There have been that many sins in my life."

"Hm. And according to what you said about never staying interested more than a few months, there are going to be hundreds, perhaps thousands more."

Devon didn't answer. He couldn't. A deep loneliness gripped him. Was she right? Was he doomed to spend his life wandering from bed to bed, searching for the perfect woman, a woman he was beginning to think didn't exist?

Of course, Kat was close to his vision of perfection, and coming closer all the time. She was smart, attractive, capable, strong, and passionate . . . He frowned. Was she getting closer to his image of perfect or was he merely beginning to mold his image of perfection until it looked like Kat?

Whatever the truth, it didn't solve the problem of his own fickleness. His own lack of strength in committing. His own tendency to hurt those who came to care for him.

Whatever he did, Devon did not want to harm Kat. She'd suffered enough. So it was with the greatest effort that he stood and pulled her to her feet. "The rain is lessening. It will be over soon."

A shadow crossed her face. "Does this mean . . ." Her gaze lifted to his face. "You don't wish to be with me now that you know—"

"No! It just means that I don't want either of us doing anything we might regret. I enjoy your company too much to allow it to turn counterfeit."

"I see," she said, disappointment deep in her voice.

He almost laughed. That must be what he looked like every time she pulled away from him. She was simply adorable. So natural and free. And he was beginning to like spending time with her a bit too much. Thank God he was leaving soon.

But the thought brought as much of a twinge of pain as it brought relief. He'd be gone and Kat would be left here, to live her life in the woods while more of Malcolm's guests came to stay. Perhaps, one day, one of them would realize exactly how special Kat was, and sweep her away. It was as if, in a moment of extreme clarity, Devon could see the future.

Bloody hell. That was exactly what would happen.

"Devon?"

He realized Kat was looking up at him. "Yes?"

She wet her lips, the innocent gesture sending his senses reeling yet again. "Devon, what if I decide that *I* want for us to be closer? What then?"

"Kat, if we were to get closer than we are now, that—"

"You think my heart would be affected."

He paused. Then nodded. "I don't want to hurt you."

"You think I would fall in love with you if we slept together. That would be my problem and not yours." She placed her hands on his chest, then tilted her mouth to his and encompassed him in a kiss.

Devon's manhood stiffened immediately. He could no more resist Kat's lush body pressed so firmly against his. Her plump breasts were so close, just a waistcoat and a shirt away from his bare chest, her hips held intimately to his.

He was afire, hot and wanting, his thoughts breaking apart, dissolving before the onslaught of her soft mouth, her delicious body.

She broke the kiss, and he realized that he was once again holding her, pulling her to him. Her green eyes sparkled into his, and she said with a definite purr to her voice, "Tomorrow, we finish this."

He knew in that second that she was right; they would finish it. And for some reason, that thought made his very soul quake.

Chapter 13

Mon Dieu! I awoke to discover that my house had sprung a leak, the cook had quit due to an unfortunate incident involving a chicken liver, and my son had written to say that if I do not provide him with financial assistance forthwith, he will be forced to become the plaything of a certain elderly lady who has no hair and very bad teeth. Remind me not to wake up again.

Madame Bennoit to her assistant, Pierre,
while searching the storerooms
for a particular shade of violet muslin to be used
for the Countess of Bridgeton's new ball gown

Fiona opened the door to the green guest chamber and peered around the corner. Breathing a sigh of relief that it was empty, she quietly closed the door behind her and crossed to the window, her skirts whispering over the thick rug.

Once there, she pushed back the curtains and lifted on her tiptoes. She could just make out St. John talking to Kat in the courtyard below.

Fiona's gaze traveled over Kat, her eyes widening. Poor Katherine had been caught in the sudden storm and was bedraggled and wet. Kat's habit appeared black and sodden, her hair fell in long strands about her face, a sopping wet scarf trailed water into a puddle behind her. Devon was no better. His breeches were now indecently molded to him, his coat open, his shirt undone. By all accounts, the two should be miserable, but instead, they were laughing.

A pang formed in Fiona's heart at the sight. They looked so happy, just as she and Malcolm had once been. Her lips quivered at the thought. She had to win the wager with Malcolm. The only thing that could save her marriage was if she could get him away from Kilkairn, back to Edinburgh where they'd been gay and carefree. Once there, she was certain he'd forget about having children, and there'd be no more discord.

Perhaps then he would realize he still loved her, if he did.

Meanwhile, she was going to have to be more underhanded in her methods. She hated that, but it was necessary. Fiona eyed Kat for a long moment, deciding that while the habit looked wondrous on Kat's generous figure, a ball gown would not be nearly as attractive, with the high waistline and voluminous folds.

Murien was, as usual, quite right. Kat, dressed in a form-fitting habit on a horse, was one thing. Kat in a ballroom was quite another thing altogether. And as much as St. John might enjoy his flirtation, he would not tolerate a companion who could not hold her own in public.

Fiona dropped the curtain just as a voice said in her ear, "What do you think you're doing?"

Her heart jumped and she fell back, pressing a hand to her pounding heart. "Malcolm! Do not sneak up on me in such a manner! I thought you were St. John's horrid valet. I vow, but the man frightens me to death."

Malcolm looked past her to the window. "Hm. Spying on Devon and Kat, were you?"

"No," she said, her cheeks heating. "I was just here to—to make certain the room was clean."

Malcolm didn't look convinced. "What a lovely hostess you are, m'dear. Always worried about the health and welfare of your guests."

She stiffened. "I do my best, though how anyone can keep a castle clean is beyond me. It's like scrubbing the earth, all it does is make more mud."

"How would you know? You've never scrubbed a thing in your life."

" 'Tis not my fault. You are the one who brought me here to this horrid damp place."

"It's my home, Fiona. I thought we could share that, at least."

There was a tiredness to his voice that twisted deep into her heart. "Malcolm, I—" She what? She loved him but would not have his children? She adored him, but could not stand the home of his birth?

His gaze met hers, searching, seeking. "Yes, love. What is it?"

"Malcolm, you know I care for you. That I—"

Could she say it? Could she tell him that she loved him dearly, desperately? And if she did, would she lose something because of it?

She looked at Malcolm, at the way he regarded her so seriously. At the curl of his hair over his ears. At the dimple in his chin that she'd kissed so many times. Fiona took a deep breath and said, "Malcolm, I love you. But I do not wish to have children until I know for certain that you will not love me the less. I have to have your promise that it will not be that way."

He stiffened, as if she'd delivered a blow of some sort. "Fiona, I love you. I think I always will."

I think. She needed more than that. More than he seemed capable of giving. "I want us to be the way we used to be, before we came here and everything became so horrid." She bit her lip, fighting the tears. "I do not wish to live here, in this castle, watching our marriage fade away."

A flicker of pain crossed his face. "Fiona, we can't go back. No one can. We can only go forward."

He was right. Her heart pained, she collected herself as best she could, lifting her chin. "Of course. Forward. We will let our marriage rest on our wager then." She met his gaze evenly. "You may think you have won, but you have not. Not yet, anyway."

Malcolm sighed, disappointment evident. "Your sister is looking for you. She's in the sitting room."

"I'll go to her at once."

"I thought you would." Malcolm's sharp gaze rested on Fiona's face. "Murien mentioned something about a ball."

Fiona heard the note of accusation. "Yes, I have decided to give a small ball. We never use the ballroom, and I thought we might do so while we have both St. John and Murien here."

Malcolm's expression hardened. "I know what you are about, Fiona. I will not let you embarrass Kat."

"Then she needn't attend. It will be her decision."

"I see. You will invite her in such a way that she cannot refuse."

Fiona nodded, suddenly feeling miserable. She didn't wish to use Kat in such a way, but Fiona had no choice.

Malcolm looked at her a moment more, then moved past her to the window. "Murien is waiting for you."

That was it. He'd dismissed her as if she were nothing more than a bothersome chambermaid.

"I—I'll go at once."

"Do so." He lifted up the edge of the curtain, his gaze on Kat and Devon. "I will be down shortly," he said absently, as if he'd already forgotten Fiona's existence.

She stood a moment more, waiting for some sign. Some indication from her husband that he cared. But no such reassurance was forthcoming.

After a long, silent moment, she turned on her heel and left the room, and Malcolm, behind her. Disconsolate, she made her way to the sitting room.

Murien whirled on Fiona as soon as she entered. There were lines of tension on Murien's usually smooth face. "Thank God you have come. I was dying of ennui."

"Yes, it has been a rather dull day. Perhaps because of the rain."

"That didn't keep St. John from going out," Murien said in a discontented voice. "I don't understand how he can continue to see Kat. Surely the attraction, if it ever was that, has paled by now. The time has come for us to separate them."

Fiona sighed at the waspish note in Murien's voice. She hated it when her sister was out of sorts. Which lately was more oft than not.

"Where is St. John now?" Murien asked. "I am so tired of sitting around, waiting on him to return."

"He is in the courtyard saying good-bye to Miss Macdonald. It appears they were caught in a rain shower."

Murien stood and raced to the mirror over the fireplace. "Why didn't you say so?" She patted her hair. "Come! If we go out on the terrace, we can see them from there."

"Yes, but—"

"Come along. I can't go alone." Murien turned on her heel and swept from the room.

Fiona stared at the empty doorway. She was beginning to believe that her sister was a wee bit selfish. Sighing, she followed Murien down the hall to the library and then out on the terrace.

They had a prime spot to witness Devon's good-bye to Kat. Though he never touched her, there was something intimate about the way they stood. Watching them, Fiona felt a wrench of jealousy. Why should Kat have what Fiona had been denied?

Murien, meanwhile, was having similar thoughts.

It burned her soul to see a man, any man, that she deemed hers, paying attention to another woman. But there were ways to deal with such inconveniences. A word here, a word there.

More was won by innuendo than by fact. Murien found a smile. "Do not fear, Fiona. I will make certain our dear friend Katherine appears at our wondrous ball."

Murien watched as Devon said one last thing to Kat and then left the courtyard. He strode away, an amused expression on his face.

Murien decided it was quite telling the way Kat gazed after him, a rather wistful look in her eyes. "I can certainly take care of that," Murien murmured.

"Take care of what?" Fiona asked, blinking as if she had just awakened from a long sleep.

Really, what had Fiona so distracted of late? It was most annoying. "Fiona, why don't you return to the sitting room and I'll join you there. I believe I should extend the invitation to our ball to Katherine."

"But I can—"

"This one needs a personal touch. I will see you in ten minutes in the sitting room, and we can begin planning the entertainment for the ball." Without waiting for a reply, Murien made her way down to the courtyard.

She caught up with Kat just as she was getting ready to mount her horse. "There you are," Murien said brightly.

Kat turned. She was soaking wet, her hair reddish and straight to either side of her face, her riding habit molded to her frame. The sight gave Murien pause, and for the first time she found herself admitting that perhaps there was more to Kat Macdonald than Murien had first thought. "Kat, I'm so glad I caught you."

"Indeed?"

There was a decidedly guarded look to Katherine's expression. No fool was Malcolm's little sister. Murien put on her best smile. "Fiona and I have been dreadfully bored, so we've been planning a little ball. Malcolm insisted we invite you."

"That was kind of him."

"Yes, well, Fiona and I argued that you wouldn't want to come, but he was quite adamant."

Kat regarded her flatly, no expression on her face.

Murien took that as encouragement. She allowed her gaze to wander past Kat. "I don't know much about horses, but that one seems rather untamed. How do you ride him?"

Kat's hand rested easily on the horse's neck. "One mile at a time."

Murien managed to keep her smile in place, but only with the utmost effort. "How humorous."

"What do you want, Murien? You didn't come to talk about my horse."

"No, I didn't. I came to give you the benefit of my advice." Murien paused as if embarrassed. "I hope you don't take this wrong, but I realize that you've been on your own for a long while. I've also noticed that you are . . . shall we say 'fond' of Mr. St. John."

Kat's cheeks colored. "I don't know where you got that idea, but what I think and feel is none of your business."

Murien's brows rose. "There's no need to be embarrassed. I'm certain you have every reason to be infatuated. Mr. St. John is all that is amiable. He is handsome, well off, of impeccable lineage, and possesses a very pleasing manner." She gave a light laugh. "I daresay half the women in the castle are enamored of him. Poor Fiona can't get the upstairs maid to do anything."

"The upstairs maid never did anything before Mr. St. John's arrival, so I fail to see a connection."

Murien's false laugh faded from her lips. Really, it was annoying to speak to someone who did not follow the customary rules of polite conversation.

"Murien, I don't know what you want, but out with it. I don't have a lot of time."

That irked. "Very well," Murien snapped, "if you wish it, I will be plain. In addition to all of his obvious charms, St. John is an accomplished flirt. He is pleasant to *every* woman he comes in contact with, including me."

Kat's hands tightened about the reins. "For your information, I am not infatuated with Mr. St. John. And second, even if I were, it would not be your place to inform me of that fact. If you wish to protect a heart, then watch for your own."

"Oh dear. I've offended you. I'm so sorry. It's just that—well, someone should drop a hint as to the way things stand."

"And how do they stand?"

It was obvious the woman was embarrassed to the teeth, which was exactly what Murien wanted. To add vinegar to the wine, she sighed softly, as if regretting what she had to say. "This is so unpleasant. But you *are* Fiona's sister by marriage, which makes us almost sisters. This is the least I can do. I just didn't want you to embarrass yourself at the ball next Wednesday."

"Embarrass? How would I do that?"

Murien smiled gently. "The ball Malcom and Fiona are holding in honor of Mr. St. John will be well attended. It is quite obvious how you feel about the man. Though you might think you were being circumspect, your face will always betray you, and everyone will know. *Everyone.*"

There was a stiff silence during which time Kat stared fixedly at Murien. Her face was inscrutable, but the way her knuckles were white on the reins told all. Kat Macdonald was boiling inside. Boiling and just the littlest bit shamed, just as Murien had planned.

Murien waved her hand. "You've been warned. Rest assured that whatever you decide, I will do what I can to smooth things over for you." Murien smiled as kindly as she could.

"I don't need anyone to smooth things over. No one would dare ridicule me in my brother's house."

"Not to your face," Murien said gently. She paused to let that sink in, then said in a staunch voice, "But you are right. You should attend the ball; after all, it is in your brother's house. I'd just forget all those who will be whispering. I'm certain Mr. St. John won't notice anything, either."

"You don't want me to go."

"Me? Oh, I don't care, one way or t'other. In fact . . ." Murien's gaze slowly traveled over Kat. "I sincerely hope you *do* come. It will make it all the more enjoyable for the rest of us."

Kat's lips thinned, and Murien knew she'd drawn blood with that one. "Murien, I don't know how to thank you."

"I'm certain you'll think of something. Perhaps, one day I'll have you do some glasswork in my house. There are a number of windows that could use some decorating glazes." Smiling over her shoulder, Murien turned and left.

She hid her triumph as best she could as she made her way back to the terrace. Kat would attend the ball now, Murien was certain of it. Better yet, Kat would be awkward around Devon, as well, wondering if he could see the same things on her face that Murien mentioned.

Overhead, the late afternoon sun shone warmly, the blue sky decorated with a faint scattering of puffy clouds. Murien decided that it was a beautiful day. A beautiful day to win.

Kat tromped into her bedchamber, Annie hard on her heels.

The housekeeper shut the door and then turned to regard Kat with a flat stare. "What's happened to put ye in such a mood?"

Kat slumped onto the bed. "Nothing." Blast

Murien Spalding and her little blond airs. Kat wasn't the type of person to develop a hatred for anyone, but Murien had certainly managed to ignite a strong dislike inside Kat's usually forgiving heart.

"Don't tell me ye aren't fashed about something," Annie said. "Ye near took off puir Donald's head fer nothing more than a cheery good afternoon."

"I did not snap at Donald."

Annie lifted her brows, her skinny arms folded beneath her breasts, one foot tapping in disbelief.

"Don't look at me like that." Kat kicked at her skirts, frustration boiling. Should she go to that silly ball? Murien would simply make a mockery of her, and Devon would . . . Kat frowned. What would Devon do?

She caught Annie's minatory gaze and suddenly remembered that the housekeeper was waiting on an answer. "I'm sorry, Annie. I just didn't wish to hear Donald complain again about the flue in the new chimney. I know it needs to be fixed but I'm not in the mood to hear him harping on it day and night whilst he—"

"He said 'good afternoon' to ye and not a word more."

Kat's shoulders slumped. She supposed she had been a little harsh. "You are right. I was just angry at—Never mind. I'll apologize to Donald as soon as I finish."

"Finish what?" Annie asked suspiciously.

Kat scooted off the bed with an energy she was far from feeling and went to the wardrobe. She threw open the door and waved at the assortment of clothing that hung there. "I'll apologize as soon as I finish deciding what I'm going to wear to Fiona's and Malcolm's ball next week."

Annie brightened. "A ball? Och now, that sounds promising."

"I don't know about that." Kat straightened her shoulders and stared at the gowns, most of them too plain to be of use. "I wish I had time to have a gown made."

Annie hopped up on the edge of the bed so that she could watch Kat pulling first this old gown and then the next out of the wardrobe. "We should order one now fer the next time ye are invited. *If* they do. I'm a wee bit surprised they remembered ye this time." She sniffed her disdain loudly. "They've been somewhat remiss aboot that in the past."

"No, they haven't. They always invite me. And I always refuse. They know I don't like their puffed up affairs and I know they would find my company at such a formal event quite onerous. But this time . . ." Kat pulled out her best gown. Of sky blue silk, it was quite fashionable. Or had been, several years ago.

She held the gown before her and looked in the mirror, mentally comparing it to the gowns Fiona wore. Good heavens, how fashion changed.

Kat sighed and dropped the gown on the bed beside Annie. "What is different about this ball is that Fiona's sister, Murien, is going to be there, and she seems to think I'll be an embarrassment."

Annie made a face. "Och, that one. She's catty, she is."

"Yes, she is." And rude and possessive, too. And if one was so inclined, one might notice that Murien's eyes were just a wee bit too closely aligned. "She's a haughty vixen, and I don't mean that in a good way."

"They say she runs with the devil," Annie said in a mysterious undertone.

Kat had to grin at that. "I can't argue with you there. She's also very determined that every man in a fifty-mile distance should pay her homage."

"Oh ho! I suppose ye're talkin' about St. John. So ye have Miss Spalding worrying that you're getting too close to him, eh?"

"I am not getting too close to him." Not yet, anyway. Tomorrow, now . . . that might be another story. Although, now that Kat had tasted Murien's poison, things seemed far less clear. If Kat did allow Devon closer, wouldn't her feelings become even stronger? Even more obvious to anyone who looked at her?

Not that she was in love; she wasn't. But she was close to it, she knew. If she looked down at her toes, she was certain they'd be flush against the line that marked friendship and love.

Perhaps it wouldn't be a good idea to allow her relationship with Devon to progress into a more physical area. Perhaps—

"Hmph. I can see why ye're hesitant about takin' up wid the Sassenach. He's well enough if ye like the tall, handsome, wealthy, titled sort o' man."

Kat sighed. "Don't start, Annie."

"Lord love ye, Miss Kat, but what's not to like in a man like that?"

Kat wisely didn't answer. She dug deeper in the wardrobe, but found nothing else even approaching an acceptable evening gown. "I should have never let Murien goad me so."

"Aye, ye haven't a decent gown."

"I know, I know. But I cannot refuse to attend now."

Annie snorted. "She taunted ye, did she? Now ye'll go, come heaven or hell, come good weather or bad. Ye'll go if ye have to walk the whole way barefoot and naked as the day ye were born."

"I was rather hoping I could find something less dramatic to wear than my bare skin," Kat said dryly. "Unfortunately, my wardrobe does not extend into our present decade." She touched the sky-blue gown on the bed and sighed. "It looks as if I'm going to have to play the part of rustic dowd for the night or not go at all."

From her position perched on the edge of the bed, Annie picked up the gown and shook it out. "Won't this do? 'Tis of quality silk, and the color would look good on ye."

"It's sorely out of fashion. I'll be a laughingstock, I suppose, but that's nothing new. At least I won't be sitting at home, moping about because some puffed-up piece of fluff ordered me to stay away. To Hades with Murien Spalding and her airs."

"That's the spirit, Miss Kat!" Annie jumped up off the bed, her thin face resolute. "And I'll help ye, I will. I might have time to turn this gown into something acceptable, if we keep things simple."

"Annie!" Kat said, touched by her housekeeper's show of spirit. "Thank you."

"Och, 'tis only right that ye go and that ye look well doin' it. Besides, I should help ye after all ye've done fer me." Annie pursed her lips thoughtfully. "The last time I saw Lady Strathmore, she had on a right lovely gown that was . . ." Annie's eyes narrowed, and she nodded, folding the gown over her arm. "What we need is one of them fashion books as are stacked in Lady Strathmore's dressing room. That fool, Jane—a lazy wench if there ever was one—tends to the upstairs. We'll borrow one of those books fer a bit and then we'll fashion ye up a gown that will show that Murien hussy just who is the real lady."

"Yes, but we've no time to—"

"Hesh, Miss Kat! We've plenty o' time. I've still yards and yards of that lovely straw-colored silk left over from making the linings for the curtains in the front room. I'll start with that and perhaps . . ." She held out Kat's old gown, shaking it a bit so that the sky-blue silk rippled in the light. "Perhaps we can put this one to use, as well. I can use the bodice and the skirts and jus' add new sleeves and perhaps—" She smiled. "I can do it, never ye fash."

Straw colored silk combined with the sky-blue—it would be stunning, Kat decided. She couldn't help but think it would add some drama to her rather drab appearance.

"Annie, do you really think you'll have it made by next week?"

"Aye, Miss Kat! Just leave it to me." Annie tossed the gown over her shoulder and went to the door.

"I'll send Donald to the castle to fetch the book. He's still lingering downstairs, moping because he thinks ye are upset with him. Then we'll have a look to see what's needed. I may have to borrow a bit of ribbon, though I've plenty of thread left."

"It seems such a huge undertaking. Can you—"

"Och now, don't ye worry! All we need is one gown, simple and elegant. 'Twill allow yer beauty to show through."

A new gown that was simple and elegant—Kat couldn't help a burble of happiness from flickering through her. "Annie, you're priceless."

A half hour later, a lone rider arrived at Kilkairn Castle. Donald, armed with specific instructions from Mistress Annie, rode up to the servants' entrance and requested to speak with her cousin Jane.

Jane was a while in coming as Lady Strathmore had decided that the castle had to be cleaned from top to bottom for the upcoming ball, a fact that had horrified Jane. Normally, she made it a point not be easily found when there was work to be done. This time, she'd hidden behind the curtain in the library and had promptly fallen asleep, propped against the windowpane. She'd been fortunate only John the footman had found her as she'd drooled a bit and marred the glass. Lady Strathmore was not the fussiest of employers, yet Janie couldn't help but think perhaps window drool was a bit much. So, sighing as if greatly put upon, Jane had wiped the window with the dust rag she'd let drop to the floor on the onset of her nap, then trudged back to the kitchen.

She halted on seeing such a huge man waiting on her. "Och now, who be ye?"

"Donald. Mistress Annie sent me to ye."

Jane looked the man up. Then down. She lingered on the appropriate places and raised her brows in admiration. "Annie has always been a good cousin to me."

The man's brows lowered.

Janie quickly said, "So ye're one of the lads from the cottage, eh? Fairly large, aren't ye?"

"I'm no' the largest."

Well! That was difficult to imagine. The giant who stood before her was every bit of six and a half feet tall, his head barely clearing the ceiling. He was a fine-looking man, too, Jane decided. With large hands as could hold a lass just right whilst tupping.

Suddenly feeling more awake, Jane smoothed her hair and hoped she didn't have a red spot on her forehead from napping against the window. "Whot's Annie wantin' from me?"

Donald glanced around the busy kitchen. Preparations were already under way for the ball and there was a fervid air to the many maids and cooks who ran hither and yon. 'Twasn't a good place for private speech. "Mistress Annie wrote ye a note. Can we speak somewhere where there's less noise?"

Jane pursed her lips. "There's a shed by the barn."

"A shed?" Donald blinked. "There's no need fer that. Everyone is in here so no one would hear us talkin' if we just went outside."

"But the shed is very private." She leaned forward

and placed her hand on his thick, bulging arm. "No one will even know we're there."

Donald shook his head. "Mistress Annie said I was to hurry, so the courtyard 'twill do." He turned and went back the way he'd come.

Jane sighed her disappointment as she followed him. She wondered what Annie could possibly want. Annie was always in a tizzy about her position with Miss Kat. Which was a silly thing to be, because everyone knew it was more of an honor to work for the viscount and viscountess in the castle than to work for Miss Kat in her cottage in the woods. Although . . . Jane looked once more at the massive man who walked before her, noting his tight rump and muscular thighs. Perhaps there were some benefits to working in the cottage for Miss Kat, after all.

Donald led the way to an area near the outer wall. Except for a few maids gathered on the other side of the garden, they were quite alone. He reached into his pocket and withdrew a crumpled note. "Mistress Annie said to give this to ye."

Jane opened the hastily scribbled note, smoothed it out, and then squinched her eyes at it.

Donald looked at her with suspicion. "Can ye read?"

"O' course I can read," Jane said indignantly. "Not well, of course. But well enough." She squinted back at the paper, slowly working her way through the rather scrambled writing. "She wants a book?"

Donald nodded.

Jane studied the note a bit more, then nodded

once. "What Miss Kat needs is one o' Lady Strath-more's fashion plate books."

"Can ye get one for us?"

Jane folded the note and carefully stowed it in her pocket, taking the time to admire Donald's wide shoulders and how he dwarfed even the huge shrub-bery around the herb garden. "Possibly."

"What do ye mean 'possibly'? Are ye goin' t' help Miss Kat or no'?"

"I'll have to steal from me own mistress."

"Borrow," Donald said firmly.

"If she don't know 'bout it, then 'tis stealin'."

He eyed her for a long moment, his eyes traveling over from her head to foot. Eyes of dark blue that left a shiver everywhere they went.

Janie wished she'd worn her good gown today of all days. She had to settle for thrusting her bosom forward and sucking in her gut. She wished she had the time to comb her hair, too.

"I have to hurry back," he finally said. "Mistress Annie said 'twas important we no' waste any time in gettin' that book to her."

"Then ye'll have to make sure she gets it. But first we're goin' to have to visit the shed."

He blinked slowly. "The shed?"

"I want a kiss," she said firmly, giving him a direct look that gave him pause. "And more."

Lord love the woman, but she was daft, she was. But she was also young, clean, and rather attractive with her brown hair and blue eyes. Besides, he was not a man who took well to returning from an er-rand empty-handed. Not Donald.

She wet her lips. "The woodshed behind the stables is empty."

Donald rubbed his neck. The things he had to do for Miss Kat. Still, he was not about to give this hot young miss a ride for nothing. He wasn't one who liked his women ordering things about as if they thought they was better than he.

He eyed her up and down as boldly as she had him. "We don't need a shed."

"We don't?" She glanced around, finding the small knot of giggling women on the other side of the garden, watching them with knowing glances.

"We don't need a shed or any other place. Here will do just fine." He reached down and undid his belt. Several of the maids began to giggle, whispering furiously to one another.

Jane caught his wrist, casting a furiously red-faced glance at her friends. "Whist now! Not here!"

"No? But—"

"The woodshed," she hissed. She caught his gaze and must have realized he was teasing, for a smile broke over her features. "The woodshed?"

He didn't move.

She added softly, "Please."

There it was. He reached down and patted her bottom in a way that pleased her very much. "Very well, ye little strumpet. To the woodshed wid ye. But don't go gettin' any ideas. This is fer Miss Kat and no one else."

Face pink with pleasure, Jane sniffed, then sashayed off, nose in the air, wiggling her hips as she went.

Following behind, Donald noted that not only was she pleasantly brass, but she had a lovely sway to her cart, too. And he was a man who appreciated swaying carts.

Feeling rather pleased with himself, Donald closed the shed door behind him. It was amazin' the things he had to do fer the mistress.

Chapter 14

Ah, ma chère. You are wrong when you say this is not the time for love. Love makes its own time. It always has.

Madame Bennoit's assistant, Pierre,
to Sabrina, Lady Birlington's kitchen maid

*L*ife, Devon decided, was a complex proposition. Just when you thought you had everything figured out, something would occur to prove you wrong—again.

Wet and bedraggled, he found the library, where he knew a fire would be waiting. He was right; a merry blaze met him as soon as he opened the door. To his relief, the room was also empty.

He made his way inside, found a chair, and pulled it close to the flames, then dropped into it and stretched his booted feet before him.

His mind was so full of the day that it raced. He was aflame with Katherine Macdonald. Tomorrow was much, much too far away, and the knowledge was torturous.

Devon reached over and retrieved the three-week-old edition of the *Morning Post*. He would read and get his mind off such things as Kat's luminous green eyes or the curve of her hips as she rode Lady through the fields.

He idly leafed through the paper, seeing nothing to stop his rapid thoughts. Finally, irritated, he threw it down. In a way, it was strange seeing a remnant of his previous life. Since he'd come to Kilkairn, he felt as if he'd been living in a distant, mystical land. Even Kat in her sturdy little cottage in the woods, surrounded by her seven scowling giants, seemed unreal.

But real she was, as evidenced by his growing feelings. And they were growing, he admitted. Though not in his usual manner. Normally, by this point in a relationship, he was well on his way to proclaiming his love. Somehow he knew Kat would not appreciate such an impulsive, and eventually worthless, display. If he told her he loved her, he'd better mean it with every ounce of his heart, soul, and body, for she'd accept nothing less.

Up till now, his life wasn't a very pretty picture. If he ever wanted a relationship that was more, then *he* would have to be more, do more, give more. That fact was slowly becoming obvious to him.

He moved restlessly. It was strange, but he didn't miss London nearly as much as he had expected. He remembered his astonishment at discovering that his brother Chase planned to close his London residence except for a paltry two months of the year, so that he could reside in the manor house he'd purchased near his new bride's childhood home.

Devon couldn't imagine how his sophisticated, onetime dissolute brother would find anything to do in the country. Yet when he'd mentioned his concerns to his brother, Chase had laughed and then categorized about two hundred chores and efforts he and Harriet already had planned, including a new system to shear sheep and store wool that he'd been certain would revolutionize the entire industry.

It was then that it had dawned on Devon how much Chase had changed. Now, though, he wondered if perhaps Chase hadn't changed at all, but had only found a place to expend his energies. Energies he'd been wasting before he met Harriet.

Devon grimaced. It was all nonsense. Chase might have needed to change, but God knew that Devon didn't. Except for his irresolution with women, he liked who he was and what he was, and if he sometimes worried about his inability to feel anything substantial, it was merely because he wasn't yet ready to settle down. Yes, that was all it was.

A soft knock sounded at the door.

"Come in," Devon said over his shoulder, glad for the interruption.

The door opened and Tilton entered, dressed and pressed into the perfect rendition of the perfect gentleman's gentleman. "I beg your pardon, sir. May I have a word with you?"

"Of course."

"Thank you." Tilton came to stand beside Devon's

chair, standing a precise two feet from the arm. "Sir, I still have not located the talisman ring."

"Blast!" Yet another thing to add to his list of things to think about that he'd rather not.

"Indeed, sir. I took the chamber apart but other than discovering a ruby cravat pin that most definitely was not yours, I found nothing."

Devon scowled. He'd been certain Tipton would find that damned ring, so certain that he hadn't really bothered to think about it. Now, though . . . Devon rubbed a hand over his face, wondering what he should do next.

He remembered seeing the ring on Mother's hand, the light catching the carvings whenever she moved. It was the one thing that was uniquely hers. He suddenly realized how much the ring meant, not just to him, but to his brothers and sister. "Damn, damn, damn. We have to find it."

"Yes, sir. I shall continue to make discreet inquiries among the servants, though so far, no one seems to know a thing."

"The hell with discreet. Offer a reward. I have to find that bloody thing before next week." When he would leave.

The thought depressed him, a feeling he resolutely repressed. "I will ask Lord Strathmore about it."

"Yes, sir." Tipton eyed Devon's wet riding habit. "You will be changing prior to visiting His Lordship, I presume?"

"No. I want to see him now."

"But you're wet."

"I won't sit on any of his good chairs. Only the old ones that appear ready to fall apart."

"How fortunate for the good chairs," Tipton said, eyeing him severely.

Devon hefted himself from his seat, glad to have something to do other than mope about. "And how unfortunate for my arse; most of the bad chairs have fallen springs. I daresay I will be sorry I did not heed your advice and change my clothing."

"You always are sorry for ignoring my suggestions, and yet you are never slow in disregarding them."

Grinning, Devon left the room in search of Malcolm. He found him standing outside the sitting room, loitering in the hallway as if listening to the murmured conversation inside.

Malcolm gestured for him to be quiet.

"What are you doing?" Devon asked.

"They are discussing the ball. I want to know who they are inviting."

"Oh. May I ask why?"

"Because it's all a plot. I know it is. I just cannot discover what their intentions are."

It was interesting how a perfectly sane man could become insane once he married. Keeping his voice low, Devon said, "Malcolm, I have lost something."

"Oh? What?"

"The talisman ring."

"The talisman ri—" Malcolm snapped his mouth closed. Silence issued from the room inside for a moment, and then the murmured conversation continued.

Malcolm grabbed Devon's elbow and dragged him around the corner. "Good God, when did that happen?"

"A day or so now. I told Lady Strathmore about it, and she said she'd ask the servants. Do you think she has?"

"I don't know, though she's said nothing to me. I'll ask about and see what I can discover." Malcolm's frown deepened. "Devon, what if someone finds it?"

"I hope they will return it to me. Though I don't want to be burdened with it, it did belong to my mother, and it is rather precious because of that."

"No, no. I mean . . . if the ring is in someone else's possession, would *they* end up married?"

Now there was a thought. Devon considered it. Finally, he shook his head. "I don't think so. I mean, it is called the *St. John* talisman ring."

Malcolm didn't appear convinced. "I hope you are right. I also hope that neither Fiona nor Murien have found the thing."

"What would they do with it?"

Malcolm frowned. "I don't know, but the way they're scheming, 'tis a possibility one or the both o' them had their hands on it."

"You're being a bit hasty."

Malcolm sighed, his shoulders slumping. An apologetic smile flickered over his face. "Perhaps 'tis just mislaid, as you said. I'll go and see if I can't find that lazy butler. Perhaps Davies has some knowledge of your ring."

Devon didn't think he'd ever actually seen the

butler at Kilkairn. "I hope Davies knows where the ring is. I must find it before I leave."

Malcolm nodded. "We shall. Never fear. It is too dangerous to leave lying around. Meanwhile, you had best dress for dinner. You look a bit wet."

Devon nodded. "I shall. Thank you for your assistance, Malcolm. I appreciate it."

"I'm looking for that dismal artifact more for my own good than yours. 'Tis the last thing I want lying about where an innocent male might chance upon it." With that, Malcolm headed downstairs, yelling for Davies as he went.

Devon watched him go. Why couldn't his mother have had a ring that caused increased health or stamina? Anything other than an illness that might lead to marriage. It really wasn't fair.

Sighing, he turned and made his way to his own room, wishing he didn't have to attend dinner that evening.

Dinner was every bit as horrid as Devon feared. Fiona was flushed and talkative, a desperate sparkle in her eyes. Once or twice Devon caught her staring at Malcolm with such a look of longing that it startled him.

Malcolm, for his part, spent most of the meal prying for hidden meanings behind his wife's every statement, while Murien did her best to play the part of The Perfect Companion.

By the time he and Malcolm retreated for brandy, Devon was ready to plead tiredness and retreat to the relative quiet of his room. But once there, he found himself resenting the stillness, for it left him far too free to think about Kat.

He stood restlessly and wandered to the window, pushing aside the heavy curtain and looking out at the starlit night. What was Kat doing now? Was she working with the lads? Was she thinking about the promises she'd made him? Was she even awake? As late as it was, she was most likely in bed, sound asleep.

That brought to mind more important questions. What did she wear to bed? A long flannel nightgown devoid of lace or trim? Somehow, he couldn't imagine her in anything so mundane. Perhaps a thin cotton rail, tied with ribbons and bows? But no. That was too ordinary. Perhaps she just wore a silk chemise. One with little tiny flowers embroidered around a low neckline. A neckline that outlined the curve of her generous breasts—

He turned from the window and grabbed up his coat, his imagination—and other parts of him—afire. It was almost midnight, and by the time he arrived at her house, it would be tomorrow already. Perhaps, in addition to showing her that he was earnest in his desire to forward their relationship, he could also model the virtue of promptness.

Grinning at his own whimsy, he made his way through the moonlit night to the stable, where he woke, then handsomely bribed, a sleepy groom to saddle Thunder.

Kat tossed her scarf on the dressing table and then found her comb. Sighing heavily, she sat in front of the oval mirror and made a face. "Comb your hair and stop thinking about That Man."

As usual, she didn't listen to herself, for the third time she drew the large toothed comb through her hair, she caught herself wondering what Devon was doing now. Was he playing billiards with Malcolm? Listening to Fiona talk about the upcoming ball? Or walking a moonlit path with Murien?

"Ow!" The comb hit a tangle. That was the problem with having thick hair, it got mussed far too easily.

She worked the comb through the tangle and smiled when it finally slid through. "There," she told her reflection in the mirror. "See what a little work will do?"

Her reflection grimaced back at her. Work was one thing, but wanting the impossible was another, which was what spending an entire day with Devon St. John tended to do to her. The man had a gift for inspiring confidences and appearing earnest, both talents that made him a dangerous man indeed.

It was funny; when she was with Devon, everything seemed so *right*. But then, when she wasn't with him, the doubts began creeping in. The damning little thoughts that asked her what she thought she was doing, spending time with a man who, by his own admission and Murien's insinuations, changed his affections as easily as most people changed their clothing.

Kat pulled the comb through her hair one last time, then braided it. The situation with St. John was too perplexing to consider this late at night. Perhaps, when she saw him tomorrow, she'd know the answer. One made all the easier by warm sunlight and a new day.

A scratch sounded at her window. Kat paused in braiding her hair, but the sound did not come again. She finished braiding, then rose and carried the candle to the bed.

Another scratch sounded, and this time she could tell it was the tree limb that, when the wind blew from the south, bent until the branches scraped the casement. She frowned. It hadn't seemed that windy before . . . was there a storm blowing in? She went to the window and flipped the latch, then pushed it open.

"Kat!" came a strident whisper.

Kat jumped, pressing a hand to her heart.

"Kat!" came the voice again, this time closer.

She blinked, then leaned forward. The tree branch was bent toward the house, but there was no wind. What there was, however, was a large man, steadily climbing the tree to her bedchamber. "St. John!"

He paused, grinning up at her. His teeth flashed in the pale moonlight. "It's after midnight." He was a scant six feet away now, and she could make out the shape of his face, a shadow of nose and eyes and smiling lips.

"I know it's after midnight. What are you doing here?" she asked, astounded and perplexed and frightened just the teeniest bit. He was getting closer with each moment, climbing with the surety of a man who had clambered countless trees as a lad.

She suddenly realized that he'd said "tomorrow."

Good heavens, he was coming because she'd promised . . . What *had* she promised?

But she knew what she'd promised . . . and she'd meant it, too. Or she had until Murien had let her know how far gone Kat already was. The truth was that she already cared too much for St. John to have a simple dalliance with him. If she wasn't careful, she'd reveal her feelings and damn what friendship she and Devon did share; a friendship far more precious than any Kat had ever had.

She pressed a hand to her cheek. Her heart was pounding, her palms damp, her throat tight. Part of her felt as if she should flee. But another part of her was flattered and excited and . . . happy. Devon St. John was climbing a tree outside her window. Her window and not Murien Spalding's, the most beautiful woman in Scotland.

He was now almost at eye level, the light from the room spilling over his face. Excitement gleamed in his eyes. "You said we would settle this thing between us 'tomorrow.'" He placed a hand on her window casement. "It is now 'tomorrow.'"

At his words, her body whispered needfully that she should move, just a step or two, and then he would be in her bedchamber and all the heated thoughts and late night longing she'd suffered would be sated. But her mind ordered her to stay put, not to be swayed by soft words.

Which was right, her mind or her body? It was torture, this double yearning to do and not to do. Kat clenched her teeth against it all.

His gaze met hers, softly quizzing. "I can't climb in unless you step back."

The old fears and questions tumbled back into her mind. "I-I do not know if I should let you in or not."

"Are you asking my opinion?" His teeth flashed whitely in the uncertain light. "For if you are, I think you should let me in so we can—"

"I'm quite certain I know what *you* think. I just don't know what *I* think."

"Whatever you decide, you'd best make up your mind quickly. I might fall at any minute. These branches are not very stable."

He was laughing at her, she could tell. And she didn't like it one little bit. "Of course, as hard as your head seems to be, one little tumble won't kill you."

"Won't it? Kat, what are you afraid of? You don't trust anyone of the opposite sex other than your lads and your brother. Meanwhile, you stay here, hiding from the world and anyone who might hurt you."

He thought she was afraid. How ludicrous! "You are sorely mistaken; I am not afraid. Not of you or anyone else."

"I see." He was silent a moment before he said, "What if I just come in long enough for a drink of water?"

"There's water in the barrel by the barn."

"Oh." He leaned on the casement with his free arm, the candlelight smoothing a golden path across his handsome face. "I'll get some water on my way out. But . . . I'm also a little chilled."

"Then you'd best return to your room at Kilkairn."

He glanced past her to the crackling fire in her

room. "But your fireplace doesn't smoke. What if I just came in long enough to warm myself a bit?"

She crossed her arms and looked at him.

He heaved a sigh. "You are the most stubborn woman. Very well, I'll leave. But I must rest first. May I come in and just—"

"No!" Heavens, but he was a determined individual. "Good night, Mr. St. John." She placed her hand on the casement to close it, expecting him to move out of the way.

Instead, he drew back instantly—and then disappeared from sight. The place where he'd been was filled with a horrid black stillness.

She gasped and rushed forward. "Devon—!"

He was still there, crouching on the thick tree limb that held him, hanging onto the branch above. His teeth gleamed faintly in the dark. "You would miss me if I was gone; admit it."

"I am not admitting anything," she said, though her heart still trembled in place. "That was a horrid trick."

"I'm a desperate man. Climbing up was one thing, climbing down in the black of night is another." He moved back into place, leaning in the casement as he smiled at her, that wistful lopsided smile that always made her melt just the tiniest bit on the inside.

"Kat, my love, what if you chose a chair for me and I promised to stay in it?"

Her gaze narrowed. "You wouldn't get up?"

"The seat of the chair and I would never part. Not unless you invited us to."

That seemed like a fair offer. Besides, if he stayed in the window, one of the lads was bound to see him. Simon in particular was a restless one and was frequently up and about in the wee hours of the morn.

Kat closed her eyes. "This is madness, but . . . blast it! I suppose I might as well."

And with that, Kat Macdonald made a monumental decision, one she'd mull the rest of her days. She stepped out of the way and let Devon St. John climb into her window.

Chapter 15

*Every oncet in a while, I gets a pain in me head and
I'm never sure if it is because of somethin' I've done,
or somethin' I need to do.*

Lady Birlington's maid Sabrina
to Cold Bob, the fishmonger,
at the market early one morning

*D*evon climbed the rest of the way in, stepping
over the sill with ease. He paused to close the
window, the sound unnaturally loud in the quiet.

"You cannot stay long." There was a defensive
note to her voice.

He turned to answer her, but though he wanted to
reply, her night rail prevented him. All he could do
was nod. Nod and stare, for she was wearing a gown
of pale green silk that flowed to her feet, clinging las-
civiously to every curve she possessed. Worse—or
better, depending on whether he enjoyed the lush
torture she presented—the neckline was low, expos-
ing rounded curves that made his mouth water.

"Yes, well," she said, her heightened color letting

him know she was aware of his regard, "the next time you decide to clamber up a tree and into a woman's room, you might want to make more noise."

"Noise?"

"Yes. Whistle or something. I could have mistaken you for a reiver, come to steal my jewels. 'Tis a wonder I didn't call for one of the lads."

"I don't whistle. Not well anyway."

"Then sing. That would work, I suppose."

"No," he said firmly. "I am not going to sing, not even for you. I respect my fellow man too much to put them through such a parody of talent."

"That is very kind of you."

"I made that decision after being forced to listen to I know not how many musicale performances by anxious mamas who think men admire women who can warble a song."

Her lips twitched. "Poor you, having to endure such."

He tried not to stare too long at her soft, full mouth. "I never heed the matchmaking mamas. But they have made me more aware of the fact that just because we think we're talented, does not make it so."

"A wise lesson."

An awkward silence then fell, as if they'd used all their stored-up banter and were now completely wordless. Kat glanced nervously around, then cleared her throat no fewer than three times.

Devon finally took pity on her. "I believe I was

supposed to occupy a chair. Shall we sit?" Now that he was there, he had all the time in the world.

"Sit?" She glanced at the bed, then at the chairs, as if dragging her mind from one to the other. "Oh yes! Of course we may sit." She led the way to the chairs, her gown revealing the tantalizing outline of her thighs as she moved.

Devon had to force himself to breathe. God, but she was beautiful. He eyed the long red-gold braid that hung down her back and wondered what her hair would look like splayed over a mound of white pillows. His blood heated.

She took her seat, sitting on the very edge of the chair, her hands clasped on the arms of the chair. The second he took his place across from her, she said, "Why are you here?"

"I was just riding by and thought to see what you were doing."

"At midnight?"

"It's twenty after," he pointed out politely.

Her gaze narrowed.

He shook his head sadly. "Oh ye of little faith."

"I have faith. Just not in men who knock on my window in the middle of the night."

"I should have used the front door, but I was bored and this seemed an adventure." He could tell from the quiver in her voice that she was nervous and fearful and just the tiniest bit excited. He smiled a little, knowing exactly how she felt. In his own way, he felt the same.

She folded her hands in her lap, her feet perfectly

flat on the floor before her. The prim gesture was very much at odds with her decadent gown. "Devon, I am not an adventuresome woman. I don't believe you should—"

"Nonsense. You are very adventuresome. You live here, alone except for the company of your servants and seven scowling giants. You are building a business that by all accounts is getting to be extremely profitable. And you can ride like an angel. How much more adventuresome do you need to be?"

Kat bit her lip. She'd never really thought of herself that way before but . . . he was right; she did take risks. Only not with her heart.

She was trying to figure out how to say this when he stood.

From her chair, Kat immediately leaned away, too aware of his proximity and her own lack of clothing.

"I am just going to get a drink of water," he said in a calming voice. "May I?"

Her cheeks heated. She didn't mean to overreact, but she was too nervous to think. "Of course. Pray help yourself."

She watched from beneath her lashes as he went to where Annie kept a pitcher and glasses. Devon poured himself a glass of water. Then he turned and leaned against the low edge of the dresser.

He finished the water and set the glass on the dresser, his eyes wandering over Kat. "That's a lovely gown," he said, his voice low and deep.

She had to fight the urge to shiver. The silk night rail had been a gift from Malcolm. Kat sometimes wondered if he'd perhaps ordered it for Fiona, but when it had arrived, it had been too large for her petite frame and thus it had been passed on to Kat. However it was, she loved the feel of the silk against her skin and she wore it often. Of course, she'd never worn it in front of anyone else, and she now found herself achingly aware of every inch of fabric that hugged her bare skin.

Devon absently picked up her white scarf from where she'd placed it earlier. He ran it through his hands. "I am intrigued by you."

"By me? Why?"

"Because you are such an interesting mixture of vulnerability and bravery. I wonder what I can do to prove to you that I am worth trusting."

"If we had several years to debate it, it is quite possible I might eventually come to do so. But you will be leaving soon."

Devon nodded but didn't reply. He was looking at the scarf, a strange expression on his face.

"Kat," he said, his gaze still on the scarf, "I think I know how to prove myself to you." He draped the scarf over his arm and walked toward her.

Her heart thudded faster. "What . . . what are you doing?"

"You've been wounded by words—told things that were not true. So I will prove myself in deeds."

"Deeds?"

"I am going to prove to you by action that I am worthy of your trust."

She gripped the arms of her chair. "Why . . . why is that important to you?" She waited with bated breath for his answer.

"Because if you never trust someone again, then you will be lonely the rest of your life. I don't want that to happen to you."

"I am not alone. I have Malcolm. He is all I need."

"You need more than that. You need friends, acquaintances . . . lovers."

Lovers. Not "lover," but "lovers." That certainly said a lot about Devon St. John. Kat eyed him with a dark frown. "It is none of your concern what relationships I choose or don't choose to have." Or whom she chose to have them with, for that matter. Although, if she were honest, in the years since Stephen, she hadn't really been attracted to any man. Except Devon.

His mouth quirked into a half smile so delectable that her heart thudded an extra beat. "Kat, do you think you can trust me for five minutes."

"Five minutes?"

He nodded. "During that five minutes, I can do anything to you that I want providing it doesn't hurt you in any way."

"Do?" her voice quavered just a bit, but Kat couldn't help it. Her entire body was afire with his suggestion. "What—" She licked her dry lips. "What would you do?"

"Nothing to cause you harm. Only pleasure."

It was a ludicrous idea, although . . . it intrigued her. "What if I wanted you to stop?"

"Then you say 'stop' and I stop." His gaze dripped over her, lingering on her breasts before returning to her face. "And I promise only to touch you in ways that will keep you gasping in delight."

Kat's face heated until she thought it would catch fire. "I—I don't know—"

He was before her now, standing in front of the chair. He looked so handsome. But it was more than that. Between them pulsed a physical longing that swept over them both like waves of the sea. It was a feeling Kat had almost forgotten.

The truth was, she wanted this man. But she also knew that she had begun to care for him and that any other step in their relationship would only jeopardize her heart all the more.

The question was, could she continue without further risking her heart?

He knelt before her. "Five minutes, Kat. No more."

She swallowed, aware that she only had to reach out and an entire world of pleasure was hers. "Why?" she finally managed to whisper. "Why me?"

He lifted his hand and lightly traced the line of her cheek. "Because you are the most exciting, beautiful, intelligent woman I have ever met."

When he put it that way, she *felt* exciting, beautiful, and intelligent. Strange how something as simple as a few words could have so much of an impact on her heart. But it was more than words; his gaze was painfully sincere.

"Very well," she heard herself whisper. "You have five minutes."

His eyes flared. "You will not regret it."

"What—" She had to lick her lips to continue. "What do we do now?"

"We are going to build your trust."

"How?"

"Very, very slowly." He held out his arm, the scarf fluttering at the movement. "Lean forward and place your feet flat on the floor."

She did as he asked, though it brought her knees against his chest.

"Afraid?" His voice was dark, deep, seductive.

Kat sent him a glance, one she hoped was quelling and disdainful. "Should I be?"

"With me? *Never*."

One word. But spoken with such meaning that it gave her pause.

He took the scarf and ripped it down the middle, into two long pieces.

"Wh—" She blinked in astonishment as he took one of the pieces of the scarf, placed the end in the palm of her hand, and then began wrapping it about her wrist. While she watched, amazed, he took the other end of the scarf and wrapped it around the arm of the chair until her wrist was bound to the chair. "Devon, I cannot—"

He placed the loose end of the scarf in her hand. "All you have to do is let go and unwind it and you will be free. You are in control, Kat. Not me."

He was right. As long as she held the end of the scarf in her hand, she had the ability to release herself. She watched bemused as he did the same to her other wrist.

Kat couldn't quite believe what was happening to her. She was dressed in the decadent silk night rail in her own bedchamber, bound to a chair in front of a handsome man.

"Now," Devon said, standing. "Here is where we begin. Do you mind if I take off my coat?"

It was very warm in the room, she thought. Actually, it was a lot warm, though little of that had to do with the fire. "Of course you may take off your coat."

He did so, revealing a narrow waistcoat of deep blue. He tossed the jacket over the back of the chair he'd abandoned earlier. "Now. May I remove my waistcoat and shirt?"

Dear God, he was undressing right in front of her. A delicate shiver traced down her back, shimmering across her skin and making her breasts swell in response. Somehow, she found herself answering in a hushed, husky voice, "Yes."

Within moments, his waistcoat and shirt had joined his coat on the back of the chair. He stood before her, broad-shouldered and narrow-hipped, his arms powerful, his chest covered with crisp, curly hair. Her fingers itched at the sight, for she wanted nothing more than to touch him.

She twisted against the bonds that held her hands.

"All you have to do is release them and they are gone." He knelt before her, his face level with hers. "You are in control, Kat. You decide what you want. And if you ever want me to stop, no matter when, no matter what I am doing, I will do so." He bent forward then, his lips to her ear. "You can trust me."

She turned her face until her cheek was pressed to his. Her entire body thrummed with awareness, with need. She wanted him to touch her, to kiss her.

He pulled back slowly, his skin brushing hers as

he found her mouth. He kissed her deeply, passionately, his lips hot and firm. She moaned against his mouth, leaning forward, letting all her passion flood through the embrace.

He left her mouth to kiss her cheek, her neck, the neckline of her gown, his lips teasing, caressing. She pressed forward, offering herself to him, wanting more.

Devon's head dipped lower until his mouth was on the crest of her breast. Her nipples hardened, abrading the silk gown and tightening. She threw back her head, reveling in the sensation.

The scarf bonds tightened as she unthinkingly attempted to bring up her hands to cup his head, hold him to her. But she did not release the ends. There was something freeing about letting him have his way, about having the ability to stop it, yet not.

He slid down and pressed his mouth to her breast through her gown. She gasped, then stopped as he tongued her nipple, her gown growing damp from his efforts. The sensation of that mouth through the thin material of her gown, of the hot, damp clothing over her nipple, made her shudder already.

It felt so good, so wondrous that she could scarcely stand it. And the fact that his bared shoulders were so tantalizingly close made her torture all the more exquisite.

He slid farther down, his hands tracing the shape of her waist, her hips, her legs. On to her feet. There he stopped, meeting her gaze for a long moment. "If you want me to quit, all you have to do is say one word."

She nodded, but made no effort to say anything.

He smiled, his hands now resting one on each ankle. "This is for you, my love." He lifted up the bottom of the night rail, sliding the silk along her bare skin, pushing the material until it rested on her knees. Then he bent and kissed the inside of each ankle, sending tremors of feeling pulsing through her.

Kat had to fight a moan. The stifled noise seemed to inflame him, for he slid his kisses from her ankles to her knees. Cupping an ankle, he gently pushed up her night rail even more, parting her legs as he did so. Cool air wafted over her calves and the insides of her thighs.

She felt like a complete wanton, sitting exposed before him. But somehow, she couldn't help it. Couldn't stay away, couldn't pretend that this attraction wasn't burning through her.

He pressed a kiss to her inner thigh, the movement sudden and unexpected. So strong was her reaction that Kat thought she'd shoot right out of the chair. "Devon," she gasped.

He stopped immediately, his gaze meeting hers. "Yes?"

She knew she had but to say one word and he'd stop. She could also release the scarf ends and be free to put her gown back in place, and resume her life of unending dignity. She looked down at herself, at the wet circle he'd made around her nipple, at the way the silk gown was bunched almost to her hips.

At the sight of her own legs bared and splayed, Devon kneeling between them.

God help her, she didn't want to stop. Not now, not ever. She lifted her eyes to his and said not one word, but two. "More, please."

Chapter 16

*I've had me share of the fair sex. 'Tis a pity the fair
sex thinks they've already had their fair share of me.*

Cold Bob, the fishmonger,
to young Peter Franshawe,
tutor to the Duke of Draventon's son
after a chance meeting in a pub

*D*evon leaned back, the candlelight caressing his
face, tracing the line of his jaw. He looked so incredibly handsome that Kat's breath stuttered. This
must have been what the angel Gabriel looked like, a
vision of masculine beauty that locked the eye and
sent a piercing ache straight to the heart.

Kat cleared her throat, wondering if her thighs
looked fat from the angle Devon could see them. She
suddenly wished for a cover. "I am a little cold."

His brows lifted. "Afraid?"

The soft words hung in the air between them.
Kat's jaw tightened. "Of you? No. Of course not."

"Good. There are a lot of things I'd like you to feel
when you look at me. Fear isn't one of them."

That was certainly unfortunate because a sort of fear was shivering through her that very instant. Fear that her feelings were already so deeply engaged that she could not back away. Not that her body was retreating from him. Oh no. God forbid that Devon touch her any more intimately than he already had or she'd explode into a conflagration of white-hot flames.

The fact was that Devon St. John inspired fear and more; he was also directly responsible for every last twinge of lust, desire, and unmitigated longing that had wracked her nights ever since she'd met him. And it was time she stopped fighting it and accepted the simple fact that she wanted him.

Slowly, she released the ends of the scarf and tugged her arm free, first one, and then the other. He rocked back on his heels, disappointment flickering across his face.

She unwound the scarf scraps from her wrists and collected them in a ball. Devon stood, looking down at her with an inscrutable expression. "Kat, I—"

She pointed to one side.

His gaze followed her finger, his eyes widening when he realized she was pointing directly at the bed.

She handed him the scarf scraps. "You can tie me up there, if you'd like. I think it might be more comfortable for us both."

Devon blinked bemusedly at the scarf ties, a gradual dawning crossing his face. "Kat, are you certain—"

"More, please," she said again, only this time she

stood and walked to the bed, not waiting to see if he would follow.

She stopped by the bed and reached up to undo the single tie that held on the pale green night rail, hesitating just a second when it dawned on her that for the first time in she didn't know how many years, a man was going to see her naked. And not just any man, but Devon St. John, one of London's most sought after, most feted bachelors.

He was used to having the most delicate and dainty women of the *ton* undress before him every day, if what Murien hinted was true.

Kat's lips quivered suddenly. She wished she hadn't grown so fond of pastries these last few years. But who could have foreseen that a beautiful, incredibly handsome man would even now be waiting for her to undress, his eyes dark with passion.

Life was a mystery. And so, too, was Devon St. John. She only hoped that he would not cease to be attracted to her once he saw her for what she was— too tall, too large, too awkward, too loud, and too . . . undainty.

The horrid thoughts froze her fingers over the ties.

Just as she was preparing to force her fingers into behaving, a pair of warm hands closed over hers. Devon's voice sounded in her ear. "You're going to maul this lovely gown. That, my sweet, is my job."

The humor lacing his voice made her relax somewhat. "I'm sorry. I'm not used to undressing on demand."

He quickly undid the tie, but made no move to

step away, his body warm against her back, his hands slowly sliding up and over her shoulders. "There. Now you are untied."

So she was. She took a deep breath and pulled her gown loose about her neck, but didn't remove it any further. In fact, she clutched it to her, feeling as bare and vulnerable as if she were suddenly seventeen once more, and thrust into the unwelcome arms of Edinburgh society. She couldn't bring herself to turn to face Devon, so she said with a nervous laugh, "I'm certain you made many of the women of the *ton* very happy."

There was a short silence, and then he leaned forward to wrap his arms about her. "Kat, don't be afraid. Not of me. You are one of the most natural, passionate women I know. I don't want you to feel less because of me."

"Less?"

"I won't pretend I don't wish to see you without that blasted gown. I do. So much. But not at the price of your pride."

Her pride. Was that what was holding her back? She considered this and then decided he was right. It astonished her that he seemed to understand her so well.

Her first impulse was to turn toward him, wrap her arms about his neck, press her body to his, and kiss him as deeply and passionately as he had kissed her only a day ago.

And after she thought about it, she realized it was also her second, third, and fourth impulse, as well. She wanted to kiss him. Kiss him and more. *Much* more. She wanted to kiss him, taste him, feel his mouth on her lips, her skin. She wanted to touch him, and feel him against her, inside her—

Stop it, she warned herself abruptly. Already her body was responding to Devon's intoxicating closeness. She didn't need her vivid imagination adding more stress to her already fractured brain.

Devon watched the play of emotions on her face, fascinated despite the raging ache in his loins. He had never known a woman whose face showed her feelings so clearly, and he didn't think he would ever tire of seeing her myriad expressions.

Her gown dropped to the floor.

Devon's breath stopped as he slowly took her in, from feet to glorious crown of hair. She was magnificent, even more lush and beautiful than he'd imagined. Long-limbed and rounded, every lush inch of her made his mouth water, his heart pound, his manhood rise in eagerness.

She crossed her arms over her breasts, drawing his attention back to her face. "I am not going to be the only one without clothing."

Her chin was jutting stubbornly, challenge in every line of her rich body. Devon undid his breeches and stepped out of them with an alacrity that had everything to do with the sight of the beautiful woman before him.

Kat eyed him up and down, her tongue coming out to wet her lips before she turned and climbed into the high bed. Devon watched her bemusedly, his body a raging river of want and need. Bloody hell, what was he supposed to do now? He had promised himself to be noble, to take his time and be gentle.

But he was caught by the sight of her plump white shoulders, by the smoothness of her pearly skin, by the silken threads of her hair curling at the juncture of her thighs. God, but she was magnificent. He wondered how he could have ever thought thin, tiny women would please him. They were pale wraiths in comparison to the sensuous woman before him.

He couldn't wait a moment more. He joined Kat on the bed, climbing in beside her. Immediately the smell of lavender and jasmine sent a wave of anticipation through him.

Devon lifted up on one arm and admired the prize he'd captured. Never, in all his experiences, had he seen such lovely breasts. Full and ripe, they would fill a man's hand and more. Each soft, abundant mound was topped with a guinea-sized areola, dusky pink and nipped with excitement. Beneath that, her stomach rounded down to—

He closed his eyes. She was going to kill him. Already his heart was racing, his stomach quivering, his manhood painfully erect.

He'd always loved women, loved sex. He reveled in a woman's unique scent, in the feel of her beneath him, around him. But this . . . this experience was different. More vibrant with taste, feel, color. There was something about Kat that inflamed him, aroused him, drove him mad with desire.

"I don't think we're going to use the scarf this time," he said hoarsely. "Kat, I want you completely with me. Without anything between us."

"As you wish," she said, her voice soft and breathy. "Just touch me, Devon, and hold me. I want you so badly." She ran her hands over his bare arms, across his shoulders, and then down his chest, her touch like lightning.

His tenuous control shattered and broke into a million tiny pieces. All that was left was the raging desire to make love to Kat. To hear her soft cries and make her moan with pleasure.

He took her in his arms and kissed her, his mouth covering hers, his tongue seeking. She clutched at him, opening her mouth beneath his, pressing closer. Devon cupped her to him, his hands spanning her luxurious curves.

The kiss deepened, fanning the flames ever higher. Her arms snaked around his waist, and to his pleased surprise, she pulled him even more tightly to her, pressing her hips to his.

Devon had pleasured many women and had left them all smiling happily. He knew the value of a woman who unapologetically enjoyed the physical act with all of her soul. And Kat was definitely one of those few. He gave himself over to pleasing her completely.

Kat was drowning in a sea of passion, of tangled blankets and a complete commitment to her own madness. A madness that had been threatening her own peace ever since she first laid eyes on Devon St. John.

God, but he was magnificent! All lean, rippled muscle and a firm arse that filled her with the be-mused desire to nip it.

He was sublimely unapologetic in his nakedness, his attention focused on her breasts. Kat was used to men looking at her breasts; they had been doing so since she was fourteen. But somehow this was different; Devon held his hand flat over her nipples, rubbing his palm over them. They immediately hardened and peaked, but Devon continued his ministrations, as if seeking something more.

Soon she was panting, her body aching, her thighs moist with longing. "Devon," she said. "Please."

"Not yet," he whispered. "Not yet."

He grasped her rounded rump firmly, kneading and pressing. She moaned, squirming slightly, growing hotter by the second. He could see the moisture glistening on her inner thighs, and his own body tightened at the sight. She was so ripe, like a plucked peach, ready to be devoured. "Tell me what you like."

"Like?" She gasped when his fingers brushed her center.

"Do you like this?"

"Oh yes!" she gasped.

He knelt between her legs, savoring the warmth of her skin, the scent of her secretmost place. He bent forward and kissed her there, gently but urgently. She planted her heels and arched upward at the shock of the touch.

He waited only a moment before he did it again. And again. Soon she was panting, her knees splayed as he pleasured her. After a moment, he lifted his head. "Tell me, Kat. I want to hear you say it." He bent and traced a line across her most sensitive spot.

"Oh God, I love it. Don't stop." She squirmed

madly, rubbing against his mouth. He sucked her gently, then with increasing fervor. She trembled against him, her hands in his hair, clutching, pulling, trying to get closer, and at the same time trying to escape. "Devon! Don't stop. Never stop."

Her gasped request set him to even more frenzied ministrations. He slowly slid his thumb into her, marveling at her tightness.

God but she was hot and wet. He wanted to plunge into her, to run his hands over her flesh and taste her until she cried out in wonder and happiness.

That was what he wanted, more than anything. Just as he had the thought, she lifted and stiffened, then said his name as the pleasure overtook her. Devon bent to capture her once more, tasting her and increasing the pressure of his tongue.

The musky-sweet scent of her and the ripe, womanly taste were more than he could take. As her shivers subsided, Devon lifted himself above her and positioned himself between her thighs. He was so ready for her that he ached, his mind a fevered flash of desire.

He was just ready to press forward when she clutched at his arms. "Devon."

There was something about her voice, some hint of desperation or fear that made him pause, rigid and fierce as he was. He had to clench his jaw, but for her sake, he kept his control.

"Are you certain you want this?"

He almost laughed. Instead he pressed an unsteady kiss to her forehead. "I want this more than anything I've ever wanted in my life."

Relief, wonder, laughter, and unmitigated lust warred for expression on her face. To Devon's relief, lust won the day, and she clamped her legs around his waist and lifted her hips to his.

He closed his eyes as he slid inside her, the overwhelming heat sending a shudder all the way to his toes. She gasped at the fullness of him, but only for a moment. Soon she was murmuring in his ear, clutching at his shoulders, moving more and more frantically as the pressure inside built.

Devon had to grit his teeth to keep from spilling into her. She was so tight, so hot, so incredibly sexy as she moved against him and writhed seductively. She had a body built for love, his hands roaming freely, touching and tormenting.

Just as Devon's tenuous control began to slip, she came yet again, arching her back and bucking wildly.

Devon had to grasp her hips to hold on; the exquisite heat and her unbridled passion pushed him over the edge. He thrust forward, burrowing deeply as he came in a rush of heat, and then collapsed on the bed.

How long it took him to regain his breath, he'd never know. But minutes passed before he could even speak.

Never had he known such passion, such earthy sweetness, such complete surrender. Never.

Devon raised on his elbow and looked down at Kat. Her eyes were closed, her face turned to one side, her braid was still intact, if somewhat frayed.

He toyed with the silken strands that had fallen loose, a smile on his face. What an experience. It had been even more than he'd expected.

He bent and kissed her neck. "Kat, my love, are you well?"

A smile curved her lips, but she made no move to face him.

"Shy?" he asked.

That got a glance. "After that? I think not. I am just too winded to move."

He chuckled, scooping her to him, soaking in the feel of her silken skin against his. "That was incredible, my love. Simply incredible."

"Mmmmm," she answered, burrowing against him, her arms about him. "It was lovely. And next time, we'll use the scarf."

He chuckled, a deep satisfaction warming him. He pressed a kiss to her forehead. "As you wish, my lady."

A lovely peace filtered through him as he held her, their hearts returning to a normal rhythm, their legs entwined in a most intimate manner.

The bed was lovely, full of pillows and far more comfortable than the rock-hard mattress he had to sleep on at Kilkairn. And certainly his bed didn't smell of lavender and Katherine Macdonald, which was a lovely scent he could quite easily become enamored of.

The thought held him, and he turned to press his cheek against hers, holding still so he wouldn't wake her. He'd never felt this way before, such a sense of completeness. It was a good thing he was leaving soon, before this magical feeling left.

It was much later that he sighed, kissed her forehead, and slowly climbed from the bed.

Ten minutes later, Simon entered the workshop and lit a lantern by the door. Then he walked to the back of the room to a large red door.

He kicked it open and then held the lantern aloft, lighting a room lined with neat cots. The inhabitants of the room began to stir, cursing at the brightness.

"Bloody hell, Simon," Donald said. "Put down the lantern!"

"What do ye want now?" muttered Hamish, leaning on his elbows and squinting toward Simon. "Was I snorin' again?"

Simon plunked the lantern onto the table that stood to one end of the room and then sat in one of the chairs. "We need to talk."

"Now?" Neal asked, knuckling his eyes.

"Aye, now. I couldna sleep, so I went to the kitchen to see if Annie had left out a little somethin' to eat."

"Ye'd better have a reason fer wakin' us other than Annie forgettin' to leave ye a hunk of cheese," Will said, sitting up and yawning.

"I have a better reason," Simon said grimly. "I saw the Sassenach. He was climbin' down out of Miss Kat's window usin' that old oak."

To a man, they came awake.

"That bastard," Donald swore, jumping to his feet.

"I get to kill him first," Neal said, standing, fists ready.

"No, 'tis fer me to do the killin'," Hamish growled. "Ye can do the dismemberin'."

Simon sighed. "Whist now, I know how ye're all feeling. I was the same. I even thought of takin' him off his horse and doin' the deed right there by me-self. But 'twould not answer. Miss Kat would skin us alive. Lads, I think the time has come to invite the Sassenach to a meetin'."

Silence met this suggestion. Finally, Hamish sighed and said, "I suppose ye're right. Miss Kat needs a beau. The Sassenach is a beau."

"But will he be good to her?" Will asked.

"He will be if we have anything to say about it," Simon said grimly.

One by one, the men nodded. Finally, Donald looked at Simon. "We're agreed then. The time has come to invite the Sassenach to a meetin'. And you, Simon, are the one who will do it."

Chapter 17

My lord, I am happy to report that your son has all the makings of a fine young gentleman once he gets over an unfortunate tendency to pinch the maids.

the dashing Peter Franshawe,
tutor to the Duke of Draventon's son,
to the duke during their daily progress meeting

*D*evon awoke the next morning to the sounds of tradesmen and hammering, carts rumbling over the drive, and the low murmur of a crowd. For a moment, he thought he was still in London, that perhaps Kilkairn Castle and all its occupants were naught but a dream.

The idea made him sit bolt upright, and it was with relieved eyes that he realized he was indeed at Kilkairn, the familiarity of the green chamber setting his mind at ease. Memories came flooding back and he turned onto his back and linked his hands behind his head, dwelling on each moment of the night before.

It had been amazing, an experience he would

never forget. He'd known Kat would be a passionate lover. But he hadn't realized how that would increase his own pleasure.

But most astounding of all was that though he'd slept with her last night, he'd awoken this morning, anxious to see her again. That was yet another first, in a series of firsts.

His gaze wandered over the room. Perhaps he should rise and see her. Had she awoken yet? Had she thought about him?

Good God, I'm acting like a lovesick puppy. He blinked, then sat upright. Love? Surely not. What he felt was merely explosive lust and . . . something else. Respect, perhaps. He knew of few women with Kat's capabilities or heart. So it was not love that he felt. Not unless . . .

His gaze fell on the empty candle dish beside the nightstand.

What if the talisman ring had *caused* him to fall in love with Kat? *Real* love. Bloody hell, what if the ring had meant for him to fall in love with her all along and he, thinking to trick it, had merely played into its nefarious plans and—

"Bloody hell, what is wrong with me?" he muttered. The ring had no power; that was nothing but an old wives' tale that his mother had made up to amuse six very active children. Not that it mattered, the ring was not in his possession, but someone else's.

He frowned. Unless, of course, Tilton had found it.

Downstairs, someone shouted and then dropped something with a large thump that seemed to echo down the hallways. "Bloody hell, what is all the din?" He got up from bed and began rummaging about for his clothing.

The door opened and Tilton entered carrying a tray. He raised his brows on finding Devon half dressed. "Pray tell me the buff breeches and green coat are an effort to amuse your host and not an honest attempt at fashion."

"What? This coat and breeches? I wore them to the Whythe-Stanhopes' and everyone complimented me."

"Hm. Did they appear to be smirking when they made their comments? Or perhaps the wine was flowing freely? I believe I have heard that the Whythe-Stanhopes are notorious about spiking the punch at their own parties."

Devon eyed his valet with a narrow gaze. "Are you accusing me of being out of style?"

"I would never presume to do such a thing," Tilton said primly, setting the tray on the night table, "no matter how true such a statement might appear to others."

Devon looked down at his breeches for a moment. Then he sighed. "Damn it, now you have me wondering if perhaps you're right. Find me another coat to wear."

"Excellent, sir." Tilton uncovered the dishes on the tray. "Perhaps you should eat while I do that very thing."

Devon was more than willing to eat; his stomach was rumbling so loudly he was beginning to think that was what had awakened him rather than the mill downstairs. "What is going on to cause that racket?"

"Preparations for the ball, sir. Apparently Lady Strathmore has been most lavish in her preparations and His Lordship has been complaining about it since."

"I see." Devon had forgotten the ball. Lately, it seemed that he'd forgotten a lot of things. He yawned and stretched.

Tilton shot him a sharp glance. "Tired, sir?"

"Somewhat."

"Yes, sir. Sleep riding will do that to you."

"Sleep riding? What are you talking about?"

"Merely that after you went to bed last night, you apparently got up, dressed, and went for a ride."

"I was awake. And yes, I know I did. How did *you* know? It was late and I thought you were already abed."

"I was, sir. However, the lower footman's youngest brother was apparently roused from his warm cot and offered a large sum to saddle your horse." Tilton met Devon's gaze evenly. "I assured the entire staff that you frequently rode out while still sleeping. They were intrigued of course, and I had to answer a thousand questions, most of them having to do with what would happen if you were sleep riding and had the sudden need to relieve yourself—would you be awake enough to realize it. After we surmounted that hurdle, they began to ask why you would ride in your sleep to His Lordship's sister's cottage. I fear I had no answer for that."

Devon didn't like the sound of this at all. "The staff all know, then, where I went?"

"Oh yes, sir. The wagering has been fierce. Some seem to think Miss Spalding may yet have a chance."

"What about my sleep riding? Didn't anyone believe that?"

"A few of the more dewy-eyed ones, but not enough. It would not surprise me if the story filtered back to His Lordship."

Wondrous. Devon wondered what Malcolm's reaction would be to such information, and a faintly sick feeling tightened his stomach. "Any word yet on the lost ring?"

Tilton shook his head, a frown creasing his brow. "No, sir, and I've interrogated the entire staff. No one has even seen it. I asked your footman, Paul, to make inquiries among the stablehands."

Devon took a sip of his juice to cover his relief. It was reassuring to know that the ring hadn't unknowingly been in his possession last night, when he'd been with Kat. He didn't want to think of their time together as ordained by some family myth. He wanted it to have been of her own free choice and nothing more.

Strange how that mattered. He wondered why, then shrugged it off. Devon finished his breakfast, changed his coat for another, and then made his way downstairs. Malcolm was on the main staircase, looking about the great hall with wonder. Devon waited for some sign that his friend had heard about his late night visit, but it quickly became obvious that Malcolm was as yet unaware of anything other than the fact that his house was being turned upside down.

Boxes were stacked everywhere, as were large folds of silver and blue cloth. Tables had been removed, chairs lined up, and every servant Devon had ever seen at the castle was in evidence, scrubbing and polishing and cleaning.

Devon wondered if any of them had ever worked so hard. He watched the small army, then said to Malcolm, "I thought this was to be a small, private ball."

"So did I," Malcolm said grimly. "Apparently that was a misconception. Every person within fifty miles has been invited to attend."

"How horrid," Devon said. And it was. The last thing he wanted to do was spend his last few precious days doing anything but being with Kat.

The thought of leaving was beginning to bother him. He absently rubbed his chest where a faint pressure seemed to lurk. What was it about her that tugged at him so? At first, she'd been his haven from the lure of the ring to keep him from becoming enamored of the she-witches of the world, women like Murien, for example. But then he'd begun to enjoy being with Kat for Kat's sake.

But that was to be expected, he supposed. After all, other than Kat, what amusement had there been at Kilkairn Castle? None. Malcolm, usually the brightest of companions, was consumed with his argument with his wife. And while riding was certainly a pleasant thing to do, Devon certainly couldn't be expected to do that alone. So that just left Kat.

A faint sense of relief filtered through Devon. Once he left the isolation of Kilkairn and found himself home once again among the glittering ballrooms of London, he'd forget all about Kat Macdonald.

Of course, he couldn't leave at all until he found the talisman ring. Brightening a little, he asked Malcolm if he'd discovered anything about the ring. To his surprise, Malcolm hesitated, then nodded. "I heard one thing from one of the lower housemaids, but . . . I need some time to make certain of the facts."

"Take your time," Devon said, waving a hand. "I'm in no hurry."

Malcolm eyed him curiously. "What about your business in Edinburgh?"

"For now, I'll send a letter and postpone the meeting. I'm certain they will not mind." Of course, Devon's brother Marcus *would* mind. But Marcus was in London, and by the time he discovered that Devon had changed the meeting date, there would be precious little he could do about it. "I cannot leave without that ring."

Malcolm seemed to agree, but before he could say anything, another group of workmen came clomping into the hall to add to the growing stack of boxes.

"Bloody hell, what is Fiona doing?" Malcolm asked.

Devon didn't know or care. He just wondered if Kat would be attending. He hadn't realized he'd spoken the words aloud until he saw Malcolm's lowered brow.

"I don't know if she'll come or not; she's funny about these things. But why are you asking? Are you wishful to see her?"

Devon was wishful to see her, taste her, touch her, and do everything in between. But all he said to Malcolm was "I was just wondering, that's all."

"Hm," Malcolm said, uncertain how to read the casual statement. Certainly there was a spark of interest there, only . . . was it good interest, or self-absorbed masculine interest?

For Kat's sake, he hoped it was not the latter. "It would surprise me if she attended. She's not usually one for such things."

Another stack of heavy boxes were being unloaded and he had to move so that the servants could clean the floor. When it came to getting things organized for an event, Fiona became a little general, ordering people about and making lightning-fast decisions.

His heart swelled a little at the thought. Lately, he'd caught her looking at him in a sad way, as if debating a horrible, difficult decision. Was she on the verge of deciding she'd had enough, that their marriage wasn't worth fighting for?

Malcolm wiped a hand over his tired eyes. The wager had been a horrid, foolish idea and had alienated them even further. He wasn't even sure if he really wanted to win.

Throat thick, he waved a hand at Devon. "I won't be able to play billiards this evening. Fiona has assigned us all a list of duties, and I must see to it that the library is readied."

"Is there anything I can do?"

"Just stay out of Fiona's way. She's a tyrant when it comes to these things."

Devon bowed. "That, I can do. In fact, I'll begin now."

Malcolm managed a smile, answering St. John's further comments as best as his aching soul would allow. Eventually Devon excused himself and Malcolm watched him go, wondering what had the lad in such a merry mood.

Well, Malcolm hoped Devon enjoyed it while he could. God knew that the second he fell in love, his happiness would be limited.

Sighing heavily, Malcolm quit the great hall and retreated to the peacefulness of his library.

Kat awoke with a pleasant, satiated feeling. It had been so long since she'd felt that way that she had to stop and think of the cause. As she stretched, her muddled morning mind stretching along with her, her ankle became entangled in something. She bent down to free herself and saw it was a strip of a white silk scarf.

Her cheeks heated as her memory came flooding back. She and Devon had made love in this very bed. And not just love, but exquisite, breathtaking love. Her breasts tingled with the memory of his hands, his mouth, of the way he'd tasted her and the power of his body over hers.

She shivered and gathered a pillow close, snuggling her cheek against it. If she breathed deeply enough, she could still smell him, the faint scent of sandalwood clinging to her sheets.

There was a knock before the door opened and Annie came in carrying something over her arm, Simon and Hamish following her. They were carrying the large brass tub and arguing about something, though they did break off their bickering long enough to wish her a good morning.

"Up, ye sleepyhead!" Annie called out merrily. "Ye've a bath to take and measurements to take afore I cut the cloth for yer gown."

Kat started to sit upright, but then remembered that she was as naked as the day she was born. Belatedly she snatched up the cover and held it before her.

Simon and Hamish were still arguing in heated whispers about a meeting of some sort, and had missed her error. But Annie's eyes widened, her gaze seeking and then finding the discarded night rail pooled on the floor. That sent Annie scurrying, admonishing the men to begin fetching the pails of water as soon as it was hot. She whisked them from the room and closed the door.

"Och, Miss Kat, ye went and fergot yer night rail. 'Tis on the floor." Annie placed Kat's old ball gown over the back of a chair and went to collect the forgotten night rail.

Kat held the covers a bit tighter. "I, ah, got very hot last night. So I took it off and threw it on the floor. I meant to pick it up, but I slept in."

"Hmph." Annie's gaze scrutinized her features. "I canno' fer the life o' me believe ye were so hot that ye took off yer rail. 'Twas cool last night after the rain."

Kat didn't know what to answer, so instead she

glanced at the old gown and said, "I'd forgotten about the ball."

Annie stopped, astonishment on her face. "How can ye say that? 'Tis to be a grand affair."

"I know, I know! I'm just a little—" What was the word? In lust? She certainly wasn't in love, that would require . . . well, it would require a man who was capable of caring about one for more than a two-month period.

A little of her happiness dimmed. He would leave soon, and she needed to remember that, first and foremost. Her heart sank as she realized how soon he would be gone. "I am looking forward to the ball." If nothing else, it might well be one of her last chances to see him, talk to him, laugh with him.

Ever.

Somehow, before this moment, the enormity of that fact had escaped her. In a way, she'd used it as a shield to protect her from caring too much. But somehow she had allowed her heart to become entangled. She loved him. With all her heart, she loved him.

The realization stole her breath. Tears threatened to clog her throat. Good God, when had that happened?

She loved a man who had plainly told her that he would not, could not love her.

Now what would she do? She had thought being with him was a safe venture. Safe because he wasn't the staying kind, safe because he hadn't once tried to pretend that he was something he was not. Now she realized that those facts had merely made him more dangerous.

"Ye should be excited," Annie chatted on, "for 'twill be a fine ball. Now come, listen to what I have planned fer yer gown."

Annie began to talk and Kat forced herself to smile, though she felt far from it.

It wasn't quite so difficult to really smile once she heard Annie's idea for the gown. The housekeeper had outdone herself. She would use the straw silk borrowed from the saved curtain linings to make a slashed overdress with puffed sleeves and decorate it with no fewer than eight tiny, hand-sewn rosettes of blue silk from Kat's old ball gown. Annie would then use the remaining blue silk as insets in the sleeves and for the petticoat, which would be revealed in the slashes on the overdress. The overall effect would be simply beautiful and, when combined with Kat's reddish hair, breathtaking.

At least when Devon saw Kat for the last time, she wouldn't be wearing a gown smudged with soot. She lifted her chin a little. Whatever else she did, she would not let him see how much she cared. This time, she would keep her pride intact, no matter the cost.

She caught sight of Annie's speculative gaze and hurried to paste a smile back on her lips. "Annie, it will be a lovely gown."

Annie beamed. "'Tis glad I am to hear that ye think so, Miss Kat. Ye know, ye look a mite flushed." Annie laid her hand across Kat's brow. "Are ye taking an ague?"

Kat shook her head. "'Tis excitement, that's all." And not just over the ball.

"Hm. Well, 'tis to the bath wid ye and then we'll see how ye're feeling." Annie went to the wardrobe and fished about for one of Kat's robes. "Here, put this on. Ye don't need to be getting cold afore ye soak in the tub."

A clattering in the hallway preceded Simon and Hamish's reentry. They carried two large steaming buckets, which they tipped into the brass tub. "One more trip will do it," Hamish said, his gaze fixed on Kat.

"Mornin' Miss Kat," Simon said, eyeing her even more closely than Hamish.

There was something odd in the way they looked at her, but Annie didn't give them time to say anything. She sent them to fetch more water while she straightened the room. Finally the tub was filled to the brim, and Annie sent the lads on their way.

Annie went to the tub and added some scent, then dipped her elbow into the water. "Perfect! Come along, now. Into the tub wid ye."

Kat didn't wait. She gratefully slid into the lavender-scented water. Perhaps her troubles would melt away if she just stayed here. Surely Annie would bring her food and the lads would keep the glasswork going . . . Why, she could stay here for the rest of her life and no one would ever know. Kat's lip trembled. Who really needed her anyway?

Stop that, she told herself. *You are being silly.* And she was, but somehow she couldn't help it. Her heart was trying valiantly not to show its cracks, and all the while it was trembling, falling to pieces. To stop from thinking too much, she scrubbed herself thoroughly, trying to rub away the hurts. It helped . . . a little.

Annie leaned out the window. "By the saints, 'tis that Sassenach of yours."

Devon? Here? Now what was she to do? If she saw him and he guessed how she felt, it would ruin everything together. But if she didn't see him, he would know something was amiss.

Which was better? Kat took a deep breath. She could do a lot of things, but pretend she wasn't affected by him wasn't one of them. Not here, or now, anyway. If she waited until the ball to see him, at least then she'd be girded in the wondrous ball gown. She would smile and laugh and dance, and no one would know her secret.

Taking a deep breath, she pushed her wet hair behind her ears and then sank into the water up to her neck. "Annie, please inform Mr. St. John I will see him at the ball and not a second before."

To say that Devon took the news of Kat's defection well would be a misstatement. He didn't. He'd been at first incredulous, and then irritated, and at last angry that she could so calmly put him off when he'd come to see her time and again.

While he was *not* in love, their night together had proven something to him. It had shown him that passion did not burn itself out, that it could satisfy even as it left one hungry for more. Never in all his days had he ever had such a delightful encounter with a woman. And if he'd had his normal reaction, once having sampled her bounty, he would be itching to be off, looking for another challenge. But this time, all he wanted was to be with Kat. More and more.

And not just physically. While riding there, he'd thought of no fewer than three things he wanted to tell her. One thought involved a nice trail ride that had a pretty little abbey at the end of it. It was a tip from one of the grooms at Kilkairn and sounded as if it might be just the thing for a lazy afternoon. The second thing he wanted to tell her was how Murien had been in the stable when he'd left. She'd been loudly demanding a horse, saying she wished to ride, too. The grooms had all been skeptical and had not hurried to meet her demands. One old groom, however, had agreed to saddle a mount for her. And he had—a pathetic old slug with a lumpy gait and a bad tendency to bite.

Devon had been hard-pressed not to laugh. But he'd made certain he wasn't around when she got ready to mount the horrid thing. He didn't want Murien tagging along when he came to visit Kat.

The third thing he thought to tell Kat was about the talisman ring and how it had gone missing. And that he could not, in all honesty, leave until it was found.

He had wondered if she would be glad, but if he agreed to her wishes he'd have to wait until the ball to discuss anything with her. It was most irritating.

It was ludicrous to wait for such a time—there were still four more days until that blasted ball. Four days of no Kat. Surely she hadn't meant it . . .

But a visit to the clearing proved him wrong. So

did a second visit. And a third. All he got from his visits was the sight of Kat's back as she whisked out of sight, and the baleful stares of her lads.

Frustrated, but refusing to make a spectacle of himself, Devon returned to Kilkairn. Preparations for the ball continued and to fill the suddenly empty hours, Devon began to assist Malcolm in the list of duties Fiona had assigned him. Devon had his servants leave the relative comfort of the inn where they'd been staying and spend the better portion of each day at Kilkairn, helping in whatever way was needed. Though he stayed busy, Devon's mood darkened with each passing hour. Without Kat, everything seemed . . . dull and lifeless. The moods of his companions were not much better. Fiona was in a tizzy, Malcolm was strangely quiet, and Murien looked as if she'd like to drag Devon off to the nearest broom closet and divest him of his clothing.

The evening before the ball, he took a long lonely ride on Thunder, conveniently missing dinner. He returned to his room well after the sun had set, muddy and tired and feeling almost despondent.

Sighing, Devon removed his coat and crossed to the window. He pulled back the curtain and stared into the distance. Cool air leaked in around the casement, making him glad for the fire, smoky as it was. The night was especially bright, lit by the full moon, the stars twinkling all around. It would have been a magical night for a midnight ride.

But only if he had Kat to share it with. God, what a coil. His last few days had been ruined. Blast it, he was locked here in a ramshackle castle with a warring couple and a marriage-minded shrew while the woman he—

He caught himself. The woman he what? Liked? Enjoyed? Lusted after? What was she? His mind seemed unable to define it, to define her.

He sighed and rested his forehead against the damp windowpane. Deep in the woods, a faint light twinkled, a glimpse of golden warmth.

He couldn't seem to stop thinking of her. Of the feel of her lips beneath his, of the fullness of her in his arms. He loved women, loved their foibles, their airs, their frivolity. They amused him, but none had ever engaged him on a serious level.

But with Kat, he found himself wondering who she was behind that enigmatic exterior. She simply did not play by the known Rules of Womanhood. She didn't flirt. She didn't laugh at his sallies unless they caught her by surprise. She didn't try to impress him or engage his interest in any way whatsoever.

She was completely devoid of the artifices most women used. Artifices that had, until very recently, amused him in a mild sort of way.

What was strange was that the more he saw of Kat, the less amused he was by what he had once considered natural feminine wiles. In fact, he was finding Murien's company onerous. What bothered him most was the realization that, had he met Murien two weeks ago, he would have been completely taken by her. At least for a month or so.

He sighed, pushing the curtain back further, to rest his shoulder against the window frame, feeling the chill of his own chamber.

He'd wager Kat's cottage was warm. There was something almost magical about that place, something uniquely comforting and homelike. Somehow, Kat had turned her cottage into everything that Kilkairn Castle was not. He sighed. Once he left Kilkairn, every day would feel like today. Every day he'd smile and talk and nod and feel utterly alone. Being with Kat had spoiled him.

He dropped the curtain and turned away. The truth was that Kat Macdonald intrigued him in a way that no other woman had. Not because he was attracted to her, but because she was a challenge, a unique, undiscovered source of amusement to his dull spirit. It had been a long while since he'd had to put forth an effort to win a woman to his bed. And such a woman, too.

He removed his boots, tossing them to one side. He had just reached for his cravat when something clinked against the window.

Devon whirled toward the sound. It came again, only with more force. Bloody hell, someone was trying to get his attention by throwing pebbles against his window. Could it be Kat? Had she missed him, too? No one else would go to such lengths to gain his attention. Malcolm would knock at the door, Fiona would never have cause, and Murien . . . well, he rather thought Murien would just walk right in and climb into his bed. And if he was not cautious, that is exactly what she would do. There was a line of brass beneath her silver polish. He could almost taste it.

Another rock hit the window, this one larger. It

clunked against the glass and fell away. It had to be Kat.

Grinning, he threw open the window and leaned out—*thunk*. A rock hit him in the forehead, and sent him staggering backward, into the long curtains that surrounded his bed.

He fell against the mattress and then lay there, blinking rapidly. Bloody hell, did she want to kill him? He straightened, carefully touching his forehead, where a bump was already swelling.

"Sassenach? Are ye there?" a heavily masculine voice called out.

It wasn't Kat after all. Irritation warred with disappointment. With one hand covering his aching forehead, Devon climbed back to his feet and looked out his window. In the courtyard below stood a huge, hulking Scotsman, one of Kat's lads, no doubt, though it was too dark to see which. "Who the hell are you?" Devon demanded. "You almost killed me!"

"Not a'purpose," the giant said in a mild tone. " 'Twas a small rock."

Devon finally recognized the voice. It was the redoubtable Simon. Devon gingerly rubbed his forehead. "What do you want?"

"I came to see if ye'd like to wash a whisker wid us."

"Wash a whisker." What the hell did that mean? "I'm afraid I cannot wash my whiskers right this moment since I have none—"

"Come, Sassenach! The Lion and Boar has some fine ale, they do. I'll even foist the rowdies fer it."

Devon placed his hands on the windowsill and

leaned out so he could see his visitor a bit more clearly. The man didn't appear drunk, for he wasn't swaying on his feet, nor did his words sound anything other than crisp and to the point. "Ale, eh? Is that what 'washing your whiskers' means?"

"What else could it mean?" Simon asked, apparently astounded.

"What else indeed. May I ask why you're offering this wonderful invitation?"

"Because we thought ye'd like a pint."

"We?"

"The others are already at the inn. I daresay we'll be hard pressed to catch up wid 'em, especially Hamish. He seems solemn, but he can outdrink any man ye care t' name."

Devon's head ached from the rock, and his heart ached from the last few wretched days. But somewhere in the back of his mind, he could hear Malcolm's voice, suggesting that the best way to win over Kat was to win over her lads.

It was an unspoken right of passage for a man who wanted to judge another man's mettle, to invite him to partake, and then see who could withstand the torture with the least effect. And Devon recognized the aged ploy now.

But this contest of manly wills had a purpose—to win the trust of Kat's lads. If all he had to do was drink with a roomful of rowdies to win some time with Kat, he'd do it every night for a year.

"Very well," he called down. "I'll come. Wait for me there."

Simon's grin was evident even from upstairs. "Do

that, Sassenach, but dinna keep me waitin' long. I've a powerful thirst as 'tis."

"I won't." Devon started to close the window, but his gaze fell on the rock that had rolled to the edge of the bed. With a faint smile, he picked it up and then, after taking a second to judge the distance, he tossed it back out the window.

A faint grunt of pain and then a loud curse filled the air.

Grinning a little, Devon pulled on his boots and coat and headed out the door.

Chapter 18

*I don't know how my son came to do such a thing,
pinching a kitchen maid. I know he has never seen
me do such a thing. I've never taken up with anything under a chambermaid in my life.*

Duke of Draventon
to his best friend, Lord Rutherford,
while walking with that gentleman
into the gallery at the House of Lords

"Bloody hell," Devon said woozily. "I've died."

"Not yet," came a sharp feminine voice.

"Kat?" He started to lift his head, then groaned
and dropped it back on the mound of pillows holding it. The movement made his stomach clench.

"Lie still," she ordered.

As if he could do else. "My head . . . did someone
hit me?"

"The only thing that hit you was the brandy in the
bottom of a bottle."

She sounded angry. He opened his eyes again, but
had to close them right away. "The room is spinning."

"Put your foot on the floor."

"What?"

Two capable hands picked up his foot and plopped it on the floor. After a moment things settled a bit and he was able to say, "That worked."

"So will this," she said. "Sit up and drink it."

It took every ounce of effort that he possessed, but he lifted himself on his elbow and realized he was on a settee in a small room, most likely at Kat's cottage. His head felt swollen to twice its normal size, and his body ached everywhere that didn't feel ill.

Kat's face swam before his eyes, and for a second he forgot his woes and said the first words that came to mind. "I love you."

She had just picked up a glass holding some murky-colored stuff, but she paused, her clear eyes meeting his not-so-clear ones. "What did you say?"

What had he said? He blinked, trying to remember. Then his brow cleared. "I said I love you." Damn, but his memory was good, even when drunk.

"I see. Here." She placed the glass in his hand.

He was suddenly thirsty, so he took what she offered and brought it to his mouth. But before the rim could touch his parched lips, the scent assailed his nostrils, and he smiled. "This smells like a lemon tart."

"It's a tonic and it tastes horrid, so don't get your hopes up."

"Horrid?"

"Horrid."

He put the glass down, though it took him some

time to make it land on the floating table. "Don't want horrid tonics. Not today, anyway. Maybe tomorrow when I'm more the thing and horrid tonics won't make me want to vo—"

The glass was rudely thrust back into his hand. "Now." Irritation colored Kat's voice. "I haven't all day, Sassenach. Drink your tonic or get on your horse and go back to Kilkairn now."

The thought of riding a horse made his stomach queasy again. He waved a hand. "No horses."

"Then drink the tonic."

Devon held out his hand, and the glass was once again placed in his grip. He peered up at her through his lashes. "You sound angry."

"Imagine that," she said, waiting for him to finish the horrid beverage. Finally, after much hacking and wheezing, he managed to choke down most of it.

He wiped his mouth on his sleeve. "Bloody hell, what's in that? Horse urine?"

She took the nearly empty glass. "No, but only because I didn't have the time to collect any."

He blinked, and she could see that her wit was wasted. Sighing, she pulled the covers back to his chin. "Go to sleep."

"Oh I will," he assured her in a thick voice, the tonic beginning to do its magic. "I will go to sleep for you, though I'd rather sleep *with* you." His eyes cracked open, and he offered a devilish smile. "Can I convince you to join me on the settee?"

"There's not enough room," she said, her heart suddenly pounding.

"There's plenty of room if you lay atop me." He moved so that he was flat on his back. "See? You'd fit just fine."

"I have work to do today. Now no more talking."

"Very well," he mumbled. "I will sleep and sleep and sleep . . . and . . . sleep . . . an—" His head lolled to one side, his long lashes cresting his cheeks.

Kat sat back on her heels, her knees unable to support her. She could scarcely believe it; Devon had said he loved her. Of course he was drunk, but still . . . had he meant it? And even if he did, would it last more than his usual month or two, if that?

Whatever he felt, her love for him would continue forever. A wave of loneliness struck her, and she had to wipe away a tear.

Simon stuck his head in the window. "How's our Sassenach?" Behind him she could just make out Donald's and Neal's concerned faces.

"He's drunk."

An awed expression came over Simon's face. "Do ye know that it took over seven pints to get him like that? Even Hamish cannot drink so much."

"What's more," Donald added, "he's not even a Scotsman."

Neal pulled Donald away from the window, so he could have a better view. " 'Tis a record at the pub. We carved his name over the door."

Kat wondered if any man truly grew up. "Thank you for that wonderful information. If he casts up his accounts, I'll let you think about that while you're cleaning it up." Kat gathered the glass and stood.

"Come back in about three hours and you can return him to Kilkairn."

"Aye, Miss Kat," Simon said. "I'll take him meself."

"I'll help," Neal offered eagerly. In the background, Donald nodded.

That was the worst part, Kat decided. Whatever had happened last night, her lads were completely won over. Devon St. John had done more than drink his fill at the inn, he had also cajoled her men into believing him a man of epic proportions, or, as Simon had put it when he'd tenderly carried the Sassenach into the cottage that morning, " 'Tis a good one, is St. John. The lads an' I have promised to teach him the glasswork oncet he's feelin' better."

With that, Kat realized she'd lost her only allies in her attempt to keep her heart in check. Thank God Annie was still on her side, else she would have been quite alone.

The thought cast her down, and it was with a heavy heart that she finally left Devon sleeping on the settee and made her way to the workshop.

Devon waved goodbye to Simon and Neal and . . . well, whoever the other one was, then wandered into the castle, his head still swollen, though thanks to Kat's tonic, the world had ceased to tilt.

Malcolm had been wrong that winning the lads was the way to Kat's heart. Devon had won the lads, but somehow that effort had only seemed to infuriate their mistress until she would barely speak to him.

Or was she upset about something else? He tried

to think what it might be, but could not hit upon anything. Perhaps he'd said something, but his memory was somewhat fuzzy.

Sighing, Devon picked his way through the sumptuous preparations for the ball and then found his bedchamber, glad he didn't run into anyone who might require him to speak in a complete sentence. Once Devon reached his room, he fell into his bed, hoping to fall back asleep. He was too tired to think. Somehow, he'd find a way to solve all his problems, but not now.

As soon as he closed his eyes, it seemed that Tilton was there, shaking him.

"I'm awake, I'm awake," Devon mumbled.

"Excellent, sir. Perhaps you could prove that by opening your eyes."

Devon rolled onto his back. "What time is it?"

"After seven, sir. I ordered a bath so you could prepare for the ball."

Devon lifted his head to see a tub sitting in one corner of the room, already filled. "It can't be that late."

"Oh, but it is. Shall I open the curtains and prove it? The sunset is quite brilliant this evening."

"No! Do not open the curtains. My brain would shatter if I had to see a drop of sunlight." Devon collected himself and swung his feet over the edge of the bed. He waited for nausea or dizziness, but none came. Kat's tonic had indeed helped; he felt much better. He managed to bathe and dress without too much fuss and allowed Tilton to assist him into his formal attire.

"Any word on the talisman ring?"

Tilton shook his head. "I don't understand it, sir. You offered a substantial reward. I fully expected someone to come forth with some sort of information, but no one seems to know a thing."

"Well, keep looking."

"Yes, sir."

"Thank you, Tilton." Sighing, Devon prepared to join his hosts, though all he really wanted to do was find Kat and make things right.

Soon, he told himself. Very soon.

The Strathmore ball was an unusual event. Not only was it being held out of town in the midst of the season, but it was also being held at His Lordship's ancestral home. It was the first truly formal entertainment at Kilkairn in over one hundred and fifty years.

Added to that, the ball was given in honor of Mr. Devon St. John, and all of Edinburgh society was anxious to meet such a wealthy, eligible bachelor.

Fiona had planned everything carefully. She'd rented large pots of flowers in varying hues of violet and blue, so many that the room looked like a garden. Long silver swaths of material floated down the ancient walls, reminding one of waterfalls and reflecting the light of a thousand candles. She'd had the servants make bowers over each doorway and had threaded even more flowers there.

She'd also ordered ices, a large quantity of punch, and no fewer than three hundred iced cakes which were to be distributed at the first ring of midnight, each baked with a favor hidden inside. Most of the favors were worthless—small pairs of dice, a trumpery bit of jewelry, or some such nonsense—but three cakes had real jewels in them. The guests were already excitedly buzzing about the coming treat, many hovering over the table, wondering which cakes held the prizes.

The ball was bound to be a smashing success.

Devon caused quite a stir when he finally appeared. Fiona had been thorough in inviting all of society, and the great hall sparkled with beautiful people. Appearing somewhat harried, she introduced him to the guests. Devon instantly felt like a prize poodle on display, especially when he saw the avaricious gazes of the many unmarried women who had attended.

What was worse was that if Fiona had latched on to his left arm, Murien had positively stuck herself on to his right. He was most uncomfortable, especially when he read the possessive note in Murien's voice.

Devon decided to let them have their way—for now, at least. He was far too busy looking for Kat to worry about Murien, anyway.

Kat, meanwhile, was still at the cottage. The dress Annie had made was beautiful; straw colored silk over sky blue . . . the colors made Kat's hair gleam. She'd been astonished when she'd first caught a glimpse of herself in the mirror for Annie had altered the current style just enough to compliment her full figure.

She stood before the mirror in the sitting room

now, trying hard not to glance at the clock over and over. She'd thought to go at ten, but Simon had not yet brought the cart. "Where is Simon? I'm going to be late."

" 'Tis fashionable to be late," Annie said calmly as she pinned a blue silk flower in Kat's hair. "He'll be here soon. Just ye wait."

"If he's much longer, I shall saddle Trusty and ride over there myself."

Annie snorted. "Ye wouldn't dare! Not after I spent so much time a-stitchin' that gown."

Kat sighed. She really shouldn't go. People would talk; they always did and Kat hated it. But this was her last chance to see Devon. Perhaps ever.

Her heart pained her at the thought and she realized that she'd been right not to spend any more time with him other than these few moments in public. She was no longer in command of her own heart; she hadn't been since she'd realized she loved him.

A knock sounded on the cottage door and Annie bustled to open it. Simon stood on the stoop.

Kat blinked. He was dressed in his Sunday best suit of broadcloth, his hair meticulously slicked back from his forehead, his skin scrubbed fresh and clean.

"St. George's dragon," she said softly, blinking.

He reddened. "Aye, I look a fool. But Annie said 'twould be nice if'n ye had a way to the ball other than the old cart, so the lads and I got ye a surprise." He stepped back and jerked a thumb over his shoulder.

Kat peered past him into the dark. Neal and Hamish stood awkwardly beside an old carriage. The two lads were dressed in their Sunday best to match Simon's. Kat raised her brows, first at her lads, then at the carriage. "Isn't that Dr. Lambert's?"

"Aye," Simon answered. "The doctor loaned it on the condition that the lads and I help raise his new barn next week."

Annie nodded her satisfaction. "Off with ye now, Miss Kat. Now ye've a carriage like a proper lady should."

Kat shook her head, her heart filled to overflowing. "Simon . . . Annie . . . I don't know what to say."

"Don't say a word," Simon pleaded. "This collar is about to choke me. Just climb in and let's be on our way fer we're already late."

Thus it was when Kat made her appearance at the Strathmore ball, it was to find Fiona already looking wan and pale, Malcolm nowhere in sight, and Devon surrounded by society beauties, with Murien purring along beside him, looking like the cat who ate the cream.

Though Kat had been expecting such a thing, it didn't make it any easier to witness. Especially since nothing had prepared her for the sight of Devon in his ballroom finery.

Dressed in black breeches that hugged his muscular legs, and a coat tailored to fit his broad shoulders without a wrinkle, he stood out among the more provincial dressers. He'd done little to his hair except comb it back, but one unruly lock hung over his forehead, giving him a slightly dissolute look.

Added to that were the faint shadows beneath his blue eyes and the look of impenetrable boredom that he was sporting, and he was easily the handsomest and most intriguing man in sight.

Kat paused at the door, suddenly wanting desperately to turn and run. It was ludicrous to make an appearance in such a lovely ball gown; she wasn't sure now why it had mattered. From the cold glances she was already receiving, she was a pariah no matter how she dressed.

As soon as she was identified, the rumors would begin yet again, and there would be more stares, more whispers, more innuendoes—the vicious circle never stopped. Her spirit quavered at the thought.

This was not the way she'd envisioned the night. She'd thought to make an impressive entrance of some sort. To be accepted where she never had been.

She wasn't sure now why she'd thought that . . . perhaps because by falling in love with Devon, she felt new. Fresh. And even lovely.

But now, facing the harsh stare of society, she had to wonder . . . was that an illusion too?

Heart heavy, she decided to make a hasty retreat, but before she could move, Malcolm suddenly materialized.

He didn't give her time to argue, but led her back inside, tucking her hand in the crook of his arm so she couldn't escape. "Where do you think you're going?"

"Home," she said flatly.

"But you look beautiful." He eyed her up and down, growing appreciation in his gaze. "Where did you get this gown? It's perfect for you."

"Annie made it."

"She's a wonder. One day I shall steal her from you and I will never eat poorly prepared food again."

"She's a miracle," Kat agreed. She knew what he was doing—making casual talk so she could regain her composure. She loved him for it, even though she wished he would just let her go.

"I didn't even know Annie could wield a needle. Yet another reason to prize her over all other women."

"Except one," Kat said softly.

Malcolm's gaze grew shadowed. He led her across the room, nodding at this acquaintance and then that. "Except one. At least have a bit of punch."

"But I—"

"It has ice in it that cost me a bloody fortune. The least you can do is drink some of it and pretend it tastes as good as it looks."

Kat had to smile. "Is Fiona driving you to ruin?"

"Oh no. I can stand the nonsense. I just wish—" He broke off, something crossing his face and then disappearing behind a bland smile. "At least let me complain. All good hosts do, you know. It's their way of casually dropping their costs into the conversation."

"Is that why they do it?"

"Lud, yes. See those large pots of violets by the door? Fiona ordered three hundred of them and they cost me five pounds each. What's horrid is that the flowers will be dead by morning and we don't even get to keep the bloody pots."

He found the refreshment table and procured a glass of punch, then handed it to her. "Well?" he said with a challenging look in his eye.

"It's wretched, but cold. Very cold."

"There. You've made my evening better already. As much as this blasted affair has cost me, I demand to get the maximum enjoyment out of it that I can, so thank you, most lovely of sisters, for drinking my punch and admiring my ice."

Kat returned the glass to him.

"More?"

"Oh no, thank you. Let's save some ice for your other guests."

"Very well, but at midnight, you must be in line to snatch up an iced cake. You could end up with a prize, you know."

She followed his gaze to the tables where the cakes were set. "Why is everyone standing around the table now? There is still almost forty minutes before the clocks will chime."

"Because some of the prizes settled to the sides and you can almost make out what prize is in which cake." He lowered his voice. "I'm going for the third cake in the fourth row. You can see a jewel of some sort sticking out of the bottom."

"You had the opportunity to see the cakes before anyone else, so I believe that is cheating. Are you certain you wish to compromise your values in such a way as to—"

"Malcolm—" came a deep voice. "And Miss Kat."

Kat knew who it was without even looking. Blast

it, it had been a trick. Malcolm had lured her into the room and then kept her busy until Devon could find them.

She closed her eyes and tried to move her heart back into place before turning and smiling. "Mr. St. John. How are you this evening?"

"My, that was frosty," Malcolm said, sending her a frown. "Perhaps you had too much of the icy punch." He glanced at Devon. "Have you come to claim Kat's hand for a dance?"

To her horror, she realized the band was playing a waltz. "I don't dance."

"Excellent," Devon said. "I'll teach you." He took her hand in his, Malcolm slipping away without so much as another word.

"You cannot learn to dance while at a ball!" Kat said desperately.

"Why not?"

"Because I'll look a fool. And you will, too."

"Nonsense. I'm an excellent teacher. Just put your arm here, and your hand here." He placed one of her hands on the tip of his shoulder and held the other one loosely. Immediately all the unease in Kat's stomach grew warmer.

"Good!" he said, placing his other hand on her waist. A shiver immediately traveled through her, though she resolutely ignored it.

His eyes glinted into hers. "Now comes the easy part; all you have to do is follow me."

"What?"

"Just follow me," he repeated.

"But I—"

The music swelled, and he began to move. Aware that now, in reality, every eye was indeed upon her, Kat struggled to keep up, desperately counting. Several times she stumbled, and once she went left when he went right.

He sighed, his breath brushing her hair. "I can see we're going to have to work on this."

"There is no need," she said stiffly, wishing miserably she'd never come. What had she been thinking? She should have refused. It would take more drastic measures to escape now. Perhaps she could fall to the floor and have a fit; she'd once witnessed just such an occurrence at a ball years ago and the unfortunate woman had been immediately spirited away. But apparently Kat's boldness was back at the cottage along with her comfortable clothes.

How she hated that every eye was upon them. By now everyone knew who she was, and their entire dance would be scrutinized, analyzed, conjectured about, and exaggerated until it didn't resemble the truth at all.

"Kat." Devon's voice was close to her ear. "Relax, my sweet. Trust me to get us through this maze of horrid dancers."

She looked into his eyes. "What does trust have to do with dancing?"

"When you follow someone in a dance, they have to direct you because you are dancing backward and you cannot see where you are going. I've often thought men do not realize how difficult it must be to relax and let a partner you sometimes barely know lead you through a maze of dancers. But you and I, we do know one another. And if there is one thing we do have, it is trust."

She thought about this. Perhaps . . . perhaps he was right. Things had changed when she realized that being closer to him did have a cost—her own heart. But that was not his fault. He'd been honest with her from the beginning.

She met his gaze and found him regarding her, a quizzical gleam in his eyes. A smile was wrung from her at his hopeful expression. "I do trust you."

"I know," he said simply. "Relax, my lovely Kat. Let me navigate for a while." He pulled her a little closer. "Meanwhile, you rest."

She did as he suggested, though after a moment, it dawned on her that those dancing around them had a good foot between them while she and Devon had mere inches. "I don't think you're supposed to hold me this close."

He rested his cheek against her hair. "But I like it."

She was quiet a moment more, then she lifted her head to ask, "Why do men always get to lead?"

His lips quivered. "I've often wondered that myself. Perhaps we can trade off. Would you like to lead for a bit?"

Would she? She thought a moment, then nodded. "Certainly."

He smiled and let her begin leading. She wished she could say she was good at it, but she wasn't. Twice she ran them into another couple, and once they barely missed a low table by the door.

But eventually she began to understand how to do it, and she led them without incident. As she relaxed, she became aware of the feel of his chest against hers. Of his hand on her waist. Of being surrounded by him.

The music swelled and pulsed, yet somehow they were in the center of a bubble of pure bliss, a slow heat simmering about them.

Kat let herself drift against him. It was heavenly, being held like this.

Their bodies brushed, then touched, then stayed there.

A deep languor arose, and Kat closed her eyes, letting the music take them where it would.

They went slower and slower, lost in the tug of heat that rose and ebbed between their bodies. Everything else ceased to be. It was just the two of them and no one else. Finally, his arms encircled her and his mouth moved from her hair, to her cheek, to her mouth . . .

Kat was lost. She kissed him back as passionately as he kissed her, reveling in the feel of Devon, her Devon, around her, with her. His hands moved across her back, then lower to cup her bottom intimately. It was then that she realized that the music had come to a halt. As had all the talking.

In fact, the entire room was deafeningly silent.

Kat opened her eyes, breaking the kiss, stepping away so that Devon was no longer touching her. All around them stood the other guests.

Some were smiling.

Some were plainly scandalized.

Some looked too shocked to do more than stare with mouths agape. Dear Lord, but they'd all seen

Devon kissing her. Worse, he'd had his hands on her arse.

Kat caught sight of Murien's furious face, Fiona standing beside her, white-faced and grim.

Good God, what had she done? Kat didn't dare look at Devon; it had to be his worst nightmare. She turned toward him, her gaze locked on the top button of his waistcoat. "Do not say a word," she said in a low voice. "Let me—"

"Katherine."

Malcolm's voice broke over her. She turned to find him next to her.

He looked hard at Devon. "It appears as if this ball has a purpose after all."

"Malcolm, no—" Kat began.

He threw up his hand. "This is a conversation better had in private. Shall we retreat to the library?"

She nodded miserably, wishing she could find something to say to Devon. Meanwhile all around them came the whispers. They were low now, but Kat knew how this part went . . . first were the tiny whispers, followed by the slightly audible murmurs of disapproval. Next came the accusations. Those hit with gale force, ripping reputation and fate alike.

How had she let this happen? Kat had to find a way to fix things, a way to keep Devon St. John from being harmed by their mistakes.

It was with a sinking heart she walked into the library, Devon behind her, as Malcolm closed the door and turned to face them.

Chapter 19

I love happy endings. I had one myself, you know.

Lord Rutherford to his lady love,
Mrs. Montesque-Drumme,
while watching the fireworks at Vauxhall Gardens

"Pssh." Malcolm rubbed his neck and looked at his sister and best friend. "I dinna know where to begin. You know better than to do such a thing."

They didn't say a word, each avoiding the other's gaze. Malcolm wondered what he should do. "What happened out there? You two were supposed to be dancing."

"We were dancing," Kat said, her cheeks pink. "At first."

Devon nodded. "I was letting Kat lead for a while—"

"You let Kat lead?" Bloody hell, what was wrong with the man?

"Aye. And somehow, it just felt . . . good. So I kissed her and, well, that felt even better. So I suppose I forgot where I was and—" Devon raked a hand through his hair.

There was no mistaking the husky timbre of St. John's voice or the slanted glance Kat threw his way.

They were lovers. Malcolm had suspected as much, but the heated looks along with the passionate kiss and intimate hold he'd witnessed between them on the dance floor proved it beyond any doubts.

Perhaps he should—The door flew open and Murien stood in the doorway, Fiona peering anxiously over her shoulder.

Murien walked in, her hand fisted about an object. "Do not continue this farce."

"Farce?" Malcolm scowled. He'd never liked Fiona's sister, and every day he was coming to like her less if that was possible.

Murien's lip curled as she looked at Kat. "You are trying to trap Devon into marriage. Well, I won't stand for it."

Devon's frown was quicker than Kat's. "You don't know what you're talking about. Kat has never tried to entrap me or anyone else."

"She is not an innocent. Nor is she without fault. I think you should put her to the test."

"What test?" Devon asked, his irration mounting.

Murien held out her hand. There, on her palm, lay the St. John talisman ring.

Fiona gasped. "Murien! Where did you get that?"

"Thank God it has been found." Devon started forward, but Murien's fingers closed over it.

Malcolm had to unclench his jaw to speak. "You stole that out of St. John's room."

Murien regarded him with a triumphant sneer. "Only after I saw you, dear brother, borrowing it."

Malcolm's face heated. He glanced at Devon, then shrugged. "I just wanted Kat to see it."

Fiona looked from him to her sister. "Murien, you know St. John was searching for that ring. There is no excuse for what you did."

"I didn't steal it. I was going to return it to St. John as soon as—" She closed her lips over the words.

Malcolm unclenched his jaw. "You were waiting for the ring to prove its magic, weren't you? But nothing happened, so you kept it, waiting."

Murien's face flooded with color. "Don't laugh! You took it to Kat, but nothing happened when it was on her finger, either."

"Nay," Malcolm said, eyeing Murien's closed fist with interest. "Something *did* happen."

Devon's gaze went to Kat. She flushed and shrugged. "It grew warm, that's all."

Murien's expression tightened. "Warm? How warm?"

"Very. So much so that I—well, I could feel it inside."

"I don't understand." Murien peered at the ring. "I've held it and held it and it still feels cold. So cold that it makes my hand ache and—"

Fiona took the ring from Murien. "You owe St. John an apology." She crossed the room and handed the talisman ring to Devon. "Here you are, sir. I ask for forgiveness for the actions of my family."

Devon looked down at the ring. It lay against his palm, sparkling as if newly minted. That was one of the ring's odder characteristics—that it never appeared old, but always new.

Always new. The words echoed softly through Devon's mind. Would that he could keep his feelings for Kat always new. Then he'd have no compunction about marrying her.

Marrying her. Good God, where had that come from?

Did he *want* to marry Kat? His fingers curled over the ring and he searched his heart for the answer. It was not long in coming . . . the truth was that he loved Kat Macdonald. And in a way he'd never thought himself capable.

Of the many women he'd once thought he'd loved only to become un-enamored of them in a remarkably short time, he'd never once awakened with the urgent need to tell them some news or thought. He'd never before wondered about their opinions on matters near to his heart or found himself storing up questions that might loosen some bit of information about them or their thoughts and feelings.

The reason his love for Kat was so different was that *he* had been different. In getting her to open to him, he'd opened his own heart and soul to her. And in doing so, he'd found a woman of gentleness and compassion that answered something deep inside him.

He loved Kat Macdonald. And suddenly he knew

it was forever. The ring began to warm, sending a tingle up his arm. He opened his fingers and looked at it in amazement. How could he have ever run from it? From his fate? "Thank you," he said quietly, and then slipped the ring into his waistcoat pocket.

"Murien," Fiona said, turning back to her sister. "Perhaps you should join the other guests. We will be along shortly."

"But I—"

"That is all, Murien." Fiona's voice rose in frosty dismissal.

Murien stiffened. "Fiona, do not speak to me that way."

"Why not? You *stole* St. John's ring."

"Yes but—Malcolm did the same thing."

Malcolm snorted. "All I did was borrow it for a wee hour, no more. You've kept it for days. Had Kat not so obviously won over St. John, you would have the ring with you still."

"Won over?" Murien laughed. "What do you mean by that?"

"You saw them kiss and . . . other things. Everyone did."

"Yes," Murien said, a faint aura of superiority on her face. "But it doesn't matter. You cannot make St. John marry Kat for that; she's already ruined. She has no reputation to protect."

Kat's face flooded with color. Devon wanted nothing more than to pull her into his arms, but something about the stiff set of her shoulders halted him. She had her pride, and she would not welcome a gesture from him that might be interpreted as pity. So instead he sent a cool glance toward Murien. "I don't know what you're speaking about."

"Oh? Let me tell you, then. When she was seventeen, Kat—"

"I know about that," Devon said dismissively. "I just meant that I don't know what you mean when you say she has no reputation to protect. She has a reputation for many things, including her excellent glasswork, as well as her kindness, capability, caring, and intelligence."

Kat looked at him, bemusement on her face. But Murien was not so quiet. She made an impatient noise. "I don't know what you're talking about, but it's—"

"None of your concern," Fiona said firmly. "Murien, it is time you left. Now."

"But I—"

"Either you go, or I will tell Mother how you embarrassed us all by sneaking into St. John's bedchamber and stealing a family heirloom."

"You wouldn't dare!"

"Try me. And you know what she'd do. You'd never see Edinburgh again, much less London."

There was a long moment of silence. Murien looked resentfully from Fiona to Devon. "I suppose there isn't any need for me to stay, is there?"

"No," Malcolm said flatly.

"None at all," Devon added. "Even if the St. John talisman ring began to glow red-hot with your name printed on the side, I would never marry you."

Her face flushed a dull red, but she kept her head

high. "Very well. I will leave." She turned, but then paused. "Of course, that means that you have lost your wager, Fiona. And your marriage. I hope you're happy."

With those bitter words, she swept from the room, slamming the door behind her.

Malcolm looked at Fiona. "I've never heard you speak so firmly to her before."

Fiona gave a faint shrug, her shoulders seemingly weighted. "It was overdue. I-I suppose I shall return to our guests as well." She made as if to turn, but Malcolm's hand closed over her arm.

"Stay," he said softly. "Please? Perhaps you can help me sort this out."

Her eyes widened, but after a moment, she nodded.

Devon knew the time had come. He and Kat both knew the rules of society, but when they were together, the rules seemed to vanish. They became unimportant in the face of other things, like passion, and companionship, and love.

He turned to Kat and took her hand in his. "Kat, this is not the way I'd thought to do this, but I want to make things right. For now and for always. Will you marry me?"

"No."

The word echoed in the silence that followed. Devon could not believe his ears.

She bent her head. "Devon, thank you but . . . I do not want to marry you."

A thick ache arose in his throat, and he suddenly realized that though he knew his feelings, he didn't know hers. Or he hadn't until now. He raked a hand through his hair, wondering what he was supposed to do now, feel now, think now.

She didn't love him. She had refused his offer of marriage without even pausing. It had cut to his soul, and he found that he could not breathe, could not think. Love was not supposed to be painful, was it? Or so despairing. Had he known it would hurt so, he would never have allowed it to happen.

Damn the talisman ring. This was the retribution he received for having lost it. Unless . . . what if the legacy of the ring was not, as he'd thought, marriage? What if it was merely the act of finding one's true love? And in that act, many things could happen, marriage being one of them.

Or heartbreak.

Malcolm blinked as if as bewildered at Kat's answer as Devon was. "Kat, lassie, do you know what you're saying?"

"I know," she said, her gaze locked on her hands, clasped in her lap.

A mirthless smile touched Devon's lips. He had feared that blasted ring all these years because he'd thought it represented the inevitable loss of his freedom. Now that he would have welcomed that loss, he found that it was all moonshine . . . An untruth. A fabled myth.

Good God, it did not bear thinking of. Just as he was ready to accept marriage—even to welcome it— it was denied to him. She had said no.

Devon looked at Kat. It was then that he saw what his pain had not allowed him to see before: Kat was

•

crying. Not just a few droplets, either, but streaks of tears, trailing silently down her face. Her lip quivered, but no sound came out. Just a soft gasp of air as if she were drowning in her own sorrows.

Her pride, he realized. That was what was keeping them apart. It wasn't that she didn't love him at all.

Relief sang through his veins and he reached for one of his handkerchiefs, but Malcolm was quicker.

The Scotsman muttered a curse and dug a handkerchief from one of his pockets and then pressed the scrap of linen in his sister's hands. "Och, don't cry. If you feel that strongly about it, you don't have to marry St. John." He sent a hard glance at Devon. "Does she?"

Devon jaw tightened and his mind sprang into action. After a long moment, he shook his hand. "Actually, I believe she does have to marry me." His chest felt weighted, but he ignored it. If he did not say and do exactly the right thing in the next few moments, he stood to lose the love of his life. And that was what Katherine Macdonald was—the end and beginning of his life. He was just starting to realize that fact.

The real beauty of it was, he'd found his true love, his soul mate, and he hadn't needed the blasted ring at all. All he'd needed was to slow down enough to listen to his own heart. And his heart told him without question, without doubt, that Katherine Macdonald was the woman he'd been searching for for so long.

Life without her would be nothing but a long string of sad disappointments, missed laughter, and aching loneliness, and he'd already had enough of that to last a lifetime.

The problem was, though he was unwilling to face life without her, for some stubborn reason, she was all too willing to live life without him. Perhaps it was because she'd spent the years since her public humiliation telling herself she didn't want someone else, didn't need anyone else . . . but what she hadn't yet realized was that love wasn't about *needing* someone in your life. It was about *wanting* someone.

There was only one way he could fix it all—mend Kat's tattered reputation, quiet the gossips at Kilkairn Castle, and never again wonder if he could love someone forever.

Devon crossed his arms and rocked back on his heels. "Malcolm, I have been compromised and I demand satisfaction."

An explosive silence met this pronouncement. Devon didn't blame them; it was never something he'd ever thought to hear himself say.

Malcolm's brow lowered. "What are you saying, St. John?"

Devon turned to Kat. She sat still as a stone, hands tightly gripped in her lap, her cheeks pale. She'd managed to partially dry her eyes, Malcolm's handkerchief twisted between her fingers. "Kat, I hate to tell your brother our secrets, but 'tis necessary."

"Secrets?" She blinked up at him, her lashes spiked with wetness. "We have none."

"We've one or two. I just want you to know that 'tis necessary."

Her brow lowered and he could see she was trying to discern his meaning.

Meanwhile, he turned to Malcolm. "Prior to this, my reputation was spotless. Reparation must be made. I demand that Katherine Macdonald marry me."

Kat gasped. "You—but I—how could you—" She clamped her mouth closed and glared. "No," she said. "I will not do it."

"You must; you seduced me."

Malcolm's brows lowered. "Seduced? St. John, have a care what you're about."

"Your sister tempted me to run away and visit her," Devon said promptly.

Kat jumped to her feet. "I did no such thing!"

"Did you or did you not allow me into your bed-chamber through the window?"

Her cheeks red as could be, she snapped, "Yes, but only because I feared you'd fall from the tree."

"But . . . if she was inside her room, how could she tempt you?" Malcolm asked, apparently bewildered.

"She was walking around in a green silk night rail beside an open window that had a very strategically placed tree beside it. How could I help myself?"

"How indeed," Malcolm murmured, comprehension finally dawning on his face. Fiona started to say something, but he caught her hand and held it to him. "Devon, I suppose you blame Kat for the tree's existence, as well."

"I believe she planted it by her window for that very purpose."

"That tree is three hundred years old," Kat sputtered.

"Ah ha! So you admit that the seduction was planned in advance."

Malcolm stifled a laugh, and even Fiona smiled.

But Kat just glared. "I admit to nothing except allowing you into my room. That was my only fault."

"Well, now," Malcolm said. "This is far more serious than I thought. Kat Macdonald, you admit to allowing Mr. St. John into your bedroom at night."

"Only once."

Devon nodded, then added, "She also locked all her windows and doors so that the only way into the house was by climbing the tree. That is how devious she was. She had to know that a challenge like that would only inflame a man more."

Malcolm tsked. "He's right. Lass, what were you thinking?"

"You've always told me I should lock my doors!"

"And leave your window open with a tree right beside it?"

"Well no, but—"

"Malcolm, as you can see, your sister has led me down a dark path. And I, in my innocence, followed like a lamb to the slaughter."

A tremor of a smile touched Malcolm's mouth. "Well, Kat. What have you to say for yourself?"

Kat planted her hands on her hips. "I have nothing to say! Not a blooming thing! St. John, I will not let you get away with this. You were the one who wanted to come into my room. And you were the one who wanted to tie me up with scarves and kiss me and—"

"Scarves?" Malcolm looked stunned.

Devon just smiled.

"Who tied who up with scarves?" Malcolm demanded.

"Devon tied me up. He's the one who—" She stopped, her brow lowering as she stared at Devon. "Wait a moment. You tricked me. You tricked me into confessing about— Oh! I see what you were— You scoundrel!"

He blinked innocently. "Me?"

"You made those outrageous allegations because you wanted me to admit to—oh!"

Devon came to stand before her, a question in his gaze. "I'm sorry I tricked you, but I thought it would be best if Malcolm knew how things stood between us."

"Aye," Malcolm said. "There's no question in my mind, either. You'll marry this man, Katherine Macdonald or I'll see to it that ye nev—"

"No," Devon said, taking her hand in his own. "She has a choice. I don't want a forced bride any more than she wants a forced groom. But if she wants a *willing* groom, then here I am."

Fiona gave a murmur of approval.

Kat's throat grew tight. He knew her so well, knew her fears and her pride. "I don't know, Devon. I don't wish to be hurt again."

"Love, the only way you can never hurt again is to stop living. And not even you with your stubborn pride and seven scowling giants can do that."

Still holding her hand, he knelt before her. "Listen to me, Kat Macdonald. I want to marry you. It will stop the petty gossip that has so hurt you as well as give our sons a name. But if you cannot find it in your heart to come to me freely, then I will be content with whatever you allow. Even if I have to live in that tree beside your window until the winds blow me down, there I will go. I love you, Kat. I love you now and I will love you tomorrow and the day after that and the day after that. I will love you as long as you allow it."

Her heart filled and swelled and threatened to overflow. "Devon . . . how can you be so certain?"

"I always thought I fell in and out of love far too easily. Now I realize that until now, until I met you, I've never loved at all."

Kat couldn't speak. Every emotion she possessed had knotted in her throat. He loved her; she could see it in his eyes, in the way he held her hand so gently, as if afraid to hurt her. She could see it in the fact that he knelt before her so patient, so tender.

Malcolm sniffed and wiped his own eyes. "Och lassie, I think you're going to have to marry the man. 'Tis obvious he's daft about you. And if you don't, you'll regret it for the rest of your days."

He looked past Kat, his eyes meeting Fiona's. "So long as there is love, one can overcome anything."

Fiona took a hesitant step forward. "Malcolm? I—I want out of our wager."

"Out of it? But . . . my love, I believe I just won it."

"Yes, well, it was a stupid idea." Her lips quivered. "I don't know what I was thinking. I just feared that if we had a child, you would cease thinking of me as—" She bit her lip.

There was a moment of silence and then Malcolm held out his hand. "Come, love. We have let our pride do the talking for too long. It is time our hearts had some time together."

Fiona slowly put her hand in his, her eyes filled with tears. "But . . . what if we cannot agree on the things that have kept us apart?"

"Then we will learn to compromise." His gaze searched hers. "I thought winning was important. But now, like you, I am beginning to think there are times when losing can be more rewarding. Come, my love. We have a lot of talking to do, the two of us. And here is neither the place nor the time."

"Indeed," she said, laying her head on his shoulder and smiling mistily. "We really must return to the ballroom. 'Tis nearing midnight and soon it will be midnight. People will wish to claim their favors."

Malcolm turned to Devon. "May I announce that you are engaged?"

Devon looked at Kat. She took a deep breath. "I suppose we might as well." The flash of happiness in Devon's eyes warmed her heart.

Malcolm nodded his approval. "Excellent! We'll make the announcement once the cakes are gone." With that, he and Fiona walked out the door, hand in hand.

Devon pulled Kat into his arms. "See what persistence can do for a man? That's my one fault, you know. Persistence."

"One?" She quirked a brow at him.

"Aye," he said challengingly.

A faint quiver touched the corner of her mouth. "I

suppose everyone is allowed one." Kat's gaze dropped to where Devon's hand enveloped hers. "I have to know one thing."

"Yes, my love?"

"Will you promise on your life to always tell me the truth, even if you think it is something I might not want to hear?"

"Yes."

He hadn't even hesitated. That was good, wasn't it?

"I want a long engagement," she added.

"One month," he said promptly.

"One month? That's not long enough," she protested, though she had to laugh a little, too. It was flattering that he was so very, very eager.

"Kat, my love, trust me on this. A month will seem very long to both of us since I daresay your brother is even now looking for an ax to chop down that damnable tree." Devon captured her hand and placed a kiss on the back of her fingers. "A month may seem like a year under such circumstances."

Her fingers tingled where his mouth moved over her bared skin and she shivered. "You are right, as usual."

He grinned. "Mmmmm! I like the sound of that. Say it again."

"When you've earned it, and not before," she said, trying to be severe, though her grin would not stay contained. Smiling up at him, she traced a finger over the pocket of his waistcoat where the talisman ring was tucked. "You once said this was cursed."

"I was wrong. It was, and is, blessed." He took the ring from his pocket and slid it over her finger.

It rested there, warm and gleaming. This time, its effect was gentler, softer, but more lingering.

She ran a finger over the silvered runes. Perhaps that was a sign. A sign to open the cold, frozen doors of her heart and let in the sunshine, one gentle ray at time. A sign to let in Devon.

The warmth of the ring seemed to sense the change in her, for it began to tingle, running up her arm and into her heart.

She looked down at the ring. "I suppose I have no choice. The ring has decided."

Devon nuzzled her ear, a flare of delicate fire flickering over her. "I have decided. To hell with the blasted ring."

She peeped up at him through her lashes. "If I refused you, would you haunt me?"

"For the rest of my days."

"And make my life a living hell?"

Devon's lips quirked. "I wouldn't say that, precisely. I believe that parts of it would be very enjoyable indeed."

Kat laughed then, and it seemed that the ring warmed even more with the sound. "Yes, my dear. Parts of it would be very enjoyable indeed."

Epilogue

I love surprises. I love large ones. Small ones. Ones that come in boxes with bows. You simply cannot have too many surprises.

Mrs. Montesque-Drumme
to her daughter, Lady Mountjoy,
while playing cards at the Westons' rout

$\mathcal{A}$ short time later, Devon pulled Kat into his arms and danced with her around the ballroom at Kilkairn.

People were still whispering, but Kat no longer cared. "I cannot believe you wished to return here. Everyone is talking about us."

"They will be talking even more when your brother announces our betrothal." He held her a little tighter, his hips now brushing hers. "Meanwhile, let's give them something more . . . exciting to talk about."

"You are a very naughty man. I can see that I'll have my hands full trying to keep you from embarrassing me more than I've embarrassed myself."

"Which is yet another reason you love me." He sighed. "Gad, when I think of it, there are hundreds of reasons for you to love me! See why we should wed with all due haste?"

"You certainly think well of yourself."

He grinned. "I can't help it. The most beautiful woman in the room is dancing with me. I feel very superior when you're on my arm."

"Oh, if that's what causes it, then by all means, continue on." She began to say something more, when a sudden excitement began to rise in the crowd.

Voices raised in exclamation and everyone began pointing to the clock.

"Ah," Devon said. "The iced cakes. Come, my sweet. Let's see what jeweled favors we may find." He took her arm and led her forward, trying to find a way through the throng.

As they went, Kat looked up and saw Malcolm standing by the table. She lifted her arm to wave—and the clock began to chime.

There was an ebullient cry and a mad surge toward the table. Kat was knocked forward, her arm outstretched. Suddenly she and Devon were watching in twin dismay as the St. John talisman ring went flying, a silver circlet that flipped end over end, above the heads of the guests, only to drop squarely onto the table of cakes.

All around them pandemonium reigned. But for Devon and Kat, there was nothing but silence.

Kat looked up at Devon. "I-I don't know how that

happened. It fit so well; I really didn't think it was loose."

"I didn't, either. In fact, I thought it fit perfectly." He lifted up and tried to see the table and the general vicinity where the ring had landed.

He was just about to say something when he caught a glimpse of the ring sitting squarely on a small iced cake, one of the few left. As Devon looked, a slender feminine hand reached from the milling crowd and took the cake, ring and all.

And then it was gone.

Devon watched as the hundreds of guests thronged, laughing and talking, some holding their prizes above their heads, others discreetly tucking them away in reticules and pockets.

The talisman ring, so recently recovered, was gone.

Kat wrung her hands. "I cannot believe I lost it like that! What will your brother say? Isn't he supposed to receive it next?"

"Oh, I'm sure Marcus will be heartbroken." A faint smile touched Devon's mouth.

"Shouldn't we at least try to look for it?"

He shook his head. "I don't believe it would do any good. There are too many people and too many grabbing hands. Chances are, someone already has it tucked into their reticule."

"Reticule?"

"Oh yes," Devon said, smiling ear to ear. "Somewhere at this ball is the woman my brother Marcus is going to marry."

Kat looked impressed. "But . . . how will he find her? Or the ring?"

"I don't know if you've noticed or not, but when the ring wishes to be found, it is." Devon took his future bride's arm. "Meanwhile, let us talk of more important things. What do you think of an elopement? Something with a lengthy honeymoon on the continent. You may bring your lads with you, and we can gaze at stained glass to your heart's content."

"A trip abroad? Really? But . . . what about your brother? Won't he need help finding the ring? And his future bride?"

"Never fear, my dear. I'm certain *your* brother will give us a copy of the guest list for the ball. Marcus can begin there."

"But . . . there are over four hundred people here!"

"Then he had better get started quickly. He's almost forty, you know, and it is high time he found a wife. Perhaps it will liven him up some; he has gotten to be quite a tyrant of late. Meanwhile, you and I, my love, have some dancing to attend to." And with that, Devon swept his lovely bride-to-be onto the dance floor, though in the back of his mind, he was already composing the letter to his brother:

Dearest Marcus:

Life is oft full of ironies. This is one I'm sure you will enjoy . . .

What Every
Woman Knows . . .

Let's face it. No one wants to *admit* that they use their feminine wiles to catch a man . . . but the truth is we do! From the first moment he sees you in a sexy pair of high-heeled shoes to the moment he first glimpses you in your wedding gown, a man often doesn't know how much effort we've taken to dress to impress! And while blatantly trying to catch a guy is definitely a "don't," there are little touches that any woman can wear that will make a man take notice.

As for our Avon Romance heroines, they *all* know that a little bit can go a long, long way. And, sometimes, when the going gets tough, it's worth it to pull out all the stops.

Now let's take a peek as four intrepid heroines captivate the interest of the men of their dreams. . . .

Coming May 2004

Party Crashers
by Stephanie Bond

Jolie Goodman's life's a mess. Her boyfriend vanished months ago—with her car! She's broke and working in the Neiman Marcus shoe department, selling tantalizing but financially (for her!) out-of-reach footwear to the women whose credit cards aren't maxed out. And now, the police have come looking for her . . . thinking that she has something to do with her boyfriend's disappearance! But sometimes selling sexy shoes is just as enticing to men as wearing them.

Jolie glanced at the doorway leading back to the showroom, then to the fire exit door leading to a loading dock, weighing her options. She had the most outrageous urge to walk out . . . and keep walking.

Is that what Gary had done? Reached some kind of personal crisis that he couldn't share with her, and simply walked away from everything—his job, his friends, and her? As bad as it sounded, she almost preferred to believe that he had suffered some kind of breakdown rather than consider other possible explanations: he'd met with foul play or she had indeed been scammed by the man who'd professed to care about her.

The exit sign beckoned, but she glanced at the shoe box in her hands and decided that since the man had been kind enough to intercept Sammy, he deserved to be waited on, even if he didn't spend a cent.

Even if people with vulgar money made her nervous.

She fingercombed her hair and tucked it behind her ears, then straightened her clothing as best she could. There was no helping the lack of makeup, so she pasted on her best smile—the one that she thought showed too much gum, but that Gary had assured her made her face light up—and returned to the showroom.

Her smile almost faltered, though, when Mr. Beck Underwood's bemused expression landed on her.

She walked toward him, trying to forget that the man could buy and sell her a thousand times over. "I'm sorry again about running into you. Did you really want to try on this shoe or were you just being nice?"

"Both," he said mildly. "My sister is going to be a while, and I need shoes, so this works for me."

At the twinkle in his eyes, her tongue lodged at the roof of her mouth. Like a mime, she gestured to a nearby chair and made her feet follow him. As he sat she scanned the area for signs of Sammy.

"She's behind the insoles rack," he whispered.

Jolie flushed and made herself not look. The man probably thought she was clumsy *and* paranoid. She busied herself unpacking the expensive shoes. "Will you be needing a dress sock, sir?"

He slipped off his tennis shoe and wiggled bare brown toes. "I suppose so. I'm afraid I've gotten into the habit of not wearing socks." He smiled. "And my dad is 'sir.' I'm just Beck."

She suddenly felt small. And poor. "I . . . know who you are."

"Ah. Well, promise you won't hold it against me."

She smiled and retrieved a pair of tan-colored socks to match the loafers. When she started to slip one of the socks over his foot, he took it from her. "I can do it."

"I don't mind," she said quickly. Customers expected it— to be dressed and undressed and redressed if necessary. It was an unwritten rule: *No one leaves the store without being touched.*

"I don't have to be catered to," he said, his tone brittle.

Jolie blinked. "I'm sorry."

He looked contrite and shook his head. "Don't be—it's me." Then he grinned unexpectedly. "Besides, under more private circumstances, I might take you up on your offer."

Heat climbed her neck and cheeks—he was teasing her . . . his good deed for the day. Upon closer scrutiny, his face was even more interesting—his eyes a deep brown, bracketed by untanned lines created from squinting in the sun. Late thirties, she guessed. His skin was ruddy, his strong nose peeling from a recent burn. Despite the pale streaks in his hair, he was about as far from a beach boy as a man could be. When he leaned over to slip on the shoes, she caught a glimpse of his powerful torso beneath the sport coat.

She averted her gaze and concentrated on the stitched design on the vamp of the shoe he was trying on, handing him a shoehorn to protect the heel counter. (This morning Michael had given her an "anatomy of a shoe" lesson, complete with metal pointer and pop quiz.)

The man stood and hefted his weight from foot to foot, then took a couple of steps in one direction and came back. "I'll take them."

A salesperson's favorite words. She smiled. "That was fast."

He laughed. "Men don't have a complicated relationship with shoes."

Coming June 2004

And the Bride Wore Plaid

by Karen Hawkins

What is to be done with Kat Macdonald? This Scottish miss is deplorably independent, and unweddably wild. But while it's impossible to miss her undeniable beauty, it's also impossible to get Kat to act like a civilized lady. Still, even she cannot resist Devon St. John. A man born to wealth and privilege, he has no intention of ever settling down with one woman . . . until he meets Kat and realizes that his future wife will, indeed, proudly wear plaid.

Devon lifted a finger and traced the curve of her cheek, the touch bemusingly gentle. "You are a lush, tempting woman, my dear. And well you know it."

Kat's defenses trembled just the slightest bit. Bloody hell, how was she to fight her own treacherous body while the bounder—Devon something or another—tossed compliments at her with just enough sincerity to leave her breathless to hear more?

Of course, it was all practiced nonsense, she told herself firmly. She was anything but tempting. She looked well enough when she put some effort into it, but she was large and ungainly, and it was way too early in the morning for her to look anything other than pale. Her eyes were still heavy with sleep and she'd washed her hair last night and it had dried in a most unruly, puffy way that she absolutely detested. One side was definitely fuller than the other and it disturbed her no end. Even worse, she was wearing one of her work gowns of plain gray wool, one that was far too tight about the shoulders and too loose about the waist. Thus, she was able to meet his gaze and say firmly, "I am not tempting."

"I'd call you tempting and more," Devon said with refreshing promptness. "Your eyes shimmer rich and green. Your hair is the color of the morning sky just as the sun touches it, red and gold at the same time. And the rest of you—" His gaze traveled over her until her cheeks burned. "The rest of you is—"

"That's enough of that," she said hastily. "You're full of moonlight and shadows, you are."

"I don't know anything about moonlight and shadows. I only know you are a gorgeous, lush armful."

"In this?" She looked down at her faded gown with incredulity. "You'd call this gorgeous or lush?"

His gaze touched on her gown, lingering on her breasts. "Oh yes. If you want to go unnoticed, you'll have to bind those breasts of yours."

She choked.

He grinned. "And add some padding of some sort in some other areas."

"I don't know what you're talking about, but please let me up—"

"I was talking about padding. Perhaps if you bundled yourself about the hips until you looked plumper, then you wouldn't have to deal with louts such as myself attempting to kiss you at every turn."

She caught the humor sparkling in his eyes and it disarmed her, even as the thought of adding padding to her hips made her chest tickle as a laugh began to form.

"Furthermore," he continued as if he'd never paused, "you will need to hide those eyes of yours and perhaps wear a turban, if you want men like me to stop noticing you."

"Humph. I'll remember that the next time I run into you or any other of Strathmore's lecherous cronies. Now, if you'll let me go, I have things to do."

His eyes twinkled even more. "And if I refuse?"

"Then I will have to deal with you, myself."

"Oh-oh! A woman of spirit. I like that."

"Oh-oh," she returned sharply, "a man who does not prize his appendages."

That comment was meant to wither him on the vine. Instead he chuckled, the sound rich and deep. "Sweet, I prize my appendage, although it should be *your* job to admire it."

"I have no wish for such a job, thank you very much."

"Oh, but if you did, it would then be my job to wield that appendage in such a way as to rouse that admiration to a vocal level." Devon leaned forward and murmured in her ear, "You have a delicious moan, my sweet. I heard it when we kissed."

Her cheeks burned. "The only vocal rousing you're going to get from me is a scream for help."

A bit of the humor left his gaze and he said with apparent seriousness, "I would give my life trying to earn that moan yet again. Would you deny me that?"

Coming July 2004

I'm No Angel

by Patti Berg

Palm Beach's sexiest investigator, Angel Devlin, knows that a tight skirt, a hint of cleavage, and some sky high heels will usually help her get every kind of information out of any type of man. But millionaire bad boy Tom Donovan has something up his custom-made shirt sleeve, and even though Angel is using every trick she knows, it's proving far more difficult than usual to get what she wants.

Tom grinned wickedly. "I caught you."

"But you didn't come after me."

"I hoped you'd come back."

"Why? So you could personally haul me off to jail?"

Tom shook his head. "Because I liked the feel of your hands on my chest and your lips on my cheek. If I hauled you off to jail we'd end up enemies. The fact that you came back means there's a chance for more."

"You know nothing about me but my name." *And the feel of my body,* Angel thought, just barely hanging on to her composure as Tom's hands glided down the curve of her spine, then flared over the sides of her waist and settled on her hips. "Why would you want more?"

"I paid Jorge for a lot more information than just your name," he said. "I know you're a private investigator and that you cater to the ultra-rich. I know that your office-slash-home is right here on Worth Avenue in a building you share with Ma Petite Bow-Wow, the local pamper-your-pooch shop. And if Jorge knows what he's talking about, you're thirty years old, five feet eight inches tall, weigh one thirty-two—"

"Thirty-one dripping wet."

Tom grinned, his laughing gaze locking onto hers. "Should we get naked and dripping wet and weigh each other?"

"Not tonight."

"It's close to midnight. It'll soon be tomorrow."

"Are you always in such a rush to get naked and dripping wet?"

He shrugged lightly. "Depends on the woman."

"Trust me, I'm the wrong woman."

"I disagree."

The music picked up tempo and so did Tom's moves. He spun around with Angel captured in his arms, the heat of his embrace, the closeness of their cheeks, and the scent of his spicy aftershave overwhelming her, making her dizzy.

And then he slowed again. His heart beat against her breasts. Warm breath whispered against her ear. "From what Jorge told me—that you wear Donna Karan's Cashmere Mist and Manolo Blahniks if you can get them on sale—you could easily be the right woman. Of course, there's also the fact that you're soft in all the right places. And going back to your original question, *that*, Angel, is why I want more of you."

Angel laughed lightly. "Jorge was a virtual font of information."

"I figured the soft-in-all-the-right-places part out for myself," Tom said, his hands drifting slowly from her waist to her bottom.

She leaned back slightly and gave him the evil eye. "Excuse me, but we don't know each other well enough for you to touch me where you're touching me."

A grin escaped his perfect lips. It sparkled in his eyes and made the dimple at the side of his mouth deepen as his fingers began to slide again, but not up to her waist. Oh, no, lascivious Tom Donovan's fingers slithered down to her thighs.

That was the first really big mistake he'd made since he'd chosen to follow her.

His fingers stilled, his eyes narrowed, and she knew he'd found the one thing she didn't want anyone to find.

Again his hand began to move, to explore, gliding up and down, over and around the not-so-little-lump on her right thigh. His eyes focused even more as his gaze held hers and locked. "That wouldn't be what I think it is, would it?"

Angel smiled slowly. Wickedly. At last, she again had the upper hand. "If you think it's a slim but extremely sharp stainless steel stiletto that could carve out a man's Adam's apple in the blink of an eye, you've guessed right."

One of Tom's dark, bedeviled eyebrows rose. "I never would have expected a sweet thing like you to carry a stiletto."

"That, Mr. Donovan, just goes to show that you really don't know as much about me as you think you do."

Coming August 2004

A Perfect Bride
by Samantha James

Sometimes expensive clothes and shoes aren't what does the trick . . . occasionally, men simply can't resist the power of a damsel in distress . . . an ugly duckling who unexpectedly turns into a gorgeous swan. When Sebastian Sterling rescues Devon, a wounded tavern maid, he thinks she's a thief—or worse. But underneath her tattered clothes is a woman of astonishing beauty and pride, who he quickly discovers could become his perfect bride.

Jimmy pointed a finger. "My lord, there be a body in the street!"

No doubt whoever it was had had too much to drink. Sebastian very nearly advised his man to simply move it and drive on.

But something stopped him. His gaze narrowed. Perhaps it was the way the "body," as Jimmy called it, lay sprawled against the uneven brick, beneath the folds of the cloak that all but enshrouded what looked to be a surprisingly small form. His booted heels rapped sharply on the brick as he leaped down and strode forward with purposeful steps. Jimmy remained where he was in the seat, looking around with wary eyes, as if he feared they would be set upon by thieves and minions at any moment.

Hardly an unlikely possibility, Sebastian conceded silently.

Sebastian crouched down beside her, his mind working. She was filthy and bedraggled. A whore who'd imbibed too heavily? Or perhaps it was a trick, a ruse to bring him in close, so she could snatch his pocketbook.

Guardedly he shook her, drawing his hand back, quickly. Damn. He'd left his gloves on the seat in the carriage. Ah, well, too late now.

"Mistress!" he said loudly. "Mistress, wake up!"

She remained motionless.

An odd sensation washed over him. His wariness vanished. His gaze slid sharply to his hand. The tips of his fingers were wet, but it was not the wetness of rain, he realized. This was dark and sticky and thick.

He inhaled sharply. "Christ!" he swore. He moved without conscious volition, swiftly easing her to her side so he could see her. "Mistress," he said urgently, "can you hear me?"

She moved a little, groaning as she raised her head. Sebastian's heart leaped. She was groggy but alive!

Between the darkness and the ridiculously oversized covering he supposed must pass for a bonnet, he couldn't see much of her face. Yet he knew the precise moment awareness set in. When her eyes opened and she spied him bending over her, she cringed and gave a great start. "Don't move," he said quickly. "Don't be frightened."

Her lips parted. Her eyes moved over his features in what seemed a never-ending moment. Then she gave a tiny shake of her head. "You're lost," she whispered, sounding almost mournful, "aren't you?"

Sebastian blinked. He didn't know quite what he'd expected her to say—certainly not *that*.

"Of course I'm not lost."

"Then I must be dreaming." To his utter shock, a small hand came out to touch the center of his lip. "Because no man in the world could possibly be as handsome as you."

An unlikely smile curled his mouth. "You haven't seen my brother," he started to say. He didn't finish, however. All at once the girl's eyes fluttered shut. Sebastian caught her head before it hit the uneven brick. In the next instant he surged to his feet and whirled, the girl in his arms.

"Jimmy!" he bellowed.

But Jimmy had already ascertained his needs. "Here, my lord." The steps were down, the carriage door wide open.

Sebastian clambered inside, laying the girl on the seat. Jimmy peered within. "Where to, my lord?"

Sebastian glanced down at the girl's still figure. Christ, she needed a physician. He thought of Dr. Winslow, the family physician, only to recall that Winslow had retired to the country late last year. And there was hardly time to scour the city in search of another . . .

"Home," he ordered grimly. "And hurry, Jimmy."

A Heavenly Offer!

USA Today bestselling author of
And Then He Kissed Me

PATTI
BERG
I'm No Angel

"Sexy, flirty fun!" —Susan Andersen

Private Investigator Angel Devlin admits that she's no angel and likes to play by her own rules. At the top of her Most Wanted list is bad boy millionaire Tom Donovan. But, as she will soon find out, Tom has a few tricks of his own. When the two worlds come together, the result is a wildly funny, sexy love tango. As Angel comes up with a plan to get her man, she will prove that 'good girls' aren't the only ones who get to *heaven*.

Buy and enjoy *I'M NO ANGEL* (Available June 29, 2004), then send the coupon below along with your proof of purchase for *I'M NO ANGEL* to Avon Books, and we'll send you a check for $2.00.

- -

Mail receipt and coupon for *I'M NO ANGEL* (0-06-054476-7) to:
AVON BOOKS/HarperCollinsPublishers Inc.
P.O. Box 767, Dresden, TN 38225

NAME

ADDRESS

CITY

STATE/ZIP

*Offer valid only for residents of the United States and Canada. Offer expires 10/1/04.

INA 0604

Experience the magic of
New York Times bestselling author

VICTORIA ALEXANDER

HER HIGHNESS, MY WIFE
0-06-000144-5•$6.99 US•$9.99 Can
Lord Matthew Weston is determined to tame the
green-eyed beauty he impetuously married, and change
Tatiana from a perfect princess to his passionate bride.

LOVE WITH A PROPER HUSBAND
0-06-000145-3•$6.99 US•$9.99 Can
Well educated but penniless, Miss Gwendolyn Townsend
is shocked when it's discovered a match has been
made between her and the Earl of Pennington.

THE LADY IN QUESTION
0-06-051761-1•$6.99 US•$9.99 Can
Identical twins, sensible Delia and mischievous
Cassandra Effington were the most delicious debutantes
to ever waltz across a London ballroom. No one ever
expected Delia to be the one to get into trouble . . .

THE PURSUIT OF MARRIAGE
0-06-051762-X•$6.99 US•$9.99 Can
Delicious debutante Cassandra Effington wagers
the Viscount Berkley that she can find him an ideal
bride before *he* finds her the perfect match.

www.AuthorTracker.com

Available wherever books are sold   VA 0304
or please call 1-800-331-3761 to order.

The seductive allure of *USA Today*
bestselling author

KAREN HAWKINS

and her devilishly charming St. John brothers

AN AFFAIR TO REMEMBER
0-380-82079-X•$5.99 US•$7.99 Can

The Earl of Greyley is desperate for a governess who can deal with
five unruly orphans. But the only person capable of handling the
adorable little terrors is the one woman he cannot abide.

CONFESSIONS OF A SCOUNDREL
0-380-82080-3•$5.99 US•$7.99 Can

Brandon St. John suspects the lovely Lady Verena
Westforth of hiding a valuable missive. With a sensuous
kiss and a passionate caress he intends to lower Verena's
guard and find the item in question.

HOW TO TREAT A LADY
0-06-051405-1•$5.99 US•$7.99 Can

To save her family from ruin, Harriet Ward invented a wealthy
fiance. But now the bank wants proof of the man's existence.

AND THE BRIDE WORE PLAID
0-06-051408-6•$6.99 US•$9.99 Can

Devon St. John has found the St. John Talisman Ring which
curses the holder by clasping a wedding band on his finger
when he least expects it. Devon vows he will never give up his
beloved freedom—even when a temptress's impulsive kiss casts
a tantalizing spell . . .

Available wherever books are sold
or please call 1-800-331-3761 to order.

AuthorTracker
www.AuthorTracker.com

HAW 0604

Delightful romance from
USA Today **bestselling author**

KAREN HAWKINS

THE ABDUCTION OF JULIA
0-380-81071-9•$5.99 US•$7.99 Can

Julia Frant has secretly loved Alec MacLean, the wild
Viscount Hunterston from afar. So when he accidentally
snatches her instead of her lovely, scheming cousin for an
elopement to Gretna Green, Julia leaps at the chance to
make her passionate dreams come true.

A BELATED BRIDE
0-380-81525-7•$5.99 US•$7.99 Can

When Arabella Hadley finds an unconscious man on her
deserted country road and sees that it's Lucien Devereaux,
the handsome, dissolute Duke of Wexford—a man who
broke her innocent heart years ago, she's tempted to leave
him there.

THE SEDUCTION OF SARA
0-380-81526-5•$5.99 US•$7.99 Can

Lady Sara Carrington chooses the Earl of Bridgeton,
England's most notorious rake to teach her how to seduce a
man. But when "demonstration" kisses become burningly
real, it's clear that Sara is using those lessons to catch *him*!

Available wherever books are sold
or please call 1-800-331-3761 to order.

AuthorTracker
www.AuthorTracker.com

HAW1 0504

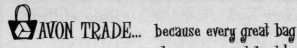

AVON TRADE... because every great bag deserves a great book!

SARAH WEBB

Always the BRIDESMAID
A Novel

Paperback $13.95
ISBN 0-06-057166-7

BABE IN TOYLAND

eugenia o riley o olson

Paperback $13.95
($21.95 Can.)
ISBN 0-06-057056-3

Miranda Blue Calling

a novel by Michelle Curry Wright

Paperback $13.95
($21.95 Can.)
ISBN 0-06-056143-2

CAROLE MATTHEWS

THE Sweetest TABOO

Paperback $10.95
ISBN 0-06-059562-0

Temporary Insanity
a novel

LESLIE CARROLL

Paperback $13.95
($21.95 Can.)
ISBN 0-06-056337-0

Elegance
KATHLEEN TESSARO

True love never goes out of style

Paperback $10.95
ISBN 0-06-052227-5

Don't miss the next book by your favorite author.
Sign up for AuthorTracker by visiting *www.AuthorTracker.com*.

Available wherever books are sold, or call 1-800-331-3761 to order.

ATP 0604

New York Times **bestselling author**

STEPHANIE LAURENS

Don't miss the delectable romantic intrigue devised within
the walls of the Bastion Club, an elite society of gentlemen
dedicated to determining their own futures when it comes
to that most important step of all—marriage.

AVAILABLE NOW

The Lady Chosen

0-06-000206-9/$7.99 US/$10.99 Can

Tristan Wemyss, Earl of Trentham, never expected he'd need
to wed within a year or forfeit his inheritance. Unfortunately,
matrimony is the last thing on the mind of the
enchanting beauty living next door.

A Gentleman's Honor

0-06-000207-7/$7.99 US/$10.99 Can

The second member of the Bastion Club, Anthony Blake,
Viscount Torrington, is a target for every matchmaking mama
in London. None of their flighty daughters can fix
his interest. But a certain lady does . . .

Look for the next Bastion Club novel in Fall 2004!

(((•))) **AuthorTracker**

Don't miss the next book by your favorite author.
Sign up now for AuthorTracker by visiting
www.AuthorTracker.com

Available wherever books are sold
or please call 1-800-331-3761 to order.

LAUA 1203

PELICAN BOOKS

THE BEGINNINGS OF
ENGLISH SOCIETY

Dorothy Whitelock was educated at the Leeds Girls'
High School and at Newnham College, Cambridge,
where she read for the English Tripos. After six years
of research work, in Cambridge and at the University
of Uppsala, she became in 1930 Lecturer, and later
Fellow and Tutor in English language, and Vice-
Principal, at St Hilda's College, Oxford. She was
Elrington and Bosworth Professor of Anglo-Saxon
in the University of Cambridge from 1957 to 1969.
She is an Honorary Fellow of Newnham College,
Cambridge, and of St Hilda's College, Oxford. She
is President of the English Place-Name Society.
Published works include *Anglo-Saxon Wills*, *Sermo
Lupi ad Anglos*, *The Audience of Beowulf*, *English His-
torical Documents c. 500–1042*, *Changing Currents in
Anglo-Saxon Studies* (inaugural lecture), *The Anglo-
Saxon Chronicle: A Revised Translation*, and *Sweet's
Anglo-Saxon Reader*, 15th edition.

THE PELICAN HISTORY OF ENGLAND

1. Roman Britain
IAN RICHMOND

2. The Beginnings of English Society
(From the Anglo-Saxon Invasion)
DOROTHY WHITELOCK

3. English Society in the Early Middle Ages
DORIS MARY STENTON

4. England in the Late Middle Ages
A. R. MYERS

5. Tudor England
S. T. BINDOFF

6. England in the Seventeenth Century
MAURICE ASHLEY

7. England in the Eighteenth Century
J. H. PLUMB

8. England in the Nineteenth Century (1815–1914)
DAVID THOMSON

9. England in the Twentieth Century (1914–63)
DAVID THOMSON

DOROTHY WHITELOCK

THE BEGINNINGS OF
ENGLISH SOCIETY

PENGUIN BOOKS

Penguin Books Ltd, Harmondsworth, Middlesex, England
Penguin Books, 625 Madison Avenue, New York, New York 10022, U.S.A.
Penguin Books Australia Ltd, Ringwood, Victoria, Australia
Penguin Books Canada Ltd, 2801 John Street, Markham, Ontario, Canada L3R 1B4
Penguin Books (N.Z.) Ltd, 182-190 Wairau Road, Auckland 10, New Zealand

—

First published 1952
Second edition 1954
Reprinted 1956, 1959, 1962, 1963
Reprinted with revisions 1965, 1966, 1968
Reprinted 1971
Reprinted with revisions 1972, 1974
Reprinted 1976, 1977, 1979

—

Copyright 1952 by Dorothy Whitelock
Copyright © Dorothy Whitelock, 1954
All rights reserved

—

Made and printed in Great Britain by
Hunt Barnard Printing Ltd, Aylesbury
Set in Monotype Baskerville

Except in the United States of America,
this book is sold subject to the condition
that it shall not, by way of trade or otherwise,
be lent, re-sold, hired out, or otherwise circulated
without the publisher's prior consent in any form of
binding or cover other than that in which it is
published and without a similar condition
including this condition being imposed
on the subsequent purchaser

CONTENTS

	PREFACE	7
I	THE HEATHEN ENGLISH	11
II	THE BONDS OF SOCIETY	29
	Loyalty to one's Lord	
	Duty to one's Kin	
III	THE KING AND HIS COURT	48
IV	FINANCE AND ADMINISTRATION	64
	Finance	
	Royal Officials	
V	THE CLASSES OF SOCIETY	83
	The Nobleman	
	The Churl	
	The Slave	
VI	TRADE AND TOWN LIFE	115
	Trade	
	Towns	
VII	THE LAW	134
VIII	THE CHURCH	155
IX	EDUCATION AND LATIN SCHOLAR-SHIP	189
X	VERNACULAR LITERATURE	204
XI	ANGLO-SAXON ART	223
XII	CONCLUSION	241
	SELECT BIBLIOGRAPHY	244
	INDEX	249

PREFACE

THIS book does not set out to give an account of Anglo-Saxon political history, but to assemble from various sources what can be learnt about the ways of life of the English between their settlement in Britain in the middle of the fifth century and their conquest by the Normans in 1066. It examines the principles of society brought from their continental homes, and how these developed in the new land. It deals with the modifications which Christianity introduced and the art and literature which it inspired. A detailed knowledge of political events, of dates, or of kingdoms and kings, etc., is not necessary for the understanding of these chapters. It is enough that the reader should know that Christianity first reached the English in 597 and within a century had spread over the whole country; and that the period can be divided into two, a pre-Viking period, when England consisted of several small kingdoms, and a post-Viking period, when the kings of Wessex were the only English rulers. The Viking raids began with a few isolated attacks at the very end of the eighth century, and became a serious menace between 835 and 878, the year in which Alfred's victory at Edington prevented the extinction of Christian culture in England. By this date the Danes had already begun the settlement of East Anglia, Northumbria, and the North-East Midlands. By 954 these areas had all been recovered for the English crown by Alfred's son and grandsons, but they retained many signs of Scandinavian influence in their language, their place-names and personal names, their administrative divisions and assessment, their law and social customs. A period of peace in the middle of the tenth century, in which took place a great monastic reform and revival of learning, was followed by renewed Danish attacks from 980, which continued throughout the reign of Ethelred the Unready and culminated in the conquest by Cnut. Danish kings, Cnut and his sons, reigned from 1016 to 1042, when the English line was restored in the person of Edward the Confessor. The reader who desires detailed information on these matters is referred to Sir Frank Stenton's *Anglo-Saxon England*, a work to which this present book is deeply indebted.

A few terms used in this book will require explanation. While the names Kent, Essex, Sussex, East Anglia, will occasion no difficulty, it should be noted that Northumbria describes all the lands in English hands north of the Humber, reaching, at the period of their greatest extent, at least as far as the Forth on the north, and to the Irish Sea on the west; that Mercia was in the days of settlement a western outpost in the valleys of the Upper and Middle Trent and its tributaries the Tame and Dove, but, as its kings conquered their neighbours one by one – among them the Middle Angles to the south-east, the *Hwicce* of the Severn valley, the *Magonsæte* about Hereford, the dwellers round the Wrekin – the term Mercia comes to be employed to denote an enormous kingdom bounded by the Humber and the Thames, the Welsh Border and the East Anglian frontier, and from the eighth century it includes London; and that Wessex similarly developed from small beginnings, in Hampshire, Wiltshire, and the Upper Thames valley, until it denotes the southern counties from Surrey to the Bristol Channel and the Cornish border.

Wherever possible, Anglo-Saxon terms have been given modern equivalents; but this is impossible with certain weights and measures. We do not know the capacity of a 'sester' or an 'amber'; a 'mancus' was a weight of gold of about 70 grains, and was considered equivalent to thirty silver pence; a 'mark' was a Danish weight made up of eight 'ores', and there were two systems current in relating it to the native coinage, for we find on some occasions 20 pence reckoned to an 'ore' of silver, and on others 16; the shilling referred to in our records is not usually a coin, but merely a unit of count, denoting 20 pence in early Kent, fourpence in Mercia and early Wessex, fivepence in Wessex in later times; a pound, then as now, contained 240 pence. But all references to money are misleading unless one bears in mind the high purchasing power of the Anglo-Saxon penny (a silver coin), and it is well to remember that 30 pence was the legal price of an ox, fourpence or fivepence that of a sheep. All other terms used in this volume are explained on their first occurrence, except that the nature of the office of an 'ealdorman', the king's highest official, is not discussed until pp. 77–80. In spite of the loss of consistency, I give personal names which are still in use, and those of kings, in their familiar, instead of their Anglo-Saxon form. I retain the well-known nickname 'the Unready', though I should prefer to render it 'of Evil Counsel', or perhaps 'the Treacherous'.

All workers in this field of study must alternate between thankfulness that so much information from so early a period has survived, and irritation that it is so unevenly distributed, whether as regards period, or locality, or subject. It might have been possible to fill up some of the gaps by imaginative surmise, but I have preferred to restrict myself to what the surviving evidence states or implies.

While it would be impossible to enumerate in brief space all the scholars whose work has been utilized in this book, I should like to take this opportunity of recording my debt to that great scholar the late Professor H. M. Chadwick, who first aroused my interest in the Anglo-Saxons and to whose careful training I owe more than can be expressed; and I wish to thank Professor Bruce Dickins for his constant help and encouragement, and Sir Frank Stenton, whose reading of this book in manuscript was only a final service to a work which his interest over many years has brought into being.

CHAPTER I

THE HEATHEN ENGLISH

ENGLISHMEN in Anglo-Saxon times were aware of the Germanic origin of their race, and most educated men after the first half of the eighth century could probably have added that their forefathers came of three of the bravest nations of Germany, the Angles, the Saxons, and the Jutes, and first landed in the romanized province of Britain in the year 449. They would have derived this knowledge, directly or indirectly, from the writings of the great historian, Bede, whose most famous work, his *Ecclesiastical History of the English Nation*, which he finished in 731, contains a chapter on the origin of his race much used by later writers. It matters little for our present purpose that when chroniclers liked to calculate the number of years that had elapsed since 'the Coming of the English' their choice of 449 as the date of this event went beyond the original statement of Bede; or that the conflicting evidence of our early sources of information makes it impossible to assign a precise year to the beginning of the English settlement in Britain. Neither need we worry overmuch whether Bede's attempted reconciliation of this tradition of threefold origin with the political divisions of his own day can be accepted as accurate in every detail. Slightly older Northumbrian writers do not observe Bede's racial distinctions, but call their own people Saxons, though the Northumbrians are Angles according to Bede. Even Bede himself does not keep during the rest of his work to the division laid down in this one chapter. Although there is enough supporting evidence to show that Bede's division had some basis of fact, it is difficult to avoid the impression that by his day these differences of origin were no longer felt to be important. St Boniface was not excluding Saxons and Jutes when in 738 he addressed a letter to 'all God-fearing Catholics sprung from the race and stock of the Angles', but meant all the inhabitants of England, and King Alfred, a Saxon, uses the term 'Angle-race' in just this sense, and consistently calls his native language English, not Saxon. (In this book, the term English is used to refer to all the Teutonic races in Britain, no matter what their origin, and to their common language.)

What is interesting is that the invaders remained so conscious of their Germanic origin. Bede's older contemporary, St Aldhelm, uses 'our stock' and 'the Germanic race' as parallel expressions, and St Boniface was probably as yet unfamiliar with Bede's historical work when he wrote home from Germany in 738 asking for support for a projected mission to the continental Saxons: 'Have pity on them, because even they themselves are wont to say: "We are of one blood and one bone".' In fact, this strong sense of kinship with the Germanic tribes on the Continent led the Anglo-Saxons to attempt their conversion even before the last strongholds of heathenism in England had fallen. From the remains of their secular poetry we can see that they took an interest in the early history and traditions of all the Germanic peoples, as in their own.

Bede brings the Saxons from the country held in his own day by the 'Old Saxons', that is, the region of the lower Elbe, the Angles from Angeln, on the neck of the Cimbric peninsula, the Jutes, by implication, from the land north of this, now called Jutland. King Alfred (871–99) was familiar with this tradition, for he says 'in those lands dwelt the English before they came hither' after he has mentioned Jutland, *Sillende* and many islands as lying to starboard when the traveller Ohthere sailed down the Cattegat from Norway to Schleswig. It has sometimes been questioned whether Bede was correct in placing the homeland of the Jutes where he does, for the archaeology and institutions of Kent, where the Jutes settled, have affinities, not with Jutland, but with the Frankish territory by the Rhine. Agreement has not been reached regarding the implications of this fact. However, it remains unchallenged that the majority of the invaders of Britain came from North Germany and the Jutish peninsula. The Jutes spoke a language closely related to that of the Saxons and Angles but also akin to Frisian; even if they did come from the Rhineland, they would still come from a Germanic district, though from one more exposed to influences from the Roman empire.

*

It is not necessary to suppose that even in their remoter homes the invaders were entirely unfamiliar with Roman culture. Articles of Roman make found their way to the Baltic shores by trade, and also as loot, for already in the late third century Saxon pirates had become such a menace to the Channel and North Sea coasts that the Romans built a series of forts from the Wash to the Isle of Wight, which were known as the forts of the Saxon Shore. Saxon raiders appear to have penetrated far inland in 429, but the 'Coming of the Saxons', often referred to in later Anglo-Saxon writers, differed from such raids in that it was the beginning of a settlement, at first, if we may accept an early tradition, by peaceful agreement as allies, though a subsequent revolt led to the conquest of the eastern part of the island. Reinforced by a continual stream of immigrants, the invaders pressed further and further west, until eventually they held almost the whole of what is now England, the east of Scotland at least as far north as the Forth, and the Solway Plain.

The newcomers came to a land that differed much
from the England of to-day. It was heavily forested, with
great stretches of continuous woodland, such as the
forests of Selwood, Wychwood, Savernake, Wyre, Arden,
Sherwood, Epping, Kinver, Morfe, the Chilterns, and
the Weald, all far more extensive than their modern
remnants. The Weald stretched from Hampshire to
Kent, 120 miles long and 30 broad, according to a late
ninth-century writer. The amount of available arable
land was reduced also by the presence of large areas of
marshland, not only in the eastern counties; Romney
Marsh was undrained, and there was a great expanse of
fenland in Somerset from the Mendips almost to Taun-
ton. The areas under cultivation were on the whole small,
surrounded by woodland and waste; but there was an
exception to this: contrary to modern conditions, the
chalk and oolite plateaux, such as Salisbury Plain, the
Berkshire Downs, and the North Downs, were cultivated
as arable. The river valleys in these areas were deserted
until the English cleared and cultivated the heavy soils
of the lowland valleys. The view that this was because
they used a heavy plough previously known only in the
areas of Roman Britain where Belgic tribes had settled is
no longer generally held.

The land was crossed by a network of Roman roads,
connecting the cities and military stations with one
another, and with the defences like the great Wall and
the forts of the Saxon Shore. Yet it was no flourishing
Roman civilization that the invaders found. Long before
the Romans withdrew their forces in 410 urban life in
Britain had begun to decay. According to Collingwood,
it had always been from the economic point of view a
luxury, with a political and cultural function. The population in the cities had shrunk and the buildings were
falling into disrepair. Few of the villas, which in many

areas formed the basis of Romano-British rural economy, had survived the barbarian raids of 368, and subsequent raids had wrought further destruction. The centralized Roman administration had broken down, and petty rulers of native race had established control over areas of varying extent, though, from time to time, one of them may have exercised some sort of overlordship over his fellows. It was one of these, known already to Bede as Vortigern, who invited Saxon allies to settle in the east of the land.

It is not, therefore, greatly to be wondered at that in general the earliest English settlements were not closely related to the Roman road system planned to meet the needs of a centralized administration which was no longer in existence. Left unrepaired, many of these roads would rapidly become unusable over long stretches, though the more important of them were brought back into use as the necessity for intercourse between the settlements increased. Nor did the invaders take naturally to town life. Some Roman cities, Silchester, Caister-next-Norwich, *Viroconium*, Verulam, for example, were never re-occupied, others not immediately. Cambridge was derelict in Bede's day. Even in places where continuous occupation seems likely, important centres like London, York, and Lincoln, the English settlement grew up beside, and not in, the Romano-British town. After all, a population unaccustomed to city life, not possessing a system of economy that enforced centralization of population, would hardly choose to inhabit decaying stone buildings which they did not know how to repair. They themselves were accustomed to build only in timber, or lath and plaster, and it seems clear that they did not retain the services of Britons skilled in masonry, if indeed any such existed by the time of the invasion. After the conversion of the English to Christianity, the early church builders always found it necessary to import masons from abroad. These sometimes re-used Roman masonry for their work; but at the time of the settlement, the invaders could have had little use for buildings whose amenities they did not know how to enjoy.

Nevertheless, even in their partly derelict condition, the monuments of Roman civilization were impressive enough to people unaccustomed to stone buildings, paved roads, and massive ramparts. Small wonder that they called these things 'the work of giants' in their poetry, as, for example, in a gnomic poem prefixed to one manuscript of the Anglo-Saxon Chronicle:

Cities are visible from afar, the cunning work of giants, the wondrous fortifications in stone which are on this earth.

In later days, there was a tendency to build monasteries in disused Roman forts, as at Reculver, *Othona*, Dover, and probably at Coldingham. The Irishman Fursey was given a deserted Roman fortress, probably Burgh Castle, Suffolk, in which to found a monastery. This practice may be accounted for on practical considerations – the protection afforded by the existing walls, the supply of masonry ready to hand – yet one wonders whether any feeling was involved that the continual prayers of men and women devoted to God would put to flight supernatural powers that might inhabit these places.

Educated men like Bede looked with admiration on the remains of the Roman period. He mentions the cities, temples, bridges, and paved roads surviving to his own day. The anonymous writer of the earliest life of St Cuthbert, in telling how the saint saw by second sight the defeat of the Northumbrian forces at *Nechtansmere* in 685, says it was while he and others 'were looking at the wall of the city (Carlisle) and the fountain in it formerly built by the Romans in a wonderful fashion, as

Waga, the reeve of the city, who was conducting them, explained.'

To the Christian Anglo-Saxon poets, these tangible signs of the decay of a civilization more magnificent than their own provided an opportunity for moralizing on the theme of the transience of earthly splendour:

Thus the Creator of men laid waste this habitation, until, deprived of the revelry of the citizens, the old works of the giants stood desolate.

We cannot guess which of the deserted cities gave rise to this poem, but there is another, with a reference to hot springs, which is believed to refer to Bath. The poet's imagination peopled it in the past with men 'glad at heart and bright with gold, adorned resplendently, proud and flushed with wine; they shone in their war-gear; they gazed on treasure, on silver, on cunning gems, on riches, on possessions, on precious stones, on this bright citadel of a spacious kingdom.' All this was changed by 'the mighty fate'.

It is possible that the stone remains of the Roman period did more than inspire the first settlers with super-stitious awe and the Christian moralists with a fruitful theme. It has been suggested that Roman sculptured remains in the north of England formed the inspiration of a school of Christian sculptors, who produced figure sculpture of outstanding merit in the late seventh and eighth centuries, a time when no other part of Europe was producing sculpture in the round.

*

The monuments of Roman Britain remained to impress the invaders. What happened to the native population? Few scholars would now maintain that they were com-pletely massacred or driven out, even from the earliest areas of settlement. More and more, archaeologists are recognizing Romano-British influence on objects found in Saxon cemeteries. In the later settlements, in the West, we find Welsh inhabitants far above the condition of serfdom. A British strain in the personal names of the Anglo-Saxons, especially visible in Northumbria, is witness to a small amount of intermarriage. Yet it would be grossly inaccurate to visualize the invaders as a mere military aristocracy over a large subject population of native origin. The Anglo-Saxon word for a Briton came to be used as a common noun denoting a slave, a fact which tells its own tale of the normal status of the Britons who remained in the parts conquered by the invaders. The influence of the natives on the language of the newcomers was almost negligible; they passed on to them many river-, forest-, and hill-names, and the names of Roman cities, but the invaders gave new names to their own settlements, and, except on the western fringes of the country, no place-name supplies a certain instance of a British habitation name or personal name. A bare handful of words of British origin became part of the English language. All this is incompatible with any view that the invaders were comparatively few in number and were absorbed into the pre-existing population. So also is the desertion of the upland villages on the downlands in favour of the valley sites that the English cleared and worked with their own heavy plough.

There is, in fact, little indication that the invaders' civilization was affected to any appreciable extent by the outlook and institutions of the pre-English inhabitants. The Anglo-Saxons regarded themselves as Germans, and continued to repeat the songs and legends which they had brought over with them – including versified catalogues of the kings and tribes of Germany and the North. The main outlines of English society – apart from those elements introduced later by the adoption of Christianity

– are already distinguishable in the account of the German peoples on the Continent, written by Tacitus in the first century of the Christian era, and can often be paralleled in later accounts of other races of Germanic origin, especially in the rich literature of the Scandinavians. Though neither of these sources can be used unreservedly as evidence for conditions in England, their statements may sometimes allow us to interpret more clearly something that is only hinted at in our own, in some respects, more scanty, records.

*

The Christian religion was established in Britain before the English came, but there is no evidence that any of the invaders deserted in its favour the rites of their forefathers which they brought with them. Thanks to Tacitus, we know something of what these were. He describes a sanctuary of a goddess called Nerthus, which was shared by a group of tribes to be located in North Germany, the Cimbric peninsula and islands, among whom the Angles are specifically mentioned, while the Saxons and Jutes are possibly referred to under other names. He says:

There is on an island in the ocean an inviolate grove, and in it a consecrated car, covered by a robe; only one priest is allowed to touch it. He perceives when the goddess is present in the sanctuary, and accompanies her with great reverence as she is drawn by heifers. Then are days of rejoicing, and festive are the places which she honours with her coming and her stay. Men go not to battle, nor do they carry arms; all iron is locked away; then only are peace and quiet known, then only are they loved, until the same priest returns the goddess to her temple, when she is weary of intercourse with mortals. Thereupon the car and the robes, and, if you wish to credit it, the divinity herself, are washed in a secluded lake. Slaves perform this, who are immediately swallowed up by the same lake. Hence arises a mysterious terror and a pious ignorance, what this may be which is seen only by those about to die.

There is no direct evidence that the English continued to worship Nerthus in Britain. Her cult survived in Scandinavia, where, however, she suffered a change of sex, for her name corresponds exactly with that of the Scandinavian god Njörthr, the father of Freyr and his sister Freyja, all three being fertility gods. But evidence for the heathen religion in England is hard to come by, for our records owe their preservation to Christian writers who had no great interest in heathen religion. There are, however, hints of fertility cults, and we learn most where the writer is probably no longer aware of the original implications of the material he has happened to preserve. For example, the twenty-second letter of the Anglo-Saxon runic alphabet bore the name Ing, and a poem about this alphabet contains the cryptic verse:

Ing was first seen by men among the East Danes, until he afterwards departed east over the waves; the waggon followed. Thus the Heardings named the hero.

It seems a far cry from here to the great god Freyr of Scandinavian mythology, who, in the words of the Icelandic author Snorri Sturluson, 'rules over the rain and the shining of the sun, and over the produce of the earth as well; and it is good to call on him for fruitfulness and peace.' Yet Freyr only means 'lord', and the god is also called Ingunar-Freyr and Yngvi Freyr. The branch of the Germans to which the North German tribes belonged derived its name, Ingvaeones, from him. The waggon in the English poem probably refers to some cult progress like the one Tacitus describes.

An obscure reference like this to a forgotten fertility god would be insufficient to prove the continuance of fertility cults after the invaders left their continental homes and ancient sanctuaries, unless it were supported by other evidence. Some measure of support is given by the existence of a charm for ensuring the fertility of one's land, for it has been only imperfectly christianized, and includes an invocation to Erce, mother of earth. Erce is presumably the name of a goddess, and Bede tells us the names of two other goddesses, Eostre, from whom he derives the name of a spring festival which gave its name to the Christian Easter, and Hretha, of whom nothing further is known. Bede tells us also that the first night of the heathen New Year was called 'the night of the mothers', but what ceremonies are implied by this name we do not know. It is hardly accidental that the boar-emblem, sacred to Freyr in Scandinavian mythology, was regarded by the Anglo-Saxons as having protective powers, even though they may no longer have connected its magical efficacy with the ancient gods of peace and plenty. The emblem was placed on helmets, and one of these is described thus in the Anglo-Saxon epic poem *Beowulf*:

as the weapon-smith made it in former days, adorned it wondrously, encompassed it with boar-figures, so that afterwards no sword or battle-blade could pierce it.

It is also to be noted that the kings of Wessex included in their genealogies a certain Scyld who is mentioned in *Beowulf* and has there some attributes often associated with fertility divinities, e.g. an arrival from and departure into the unknown. The corresponding name is borne in Scandinavian sources by the husband of a fertility goddess, and both English and Scandinavian traditions assign him a son whose name seems to mean 'barley'. It looks, therefore, as if in this figure we have another trace of an old, forgotten, fertility cult.

We are not dependent on scattered references in literature to prove the worship in England of Woden, Thunor, and Tiw, gods already known to the Germans in Tacitus's time, whom Latin writers normally equate with Mercury, Jove, and Mars respectively. These three gods have left their mark on place-names in England. Woden is a frequent first element in these names, as in Woodnesborough and Wormshill, Kent, Wednesbury and Wednesfield, Staffordshire, Wensley, Derbyshire, and the lost *Wodneslawe*, Bedfordshire, *Wodnesbiorg*, Wiltshire, *Wodnesfeld*, Essex, and so on. Thunor occurs in Thunderfield, Surrey, Thurstable, Essex, Thundridge, Hertfordshire, and six times – in Essex, Sussex, Surrey, and Hampshire – before a second element *leah*, which means a wood, or a clearing in a wood. The god Tiw was worshipped in Tysoe, Warwickshire, Tuesley, Surrey, and in the lost *Tislea*, Hampshire, and *Tyesmere*, Worcestershire.

English sources do not tell us what qualities were attributed to these gods, except once, in the case of Woden; for a charm called the *Nine Herbs Charm*, which says:

> The snake came creeping, it tore a man to pieces; then took Woden nine glorious twigs, and struck the adder that it flew into nine parts,

for all its obscurity, agrees well with one aspect of this divinity in Scandinavian sources, as the god of knowledge, of intellectual attainment, who wards off evil from mankind by his wisdom. In England, the building of prehistoric monuments was attributed to him; his name is given to the Wansdyke, and one of his by-names to earthworks in different parts of the country called Grim's ditches. In contrast to Woden, Thunor 'the Thunderer' does not figure in English literary sources, but it is to be noted that among the heathen customs that the Church as late as the eighth century was eager to suppress was the observance of the fifth day of the week in honour of Jove (i.e. Thunor).

When the English accepted Christianity, they came to regard their former gods as devils. The Christian poet who drew the contrast:

Woden wrought idols; the Almighty, that is the powerful God, the true King himself, the Saviour of souls, wrought glory, the spacious heavens,

does not suggest that the old gods had never existed. An extant charm claims to be effective against 'the shot of the gods, the shot of the elves, the shot of witches'. Gradually, however, they were forgotten, so that when, at the end of the tenth century, the homilist Abbot Ælfric repeats the normal equation of classical and Germanic deities, he uses the Scandinavian forms of the names of the latter. Presumably the fresh influx of heathen settlers in the Viking age had made these forms more familiar to an English audience than those used in their own, long distant, heathen past.

Words denoting a heathen sanctuary of some kind occur in place-names in all areas of early settlement. Of special interest are Peper Harrow and the lost *Cusanweoh*, Surrey, and Patchway, Sussex, for in all three the second element (*hearg*, *weoh*) means a sanctuary, while the first is a personal name in the genitive case, so that private ownership is suggested, reminiscent of the position of the Icelandic *goði*, who combined the functions of chieftain and priest. On the other hand, the old name for Harrow-on-the-Hill, Middlesex, which means sanctuary 'of the Gumenings', and the lost *Besingahearh* 'sanctuary of the Besings', Surrey, seem rather to refer to the holy place of a family or group. Some of these places are on hill-tops, whereas the number of place-names with heathen associations that contain a word meaning 'wood' or 'woodland clearing' shows that heathen sanctuaries were often in the woods, and reminds us that Tacitus speaks of sacred groves among the Germans, and that later continental and Scandinavian evidence bears out his statements.

Some of the places which were the meeting-places of

the hundreds in later times have names containing heathen elements, a circumstance which implies that people continued after their conversion to Christianity to meet at the places where they had been accustomed to carry on their heathen rites. In so doing, they would be acting in accordance with instructions sent by Pope Gregory to the missionaries in 601, advocating the conversion of pagan temples into Christian churches, 'in order that the people may the more familiarly resort to the places to which they have been accustomed.' There is, however, little evidence that the missionaries went so far as to use a heathen building for a Christian church, though Canterbury tradition believed that St Pancras's church had once been King Ethelbert's idol-fane; we read rather of total destruction, as at the great temple at Goodmanham near York, after King Edwin's council had decided in favour of the Christian faith in 627, or all over Essex in 665, when Christianity had been re-established after a relapse into paganism in time of plague. This relapse may have brought it home to the men on the spot that the continued existence of heathen fanes had dangers greater than Gregory had realized. King Aldwulf of East Anglia, a contemporary of Bede, remembered having seen in his boyhood the temple in which his predecessor King Rædwald – not fully comprehending the demands of the new faith – had set up an altar to Christ beside those to his old gods. Bede's account makes it clear that this was never converted into a Christian church.

From this passage and other places we learn that heathen sanctuaries might include temples and images of the gods. Great sacrifices were held at certain seasons; a feast was held in the second month of the year at which cakes were offered to the gods, while the feast after the autumn slaughtering of the surplus cattle caused November to be known as 'sacrifice month'. These sacrifices were accompanied by ceremonial feastings.

A few scattered details of heathen customs can be garnered. A priest had to observe certain taboos, not being allowed to carry weapons or to ride on anything but a mare; he was believed to be able to bind the hands of his enemies by chanting spells from a high mound. The letters of the Germanic alphabet, runes, were held to have magic powers if used in the correct arrangement; they could, for example, release a prisoner from his fetters. Veneration was paid to trees, wells, and stones, and there was a firm trust in 'incantations, amulets, and other mysteries of devilish art.' The Church preached for generations against these and other superstitions – against the burning of grain 'for the health of the living and the house' after a death, against women who placed their daughters on a roof or in an oven to heal fever. People came to rely on Christian prayers, holy water, and the relics of saints to protect them from the evil powers with which they felt themselves surrounded, and which could be fitted into the Christian scheme of things as the monstrous offspring of Cain, from whom sprang 'ogres and elves and ghouls, and giants who fought against God for a long time.' Place-names afford ample evidence of the prevalent belief in such creatures, for various words for demon and goblin are common in them. The hermit St Guthlac had to fight long and earnestly against the fenland demons whom his coming had displaced. *Beowulf*, the greatest poem in Anglo-Saxon literature, is devoted to the freeing of human habitations from the ravages of supernatural creatures that inhabit the fens and from a dragon residing in a prehistoric burial-mound. The audience for whom the poem was composed would not have felt these themes either fantastic or trivial. The charms which kept away these evil influences were christianized, so that it is rare to find, among those that survive, an uneradicated heathen reference like the ones mentioned above.

From the fragmentary evidence for Anglo-Saxon heathenism, it is not possible to form a clear idea of the pre-Christian views of an after-life, or of the connexion between religion and ethics. Their practice of burying goods with the dead would imply some belief in a future life in which these will be of use, but if we can take at its face-value the speech Bede puts into the mouth of a pagan Northumbrian nobleman, comparing human life to the flight of a sparrow through the king's hall, 'coming in from the darkness and returning to it', this belief was very indefinite, or else it failed to convince the upper classes. No one at the council is reported to have disputed the nobleman's statement. There is certainly no evidence to justify the putting back into this period of the Scandinavian conceptions in the Viking Age of a Valhalla and 'a twilight of the gods'.

The language used on the same occasion by Coifi, the Northumbrian high-priest, suggests that what was expected of the gods was material benefit in this life in return for the due observance of their rites, for he complains to the king:

Not one of your men has applied himself to the worship of our gods more zealously than I, and nevertheless there are many who receive fuller benefits and greater dignities from you than I . . . But if the gods were any good, they would rather wish to help me, who have taken care to serve them the more assiduously.

But it must be remembered that Bede was not in a position to paint a fair picture of the heathen point of view, and it is perhaps best to leave it an open question how far the heathen English connected divine favour with obedience to an ethical code. We may be sure, however, that the breaking of oaths sworn on sacred things was considered to bring down the wrath of the gods, and we are told by Tacitus that the assemblies of the Germans were placed under divine protection, which would make a breach of their peace an act of sacrilege. One of the least Christian features of extant heroic poetry, a feature perhaps inherited from heathen times, is that men seem more concerned with the reputation they will leave behind them than with divine rewards in this world or the next. This view is expressed concisely in *Beowulf:*

Each of us must experience an end to life in this world; let him who can achieve glory before he die; that will be best for the lifeless warrior afterwards.

The poet's final comment on this hero – and the concluding words of the poem – is that of all men he was 'the most eager for glory.' The poet who wrote this was a Christian, and his hero wins his glory by virtues not incompatible with a Christian code. Yet it emphasizes the difference between this remark and a strict churchman's point of view to note that the tenth-century homilist Ælfric uses an equivalent term to explain what is meant by the deadly sin of pride.

It is often held that Anglo-Saxon poetry is permeated by a strong belief in the power of fate, inherited from heathen times, and some have even seen a conflict between a faith in an omnipotent Christian God and a trust in a blind, inexorable fate. To me, this view seems exaggerated. The word used for fate can mean simply 'event', 'what happens', and though there are passages where some degree of personification is present, such as 'the creation of the fates changes the world under the heavens' or 'woven by the decrees of fate', I doubt if these are more than figures of speech by the time the poems were composed. If they are inherited from the heathen past, they may indicate that men then believed in a goddess who wove their destiny, but the poet who says 'to him the Lord granted the webs of victory' is unconscious of a heathen implication in his phrase. It would be natural enough that, even while yet heathen, the Anglo-Saxons should feel that man's destiny is outside his own control, but stronger evidence would be necessary before we could assume a belief in the fate-weaving Norns at the foot of the world-tree Yggdrasil, as described in the much later, poetic, mythology of the Scandinavians.

CHAPTER II

THE BONDS OF SOCIETY

Loyalty to one's Lord

THE strength of the bond between a man and his lord in the Germanic races impressed Tacitus in the first century, causing him to write some famous words that find an echo throughout Anglo-Saxon literature. Having mentioned that the loyalty is personal, not tribal, for a successful chief may attract to him men from many tribes, and that chieftain and followers vie with one another in showing courage on the battlefield, Tacitus continues:

Furthermore, it is a lifelong infamy and reproach to survive the chief and withdraw from the battle. To defend him, to protect him, even to ascribe to his glory their own exploits, is the essence of their sworn allegiance. The chiefs fight for victory, the followers for their chief.

In return for their service the men expect horses and weapons, and feasting in the lord's household; they covet the place of highest honour in it.

The acceptance of Christianity made no difference to this attitude, and several centuries after Tacitus it is a very similar picture that is painted in the Anglo-Saxon poetry of Christian date. The lord has his band of followers, often called *gesithas* 'companions', who share 'the joys of the hall' in time of peace and who should be prepared to die for him in time of war. Thus the aged Beowulf looks back with satisfaction on the services he performed for his lord, King Hygelac:

I repaid him in battle for the treasures which he gave me. . . .
Ever would I be before him in the troop, alone in the van.

The fragmentary poem on the battle at *Finnesburh* tells us that 'retainers never repaid better the bright mead than his young followers did to Hnæf.' Beowulf himself was not so well served, and his young kinsman Wiglaf speaks bitter words of reproach to the men who have failed to come to their lord's support:

He who wishes to speak the truth can say that the lord who gave you those treasures, that war-gear that you stand up in – when he often gave to men on the ale-benches in the hall, as a prince to his thanes, the most splendid helmet and corslet that he could find, far and near – entirely threw away this war-gear, when battle befell him.

Such conduct earned lasting infamy, and Wiglaf goes on to draw a grim picture of the future dishonoured life of the men guilty of desertion.

As in Tacitus, the lord takes the honour of his followers' exploits, and King Hygelac in *Beowulf* is called 'the slayer of Ongentheow', although the deed was done by two of his thanes, whom he richly rewarded. The retainer brings the spoils he has won to his lord. Beowulf gave to King Hygelac the gifts he had been given for his services in Denmark, and on another occasion he expresses his satisfaction that by killing the Frankish champion, Dæghrefn, he had denied him the triumph of bearing in person to his lord, the king of the Franks, the armour of Hygelac, who had been killed in battle, almost certainly by Dæghrefn himself. The minstrel Widsith gave to his own lord on his return to his native land the magnificent ring which King Eormenric had bestowed on him. His lord had given him a grant of land. Grants of land by a king to his thanes are mentioned elsewhere in verse literature.

The bond between lord and retainer went deeper than material benefits on either side. The giving of arms and treasure, which was ceremoniously performed, had a

symbolic significance, and it is not mere material loss
that inspires the following lament for a dead lord contained in a poem generally known as *The Wanderer*:

All joy has departed. Truly does he know this who must long
forgo the advice of his dear lord. When sorrow and sleep both
together often bind the wretched lonely man, it seems to him in
his mind that he embraces and kisses his liege lord, and lays
hands and head on his knee, as sometimes in days of yore he
enjoyed the bounty from the throne. Then awakens the friend-
less man; he sees before him the dark waves, the sea-birds dip-
ping, spreading their wings, frost and snow falling, mingled
with hail. Then are the wounds of his heart the heavier, the
sore wounds after his dear one; his sorrow is renewed.

The relationship of lord and follower involved the
duty of vengeance by the survivor if either were slain –
or, at the very least, the exaction of a compensation high
enough to do honour to the slain man. A story that told
how the followers of a Danish prince Hnæf succeeded in
apparently hopeless circumstances in avenging their lord
by killing his slayer, the Frisian king Finn, was apparently very popular, for not only is there a fragment of a
poem about it among our scanty remains, but also it is
told in *Beowulf*, in so allusive and obscure a fashion as to
show that the poet expected his audience to be already
familiar with it. *Widsith* refers to it also.

It is not only in poetry that we find instances of loyalty
to the lord. It was no mere literary convention. The followers of Oswald of Northumbria in the seventh century
and of Æthelbald of Mercia in the eighth accompanied
their lords in exile, and a little later we find Charles the
Great asking the archbishop of Canterbury to inter-
cede with King Offa of Mercia that some English exiles
should be allowed to return, now that the lord whom they
were accompanying in exile is dead. At the beginning of
this century, Bishop Aldhelm of Sherborne wrote to persuade the clergy of Bishop Wilfrid of Northumbria that

it was their duty to share his exile, and mentions as a matter of common knowledge that a layman who refused to go into exile with his lord would be an object of scorn and ridicule. Greater sacrifices than voluntary exile were made. In 625 Lilla, a thane of Edwin of Northumbria, thrust his own body between the king and an assassin's stroke, and died in his lord's defence; in 666, Bishop Wilfrid's retinue swore to fight to the death, if need be, against a vastly superior force of heathen South Saxons; in 685 King Ecgfrith fell at *Nechtanesmere*, 'all his body-guard having been killed', and the absence of any comment on or any elaboration of the incident may indicate that it was what was normally expected. An incident of 786 is recorded much more fully; when the thanes of King Cynewulf of Wessex were roused from sleep to find that their king had been killed in a surprise night attack, they refused all offer of terms in spite of their hopeless position, and 'continued to fight until they all lay dead, except for one Welsh hostage, and he was severely wounded.' In their turn, men of the opposing party who were offered quarter on grounds of kinship by Cynewulf's main forces when they arrived on the scene, equally indignantly rejected the suggestion, preferring to stand by their leader to the end. The passage in the Anglo-Saxon Chronicle which records this incident stands out from the annals surrounding it in its fullness and circumstantial detail; it may have been drawn from an oral account handed down for some time before it was written down. The story is told with some measure of narrative art, but there is no reason to doubt the truth of the facts it records. The same annal relates that a swine-herd took vengeance on the slayer of his lord, Ealdorman Cumbra, so we see that it was not only the aristocratic classes that recognized this obligation. The lord's duty to take vengeance or exact compensation for the slaying of one of his men was recognized by the law, which allotted a 'man-compensation' to the lord, in addition to what must be paid to the kindred of a slain man.

It is true that beside these instances of loyalty one must set acts of treachery and violence that sometimes violated the tie between lord and man. In 757, Æthelbald of Mercia was murdered by his own bodyguard – a later generation than those who had shared his exile more than forty years before – and the following year Oswulf of Northumbria similarly perished at the hands of his retainers. In 796 the death of Ethelred of Northumbria was engineered by one of his own nobles, an act that caused Charles the Great to describe the Northumbrians as murderers of their lords. Such incidents were looked on with horror, and Ethelred's death was duly avenged by his thane Torhtmund.

In Christian times the man who took service under a lord swore the following oath over relics:

By the Lord, before whom these relics are holy, I will be loyal and true to N, and love all that he loves, and hate all that he hates, (however) in accordance with God's rights and secular obligations; and never, willingly and intentionally, in word or deed, do anything that is hateful to him; on condition that he keep me as I shall deserve, and carry out all that was our agreement, when I subjected myself to him and chose his favour.

A story in Bede illustrates well the binding force of the oath of allegiance even in heathen times. When Edwin of Northumbria had taken refuge with King Rædwald of East Anglia, he felt that he could not break his pact with this king even on the strong provocation of discovering that he was meditating betraying him to his enemies for money. Rædwald's wife dissuaded her husband from so shameful an act, stoutly declaring that his honour should be more precious than any treasure.

This story shows also that the tie was a personal, and

not necessarily a tribal one. Edwin, it is true, was a fugitive from his own race, but men might voluntarily take service under the ruler of another tribe. One of the things that was distressing Bede towards the end of his life was the danger threatening the defences of Northumbria because of the kings' too lavish and indiscriminate gifts for religious, or supposedly religious, purposes, for thus their resources were impoverished and the young men of the country driven to take service outside where there was hope of more substantial reward. Besides fugitives and voluntary guests, even hostages were expected to repay the host's hospitality with service in time of war. We have mentioned one instance above, and another occurs in the late tenth-century poem on the battle of Maldon, where a Northumbrian hostage fights on with the bodyguard of Brihtnoth, ealdorman of Essex, after their lord has fallen.

The ideals referred to by Tacitus are still being expressed nine hundred years after his time. In the late tenth-century *Life of St Edmund*, the author, who claims to derive his information from St Dunstan, who had it from the saint's swordbearer, puts into Edmund's mouth a speech on heroic lines, expressing his determination not to live after his slain followers, nor to save himself by flight. A very few years later, the poem on the battle of Maldon tells how Brihtnoth's retainers fought on, after his death and the flight of his army, with no hope of victory, but with determination to avenge his death, as a due return for his gifts and favours. The heroic code is nowhere stated more completely or more simply than in the lines:

Quickly was Offa cut down in the fight; yet he had carried out what he had promised his lord, when he vowed to his treasure-giver that both together they should ride safely home into the stronghold, or fall in the army, die of wounds on the field of battle. He lay as befits a thane, close by his lord.

Sentiments such as: 'the steadfast men round Sturmer will not need to taunt me, now my lord has fallen, that I journeyed home lordless'; or 'he cannot waver who plans to avenge his lord in the army, nor care about his life'; or 'I will not retire, but I intend to lie by the side of my lord, of so dear a man' – have been thought to contrast strangely with the sad tale of treachery and cowardice told in other sources for the reign of Ethelred the Unready (978–1016). Yet heroism was not altogether dead in his reign. In 988, the men of Devon 'who chose rather to end their lives by a death in battle than to live ignobly', led by Streonwold, carried the day in spite of heavy losses; the chief men of the East Angles fell fighting in 1004; the men of Cambridgeshire stood firm at Ringmere in 1010. The speeches in the Maldon poem, which was composed for an audience very familiar with the persons mentioned, probably with the incidents also, may represent, at the very least, a translation into words of sentiments to which their deeds had borne ample witness. When they followed men like Brihtnoth of Essex, or Streonwold of Devon, or Ulfcytel of East Anglia, the English of Ethelred's day could maintain the heroic standards.

*

The lord's gift of armour and horses to the man who entered his service developed into the legal due called 'heriot', which means literally 'war-gear', and which was paid to the lord on the death of his man, representing originally the return on the follower's death of the lord's gift. This payment was remitted when the man fell 'before his lord' on a campaign. To the end of the period it tended to be paid in kind, a fact which suggests that it was felt to have symbolic significance. For example, a tenth-century ealdorman declares:

And I bequeath to my royal lord as a heriot four armlets of three hundred mancuses of gold, and four swords and eight horses, four with trappings and four without, and four helmets and four coats-of-mail and eight spears and eight shields.

A law of Cnut in the eleventh century states the heriot due from different ranks mainly in terms of horses and weapons.

Though the heriot might represent in concrete form a man's sense of obligation to his lord, the principal payment made to a follower in Anglo-Saxon times was in land. Such donations are occasionally mentioned in poetry, more frequently in historical sources. Benedict Biscop, the founder of the twin monasteries of Monkwearmouth and Jarrow, had been a thane of King Oswiu of Northumbria (641–70) before he entered religion at the age of twenty-five, and had received from him a grant of land suitable to his rank; and it is clear from a letter which Bede wrote to Archbishop Egbert in 734 that he considered that a young thane had a right to expect an endowment of land from his prince, to enable him to marry and set up an establishment of his own. Numbers of charters survive in which kings grant land to an individual ealdorman or thane 'on account of his faithful service', but sometimes the words 'and because of his acceptable money' are added, and one cannot be certain that even those without this tell-tale phrase are not in many cases sales masquerading as gifts.

The man got something more than all this from his lord: he got protection. No one would be eager to molest a man who had a powerful lord ready to demand compensation or to take vengeance. The lord took responsibility for the man's acts; he had to produce him to answer a charge in court, or pay the damages himself, and it would be to his interest to defend his man from a wrongful accusation. He was held responsible even for deeds committed before the man entered his service, and would therefore be unwise too readily to accept an unknown man. This may explain why in the poem *The Wanderer* the man bereft of his lord finds it so difficult to find a new protector. The lord's responsibility for his followers is the aspect of this relationship which stands out most prominently in the laws.

*

The Christian Church did not come into conflict with the Germanic principle of loyalty to the lord. It added its sanctity to the oath of allegiance. Vengeance taken for a lord's murder is regarded as a laudable act by no less a churchman than Alcuin himself, whom we find in 801 recommending to Charles the Great a certain Torhtmund, 'a faithful thane of King Ethelred (of Northumbria), a man approved in faith, strenuous in arms, who has boldly avenged the blood of his lord.' But Ethelred was a king foully murdered, and we are hardly justified in assuming from Alcuin's attitude on this occasion that he would in general have approved of acts of vengeance, rather than the alternate procedure, which the Church encouraged, of accepting compensation. How ready the Church was to admit the binding force of a man's duty to his lord can be seen in the *Penitential of Archbishop Theodore*, for this text, unyielding though it normally is in its stern attitude to what the Germanic code regarded as not merely justifiable but laudable homicide, imposes only a slight penance on the man who commits homicide at his lord's command. It placed this act on a level with killing in battle, and considered the lord's command a greater extenuation of homicide than the desire to avenge even a close kinsman.

Moreover, when the claims of the lord clashed with those of the kindred, the idea becomes established during the centuries after the conversion that the duty to the lord should come first. This was expressly stated by the followers of the King Cynewulf mentioned above, for they declared unequivocally that 'no kinsman was dearer to them than their lord' and were willing to run the risk of kindred murder in order to avenge the king's death. The laws of King Alfred allow a man to fight, without becoming liable to a vendetta, in defence of a wrongfully attacked kinsman, but not if this involves fighting against his lord: 'that we do not permit'. This attitude agrees with the tremendous horror at the crime of treachery to a lord expressed by this king in the introduction to his code. Possibly, however, the inclusion of this proviso in the legislation would have been unnecessary if in practice the claims of kinship and affection had not sometimes overridden those of duty to the lord.

The homilists, like the poets, have many passages in praise of loyalty and condemnation of treachery. To Archbishop Wulfstan in 1014 there is a betrayal worse than deserting a lord on the battlefield, or even than plotting his death: 'for the greatest of all treachery in the world is that a man betray his lord's soul' – that is, entice him to sin. The Church taught that other services than vengeance could be rendered for a departed lord, i.e. the taking of alms to Rome, or the making of grants to religious houses, for the good of his soul. A paragraph that sums up the Christian view of loyalty occurs in Cnut's laws and is probably from the pen of Archbishop Wulfstan. It concludes:

> For all that ever we do, through just loyalty to our lord, we do to our own great advantage, for truly God will be gracious to him who is duly faithful to his lord.

Duty to one's kin

The bond of kinship may at times have had to yield before the claims of the lord, but it was nevertheless very important in Anglo-Saxon society. Every individual depended on the support of the kindred in all the affairs of life, and the poetry shows that the position of the kinless man was regarded as wretched indeed. Beside the lament for a dead lord quoted above could be placed a dirge in *Beowulf* by the last member of a kindred. He placed his ancestral treasures in the grave-mound and 'sad at heart he uttered his grief, alone after them all he wandered wretchedly, day and night, until the surge of death touched his heart.' Another poem speaks with sympathy of the man who must be alone – 'better would it be for him that he had a brother.' This poet is thinking of the everyday affairs of life, but usually, both in literature and in the laws, it is in connexion with the vendetta that we hear most of the claims and obligations of the kindred.

If a man were killed, it was the duty of his kindred to take vengeance on the slayer or his kindred, or to exact compensation. The fear of the action of the kindred was originally the main force for the maintenance of order, and to the end Anglo-Saxon law regarded homicide as the affair of the kindred, who were entitled to receive the 'wergild', i.e. 'man-price', for any of their members slain. Vengeance was no mere satisfaction of personal feeling, but a duty that had to be carried out even when it ran counter to personal inclination, and a favourite theme in Germanic literature was provided by any situation when this duty clashed with other feelings, such as friendship or marital affection. The duty was incumbent on both paternal and maternal kinsmen, and the kinsmen of the slayer were all liable to it unless they repudiated the slayer and thus dissociated themselves from responsibility. But in that case they could not afterwards carry on a vendetta for him or receive compensation if he were slain; they had renounced their rights to claim kinship with him.

A composition, in money or property, could be accepted without loss of honour provided it was adequate to the rank of the slain man. This was so already in the time of Tacitus, but it was always open to the injured kindred to refuse settlement and carry on the vendetta if they preferred. Alfred's laws seem to have tried to change this, but without success. Fixed compositions for homicide, in proportion to the rank of the slain man, were established early, at first expressed in numbers of oxen; and the rate at which a man must be paid for if he were killed, i.e. his wergild, became so much the most important mark of rank that the various social classes were sometimes described by terms derived from it, e.g. (men) of two – or six, or twelve – hundred (shillings). It was a great grief and humiliation if a kinsman lay 'unavenged and unatoned for'. In such a situation the old King Hrethel in *Beowulf* found life unbearable; he took to his bed and died when one of his sons accidentally killed another, for there could be no vengeance nor compensation within the kindred:

That was a fight unatoned for by money, though grievously committed, weighing heavily on the spirit; yet the prince had to lose his life unavenged.

The vendetta was not a wild act of lawlessness; the conditions under which it was carried on, and the details of the procedure, were carefully regulated by law. There were definite rules as to the division of the financial responsibility between the slayer, and his paternal and maternal kinsmen, the latter being responsible for only half as much as the former. In the same proportion as they paid for the act of one of their members, they received if they were the injured party. A portion of the wergild went to a group of very close relations, and the law was specific as to the amount of this and the limit of time in which it must be paid. In Kent it had to be paid 'at the open grave' and the rest of the wergild within forty days. There were strict regulations regarding the circumstances in which vengeance was permissible. It was illegal to carry on a vendetta against a man who had committed homicide when defending either his lord, his man, or his kinsman from wrongful attack, or who had killed a man whom he had caught in the act of violating his wife, daughter, sister, or mother, provided he killed him on the spot.

Similarly it was illegal to wage a vendetta on behalf of a man who had met his death as a convicted thief, or perpetrator of some other capital crime. His kinsmen were bound to give an oath that they would take no steps to avenge him. If they held that he had been unjustly executed, they must bring an action to prove this before they could legally take vengeance or exact compensation. The *Beowulf* poet compares Hrethel's grief for the loss of his son with that of an old man who sees his son's body swing on the gallows, for both were debarred, though for different reasons, from the consolation of an effective vengeance or an adequate compensation, and their dead lay dishonoured. Finally, a slayer's guilt had to be proved before vengeance could legally be taken. A man accused of homicide had the right to deny it by oath, with the support of oath-helpers, according to the normal procedure of the courts. Probably a homicide would usually admit his act, for attempted concealment turned it into murder, to be classed with slaying by secret means, poison or witchcraft, which could not be expiated by money payments. Among the local abuses of law that the legislation of the reign of Ethelred the Unready (978–1016) aimed at correcting was a practice that had grown up in the North which regarded as valid an accusation of homicide if made on the day of the slaying, apparently regardless of whether proof were forthcoming that it was directed against the proper person or not.

*

When the English were converted to Christianity, it was unavoidable that there should be a clash between Christian and pre-Christian ethics in this matter of vengeance. It may be this that lies behind an incident reported by Bede, in which King Sigeberht of Essex was killed by two of his heathen kinsmen because they were angered by his habit of forgiving his enemies the wrong done to him. They may have felt that by this leniency he was failing in his duty to protect his kindred. However that may be, the *Penitential of Archbishop Theodore* states in unambiguous language:

If anyone kills a man in vengeance for a kinsman, let him do penance as a homicide, seven or ten years.

This attitude must have come as a shock to the early converts to Christianity, and even this penitential yields a little by assigning a shorter penance if the vengeance taken was for a brother.

The Church was eager to encourage settlements by composition. This was, of course, no new thing, and already in heathen times attempts were sometimes made to secure more lasting reconciliation of opposing families by means of diplomatic marriages, though the hero of *Beowulf* makes the comment:

Normally it happens but rarely that the slaughterous spear lies quiet even for a short time, after the fall of men, though the bride be fair.

The Church threw its authority on the side of compensations, remitting, according to the penitential already mentioned, half the penance to the homicide who is willing to pay the wergild to the injured kindred. Bede relates how Archbishop Theodore used his influence to bring about a settlement after King Ecgfrith's brother had been killed by the Mercians. But this way out of the dilemma was not always open. There remained the problem of dealing with the slayer who either would not, or could not, pay the wergild. It is this which keeps the vendetta alive throughout the whole Anglo-Saxon period. The law could try to bring pressure on the slayer and his kindred to make them pay, but homicide was an expensive matter, and the man of a poor family could not be allowed to get off scot-free.

The Church took care to fit its own members into the scale of wergilds, equating a priest with a thane. But a man left his kindred when he entered religion and compositions were paid to his monastery. The *Dialogue of Archbishop Egbert of York* concerns itself with the position that arises when the slayer of an ecclesiastic cannot pay the wergild, and declares that he is to be handed over to the king for punishment 'lest the slayers of the servants of God should think that they can sin with impunity.' The natural inference is that he assumes that, when the slain man is a layman, the kindred will carry on the vengeance, if no compensation is obtainable. The Church cannot do this; so the king must act for it. We have already seen that in some circumstances Alcuin considered vengeance a praiseworthy act.

The modifications in the laws of successive Anglo-Saxon kings of the regulations governing the blood-feud are themselves adequate evidence of its continued existence. King Alfred forbade violent action against an adversary before justice had been demanded of him; King Edmund (939–46) prevented the slaying in vengeance of anyone except the actual perpetrator of the deed. He laments the prevalence of feuds:

The illegal and manifold fights which are among us distress me and all of us very greatly.

His laws go into detail on the elaborate precautions to be taken when a slaying is being compounded, showing how easy it was for enmity to flare up again if the parties were brought face to face. First, the slayer is to deal with the kindred of the man he has slain through a go-between, who is to obtain for him, under security, a safe conduct, so that he can come forward and give pledges and securities for the wergild. After that, if anyone attacks him, it is regarded as a breach of the king's protection, punishable by a heavy fine.

The prevalence of feuds in King Edmund's time was probably in part due to the influx of Danish settlers into the north and east of England at the end of the previous century, for in all the Scandinavian lands vendettas were very common, and there was an opinion current that to pursue vengeance was a more manly course of action than to accept compensation. It is certainly from the north of England that we get the most vivid account of a feud, one that lasted for three generations, on until after the Norman Conquest. Earl Uhtred of Northumbria roused the enmity of Thurbrand, a member of a rich landed family in Yorkshire, and he engineered the murder of Uhtred in 1016, as he entered the hall at *Wiheal* to make his submission to Cnut. Uhtred's son Aldred avenged his father by killing Thurbrand, and the feud descended to the latter's son Carl, but by the intervention of friends a settlement was made, and mutual reparations were paid. It seemed so complete, that Aldred and Carl became sworn brothers and planned to go together on a pilgrimage to Rome; but they were hindered by a storm, and, while they were together at Carl's house at Rise, something – we are not told what – must have caused Carl to remember old grudges, for he slew Aldred in Rise wood. The feud then lay dormant for a long time. It was not until 1073 that Earl Waltheof, the son of Aldred's daughter, avenged his grandfather's murder by sending assassins who killed all Carl's sons and grandsons as they were feasting at the house of the eldest son, Thurbrand, at Settrington – all except two, one whom they spared for his excellent disposition, and one who was not present.

Conditions in the North after the Viking Age were undoubtedly much wilder than elsewhere, yet even in the more civilized South the blood-feud survived till quite late, as is shown clearly by an incident as late as the episcopate of Bishop Wulfstan of Worcester (1062–95), in whose diocese the five brothers of a slain man refused to come to terms even though the slaying had been accidental; they said that they preferred to be excommunicated rather than fail to avenge their brother, and it required a miracle to make them change their minds.

*

Though the laws concern themselves principally with the kindred in its relation to the blood-feud and the wergild, people depended on their kinsmen for many other kinds of support; but the obligations within the family were known by custom and are rarely expressly stated in our sources. We know that close kinsmen, at any rate, arranged marriages and settled the terms of marriage agreements for their members, and that a woman's kindred continued to watch over her interests after her marriage. The nearest kinsmen looked after the estate of a child whose father died while it was a minor. Kinsmen were responsible for seeing that an accused member came forward to answer a charge, and if he did not, and became an outlaw by default, they were forbidden to harbour him under pain of heavy penalties. It is possible that at one time they acted as oath-helpers to support his oath of his innocence.

There are some signs that in the later Saxon period the kindred was no longer an adequate force to maintain order, either from the point of view of the state or of the individual. Homilists complain bitterly of the decay of this bond:

Now too often kinsman does not protect kinsman any more than a stranger, neither a father his son, nor sometimes a son his own father, nor one brother another.

On the other hand, the laws have from time to time to deal with the abuse of power by a too powerful kindred, which tries to prevent the proper operation of the law in relation to its own members. King Athelstan (924—39) ordered the transportation to another district of persons of a kindred so powerful that they could not be restrained from crime or from harbouring criminals. The kindred's responsibility for producing its members to answer a charge proved insufficient to bring men to justice, so an artificial association was imposed from above for this purpose. According to a law of Cnut which may be quoting an older source, every adult free man was to be in a 'tithing', that is, a group of ten men who acted as sureties for one another's behaviour, 'and his surety is to hold him and bring him to answer any charge.' Men also formed voluntary associations of a semi-religious, semi-social character, called gilds, which reinforced the kindred in some of its protective functions. Statutes of such gilds have survived from the late tenth and the eleventh centuries from Exeter, Bedwyn, Abbotsbury, Woodbury, and Cambridge. The thanes' gild in Cambridge took on the responsibility of carrying on the vendetta after a wrongfully slain gild-brother, and also undertook to support any of their members who slew a man in a necessary feud, and to help him to pay the wergild. If, however, any member killed a man without good reason, 'foolishly', he had to bear the feud alone. These statutes thus supply evidence, if such were needed, that the blood-feud was still prevalent in late Anglo-Saxon times. A rather similar organization was formed in London already in King Athelstan's time. It seems to have concerned itself primarily with common action to suppress cattle-lifting, but it also declared its members to be 'all in one friendship and one enmity', that is, that they would avenge one another's wrongs.

CHAPTER III

THE KING AND HIS COURT

THE Anglo-Saxons were familiar with the institution of kingship already in their continental homelands, and long after they settled in Britain they continued to tell stories of kings who reigned in continental Angeln as far back as the fourth century, one of whom, Offa, reigning twelve generations before his famous Mercian namesake and descendant, was remembered as the king who established the Eider as the boundary between the Angles and the *Swæfe*, their southern neighbours in their homeland. Most royal families in England claimed to be descended from gods, Woden in most instances, Saxneat, a god worshipped also by the continental Saxons, in the case of the royal house of the East Saxons. It is probable that in very early times the heathen kings had some priestly functions.

Until the great Danish invasion of 865–78, England was divided into several kingdoms, though for long periods those south of the Humber were united under an overlord known, according to a ninth-century authority, as a *Bretwalda* 'ruler of Britain'. This was no mere empty title; subject kings paid tribute to their overlord, they attended him from time to time at his court, they obtained his consent to their grants of land, they fought under his leadership in time of war. An Anglo-Saxon poet may well have contemporary parallels in his mind, of a *Bretwalda* calling his subject kings to his standard, when he describes the gathering of Pharaoh's host in the following words:

He had chosen the flower of the nations, two thousand famous men of noble birth, kings and kinsmen. . . . Therefore each of them led out his men, every warrior whom he could assemble in time.

By the time Bede was writing his *Ecclesiastical History* this overlordship had been held in turn for single reigns by Sussex, Wessex, Kent, and East Anglia, and for three successive reigns by Northumbria. Wulfhere of Mercia held similar power in the late seventh century, and during the greater part of the next century Mercia, under its kings Æthelbald and Offa, was supreme over all the lands south of the Humber. The supremacy of the West Saxon kings, which was established early in the ninth century, proved permanent because the other kingdoms were destroyed by the Danes. When the kings of Wessex had reconquered the Danelaw in the tenth century, they became henceforward rulers of a united England.

The richly furnished ship-burial at Sutton Hoo suggests that even the kings of heathen days had considerable wealth at their disposal, and, as the smaller kingdoms became absorbed into those of more powerful rulers, the kings' dignity increased and their courts became more impressive. Bede speaks of the pomp upheld by King Edwin of Northumbria:

Even in time of peace, as he rode with his thanes between his cities, villages, and provinces, his standard-bearer was wont always to go before him; and also if he walked anywhere along the streets, that kind of standard which the Romans call 'tufa' and the English 'thuuf' was borne before him.

Eighth-century poets, who are clearly drawing on their knowledge of contemporary courts when they speak of the kings of ancient Scandinavia or of Israel, describe a somewhat elaborate court-etiquette, and refer to the material splendour of gold-inwrought tapestry, tessellated pavements, drinking-cups of precious metals. Later kings were no less concerned with their visible splendour; in the midst of all his many activities, King Alfred found time to supervise the building of halls and chambers and the production of objects of beauty, inviting to him craftsmen from many nations to this end. His great-grandson King Edgar showed by his impressive coronation ceremony at Bath in 973 that he grasped the political value of external magnificence.

*

The king was in a unique position at law. His mere word was incontrovertible, and he need not support it with an oath. An attempt on his life, whether directly, or by harbouring his enemies and outlaws, cost life and all possessions. It is obvious, therefore, that the slaying of a king by any of his subjects was a crime that could not be compounded for, and thus when documents mention the amount of the king's wergild – that is, the price to be paid for him if he were killed – they must be concerned with settlements between warring factions or nations, such as the occasion when the men of Kent paid to King Ine of Wessex in 694 the sum of thirty thousand (pence), to obtain peace after they had burnt Mul, a member of the West Saxon reigning house, and his followers some years previously. In a text dating from the post-Viking period and written in the north of the country, a king's wergild is set at fifteen times that of a thane, and half of it is to be paid to his kindred, half to the people. Mercian law only demanded a wergild approximately six times that of a thane, but this evidently refers only to what was paid to the kindred, for an equal amount, called a 'royal payment', is to be paid in addition. We have no direct evidence for Wessex, but the amount paid for Mul is the wergild of a Mercian king, without the 'royal payment'. This would not be called for in this instance, for Mul was, at most, only a sub-king.

If anyone fought in the king's house, he forfeited all that he possessed, and his life was at the king's mercy.

Increasing importance was attached to the sanctity of the king's person as the period advanced. King Edmund (939–46) decreed that no man guilty of bloodshed was to presume to come into the king's neighbourhood until he had done penance for his crime and undertaken to make reparation to the kindred. This king, as we have seen, was greatly concerned to decrease the number of blood-feuds, and a regulation which in effect forbade the appearance at court of anyone concerned as a principal in a feud must have been effective in the desired direction. Later codes extend this prohibition to other categories of offenders, and state also that if an excommunicated man comes into the king's neighbourhood, he is to forfeit both life and goods. Popular tradition interpreted the king's neighbourhood as extending on all four sides of the gate of the house in which he was residing 'three miles and three furlongs and the breadth of three acres, and nine feet and nine "spear-hands" and nine barley corns.' Men liked to be precise on such matters.

A very heavy fine, 120 West Saxon shillings, a sum equivalent to twenty oxen, was due to the king for various crimes regarded as a breach of his protection, and for forcible entry into his house, while lesser offences had smaller fines. He might give his special peace to particular individuals or places or occasions, and if he did, the penalty for breach of this peace varied according to whether it had been given by the king in person, or through a subordinate. The homilist Ælfric draws the following parallel to illustrate and bring home to his hearers the difference between the old dispensation, given by God through his prophets, and the new, given by Christ himself:

One thing is the ordinance which the king ordains through his ealdorman or his reeve; quite another is his own command in his presence.

The law draws a distinction between a breach of the king's peace, 'given with his own hand', which incurs the death penalty, and a breach of the peace given by the ealdorman or the king's reeve, which can be compensated for by fines. These increase in size with the importance of the assembly in which the peace was pronounced, and in the northern Danelaw they were so heavy that they must have been beyond the capacity to pay of any but the wealthiest of men. It seems probable, therefore, that the responsibility for payment lay with the whole district if it failed to produce the disturber of the peace, or if, having produced him, it chose to redeem him from death. Such arrangements were in force elsewhere: at Dover in the Confessor's time there was a special king's peace from Michaelmas until St Andrew's day 'and if anyone broke it, the king's reeve took a fine from all in common.' In dealing with corporate acts of violence or disobedience, kings sometimes used more summary methods than levying fines: they ravaged the district concerned. King Eadred ravaged Thetford in 952 when an abbot had been murdered there, and King Edgar ravaged Thanet in 969 because of the ill-treatment there of some York merchants. Similar violent measures were taken by the unpopular kings Ethelred the Unready (978–1016) and Harthacnut (1040–2), but it is clear that respected and efficient rulers on occasion took this line of action.

*

The Church made its contribution to the idea of the dignity and sanctity of kingship. Kings state in their regnal styles that they reign by the grace of God, and towards the end of the eighth century the practice of an ecclesiastical coronation was introduced from the Continent. It grew in importance, special emphasis being laid on the anointing of the king. A coronation order was composed by Archbishop Dunstan for Edgar's delayed coronation at Bath in 973, and this order later influenced the forms used abroad. The ceremony at Edgar's coronation made a great impression, and a Latin writer some thirty years later gives a full account of it, including the oath sworn by the king. There also survives a vernacular version of this, as given by King Ethelred at his coronation at Kingston, and it is as follows:

In the name of the Holy Trinity! I promise three things to the Christian people subject to me. First that God's Church and all Christian people of my dominions shall keep true peace. Secondly, that I forbid to all ranks robbery and all injustice. Thirdly, that I promise and command justice and mercy in all judgements, that the gracious and compassionate God, who liveth and reigneth, may through that grant us his eternal mercy.

By the early eleventh century it could be declared that 'A Christian king is Christ's deputy among Christian people.' We can see the influence of this theory. Whereas in 757 a West Saxon king was deprived of his kingdom 'on account of his unjust deeds' by the West Saxon council, and Alhred of Northumbria was deposed in 774, Ælfric at the end of the tenth century can state as an accepted fact that a king cannot be deposed. He says:

No man can make himself king, but the people has the choice to elect whom they like; but after he is consecrated king, he has authority over the people, and they cannot shake his yoke off their necks.

Archbishop Wulfstan considered the expulsion of King Ethelred in 1013 as 'a very great treachery', second only to the betrayal of one's lord's soul.

Though the king was elected, the choice was normally limited to members of the royal family. In early times, any man who could trace his descent back to the founder of the royal dynasty considered that he had a claim to the throne, and much conflict was occasioned in some king-

doms by rival claims. It became increasingly the custom
to elect the eldest son of the last king. This custom was
broken when King Alfred was chosen to succeed his
brother in 871, but his predecessor's sons were young,
and, with an invading army in the country, it was hardly
the time to elect a child. On King Alfred's death, his
eldest son was chosen, and an attempt by the son of
Alfred's elder brother and predecessor to obtain the
throne was foiled. After this we hear of no further suggestion that a king should be chosen from this elder branch,
though it included men of standing and capacity. Even
after the murder of Edward the Martyr in 978, when his
brother Ethelred was still a minor, there seems to have
been no thought of passing over a descendant of Alfred
in favour of an adult descendant of a more distant king.

The election of a king was frequently nothing more
than the acknowledgement of the obvious successor, but
when such was lacking, some decision among various
possibilities might have to be made. The body responsible
for the appointment was the king's council of 'wise men',
which was made up of the archbishops, bishops, the
abbots of the greater abbeys, the ealdormen, the more
important king's thanes, and sometimes the king's
priests. They were not always in unison regarding the
succession to the throne; when Cnut died in 103⅘ one
party wished to elect his son Harthacnut, absent in Denmark, but another wished to postpone decision until his
arrival, and appoint Cnut's illegitimate son Harold as
regent meanwhile, and this party prevailed. A more
remarkable disagreement occurred in 1016, under
abnormal conditions. King Ethelred died while Cnut's
Danish army was attempting the conquest of England,
and in the disordered state of the country an assembly at
Southhampton chose Cnut as his successor, whereas
another at London elected Ethelred's son Edmund.

The king's council advised him on important matters of policy, on the issue of laws and the alienation of land by charter to religious houses and others. Bede has left us a vivid picture of the deliberations of the Northumbrian council over the acceptance of the Christian faith. Offa of Mercia, as overlord of the south of England, held councils that were attended by all the greater ecclesiastics south of the Humber, but only by Mercian laymen. When all England was united under one rule, ecclesiastical and lay magnates came to the council from all parts, but after the reign of Athelstan (924–39) those from the extreme north seem rarely to have been present, and it may be that they were summoned only when matters of deep importance were to be discussed. A council at London of 989 or 990, which is unusual because of the presence at it of several northern dignitaries, is called 'the great synod', 'the great assembly', in the document that mentions it, and was probably felt to be abnormal. The king summoned his council 'from far and wide' when he needed it; the great festivals of Christmas, Easter, and Pentecost were favourite times for large gatherings, and several surviving law-codes we know to have been issued by councils that sat at these seasons, Athelstan's fifth code at Exeter at Christmas, Edmund's first code at London at Easter, Cnut's laws at Winchester at Christmas. In these three cases the meeting took place in an important borough, but the council often met at royal estates in places of no particular significance. To house so great a company with their retinues the royal residences must have been of considerable size, and Asser, King Alfred's biographer, tells us that this king gave much attention to building and improving various royal vills. Some of the company may have lived in tents. Bishop Ælfsige of Chester-le-Street had presumably made the long journey south to attend a council when his companion, Aldred the Provost, added some collects into the ritual book the bishop had with him, with the note that he did so 'south of Woodyates at Oakley (Down) in Wessex, on Wednesday, St Lawrence's Day, for Ælfsige the bishop in his tent, when the moon was five nights old, before tierce.' But we cannot be certain that Woodyates was actually the place of assembly – though a council had met there a century earlier; it may merely have been a halting place on the way to or from the council. In any case, St Lawrence's day is in August; the attenders at winter councils can hardly have been housed in tents. Others, besides Bishop Ælfsige, possessed tents. A certain Ælfric Modercope bequeathed to a bishop 'my tent and my bedclothing, the best that I had out on my journey with me' and tents are mentioned in other wills.

Men journeying to and from councils and assemblies were protected by a special peace, which meant that heavier penalties were attached to offences committed against them on their way. Travellers to the king's court could claim hospitality en route; occasionally we hear of royal grants of estates to serve as halting-places on oft-made journeys, such as the grant of Crayke in Yorkshire by King Ecgfrith of Northumbria to St Cuthbert, as a resting place on his way to York, if we are to believe the Durham tradition. A late, but probably reliable, authority says that King Edgar gave estates in England to Kenneth of Scotland, so that he could stay at them on his way to court.

*

Even apart from occasions on which the council was meeting, the king was accompanied by a large company. Ælfric divides the court of a secular ruler into officials and thanes, and King Eadred's will shows that his highest court officials were his 'dish-thanes' or seneschals, his 'wardrobe-thanes', perhaps the same official as one called elsewhere a 'bower-thane', i.e. chamberlain, and his butlers. Below these he had stewards, and he refers in general terms to other office holders, among whom would probably be 'horse-thanes', or marshals. These offices were held by men of the highest class, and added to their prestige. The court included also king's thanes who had no special office, men who corresponded to the lord's followers mentioned by Tacitus. Old English poetry divides a king's following into 'tried men' and 'young men', and this division agrees well with one distinguishable in the writings of Bede between older men with an establishment of their own, who spend only part of their time at court, and young followers who have not yet received a landed endowment. Similarly, King Alfred's court consisted of the sons of the nobility who were being brought up there and king's thanes who spent only part of their time there. Alfred had organized these so that they served him in regular rotation, one month at court and two at home looking after their own concerns.

When the Dane, Cnut, became king, his court was guarded by his 'house-carls', a term of Scandinavian origin applied to military retainers organized as a gild or fraternity, with strict rules regulating their relations with the king and with each other. They had an assembly of their own, in which were judged offences against their code. It is only in later, Scandinavian, sources that we are told about the details of their organization, of the order of precedence at banquets, of the penalties for various misdemeanours. At first they formed a guard for a king of foreign race, but they were retained by Cnut's successors, even after the English line was restored. Moreover English noblemen copied the royal court and kept house-carls of their own. The expense of maintaining the royal house-carls was met by a tax. The boroughs of Dorset and Devon, in the reign of Edward the Confessor, contributed for this purpose at the rate of one mark of silver from ten hides. By this reign, at any rate, it had become common also to reward house-carls with land.

After the conversion to Christianity, kings were accompanied by their chaplains, who acted also as secretaries. From quite early times, the business of government required some men of education at its centre, and only the ecclesiastical order could supply them. King Alfred divided his whole income into fractions earmarked for special purposes, and this would have been impossible without at least some rudimentary form of royal treasury. The king's priests were in charge of his archives also, at any rate from the tenth century, when we begin to hear of documents kept with the king's relics. Certainly by the time of King Athelstan (924–39), and probably long before, there was a royal chancery in fact, though not in name, that drew up the charters issued in the king's name. We know the name of one of the secretaries of King Alfred's father, King Æthelwulf; he was a Frank, called Felix. King Eadred left in his will fifty mancuses of gold and five pounds to each of his priests 'at his relics', five pounds to each other priest. In the eleventh century it was not uncommon for a king's priest to be rewarded for his services with a bishopric.

*

The king moved from one royal estate to another, accompanied by his court. It can have been no light matter to offer hospitality to such a company. When King Athelstan had promised to visit a lady of royal rank, called Æthelflæd, his purveyors came the day before to inspect her provisions for the royal visit, and reported all in order except that the supply of mead was inadequate. The hostess prayed to the Virgin, with the result that the

mead never failed, although the butlers served the guests
all day with drinking-horns, goblets, and other vessels, 'as
is the custom at royal banquets.' Feasting and drinking
at the king's court are alluded to frequently in the poetic
literature. The company was entertained by minstrelsy
and song, and men told tales of their experiences. In
Beowulf the aged king himself entertained the court in
this way; at Athelstan's court the young Dunstan heard
an old man, who claimed to have been the sword-bearer
of King Edmund of East Anglia, tell the story of that
king's martyrdom at the hands of the Danes. It may have
been before the assembled company that the travellers
Ohthere and Wulfstan gave King Alfred the accounts
of their voyages in northern waters and the Baltic which
were incorporated into the translation of Orosius.

Foreign visitors were frequent at the courts of English
kings. In the days when England contained several
kingdoms, the court of the overlord was attended by the
kings of subject provinces, and there were friendly visits
and marriage alliances between the various royal houses,
and an interchange of envoys on business of different
kinds. Not all of these came in good faith; King Edwin of
Northumbria nearly lost his life by receiving without suspicion the envoy of a treacherous West Saxon king. The
precautions, described in *Beowulf*, before the newcomers
are allowed into the king's presence – the herald's enquiry into their business and antecedents, and his consultation with the king before he permits them to proceed, leaving spears and shields outside – are doubtless
drawn from life. Intercourse with foreign courts across
the Channel existed even in heathen times, when Ethelbert of Kent married the daughter of the Frankish king
Haribert, and it increased as time went on. Pippin sent
letters and gifts to King Eadberht of Northumbria
(737–58), and Charles the Great and Offa (757–96) were

in constant communication, exchanging gifts and discussing the common interests of the lands they governed. Charles at one point went so far as to interfere in the succession to the throne of Northumbria. Alfred's father maintained a connexion with the Carolingian court, and married a Frankish princess as his second wife, while Asser says that Alfred's court was visited by Franks, Frisians, Gauls, pagans (i.e. Scandinavians), Welsh, Irish, and Bretons, and claims that embassies from foreign nations were a daily occurrence. We may allow a little for exaggeration, but much of what he says receives confirmation elsewhere; his information that letters and gifts came from as distant a personage as the patriarch of Jerusalem is supported by the survival of some medical recipes sent to Alfred from this source. Royal guests at Alfred's court included the Welsh king Anarawd of Gwyneth, son of Rhodri Mawr, who came in order to secure Alfred's support and was confirmed while at the court, Alfred standing sponsor and presenting him with generous gifts, as he did also the Danish king Guthrum at his baptism, which was agreed on after the Danish defeat at Edington in 878.

We hear more of visits from the non-English kings of Britain in the next century. Most of them acknowledged King Athelstan's authority and some of his charters are witnessed by the rulers of Wales, and of Strathclyde, and (once) of Scotland, present at his court when the documents were drawn up. They attest as sub-kings. Kenneth, king of Scotland, was escorted to King Edgar's court by the bishop of Chester-le-Street and the earl of Northumbria, where he received the grant of Lothian in return for his homage; and in the same king's reign a scene was enacted at Chester in 973 that impressed itself deeply on men's minds. Post-Conquest writers declare that Edgar was rowed on the Dee by eight subject-kings visiting his court. Whether this is true or not, we may be sure that something spectacular took place from the words of Ælfric, an almost contemporary authority:

And all the kings who were in this island, of the Cumbrians and the Scots, once came to Edgar, eight kings on one day, and they all submitted to Edgar's direction.

King Alfred married his youngest daughter to a count of Flanders, and several of his granddaughters were married into continental ruling families. It would be tedious to list all the references to foreign embassies and visitors that occur in the sources for the later part of our period, but some scenes are more fully reported. Hugh, duke of the Franks, sent an embassy led by Athelwulf, son of Baldwin of Flanders and Alfred's daughter, to King Athelstan to ask for his sister's hand in marriage. The mission was received before an assembly of magnates at Abingdon, and it brought an impressive set of gifts,

perfumes such as never before had been seen in England, precious stones, especially emeralds, in whose greenness the reflected sun lit up the eyes of the onlookers with a pleasing light; many fleet horses; . . . a certain vase of onyx, carved with such subtle art by the engraver that the cornfields seemed truly to wave, the vines to bud, the forms of men to move, and so clear and polished that it reflected like a mirror the faces of those gazing on it; the sword of Constantine the Great, on which the name of the original possessor could be read in letters of gold, and in whose pommel above thick plates of gold you could see fixed an iron nail, one of the four which the Jewish faction prepared for the crucifixion of our Lord's body; the spear of Charles the Great, which, when that most invincible emperor, leading an army against the Saracens, hurled among the enemy, never failed to secure the victory; it was said to be the same which, being driven by the hand of the centurion into our Lord's side, opened by the gash of that precious wound Paradise to wretched mortals;

and so on through a list of further relics, including part

of the true cross and of the crown of thorns. The suitor had taken the trouble to study Athelstan's tastes; this king was a great collector of relics and apparently not very critical of what he was told about them.

Very different gifts were brought by another embassy. This came from Harold the Fairhaired, king of the Norwegians, and the envoys, Helgrim and Osfrid, were received at York in royal fashion, and given rich gifts. Harold had sent to Athelstan a ship with a golden beak and a purple sail, surrounded within with a dense wall of gilded shields. We are not told of the political purpose of their visit.

Incidents of this kind may have been rare, but the arrival of foreign messengers and the return of English envoys were common. Foreign ecclesiastics and scholars came also, from the time of the Irishman, Adamnan, who has left us a reference to two visits to the court of King Aldfrith of Northumbria at the end of the seventh century, to the days of Edward the Confessor (1042–66), when Norman and Lotharingian ecclesiastics sought their fortune in England. To single out a few from many instances, we may mention the sensational visit to Alfred of three Irishmen who had set out without oars or rudder and with food for seven days and arrived in Cornwall after a voyage of just that length; the foreign scholars invited by Alfred to help his educational reform; the monks of St Bertin's in St Omer who came to King Edmund (939–46) when dissatisfied with a reforming abbot at home, and were given by him a monastery at Bath; the monks from Fleury and Ghent who came to help King Edgar draw up a common rule of observance for English monasteries; the Danish priest Gerbrand who came in 1022 to be consecrated bishop of Roskilde by the archbishop of Canterbury. Throughout the period, there were envoys coming backwards and forwards from the papal curia, and occasionally the important event of the visit of a papal legate.

Finally, we can add the visits of merchants bringing rare goods from abroad. The Norwegian Ohthere brought walrus tusks to King Alfred, and, if we can trust the evidence of the Icelandic sagas, it was the habit of Icelanders on trading ventures to visit the court and perhaps enter into the service of the king for a time. Thus Gunnlaug Ormstunga came to the court of Ethelred the Unready, and sang before him a panegyric singularly inapplicable to that monarch.

All the host of the generous and warlike king fears England's lord as a god; and the race of men bows to Ethelred.

We naturally need not assume that all the business of these visitors took place before the assembled court. Yet they would receive hospitality along with the members of the court and hand on news of the outside world and the tales of their own lands. As there would also be a constant coming and going of the king's messengers who bore his writ and seal to the shire-moots and to the individual magnates in all quarters of his land, one may believe that after attendance at court its members might return to their own localities with something to recount.

CHAPTER IV

FINANCE AND ADMINISTRATION

Finance

THE king derived his income partly from royal estates, which were scattered over the whole country, each in the charge of a king's reeve. Another important source of revenue was his 'farm', a food-rent paid to him by all the lands in his realm that had not been freed from this charge by special exemption. It was rendered at the royal estates, and the lands from which it was due were grouped together into units, each of which was to supply annually the 'farm of one night', that is, the provisions originally considered adequate to support the king and his court for a day. Though sometimes it was commuted into a money payment, it was normally paid in kind, in ale and corn, malt, honey, dairy-produce, and livestock. The king drew income also from the tribute of subject kings, from inheritance after foreigners, from tolls, and from fines and forfeitures incurred in the law-courts. The king's reeves presided over these and collected what was due to the king. Even when grants of the profits of jurisdiction were made to private individuals, the fines for some of the more serious offences were reserved for the king.

Besides his actual income, whether in money or in produce, the king had many rights that he could claim from his subjects. He did not need to spend his resources on the equipment or payment of an army, or on the hiring of labour to build fortifications and bridges. These obligations, like the king's farm, were distributed over

the estates of the land; exemption from them was so rare
that a charter that claims such exemption is immediately
suspect. The king is more ready to grant – for a consideration – exemption from some of his other rights,
from the duty of supplying hospitality to his messengers,
his huntsmen, and falconers, or of feeding his dogs or his
hawks. A bishop of Worcester in 855 paid three hundred
shillings to get an estate freed 'from feeding any hawks or
falcons or any huntsmen of king or ealdorman, likewise
from the feeding of those men whom we call in English
"the Welsh expedition" (a term of uncertain meaning),
and from giving lodging to them or to mounted travellers, whether English or foreign, whether nobles or com-
moners.' Certain places, because of their position, were
liable to special services. Thus an estate on the coast of
Cornwall supplied maritime guard instead of bridge-
work; Dover was responsible for giving aid to the king's
messengers crossing the Channel; the priests of the king's
three churches in Archenfield bore the king's embassies
into Wales; Wallingford owed carrying services by land
or water, as far as Reading, Blewbury, Sutton Courtenay,
and Bensington; at Torksey, 'if the king's messengers
should come thither, the men of the same town should
conduct them to York with their ships and their means of
navigation, and the sheriff should find the messengers'
and the sailors' food out of his farm'; if the king visited
Shrewsbury, the sheriff supplied him on his departure
with twenty-four horses to accompany him as far as
Leintwardine, or as far as the first house in Staffordshire;
and so on. A variety of local arrangements about guarding the king's person and helping him in his hunting
when he came on a visit are mentioned in Domesday
Book, and similarly, his rights to customary payments
varied from place to place. Six counties, Worcester,
Warwick, Oxford, Northampton, Leicester, and Wiltshire

each paid him ten pounds for a hawk, twenty shillings for a sumpter-horse; Oxfordshire and Warwickshire paid twenty-three pounds for dogs; three royal manors in Bedfordshire paid sums from 130 to 65 shillings for dogs; the city of Norwich supplied a bear and six dogs for bear-baiting.

We know from his life by Asser that King Alfred reorganized his finances. Alfred gives us his views on the subject of royal expenditure in a passage which he inserts into his translation of Boethius's *Consolation of Philosophy*:

> I desired tools and materials for the work that I was charged to perform, namely that I might worthily and fittingly steer and rule the dominion that was entrusted to me. . . . This, then, is a king's material and his tools for ruling with, that he have his land fully manned. He must have men who pray, and soldiers and workmen. Lo, thou knowest that without these tools no king can reveal his power. Also, this is his material, which he must have for those tools – sustenance for those three orders; and their sustenance consists in land to live on, and gifts, and weapons, and food, and ale, and clothes, and whatever else those three orders require. And without these things he cannot hold those tools, nor without these tools do any of the things that he is charged to do.

The division of mankind into the three orders is common medieval doctrine, and Alfred may have learnt of it from Frankish sources, for references to it begin in these about the same time, though it happens that Alfred's statement is fuller and more complete than any other known to me from so early a date.

It is interesting to compare Alfred's actual division of the income that reached his treasury. Half of it he devoted to religious uses, that is, to the men who pray. The other half he subdivided into three portions, one for the soldiers and thanes who served him in turn at his court, one for his workmen, whom he had gathered from many races, and the third for visitors who came to him from every race, far and near. The soldiers mentioned in this connexion are the king's bodyguard; the bulk of the men who fight, the rank and file, were not recompensed from the king's treasury, any more than were the largest class of the men who work, the tillers of the soil; these gave their services in return for the land they held. Alfred makes no provision in this division for the royal officials in the shires or on the royal estates, for these derived their income from a share of the royal income before it was handed over to the king, and from lands allotted to them. Grants of land lie outside the subject of this chapter in Asser. The queen and the princes were also provided for by estates assigned to them. The evidence for this is later than Alfred's time, but does not suggest that it was an innovation. The king's council about 975 took away from the abbey of Abingdon some estates which King Edgar had given there, because they were estates belonging to the king's sons. The king's wife received a gift of lands at her marriage: Emma is said to have been given Winchester, Exeter, and Rutland by Ethelred, and the last-mentioned place appears in the possession of Edward the Confessor's queen also. It is, in fact, highly probable that it became a separate county by reason of its having been a queen's dower. The Confessor's queen is shown by Domesday book to have had very extensive lands, but we cannot tell how many came to her from her own family. The same source shows that there were customary gifts to the queen in many places by the end of the Anglo-Saxon period, and they may be of ancient date. For example, she received a hundred shillings from each of the counties of Worcester, Warwick, Northampton, and Oxford, and sums from two to four ounces of gold from the Bedfordshire royal estates of Luton, Leighton Buzzard, and Houghton Regis.

*

The royal revenue so far described was planned to meet normal demands; any abnormal need for money had to be met by a special tax levied on the country. Over most of the country the unit of assessment on which it was raised was the hide, originally the amount of land felt sufficient for a peasant household, though from the beginning, Kent was assessed in 'sulungs', i.e. areas which could be worked by an eight-ox plough, while in the parts of England settled by the Danes in the Viking Age the hide was replaced by the Danish 'ploughland' which Latin sources render 'carrucata'. All over the country estates were assessed in these measures for fiscal purposes in round figures which even in the beginning could only roughly have approximated to the actual area of the individual estate. The process seems to have been as follows: a large district was given an assessment reckoned in multiples of a hundred hides or ploughlands, and this number was then divided locally among the component estates of the district in units of five or multiples of five (in the Danelaw, which calculated by the long hundred of 120, the units are usually of six, or multiples of six, carrucates). As the assessment remained fixed over very long periods, while the actual conditions might alter greatly, it tended to move further and further from any correspondence with the real size of the estates. We hear most of this assessment in relation to a tax known as 'Danegeld', but it is much earlier than the introduction of this tax, and was probably first laid down in connexion with the payment of the king's farm.

Greater sums of money than could be obtained from the normal revenue were required for the tribute to buy off Danish raids. Already in 865 the East Angles 'made peace with the Danes', and doubtless made it at a price, but even at that time the notion of buying off an invader was not new. Oswiu of Northumbria had attempted to buy off Penda of Mercia in 654, apparently from the royal treasure. After 865 the practice became only too common, and the requisite sums were obtained by special taxation. This is shown clearly by a document in which a bishop of Worcester leases one of the estates of his see in return for twenty mancuses of gold, in order to meet his church's contribution to 'the immense tribute of the barbarians in the year in which the pagans occupied London' (i.e. 872). When the Danish king, Swein, was accepted by a large part of England and resided at Gainsborough in 1013, he imposed a tribute, and seems to have employed the existing machinery in its collection; for it was a local magnate, Thurcetel, surnamed 'Salmon', who collected it from the hundred of Flegg, Norfolk, and who, learning of Swein's death as he was riding to deliver the money, brought it back and re-paid it to the contributors. In 1040 another Danish king, Harthacnut, sent his own house-carls to collect a heavy tax for the payment of his ships' crews, and at Worcester the populace rose against two of them and killed them.

King Eadred, who died in 955, left in his will sixteen thousand pounds to his people 'that they may be able to buy relief for themselves from famine and from the heathen army, if they need.' Certain prominent ecclesiastics were to hold it in trust for the benefit of groups of counties in the south of England and in Mercia. In 991 a Danish army was bought off for the sum of ten thousand pounds, and in the years that follow repeated and ever-increasing payments are made. A treaty of 994, which survives, was bought for twenty-two thousand pounds, and by 1012 the amount had risen to forty-eight thousand. It was in this year that Archbishop Ælfheah of Canterbury, held prisoner by the Danes, refused to allow the people to be burdened any further by paying a ransom for him, and died a martyr's death at the hands

of his incensed captors; and in the same year also, King
Ethelred took into his service ships of Danish mercenaries, who had left their own side because they were
shocked by the murder of the archbishop. An annual tax
was levied to pay for them, and a standing force of house-
carls was kept through the reigns of Cnut and his sons,
and paid by a tax known as 'army-payment'. It was
stopped by Edward the Confessor in 1051. After the
Norman Conquest it was referred to as 'Danegeld'.

*

Meanwhile another charge had become incumbent on
the land, the upkeep of a fleet. Some early kings, such as
Edwin and Ecgfrith of Northumbria, had fleets, but we
are not told who paid for their building and their manning, nor for Alfred's fleet, which he enlarged with new
and larger ships, built 'neither according to the Frisian
nor the Danish pattern, but as it seemed to him that they
would be most useful.' They were manned partly by
Frisians, and it is possible that ship-builders were among
the craftsmen whom Asser tells us the king invited to
work for him and paid out of his revenue. But it is probable that the bulk of the cost of providing and maintaining ships was borne by the land as in later times. A fleet
plays a part in the campaigns of Alfred's successors,
Edward and Athelstan, and Edgar's fleet was at Chester
in 973 when he received the submission of the Welsh and
Scottish kings. A post-Conquest writer assigns to this
king three thousand six hundred ships, and speaks of an
annual circuit of the whole island. Without accepting his
statements in full, we may reasonably suppose that the
possession of a strong fleet was one of the reasons why
Edgar overawed the foreign kings of Britain.

More information on the provision of ships is available
for Ethelred's reign (978–1016). He demanded both a

land-army and the furnishing of ships in 999, but owing to delays and incompetent leadership 'at the end it effected nothing except oppression of the people and waste of money and the encouragement of the enemy.' In 1008 the order went out that ships were to be built throughout England, 'a warship from 310 hides and a helmet and a coat-of-mail from eight hides.' They were ready the following year:

There were more of them than there had ever been before in England in any king's day, according to what books tell us, and they were brought all together to Sandwich, and were to lie there and defend this land against every raiding army. But yet we had not the good fortune nor the glory that that naval force was of any use to this land, any more than it had been on many previous occasions.

Once again, 'they let all the nation's labour thus lightly come to naught.' According to the laws of this reign, warships were to be ready every year soon after Easter.

About 1005, an archbishop of Canterbury left to the king his best ship with its sailing tackle along with sixty helmets and coats-of-mail, and about the same time a bishop of Crediton left to the king a sixty-four-oared ship. The archbishop bequeathed also a ship to each of the counties of Kent and Wiltshire, obviously to lessen their burden of supplying ships. There are traces in some counties of an arrangement of hundreds in groups of three, each group to provide one ship, and Domesday Book gives sporadic information on ship service at various places. Maldon for example supplied one ship; more often, we read of contributions in men, goods, or money: Warwick sent four boatswains or four pounds when the king led a sea expedition; an annual charge of sixpence a house at Colchester could be devoted either to provisioning the king's mercenaries or to an expedition by land or sea; if the king went against his enemies by sea, the burghers of Leicester must send him four horses to London, to carry weapons or other things where they were needed; vague references to service by land or sea are sometimes found. A document from about the year 1000 describes how St Paul's apportioned over its estates its obligation to supply forty-five seamen.

From 1012, when Ethelred took into his service forty-five Danish ships, a standing fleet was kept, and charged for at the rate of eight marks (i.e. over four pounds) to the rowlock. This amounted to a heavy burden, and the fleet was disbanded by Edward the Confessor in 1049 or 1050. By the end of his reign some of the Channel ports had responsibilities for sea-defence; thus at Lewes 'if the king sent his men to guard the sea, without going himself' all the men of the borough, no matter on whose land they dwelt, paid twenty shillings, which was given to 'those who had charge of the arms on the ships.'

*

The king's rights with regard to the calling out of the army are not specified in detail in the laws. These give the penalties for disobeying a summons, and for desertion from the army, and state that all penalties for crime are increased when the army has been called out; but they do not say if there was a limit to the number of men whom the king could demand, nor do they specify the minimum equipment in weapons and provisions that each man must bring with him, though King Athelstan legislates to ensure that shields shall be of a proper quality. He forbids the covering of them with sheepskin (instead of ox-hide). In times of crisis, it is probable that every able-bodied man could be summoned to the host. This was done in 1016, but the mere fact that the chronicler troubles to state this expressly implies that it was not the normal proceeding. It is only when we reach Domesday Book that we are told how many men must go

from estates of a certain size. A normal rate in Edward
the Confessor's time seems to have been one man from
five hides, but there are differences in local custom as
each place made its own bargain with the king. In Berkshire, a man went from five hides with provisions for two
months or four shillings from each hide instead; at
Malmesbury, the king had the right to one man from five
hides, or a pound; Oxford ought to send twenty men, but
could buy itself free at the rate of a pound a man; at
Warwick 'when the king went by land', ten burgesses
went on behalf of all the others; Leicester supplied
twelve. We are told that Exeter performed the same
service as five hides of land, and the three small Devon-
shire boroughs, Totnes, Lidford, and Barnstaple, together
performed the same service as Exeter. This seems to let
the Devon boroughs off lightly, but between them they
also paid annually a mark of silver for mercenaries. The
Dorset boroughs pay at exactly the same rate, a mark of
silver for ten hides, 'for the needs of the house-carls', and
nothing is said of obligations to the host when it was
summoned. We cannot be sure that any of these arrangements are of great antiquity. A law of Athelstan's, in the
first half of the previous century, ordering every landowner to have two well-mounted men for each plough in
his possession, suggests, if it applies to the obligation of
military service, a very much heavier demand, and it is
possible that later kings aimed at smaller contingents in
order to improve the quality of their equipment. The
traditional armament of the Anglo-Saxon churl, spear
and shield, had become inadequate for changed conditions of warfare.

Domesday Book occasionally tells us something of the
arrangements made locally as to who was to perform the
military service due from an estate, as in this passage
relating to land in Lincolnshire:

The men of the Wapentake of Candleshoe, with the consent of the whole Riding, testify that in the time of King Edward Siwate, Alnod, Fenchel, and Aschil divided their father's land among them equally and share and share alike, and held it in such wise that if there were a call to the king's army, and Siwate could go, the other brothers assisted him. After Siwate, a second went, and Siwate and the rest assisted him; and thus with respect to them all.

We may perhaps see a glimpse of a village council deciding who shall answer the king's summons in the specific words which Abbot Ælfric uses to translate a vaguer Latin original:

The township was ordered to equip two soldiers for the army. Then the two boys (i.e. two foundlings brought up in the village) were chosen for that military service.

King Alfred introduced the innovation of dividing the forces he could call on into two sections, only one of which was on service at any time, to be relieved by the other contingent when they had covered a set period. The Chronicle records one occasion when the serving force came to the end of its term and, having used up its provisions, disbanded before the relieving division arrived on the spot, but in general the system seems to have worked well. Certainly in the reign of Alfred's son Edward the English army proved a most effective force for the offensive warfare of reconquering the land ceded to the Danes.

Anglo-Saxon kings often led their armies in person. Indeed, at one point in 1016, the assembled host refused to act, and disbanded because the king was not present; but the circumstances were unusual, and they may well have suspected that the king's son who had summoned them was playing a lone hand. Desertion from the army was a much more serious offence if the king himself were leading it than otherwise. In this event, it was punishable by death, unless the culprit could redeem himself by payment of his own wergild; in the king's absence, desertion from the army was punished by a fine of 120 shillings. While the laws state the general penalties for such offences, Domesday Book shows that there could be local variations even in matters of this kind. Thus while the fine for neglecting a summons to the army was five pounds (which equals 240 West Saxon shillings) in Oxford and Warwick, the same offence in Berkshire and in Worcester might cost all one's lands.

*

The assembly of the army took time, and so it did not provide an adequate defence against sudden attack. This became very obvious in the era of Viking invasions, for the Danes could land a powerful force on the coast, or on the banks of navigable rivers, do great damage, and sail away with their plunder before the forces of the district could be mustered. Alfred began therefore to surround his territories with a ring of fortresses, manned and kept in repair by the surrounding districts. Long before Alfred's time, the kings had the right to demand work on fortifications as one of the three public charges on all estates, those charges which from the middle of the eighth century are almost always reserved whenever any grant of exemption from dues or services is being made. The labour for the great earthwork built by Offa on his Welsh frontier would be forthcoming under this charge, and before Alfred's time early ninth-century charters make mention of the fortification of strongholds 'against the pagans', in a few cases enlarging the obligation to include the destruction of (enemy) fortifications. Alfred's 'burghal system' was new, therefore, only in its scale, and perhaps in making more permanent arrangements for the upkeep of the strongholds. Asser complains of the failure of the people to co-operate willingly with the king in this work, which meant that in some places the forts he had ordered were incomplete, or not begun, when invasion came. It may be that the charge of making them fell heavily on some already burdened districts. It is clear that the systematic defence of his realm by this means was not completed until the reign of his son Edward, from whose time comes a document known as the *Burghal Hidage*, which gives the number of hides of land allotted to the maintenance of the individual fortresses. Edward also consolidated his advance into Danish-held territory by similar fortifications, and his sister Æthelflæd, the Lady of the Mercians, followed the same plan in the area under her control. The type of fortification differed according to local conditions; sometimes it was merely a question of repairing existing walls of Roman origin, whereas at other places an earthwork and stockade were thrown up at some previously unfortified site; a fort at Towcester was surrounded with a stone wall. It was reckoned that a fortress would require as a garrison four men to every pole of wall, and the allotment of a definite number of hides of land to the maintenance and manning of a fortress is based on the assumption that one man would come from each hide, and that eighty hides would be responsible for keeping in repair twenty poles of the wall. The laws of the next reign enjoin that the repairing of fortresses must be completed a fortnight after the Rogation days. In the reign of Edward the Confessor the demand of one man from each hide was still being made at Chester, where the reeve summoned a man from each hide in the county to repair the wall and bridge. The lord of any man who failed to appear paid to the king and earl a fine of forty (Norman) shillings, which was equivalent to 120 Mercian shillings.

The repair of bridges is associated with military

service and fortress work to make up the three public dues. One surviving document shows how this duty might be apportioned. It consists of a list of the estates whose business it was to repair Rochester bridge, with the number of piers for which each was responsible, in terms such as:

> The second pier belongs to Gillingham and to Chatham, and they have to provide planks for one pole and put three beams in position.

Royal Officials

As King Alfred remarks, 'the affairs of the kingdom' were 'various and manifold', and a reference we get to his dealing with an appeal to his judgement in a law-suit, as 'he was in his chamber, washing his hands', suggests a very busy man with no time to waste. The king needed deputies who could deal with the routine business of government in the various parts of the kingdom. This deputy was called an ealdorman, until in the eleventh century this term was superseded under Scandinavian influence by the name earl, which had previously been used in this sense only in the parts of England densely settled by the Danes. In English territory the word earl had had, as we shall see later, a different meaning, denoting, not an official, but merely a man of the upper class, but this usage was obsolete long before the eleventh century, and the way was open to adopt the term earl to replace the native term ealdorman.

The ealdormen were appointed by the king. Sometimes they were related to the royal house; one mentioned in a charter of King Beorhtwulf of Mercia in 852 is called 'his uncle's son' in the boundaries attached to the charter, and the descendants of Alfred's elder brother are some-

times ealdormen of the Western Provinces in the late
tenth and early eleventh centuries. Sometimes in the
eighth century ealdormen belong to the family that had
ruled the province as kings before its absorption into a
larger kingdom. Most often they were drawn from the
king's thanes. Their office was not hereditary, but it became usual in the tenth century to choose ealdormen
from a few outstanding families, and the same ealdormanry frequently remained in one family for more than
one generation. The sons of Ealdorman Athelstan 'Half-
King' (c. 932–58) succeeded him in East Anglia, and
Mercia was regarded as belonging to the house of Leofric
in the eleventh century.

Until the tenth century an ealdorman south of the
Thames was normally in charge of a single shire, but
later several shires are united under one ealdorman;
Æthelweard, for example, was Ealdorman of the south-
western shires at the end of the tenth century. The south
of England had been arranged in its modern shires much
earlier than the rest of England; Kent, Sussex, Essex, and
probably Middlesex represent originally independent
kingdoms, and Surrey is the 'south region', the land
south of the Thames that once belonged to the Saxons
north of it. Norfolk and Suffolk represent ancient divisions of East Anglia. But the shires of Wessex, except for
Devon and Berkshire, took their names from their chief
settlement, Somerset from Somerton, Hampshire from
Southampton, and so on, and probably arose from a very
early administrative arrangement. This superseded the
conditions of the age of settlement, when the land was
divided into smaller regions, separated from one another
by stretches of forest and waste in which precise boundaries were unnecessary.

It is less easy to discover what was the area under an
ealdorman's control in Mercia and Northumbria. The

modern shires here are of later growth, hiding to a great
extent the older division into regions, though we know
the names of the tribes of some of these. Our shires of the
East and North Midlands and of York have developed
from the areas attached to Danish boroughs after the
Viking settlement, while the shires of the South-West
Midlands, which are similarly named from a single
borough, probably owe their origin to a tenth-century
reorganization which may have taken the West Saxon
shires as its model. By this time it was no longer customary for each shire to have its own ealdorman, and
Mercia is sometimes treated as one large ealdormanry,
though sometimes smaller ones are carved out of it; but
when Mercia was a separate kingdom, it seems to have
had as many as eight, or even ten, ealdormen in office
concurrently. We do not know how Northumbria was
divided among its ealdormen in its independent days.
When it became part of the kingdom of England it was
sometimes under a single ealdorman, whereas sometimes
Yorkshire was treated as a distinct area.

Within his own area of operations, the ealdorman was
the king's representative. He led the forces of his district
in war, and presided at its judicial assembly. Like the
king, he had official estates, and rights of claiming
hospitality for his officials and messengers. A charter of
836 which frees a bishop's estate from, among other
things, hospitality to the king or ealdorman has an en-
dorsement that shows that the ealdorman's rights had
had to be bought out, for it says: 'and the bishop gave to
Ealdorman Sigred six hundred shillings in gold and to
Ealdorman Mucel ten hides of land at Crowle.' The
ealdorman received a proportion, perhaps a third, of the
fines due to the king at the law-courts, and a third of the
revenues from the boroughs within his province, at any
rate by the end of the period. He was entitled to a fine of

120 shillings if anyone fought at an assembly where he was presiding, and he had higher compensations than other men of the same class for breach of his protection, fighting in his house or violent entry into it. In the North, the only area for which evidence exists, his wergild was four times that of a king's thane. A Surrey ealdorman in Alfred's reign uses the expression 'my two wergilds', which suggests that, like a Mercian king, he may have been entitled to a wergild by reason of his office as well as the normal wergild of a man of his class.

Royal grants of land to individual ealdormen are common, but one cannot distinguish gifts in gratitude for service from sales. The wills of several ealdormen have survived from the ninth and tenth centuries, and show that they had extensive lands, but nothing at all comparable to the enormous accumulation of landed property by the families of Earl Godwine and Earl Leofric in the eleventh century that is revealed by Domesday Book. Many of the estates bequeathed in the wills can be shown to have been acquired by inheritance, and others may have been. It is difficult to judge therefore whether in general the holding of this office was highly profitable.

*

When the area under an ealdorman came to consist of several shires, we begin to hear of an official called the 'shire-reeve', that is, the sheriff. He is first mentioned in the latter part of the tenth century, but men who hold this office are sometimes referred to under the wider designation of 'king's reeve'. It is possible that the office of sheriff may have existed for some time before the first use of the specific title, but there would be little need for it while the ealdormanries were small, and in the ninth century the laws assume that a man in need of assistance will apply direct to the ealdorman, not to a sheriff. The latter was appointed by the king and took charge of his rights in the shire. He presided at the shire-moot in the absence of the ealdorman; it was the sheriff who as the king's representative took Archbishop Dunstan's oath in a land-suit in Kent between 964 and 988. When the king wished to communicate with the shire, he sent a writ addressed to the bishop, the earl, and at times the sheriff. Sometimes estates were attached to the office; by the end of the period the practice was not unknown by which the sheriff paid an agreed sum to the king as the proceeds of the shire and made what profit he could out of the actual receipts.

The term 'king's reeve' does not necessarily, nor usually, refer to the sheriff, but is in frequent use before that office came into being. It normally refers to the man in charge of a royal estate and responsible for the collection of the king's farm from the surrounding area. He presided at the 'folk-moot' mentioned in Alfred's laws; a trader had to bring the men he was proposing to take up country with him 'before the king's reeve in the folk-moot'; he collected the fines and forfeitures due to the king, and in some circumstances he had to keep prisoners at the king's estate.

The towns were similarly in charge of a king's reeve, called a *wic*- or *port*-reeve. A town-reeve of Winchester was an important enough person for the Anglo-Saxon Chronicle to record his death in 896, while that of the reeve of Bath is entered in 906. The town-reeve is mentioned by name when the king addresses a writ to a town. The duties of these reeves included the control of the tolls paid by traders to the king. The king's reeve of Dorchester rode out to find out the business of the first ships of Danish men to reach the coast of Wessex (789–802), for if they were traders it was his business to exact toll; his enquiry cost him his life. Toll had even to be paid

when slaves were purchased for the purpose of manumitting them, and so the Exeter manumissions often
mention that the town-reeve took the toll on the king's
behalf. The town-reeve's duties would be increased when
it was forbidden to buy outside a town. He had to be
present as a witness, and at the proceedings when
property was attached. He had duties of supervision with
regard to the mint in his town.

In the reign of Ethelred the Unready, we read of fric-
tion between an ealdorman and the king's reeves. In 995
two brothers had been killed while illegally defending
one of their men who had stolen a bridle. Æthelwig, the
king's reeve in Buckingham, and Winsige, the reeve in
Oxford, gave them Christian burial. Ealdorman Leofsige
complained to the king, because the brothers had forfeited their right to this. But the king, who says 'I did
not wish to sadden Æthelwig, who was dear and
precious to me', not only refused to take action in the
matter, but also granted to this reeve the brothers' forfeited estates. Later, Ealdorman Leofsige was banished
for slaying another favourite reeve of the king, a man
called Æfic, in his own home. If Ethelred made a practice of upholding his reeves without enquiry into the
legality of their actions, this may help to account for
the lack of good service and support from his ealdormen
that is one of the features of his unhappy reign.

CHAPTER V

THE CLASSES OF SOCIETY

IN the eyes of the law, the chief mark that distinguished one class of society from another was the price that had to be paid in compensation for the slaying of one of its members, which was called the wergild. There was a different scale in force in Kent – at any rate in the early period – from that current in the rest of England. A Kentish nobleman is called an earl in the seventh-century laws of that kingdom – a term which carried no connotation of office at that date – and his wergild was three hundred Kentish shillings, probably the sum originally equivalent to three hundred oxen, which was just three times the wergild of the ordinary free man, the churl. In the other parts of the country the word earl is used in this way, to denote a man of the upper class, only in poetry and in the rhyming formula 'earl and churl'; it has otherwise become obsolete, and men of this class are called *gesithas* 'companions', or in later times thanes – a word which once meant 'servant' but later went up in the world, because of the dignity involved in serving the king; or they might be referred to by a name derived from the amount of their wergild, men 'of twelve hundred', for this was the number of shillings to be paid if one of them were slain. In Wessex, by Alfred's time this amount is exactly equivalent to that paid for a Kentish earl, for a West Saxon shilling contained at that date five pence, while in Kent the shilling had twenty pence; in Mercia, and probably in Wessex in early times, the shilling only contained four pence, so that the thane's wergild was rather lower. Both in Wessex and in Mercia it was six times that of a churl, for in these areas the churl's wergild was only about half that of his Kentish counterpart. In Northumbria there was probably a similar ratio between the wergilds of the nobleman and the churl, but the position has been obscured by the fact that the only record on the subject gives the thane a wergild exactly equivalent to that of a late West Saxon thane, but seems to have reckoned the churl's wergild in terms of Mercian shillings, of fourpence to the shilling instead of fivepence. In Wessex – evidence for other areas is lacking – there was up to the time of Alfred an intermediate class of men, with a wergild of six hundred shillings. These were of the *gesith*, not the churl class, and there is some evidence to suggest that they were not entitled to the highest wergild because they possessed less than five hides of land. As there is no later mention of this intermediate class, and the phrase 'of twelve hundred and of two hundred' is used to cover the whole free population, we may assume that the six-hundred wergild was abolished. Perhaps the class entitled to it was never a large one.

The wergild was not the only line of demarcation between the various classes of free men. Similar variations existed in the compensations due to them for other injuries, such as offences against persons or places under their protection, forcible entry into their houses or fighting on their premises. The oath of a man of a higher class was valued at more than that of a churl. On the other side, the higher ranks paid greater fines when convicted of crimes; for some offences, such as the harbouring of fugitives, the offender had to pay the amount of his own wergild; for some others, the neglect of military service, for example, the man of the highest class paid 120 shillings, the intermediate class 60 shillings, and the churl 30 shillings, in Alfred's time.

The Nobleman

To the eleventh-century writer of a private treatise on the management of a large estate, called 'The Rights of Various Classes', the rights and obligations of a thane were that he held his lands by title-deed, that is to say, free from dues and services to the king except for the three public charges of military service, construction of fortifications, and repair of bridges, and with the right to bequeath them to whom he wished. The writer admits, however, that on some estates, the thane may be liable to some other services at the king's demand, watch over his person, maritime guard, guard duties in the host, provision of the equipment for a ship, the building of deer-hedges at the king's estate. Domesday Book supports him. It tells, for example, how from some lands in Kent the king has a bodyguard for six days at Canterbury or Sandwich and it is supplied by the king with food and drink.

There survive a few other private dicta as to what were the qualifications that entitled a man to be a thane. One says that a churl who throve so that he possessed five hides of land on which he paid the royal dues, should, if killed, be paid for with the wergild of a thane; it adds :

And even if he thrive so that he have helmet and coat-of-mail and a gold-plated sword, if he has not the land, he is nevertheless a churl.

Even if he had the necessary five hides, his children were not, according to this writer, born to the rank of thane; the rank became hereditary only if his son and his son's son similarly held this amount of land; otherwise they were to be paid for at the churl's rate. Another document, written probably in the eleventh century, in a somewhat nostalgic mood about things that had 'at one time' been the practice, says:

> If a churl prospered, so that he had fully five hides of land of his own, a church and a kitchen, a bell-house and a castle-gate, a seat and a special office in the king's hall, then was he henceforth worthy of the status of a thane.

So also was a merchant who had thrice crossed the sea in his own ship.

This writer does not tell us in what way things have changed. Has it become too difficult for a deserving man to receive the coveted recognition? Or are men with inadequate qualifications becoming members of the higher class? Perhaps both things are happening; the writer may feel that thaneship is now granted for other things than honest merit. On general grounds we may be sure that this rise in status would not be automatic: some ceremony, or at least some public notification, would be essential, for the community must know how much a man's oath is worth, and what it would cost to kill him. There was room for no vagueness or difference of opinion about individual cases. There is an interesting passage in an eleventh-century manuscript that shows that a churl was made a thane by an act as definite as that by which an owner manumitted his slave, or the king appointed his ealdorman – by this date called an earl. We are told in a context that shows that we are dealing with an actual fact, not merely somebody's theory as to what once was, or ought to be, the practice, that a churl became a thane 'by the earl's gift'.

Some men of the upper class possessed extensive estates, scattered over a wide area. The thane Wulfric Spott, the founder of the monastery of Burton-on-Trent in 1004, possessed seventy-two estates in addition to an unspecified number in South Lancashire and the Wirral;

the majority of his lands were in Staffordshire and Derbyshire, but he had several in Warwickshire, Shropshire, Leicestershire, Yorkshire, and Gloucestershire, and isolated estates in Worcestershire and Lincolnshire. He belonged to one of the leading families, of the type from which the ealdormen were often chosen, but at any rate by the reign of Edward the Confessor thanes with equally extensive and widespread holdings are not rare. More common, however, were men of the standing of Ælfhelm Polga, who bequeathed in his will land in twenty places, mainly in Cambridgeshire, Suffolk, and Essex, but also in Bedfordshire and Hertfordshire; or of a certain Wulfric, son of Cufa, to whom were restored in 960 fifteen estates in Berkshire, Sussex, and Hampshire, which he had forfeited a year or two earlier for some unspecified offence. The women of this class of society also might hold considerable landed possessions; for example, one called Ælfgifu left by will between 966 and 975 fifteen estates, chiefly in Buckinghamshire, though one lay as far afield as Dorset; while the widow of Ealdorman Brihtnoth, the hero of the poem on the battle of Maldon, disposed of thirty-six estates, most of which she had inherited from her own family.

Such landowners resided now at one and now at another of their estates. It would be interesting to know if a custom observed on Earl Morcar's estate at Kingsland, Herefordshire, was at all usual; there the reeve of the estate presented to his lord's wife on her arrival eighteen ores of pence, that she might be in a good mood (*laeto animo*), and he gave ten shillings to the steward and other servants. At Earl Godwine's estate at Berkeley, Gloucestershire, difficulties were caused for the purveyors by his countess's refusal to eat any food grown on the estate 'because of the destruction of the minster.' We know nothing of the circumstances in which Berkeley minster came to an end, but it is clear that the countess felt that a curse might descend on the users of the land. Her husband had to buy an estate at Woodchester for her to live off whenever she was at Berkeley. Many land-owners possessed a house or houses in their county town, and the greatest magnates, lay or ecclesiastical, would find it convenient to have one in London.

We know from written sources and from excavations at Yeavering, Northumberland, and Cheddar, Somerset, that their houses were commonly built of wood, and in the early days consisted of a single-storied great hall, used for meals, entertainment, and all the main daily business, and as sleeping quarters for the re-tainers at night, with smaller, detached buildings, called 'bowers', for the various domestic offices, and for the bedrooms of the owner and his family and his guests. The whole was surrounded by an earthwork and stockade, and was known as a *burh*, that is, a fortified residence. Such arrangements are implied in the poems, and in the account in the Anglo-Saxon Chronicle of the surprise at-tack on King Cynewulf in 786; the king, with his mistress, was in a 'bower' which could be surrounded by the attack-ing party, and had only one door; it was quite separate from the place where his retainers were being housed.

Before the end of the Saxon period, however, some domestic architecture was carried out in stone. Alfred built halls and chambers in both materials, and his biographer Asser does not suggest that this was an in-novation. Earl Harold's hall as depicted on the Bayeux tapestry was a stone building raised on arches, and upper storeys are occasionally mentioned from the tenth cen-tury on. One at Calne, in which a meeting was being held in 978, gave way, causing injury and loss of life. St Dunstan, who chanced to be standing on one of the beams, was, in the opinion of contemporaries, miraculously preserved. Building in stone was, however, the exception. Byrhtferth of Ramsey, writing in 1011, describes the building of a house as follows:

First, one examines the site, and also hews the timber, and fits fairly the sills, and lays the beams, and fastens the rafters to the ridge-pole, and supports (it) with buttresses (?), and afterwards adorns the house pleasantly.

The hall was furnished with trestle tables and fixed benches, which were strewn with mattresses and pillows when the hall was used as sleeping quarters. It was hung with tapestries; *Beowulf*, which mentions gold-inwoven tapestry, implies that in early days hangings were used only on special occasions, even in a royal hall, but they doubtless became more common later, and are quite frequently mentioned in tenth- and eleventh-century wills. They could be used for sinister purposes, as when the assassins of Earl Uhtred hid behind them in the hall at *Wiheal* in 1016 and murdered him when he came in to make his peace with Cnut. The Bayeux tapestry has survived to show us what could be the quality of English work at the end of the period, and it is probable that a tapestry presented to the monastery of Ely by Ealdorman Brihtnoth's widow was something similar; on it were depicted the deeds of her husband, presumably including his heroic death at the battle of Maldon. The wills supply further information about those furnishings that were valuable enough to be handed down, as they contain clauses like:

I grant to St Peter's monastery at Bath . . . the best dorsal that I have and a set of bed-clothes with tapestry and curtain and with everything that belongs with it.

or:

And to Eadgifu two chests and inside them her best bed-curtain and a linen covering and all the bed-clothes that go with it.

The objects found in the graves of the heathen period show us that already then drinking cups and elaborately decorated horns were made, and that the Anglo-Saxon chieftains valued beautiful table-ware enough to import glass from across the Channel and silver-ware from as far away as the Eastern Empire. There is no reason to suppose that their standards in this respect deteriorated in later centuries, and such objects are often bequeathed: e.g. 'a cup supplied with a lid', 'two silver cups', 'her gold-adorned wooden cup', 'two ornamented horns', 'a bowl of two and a half pounds', 'the drinking horn which I bought from the community of the Old Minster' and so on.

*

Life in a nobleman's hall was very like that at court, on a smaller scale. Like the king, lay and ecclesiastical lords had their officials: the prince Athelstan speaks of his seneschal, a bishop of Elmham of his cup-filler; Ealdorman Brihtnoth's chamberlain fought beside him at Maldon; the seneschal of the abbot of Ely held an estate of the abbey in Cambridgeshire; an eleventh-century testatrix makes bequests to two stewards. All great households included one or more domestic chaplains, whose functions were secretarial as well as religious. Great ecclesiastics, as well as laymen, kept a large retinue of retainers, and in the seventh century Bishop Wilfrid's was so large that it aroused the envy and enmity of the queen.

In the hall men amused themselves with feasting and drinking, often beyond measure. Abbot Ælfric writes reproachfully to an Oxfordshire thane who has plied him too heartily with strong drink when he was his guest. The picture given in the devil's speech in the poem *Juliana*, of men ready to renew old quarrels when they have drunk too much, and the graphic account of a riotous feast in the poem *Judith*, may have been drawn from life. Over their cups men made boasts of what they would perform, and this was regarded not only as excusable, but to be admired, provided the boast was lived up to. Brihtnoth's men, faced with certain defeat at Maldon, were reminded of the vows they had often made about stern battle, when drinking on the benches in the hall: 'Now can be tested who is brave.' A wise man will take thought before he utters a vow, but a man who promised nothing, who refused to commit himself, would probably not have been admired.

Harp-playing and song helped to pass the long evenings, and certainly the performers were not always professionals. In *Beowulf* the king himself performs to the harp, and a king's thane supplies entertainment on another occasion. St Aldhelm, who was of royal descent, was a skilled performer, and King Alfred saw to it that his sons and daughters should be taught Saxon songs. Some of the professional minstrels may have been of aristocratic rank. In the early period, at any rate, they went from hall to hall, as described by the poet of *Widsith*:

So go the singers of men, destined to wander through many lands. They tell their needs, they speak words of thanks, ever south or north they find someone wise in songs, generous in gifts, who wishes to exalt his fame before the company.

Other indoor amusements included dicing and a game akin to chess.

A thane's life was not spent between the hall and the battlefield, as one might almost imagine from poetic sources alone, nor in the sports of the field, important though these were. Stag-hunting, fox-hunting, and hawking were favourite pastimes for kings and nobles. All such men had their huntsmen and their fowlers, and it is common for services in connexion with these sports to form part of the terms by which landowners let out their lands. Trouble was taken to secure fine dogs and hawks. A king of Kent writes to the missionaries in Germany, requesting, in addition to their prayers, that they should procure for him some falcons of a kind unobtainable in his own country, and dogs of a specially fine breed were sent by King Alfred as a present to the archbishop of Reims when he wished to obtain his help with his educational reforms. A Kentish thane, late in the tenth century, bequeathed to the king two hawks and all his staghounds, and it was while stag-hunting that King Edmund was almost carried over a precipice, and made a vow, as his horse was hovering on the brink, to recall Dunstan from exile. A picture of a deserted hall in *Beowulf* includes the lines: 'No good hawk flies through the hall, nor does the swift horse stamp in the courtyard.' A verse in the *Runic Poem* gives us a glimpse of men discussing the points of a horse, and both *Beowulf* and Bede supply vignettes of young men testing the speed of their horses by horse-racing as they go on a journey.

These were the pastimes of men of rank, but they had their more serious occupations also, military duties in time of war, legal duties of attendance at assemblies, of assisting in the suppression of crime, of riding out on the track of stolen cattle. They had to keep order in their households, for whose offences they were legally responsible, having to bring the accused to answer to a charge or themselves pay the compensations; probably they were often concerned in litigation on behalf of themselves or their men. The more important of them had duties at court, and all had their obligations to the Church. When we add to all this the supervision of their estates, we realize that 'the joys of the hall' so extolled in verse can have occupied no disproportionate amount of the thane's time.

Some men of this class were literate. Alfred planned that all young men of free birth and adequate means should learn to read English. How far this dream was realized is uncertain, but laymen who could read were no rarity in the late tenth century. Bishop Ælfwold of Crediton left a copy of a theological treatise to a layman, and a casual reference to 'books and such small things' in a woman's will perhaps suggests that it was no remarkable thing for lay households to have some books. Ælfric wrote theological treatises for Wulfgeat of Ilmington and Sigeferth of Asthall, both of them ordinary men of the thane class, of no particularly distinguished position; while his patron, Ealdorman Æthelweard, was himself the author of a Latin chronicle. Byrhtferth of Ramsey assumes that some laymen may want learned matters explained to them. He says, in 1011, that priests must fully understand the 'moon's leap'; otherwise they may be put to shame 'before the king's nobility'.

*

We are less well-informed about the activities of the women of this class, but we may assume that the mistress of the house was occupied in supervising the running of it, no small matter when baking, brewing, spinning, and weaving were all done at home. A small tow-chest is one of the articles bequeathed in a woman's will. The qualities that the author of a gnomic poem regards as desirable in a queen can be taken to apply to noble ladies in general, for the poem was composed at a time when courts were small and domestic:

A woman shall prosper, be loved among her people, shall be cheerful, keep counsel, be liberal with horses and treasure; always, everywhere, greet first at the mead-drinking the protector of nobles before the band of retainers, give the first cup promptly into her lord's hand, and study the benefit of both of them in their housekeeping.

The mistress of the house herself attended to the needs of important guests, and she and her daughters presented the wine-cup to those persons whom they wished to honour; as it says of the king's daughter in *Beowulf*:

Sometimes Hrothgar's daughter bore the ale-cup before the retainers, to the nobles in turn; I heard the company in the hall call her Freawaru, as she gave the studded goblet to the warriors.

A *gesith's* wife who Bede says was healed by Bishop John of Beverley 'presented the cup to the bishop and to us, and continued to serve us with drink as she had begun till the meal was over.'

Little is said in our records about the upbringing of children in Anglo-Saxon times, and I know no evidence that there was any general habit of letting them be fostered away from home, though youths of noble birth might be brought up at court, and those destined for the Church be placed early in episcopal households. When a man died leaving a child, the law held that 'it was right that the child accompany the mother' while the kindred administered his property during his minority. It is perhaps worth noting that the gnomic poetry reveals an attitude to the education of the young which we tend to regard as modern, for it says:

One shall not rebuke a youth in his childhood, until he can reveal himself. He shall thrive among the people in that he is confident.

The activity of an Anglo-Saxon lady was not confined to her own home. She could hold land in her own right, dispose of it freely, and defend her right in the courts. She could act as a compurgator in law-suits. She could make donations for religious purposes and she could manumit her slaves. She was, in short, very much more independent than were women after the Norman Conquest. Thus we read in Domesday Book of a certain Asa in Yorkshire, who 'held her land separate and free from the domination and control of Beornwulf her husband, even when they were together, so that he could neither give nor sell nor forfeit it; but after their separation she withdrew with all her land, and possessed it as its lady.'

*

That the upper classes cared for fine apparel we know mainly from the homilists' diatribes against it, especially against priests, monks, and nuns who emulated the laity in this respect. Men wore a mantle over a knee-length tunic and trousers, and sometimes bequeath silken robes and fur cloaks. The mantle was fastened by a brooch, often of beautiful workmanship and great size, the tunic held by a belt that might have richly ornamented clasps and mounts. Gold and silver finger-rings, armlets, and collars might be worn, and much interest was taken in the elaborate ornamentation of weapons and of horse-trappings. The verse literature, which never describes clothes, can spare several lines to depict a helmet, a sword-hilt, or a coat-of-mail, and men speak with loving precision of such things in their wills, when they specify who shall have 'the silver-hilted sword which belonged to Ulfcetel', 'the sword with the pitted hilt', 'my round shield', 'the inlaid sword which belonged to Withar', 'the sword worth 120 mancuses of gold with four pounds of silver on the belt', 'a spear inlaid with gold.' How long such things could be treasured and handed down as heirlooms is shown by the bequest made by the prince Athelstan to his brother in 1015 of 'the sword which King Offa owned.' The latest king of this name, and presumably the one meant, was the great Mercian king who died in 796. One would like to know if the sword so treasured was the Avar sword sent to Offa as a gift from Charlemagne. As for horse-trappings, they are often included in heriots; gold-plated bridles and saddles adorned with precious metals occur in poetry, and we need not take this to be exaggeration. Just after the Norman Conquest the reeve of Saham, Norfolk, transferred to a man of Earl Ralf the service of five sokemen, paying between them 10s. 8d. a year, in exchange for a bridle; and the bridle whose theft, as we saw above, led to such trouble in the reign of Ethelred may have been a valuable article. One is often struck in reading documents of the period by the very great value of articles of adornment, when considered in relation to the purchasing power of money. A necklace of 120 mancuses of gold, such as one reads of in the tenth century, would have purchased 120 oxen, or 600 sheep, or fifteen male slaves, at the price assigned to them by the laws; a mancus seems fairly frequently to have bought three acres of land in the East Midlands about the same period, but naturally the price of land varied with its nature, and, as the recorded sales are usually to churches, it may be that the seller hopes to get spiritual benefits by letting it go cheaply. Nevertheless, such comparisons show that quite a few articles of adornment might constitute a large capital.

Women wore a kirtle reaching to the ground, a tunic, and a mantle, fastened by brooches that were often worn in pairs, one on each shoulder. They wore rings, armlets, and necklets, and also diadems or circlets of gold. Their wills show more interest than those of menfolk in their garments and jewellery, referring to linen and woollen kirtles, to 'her best dun tunic', 'her old filigree brooch worth six mancuses', 'a necklace of forty mancuses', 'a headband of thirty mancuses of gold.' No testatrix, however, gives the impression of having an extensive wardrobe, but probably only those garments of especial value, used for great occasions, are thought worthy of mention.

The Churl

The ordinary freeman is most commonly called a churl.
In Wessex and Mercia his wergild was only one-sixth of
that of a nobleman of the twelve hundred class, and he is
therefore sometimes called 'a man of two hundred (shillings.' A Kentish churl had a wergild of double this
amount, of one hundred Kentish shillings, a sum equivalent to four hundred West Saxon shillings, and was a man
of substance, whose normal holding was the amount of
land that an eight-ox plough could keep under cultivation, with pasture and woodland in addition. Below him
in the social scale was a class called *læt*, with a wergild
that varied from four-fifths to two-fifths of that of a churl,
whose members have been thought to be a subject population, for a corresponding term was used among some
continental German tribes to denote a class intermediate
between freemen and slaves. Over the rest of England,
the churl's holding was probably originally a hide of land,
for this term means 'household' and once denoted the
land that was considered adequate for one family. The
acreage considered necessary varied in different parts of
the country, 120 acres being reckoned to the hide in the
East Midlands in the tenth century, though in the west
country hides were much smaller – barely half this
number of acres. By the later part of the period, by a
rough equation, a Kentish ploughland was reckoned as
two hides. Below the churl in Wessex were classes of
Welsh peasants with lower wergilds than Englishmen of
the same status.

Though he apparently lived at a lower economic level
than his Kentish counterpart, the churl in the other
kingdoms of the Heptarchy was nevertheless a man with
the full rights of a freeman, and often held land that he
had inherited from his ancestors and would leave to his

children. He paid a freeman's dues to the Church, attended the popular assemblies, fulfilled his military obligations, claimed compensation for trespass into his homestead, or for fighting inside it, and was not bound to the soil – he could 'go whither he would'. He might well own more than one hide of land, for there was a widespread feeling that a property of five hides was necessary before a man began to be regarded above his class as a churl. A charter of King Ethelred in 984 mentions a 'rustic' who had had eight hides of land near the Kennet.

It is generally agreed that the position of the churl deteriorated as time went on. Even in the early days there were churls who did not own land that they could live off; by about 700, and perhaps long before, there were men who took their land at a rent from a lord, and, if they also accepted a homestead from him, he had a right to agricultural services as well as rent. When King Alfred made his treaty with the Danes late in the ninth century, peasants (churls) who occupied land for which they paid rent were set level, for the purpose of compensation by wergild if they were slain, only with the Danish freedmen, i.e. manumitted slaves. A tenth-century testatrix bequeaths along with an estate peasants (*geburas*) of whose tenure she uses the phrase in Alfred's treaty. Some late tenth- or eleventh-century entries in a Gospel-book from Bedwyn imply that occupiers of *geburland* cannot leave it at will, as the following example will show:

This is Ecgwynn's witness, that Edwin granted her that she might bring herself out of the *geburland*, free to journey into every land, in return for ten mancuses of silver, when Ælfsige held office and Wynstan was his deputy, in their witness and that of Ælfheah the priest and of all the servants of God at Bedwyn and of all the people.

We are expressly told in an eleventh-century document

dealing with the management of a large estate that there were great varieties in local custom with regard to the rights of the various classes of men, and we can never hope to get into a simple formula the differences between the minor categories of the peasant class up and down the country. This document tells us nothing about churls who lived on land of their own, for these lie outside its theme. From Domesday Book we suspect that such men existed, but apparently they were not very numerous in the South and West in late Anglo-Saxon times. Many an independent freeman may have had to purchase protection and financial help in times of stress and disorder at the cost of relinquishing some of his rights. Not all powerful men were scrupulous in observing the rights of weaker individuals, and Archbishop Wulfstan includes the lessening of the rights of freemen among the abuses of his day: 'Freemen are not allowed to rule themselves, nor to go whither they would, nor to deal with their own property as they would.' Cnut's laws complain of overbearing men who defend their followers at law either as freemen or bondmen, whichever seems easiest to them. Through one cause or another, the average peasant in the south and west of England was in this matter of personal freedom below the majority of the peasantry in the areas settled by the Danes.

The document on estate management deals with various classes that hold their land from a lord. Highest come men called *geneatas*, 'companions', who pay rent and render services mainly of a non-agricultural kind – riding services, bodyguard over their lord's person, watch over his horses, escort duties for his guests, services connected with his hunting, and so on. They seem to be represented in the Domesday survey of several counties, especially in the West Midlands, by men called *radcnihts*. The bishops of Worcester leased out a number of the estates of their see on terms very similar to these, and we may note that it was a *geneat* that a landowner in 896 sent to ride round the boundaries of a disputed estate with the claimant's representative.

We learn also what could be demanded from the *gebur*, a peasant who had been given his holding – a quarter of a hide – by the lord, and supplied with two oxen, one cow, and six sheep as initial stock, seven acres already sown, tools for his work and utensils for his house. In return, after the lapse of a year, he is to give two days' work every week, and three days at harvest time, and from Candlemas to Easter, unless he should be using his horses on the lord's service. He is to pay a rent of tenpence at Michaelmas, twenty-three sesters of barley and two hens at Martinmas, a young sheep, or twopence, at Easter. In rotation with others of his kind, he is to keep watch at his lord's fold in the period between Martinmas and Easter. In addition, he must plough one acre a week in the autumn ploughing, fetch the seed from the lord's barn, and plough three acres extra as 'boonwork', two acres in return for his pasture rights. As part of his rent, he ploughs a further three acres and sows them with his own seed. He joins with one of his fellows in keeping a staghound for his lord, and he gives six loaves to the latter's swineherd when he drives his herd of swine to the mast pasture. On his death, his lord inherits his goods.

Similar demands were made from men of this class at Tiddenham, from which an eleventh-century survey survives, but local conditions cause variation in detail. Fish-weirs on the Severn and Wye were an important source of income on this estate, so here the *gebur* must provide rods and help in the building of the weirs. At Martinmas he gives a ball of good net-yarn. Wherever there were special industries separate arrangements of this kind would be made.

The demands are heavy, but definitely limited by custom. These men are not the lowest in the scale of freemen. There is a class of *cotsetlan* 'cottage-dwellers', who may hold as little as five acres and who do services for their holding, but pay no rent; and there are free labourers without homes of their own, whom the lord is to supply with food, shoes, and gloves.

The lord did not depend entirely on the services of his tenants; he had his specialist workmen, his overseers, his herdsmen, his dairymaids, etc. Such persons were sometimes slaves, but often free. They received their perquisites by custom: the sower has a right to a basketful of every kind of seed he sows; the oxherd may pasture two oxen or more with his lord's oxen on the common meadow, and his cow may go with the lord's oxen; the cowherd is to have the milk of every grown cow for seven days after it has calved; and his cow may go with the lord's cows; the shepherd has twelve nights' dung at Christmas and one lamb of those born in the year, and a bell-wether's fleece, and the milk of his herd for seven days after the equinox, and a bowl of whey or of butter-milk throughout the summer; the woman who makes the cheeses has all the buttermilk except the herdsman's portion; the overseer of the grain gets all the corn that falls at the door of the barn; every tree blown down in the wood belongs to the woodman. Special allowances or feasts are customary on certain occasions, varying according to the custom of the district, such as Christmas, Easter, the time of 'boonwork' in the harvest, or at the ploughing; a 'rick-cup' may be given at the bringing home of the corn.

A good example of an estate very much of the type the author of this treatise had in mind is afforded by the Domesday Book account of Queen Edith's estate at Leominster, Herefordshire. It had 30 ploughs on the demesne, and 230 others, and there were 8 reeves, 8 beadles, 8 *radcnihts* (corresponding to the *geneatas* of the treatise), 238 villeins (corresponding to the *geburas*), 75 bordars (corresponding to the *cotsetlan*) and 82 persons of unfree birth. The villeins ploughed 140 acres of the lord's land and sowed it with their own wheat seed; they paid eleven pounds and 52 pence. The *radcnihts* gave 14 shillings and fourpence and three sesters of honey. There were eight mills, worth 73 shillings and 30 sticks of eels. The woodland rendered 24 shillings in addition to pannage. In its general make-up this great estate agrees closely with the treatise, though naturally Domesday Book cannot go into minute detail on local customs.

*

There was also much local variation in the system of working on the land. Our documents mainly give us information about the open-field system and we are told little about the estates where owners held their arable land in blocks, or about the isolated farms in the clearings that were being steadily won from the waste throughout the period. When the open-field system was in use, all the available arable was not cultivated in any year; part, a half or a third, was left fallow, and the part under cultivation was further divided among winter-sown and spring-sown crops. It was distributed among the various holders in strips, each strip representing a day's ploughing, and an individual holder did not receive adjacent strips, but scattered over the fields as they fell to him by rotation. Meadow was similarly divided, and each man had his definite rights in the common pastures – whether these were permanent or formed by the part of the arable that was lying fallow – in the woodlands, that were important for pasturing of swine as well as for the provision of timber and firewood and for the hunting of game, and in the fisheries or any other sources of profit belonging to the vill. Such appurtenances are often specifically mentioned in grants of land, as, for example, in a charter of 822, which gives an exhaustive list – 'fields, woods, meadows, pastures, waters, mills, fisheries, fowling-places, hunting-grounds, and whatever is contained in it.' At one time the Weald of Kent was used as unenclosed swine-pasture by the large communities which made up the Kentish people, communities whose territories became the lathes of Kent; but before long portions were assigned to individual manors. Each man had his rights in proportion to the size of his holding, and he also had his duties and obligations. We see him about 700 in association with his neighbours in the laws of Ine of Wessex, which fix the responsibilities for fencing the common fields and meadows, and discuss the amount to be paid for the hire of another's yoke of oxen. The plough was drawn by oxen, and it was assumed that a team would normally consist of eight; few churls would be wealthy enough to possess a full team, and most would have to combine with their fellows to get their land ploughed.

Under the methods of agriculture current, the land would not easily be made to produce a livelihood; it needed steady work all the year round. To quote C. S. and C. S. Orwin: 'Autumn sowing on the fallow was followed by winter cultivation of the stubble and spring sowing, after which fallow cultivation and hay-making occupied the farmer until the corn harvest finished the farming year.' Wheat and barley were the principal crops, the latter being necessary not only for bread but also to provide malt for brewing; rye, beans, and peas are mentioned sometimes, and flax was cultivated also. Owing to the shortage of feeding stuffs, only a minimum of stock could be kept throughout the winter; many beasts had to be slaughtered in the autumn and the flesh salted for winter consumption. Most men would have a small croft in which they could grow the few vegetables then in use, and the herbs required for seasoning and medicinal purposes. A much more important activity was bee-keeping, for honey was not merely their sole means of sweetening, it was the major ingredient of mead; in some parts of the country rents continued to be paid in sesters of honey after the remaining dues had been commuted to a money payment.

After a bad season, food could become very scanty before the next year's crops were garnered. The poorer men had few reserves, and a succession of bad years or the dislocation caused by wars and invading armies brought about serious famine. The destitute depended on the alms of the charitable; a testator may leave by will that a hundred poor men are to be fed annually at Ely on St Audrey's day; a king can order his reeves to supply one poor man on each of his estates every month with an 'amber' of meal, a flitch of bacon, or a wether worth fourpence, and with clothes for a year; but such mitigations were occasional and haphazard. The chroniclers and homilists speak frequently of famine, and Abbot Ælfric accepts the fact that men die of hunger as part of the divine scheme of things:

> The Almighty Ruler sometimes withdraws sustenance from men on account of sins, but nevertheless we believe that he whom hunger kills goes to God unless he was particularly sinful.

*

Not all men of the churl class were engaged in tilling the land and minding the flocks. It was men of this class who carried on the necessary crafts, often in the service of a lord. Asser mentions King Alfred's goldsmiths and crafts-men of all kinds, his falconers, hawkers, and dog-keepers.

The king's huntsmen and foresters occur frequently in our records, and are sometimes rewarded for their services with estates of considerable size, as when in 987 Ethelred gave three hides and three perches at Westwood and Farnley to his huntsman Leofwine. In the Latin dialogue composed by Abbot Ælfric to exercise his pupils in Latin vocabulary, the king's huntsman is made to say: 'He clothes and feeds me well, and sometimes gives me a horse or armlet, that I may the more joyfully ply my craft'; and in one manuscript he is made to add: 'I hold the first place in his hall.' The fowler discusses whether it is preferable to tame new birds every season or to feed the trained birds throughout the summer, and in an Old English poem we are given a sketch of his methods:

One man shall tame the proud wild bird, the hawk on the hand, until the bird of prey becomes gentle; he puts jesses on it, feeds thus in fetters the creature exulting in its wings.

Similar sketches survive of the builder, the seaman, the merchant, etc. There was an opinion current among some people at any rate, that the latter's trade, successfully carried out, ought to entitle a man to the status of a thane, and seamen such as King Edward's steersmen, who held land in Domesday Book, may not have been churls. The goldsmith also plied a much honoured craft; if he were the man of a 'mighty king' he received 'broad lands in recompense' – the poet's statement is supported by charters and Domesday Book, where several of King Edward's goldsmiths are mentioned as holders of lands, one of them, Theodric, with estates in three counties, Oxfordshire, Berkshire, and Surrey. Private persons also rewarded their goldsmiths with land; for example, the Cambridgeshire thane Ælfhelm Polga gave half a hide to his goldsmith, for him to alienate as he pleased. Goldsmiths occur as donors, not recipients, in an entry in a Gospel-book from Thorney: two, called Ælfric and

Wulfwine, who served a lady by name Eadgifu, gave two ounces of gold which, the entry says, 'is on the outside of this same book in filigree work', but which, alas, is there no longer. We hear also of the weaponsmith, who 'can make many weapons for the use of men, when for men's battles he works a helmet or a dagger or a coat-of-mail, a bright sword or a shield-boss, firmly fitted to repel the flying javelin.' The young prince Athelstan, whose will of 1015 betrays a great interest in his weapons, kept a sword-polisher. Another very skilled craft is mentioned in the Wiltshire section of the Domesday survey: a certain Leofgyth is holding in 1086 land held by her husband in King Edward's day; we are told: 'This Leofgyth made and makes orphreys for the king and the queen'. This sort of gold-embroidery was also done by Ælfgyth 'the maid' to whom Godric the sheriff gave in the Confessor's reign half a hide of land in Buckinghamshire on condition that she should teach his daughter to make orphreys; a lady, Æthelswith, practised this art at Coveney, Cambridge-shire. This shows that it was an accomplishment for a high-born woman, not merely a means of earning one's bread.

Much less exalted craftsmen are the blacksmith, who makes ploughshare and coulter, goad and fish-hook, awl and needle, the carpenter, responsible not only for various tools and utensils, but for houses and ships, the fisherman who sells his catch in the towns and could sell more if he had it, the tailor, the salter, the baker, and the cook. Sometimes these people were of unfree birth – a female weaver, a sempstress, and a male cook are be-queathed in wills and a male weaver is granted his free-dom in a manumission – but often they were free folk of the churl class.

Finally, we have the trades that catered, not for men's needs, but for their pleasures, minstrels of a humbler type than those mentioned in a previous chapter, who were probably of the thane class. These gleemen sang their lays in the market-places and the ale-houses, and their method was imitated by St Aldhelm, if William of Malmesbury's tale is true, when he stood on the bridge to attract an audience to him by his songs, later turning to more edifying matter. In the eleventh century, priests are forbidden to be 'ale-minstrels' or gleemen. Occasional glimpses are to be had of other entertainers; a buffoon figures in an account of a tenth-century miracle, and some sort of acrobat or tumbler is described in the words of the poem: 'One is agile, he has a skilful art, the gift of giving entertainment before the retainers by his actions, light and flexible.'

The churl was not, any more than his betters, entirely dependent on professionals for his entertainment; the men on an estate of Whitby Abbey in the seventh century were able to perform each in his turn with the harp – all except Cædmon. Bede speaks elsewhere of men drinking and making merry together, and listening to a traveller's account of what had befallen him on his way. Ale-houses are sometimes mentioned, in which quarrels arose only too easily and gave rise to bloodshed; vigils over the dead were seized on as an opportunity for conviviality, to the scandal of the Church, which complained also that men used the Church holidays for feasts instead of religious observance. It was not easy to prevent riotous behaviour in the churchyard, or even in the church itself. Among outdoor amusements men had bull-baiting, and perhaps cock-fighting. But in general, the routine of daily work, and its interruptions by attendance at assemblies, or the hue and cry after a thief, or the tracking of stolen cattle, or other legal duties, would probably leave men of this class with little leisure on their hands.

One knows but little of the conditions in which they

lived. The house of the average peasant was a simple
affair, with a main all-purpose room and some out-
buildings. The fire burned in an open hearth and the
smoke found its way out through a hole in the roof, which
was often of thatch, the house itself being of wood or lath
and plaster. If we could take as typical the few Anglo-
Saxon villages whose sites have been discovered and ex-
cavated, we should be forced to assume that the peasants
in the heathen period lived in extreme squalor, in
cramped huts whose floors they used as refuse heaps. But
these, later deserted, sites may have been occupied by
unusually poverty-stricken sets of men, while richer sites
remained in continuous occupation, or the huts may have
belonged to slaves; in any case, it is hardly legitimate to
use this evidence for the standard of living of the average
churl in Christian times.

The Slave

The slave had no wergild. He was a chattel, and if anyone killed him, he had merely to pay his value to the
owner. The usual price of a slave was a pound, the
equivalent of eight oxen, and the sale of a slave took place,
like that of cattle or other goods, before proper witnesses,
so that the purchaser could vouch the seller to warranty
if later anyone claimed that the slave had been stolen.
Toll was paid on the transaction, as on any other sale; in
the Rape of Lewes in the reign of Edward the Confessor
the toll was fourpence. Slaves are sometimes included in
inventories of stock, as, for example, 'thirteen men capable of work and five women and eight young men and
sixteen oxen, etc.' As a slave had no property of his own
in the eyes of the law, it followed that he could not be
punished by fines when convicted of crime, and he was
therefore liable to flogging for minor offences, and to

mutilation and death for serious crimes, unless the owner were willing to redeem him by paying the fines and compensations involved. If the owner himself ill-treated or even killed his slave, he incurred ecclesiastical penalties, but it was not the concern of the law.

Christian influence worked to mitigate the lot of the slave, preaching 'We are all God's bondmen, and so he will judge us, as we judge those over whom we have authority.' Stories were told of the intervention of saints to prevent harsh treatment of slaves. The slave obtained certain rights by custom. His right to earn for himself in his free time was admitted, and Alfred's laws ordain that slaves are to be allowed the four Wednesdays in the Ember weeks in order that they may sell what has been given to them or what they have been able to earn in their leisure time. Similar injunctions are met with elsewhere, and Archbishop Wulfstan considers the disregard of these rights as one of the abuses that have brought down on his countrymen the wrath of God, in the form of the Viking invasions. There was also a fixed standard – with, of course, local variations – of what was due to a bondman for his labour. An unfree swineherd received a little pig and his chitterlings, 'and otherwise the rights which belong to bondmen.' A bondwoman was to receive as yearly provisions eight 'pounds' (i.e. the large pound, approximating to a hundredweight) of corn, a sheep, or threepence, as winter relish, a sester of beans as Lenten relish, whey, or a penny, in the summer; while a man got twelve 'pounds' of good corn, two sheep, one good cow, and the right to cut wood. Moreover 'to all bondmen belong a Christmas and an Easter food-allowance, a plough-acre and a harvest handful, in addition to their essential right.' Slaves were sometimes able to buy their freedom, which is a further indication that in practice their right to have possessions was acknowledged.

The ploughman in Ælfric's *Colloquy* describes a hard lot:

> I go out at dawn driving the oxen to the field and yoke them to the plough. It is never so harsh a winter that I dare lurk at home for fear of my master, but when the oxen have been yoked and the ploughshare and coulter fastened to the plough, I must plough each day a full acre or more. . . . I must fill the oxen's manger with hay, and water them, and clear out the dung.

To his questioner's remark 'Alas! it is heavy work,' the ploughman replies: 'Yes, it is heavy work, because I am not free.'

Slaves often ran away. The law tried to put a stop to this by harsh penalties if the runaway were caught. According to the laws of King Athelstan (924–39), he is to be stoned to death. Anyone who abetted him, even unintentionally, was to recompense the owner. The loan of a weapon to a slave was regarded as giving him a chance to get away:

> If anyone lends a sword to a man's servant, and he runs away, the lender is to pay a third (of his price). If he provides him with a spear, he is to pay half. If he lends him a horse, he is to pay the full price.

It proved particularly difficult to prevent slaves from running away to join the Danish forces during periods of Viking ravages. The two treaties which are extant between English and Danish armies, one from Alfred's reign, one from Ethelred the Unready's reign, each contain a clause stating that neither side shall receive the runaway slaves of the other. The English slave who joined the Viking forces ravaging his district might seize the opportunity to turn the tables and pay off old grudges on his former master; Wulfstan laments that 'often a thrall binds very tight the thane who was formerly his master, and makes him a slave'; or it might happen that the slave killed his former lord in a fight, and no wergild was paid to the kindred.

*

The unfree class consisted of persons of different origins. Some were the descendants of the British population, as the use of the word for 'Briton' to mean simply 'slave' testifies. The menial tasks described in some Anglo-Saxon riddles are performed by 'Britons'. Some slaves were captives taken in the wars between the different English kingdoms. Thus the Mercian captor of a Northumbrian thane sold him to a Frisian slave-merchant in London, from whom he was ransomed by the Kentish king, son of the sister of the queen whose thane the captive had once been; and there is extant an interesting letter from Archbishop Berhtwald of Canterbury to Forthere, bishop of Sherborne, written between 709 and 712, asking him to persuade an abbot of Glastonbury to release in return for a ransom of three hundred shillings a captive girl, whose relatives have asked for his mediation, 'in order that she may pass the rest of her life with her kindred, not in the sadness of servitude, but in the delights of liberty.' The *Penitential of Archbishop Theodore* shows that it was not uncommon for people to be led off into slavery, for he found it necessary to permit re-marriage after a lapse of five years to the husband or wife of anyone led into captivity who could not be redeemed.

In times of great dearth, men might be reduced to the extremity of selling their children or other kin into slavery. Wulfstan writes in 1014:

Also we know full well where that miserable deed has occurred that a father has sold his son at a price, or a son his mother, or one brother another, into the power of foreigners.

They might even relinquish their own freedom in order to be fed, as a manumission states in vivid words: a woman sets free 'the men who gave her their heads to obtain food in the evil days.' But the commonest type of English slaves were the penal slaves, persons enslaved as a punishment for certain specific crimes, or because of their inability to pay the fines and compensations which they had incurred. The kindred of a slave of this kind must redeem him within a year, or they lost all subsequent right to his wergild if he were slain; after a year, his wife could marry again. The offspring born in slavery to slaves of any origin would be themselves unfree.

There was originally some doubt whether the Church ought to own penal slaves, and, though Archbishop Theodore pronounced in the seventh century that it could, the Council of Chelsea of 816 made their manumission on the death of a bishop obligatory. Other landowners than bishops give instructions in their wills that all the penal slaves on their estates are to be set free, and perhaps people were not altogether comfortable at owning slaves of their own race. Except in Kent in very early days, it was strictly forbidden to sell people of English race across the sea, or into the control of foreigners, by which phrase the heathen Danes are primarily meant; yet, in spite of the laws, a foreign slave trade persisted, and Bishop Wulfstan II of Worcester tried to put an end to it at Bristol after the Norman Conquest.

The redemption of captives and the manumitting of slaves were Christian acts of mercy much encouraged by the Church. Most surviving wills contain instructions for the freeing of some slaves, penal or otherwise, sometimes mentioning them by name, sometimes speaking in general terms, such as: 'and all my men are to be free, and each is to have his homestead and his cow and his corn for food.' Separate manumissions were entered on the fly-leaves or other blank spaces of gospels and service books, and have come down to us from Bath, Bodmin, Lichfield, Bedwyn, Exeter, Durham, and St Augustine's, Canterbury. Here is a typical example:

Here it is made known in this gospel that Godwig the Buck has bought Leofgifu the dairymaid at North Stoke and her offspring from Abbot Ælfsige for half a pound, to eternal freedom, in the witness of all the community at Bath. Christ blind him who ever perverts this.

The ceremony often took place at the altar, but it might instead be performed at cross-roads, to symbolize the freedom of the manumitted slave henceforward to choose his or her own path; for example:

Eadgifu freed Wulfric at the cross-roads, three weeks before midsummer, in the witness of Brihtstan the priest and of Cynestan and of the cleric who wrote this.

The essential thing was that the act should be done before adequate witnesses, who would prevent its infringement if any person were bold enough to attempt this in defiance of the ecclesiastical anathema with which most manumissions are provided. A particularly interesting manumission is one performed by King Athelstan, probably on the day of his coronation, which runs:

King Athelstan freed Eadelm immediately after he first was king. Ælfheah the priest and the community, Ælfric the reeve, Wulfnoth the White, Eanstan the prior, and Byrnstan the priest were witness of this. He who perverts this – may he have the disfavour of God and of all the relics which I, by God's mercy, have obtained in England. And I grant the children the same that I grant the father.

The manumitter retained certain rights over the man he had freed. He had the inheritance after him, and his wergild if he were killed. This was a necessary protection for the freedman, for it might easily happen that he had no free kinsmen and therefore no one to exact compensation if he were injured or slain. It was his former owner's duty to claim the compensation, otherwise the freedman could have been molested with impunity. It is an application of the same principle that makes the king the receiver of the wergild of a foreigner, who, like the freedman, will be unlikely to have kinsmen in the land to act for him. Manumission does not, therefore, put a man at once exactly on the level of a man who is freeborn, and it may be that the term half-free which is occasionally met with in our records was applied to manumitted slaves.

CHAPTER VI

TRADE AND TOWN LIFE

Trade

TRADE did not play a very large part in the activities of the early English communities, for these were to a considerable extent self-sufficing for the necessities of life; yet from the beginning most settlements had to import two very important commodities, salt and metals, the former necessary for preserving meat and fish for winter consumption, the latter essential for the tools with which a livelihood was obtained. Salt was obtained from saltpans in coastal areas, and from the salt districts of Worcestershire and Cheshire as soon as the English invaders pressed so far west. Express mention of saltpans as an important adjunct of an estate occurs fairly early in charters; for example, King Cynewulf of Wessex gave one at Lyme Regis in 774 to the bishop of Sherborne, mentioning the need of salt for ritual uses as well as for the seasoning of food; already in 716–7 King Æthelbald granted to the church of Worcester 'a portion of land on which salt is wont to be produced, at the south side of the river which is called Salwarp . . . for the construction of three salt-houses and six furnaces', in exchange for 'six other furnaces in two salthouses in which likewise salt is made, namely on the north side of the said river.' Domesday Book allows us to see something of the organization of the salt industry by the latter part of the Saxon period. It mentions 285 saltpans in Sussex alone. The chief salt town of England, Droitwich, appears as a very specialized community, in which, while the majority of the saltpans

belonged to the king or the earl, many other persons had
interests; the estates of lay landowners, even as far afield
as Oxfordshire and Buckinghamshire, sometimes have
saltpans in Droitwich attached to them, and others are
possessed by the churches of Westminster, Coventry, St
Peter of Gloucester, St Guthlac of Hereford, and St
Denis of Paris, besides the nearer churches, Worcester
and Pershore. A fuller and more interesting account is
given of the industry in Cheshire, for we learn not only
of the ownership of the salthouses, but also details relating to tolls, etc. Thus it is stated that if the earl sold any
of the salt from one salthouse which supplied his manor
of Acton all the year round, two-thirds of the toll went
to the king, one-third to himself, whereas other owners
had their salt for their own consumption free of toll only
from Ascension Day to Martinmas. The rate of payment
varied a little from place to place, but was normally
fourpence on a cart drawn by four oxen, twopence on a
horse-load, or on eight men's loads. There were prefer-
ential rates for those dwelling within the hundred or in
the county, and we get a glimpse of the salt pedlars: men
from the same hundred, who carried salt about the
country to sell it, had to pay a penny for each cart; if,
however, they carried it on a horse, they paid a penny at
Martinmas. Landowners who possessed saltpans of their
own were a minority; most people must have been dependent on pedlars such as these for their supplies.

Iron-working was carried on on a small scale at
various places, in Kent, Sussex, Northamptonshire,
Lincolnshire, Yorkshire, etc., and it was an important
industry in the forest of Dean, with the result that estates
in Gloucestershire and Somerset often pay part of the
king's farm and of their rents in blooms of iron. In this
form, iron was traded over the country, to be made into
ploughshares, fishhooks, and tools of all kinds by local

smiths, but probably from very early times there was specialization in the production of the finer goods of the weaponsmith, so that ornamented helmets, coats-of-mail, and inlaid swords would be obtained by trade, for only the wealthiest of magnates could employ workmen of such expert skill. The ordinary local smith could no doubt supply the plain spear-heads and simple shield rims and bosses required by the common man. As we have seen, specialist craftsmen were employed by the king and great nobles; it was natural also that they should be found in places where there were markets and a general concourse of people. There were eight smiths at Glastonbury in the Confessor's reign, and six at Hereford, each of whom made annually for the king a hundred and twenty horseshoes; Gloucester supplied the iron for the rivets of the king's ships.

The most important source for the supply of lead was Derbyshire. Thus in 835 Wirksworth was rendering annually to the archbishop of Canterbury lead to the value of 300 shillings, and in the reign of Edward the Confessor a group of royal manors in the county included in their farm five cartloads of lead, consisting of fifty slabs. Building-stone was another article of commerce after it became customary to build in this material, but our records reveal little about methods of quarrying and distributing it. As far as possible material of such weight would be conveyed by water, and it was thus that the brothers of Ely set out to fetch stone for St Audrey's coffin; they did not, however, seek a quarry, but found what they wanted in the deserted Roman site of Cambridge. Only sporadic mention is made of quarries, as, for example, four quarries, one for millstones, in Sussex with annual values from ten and tenpence to four shillings.

*

One must not exaggerate the self-sufficiency of the individual settlements even with regard to foodstuffs and clothing materials. It cannot have been long before certain well-placed communities found themselves able to produce supplies of this or that commodity in excess of their own needs, and to trade their surplus for necessities in which they were less supplied, or even for luxury goods. Instances that leap to one's mind are the dairy produce, especially cheese, of the Vale of the White Horse, and the manufacture of sheep-milk cheese in the Essex marshlands; here and in many other sheep-farming areas the yield of wool would be more than could be used up at home.

Very frequent references can be found to the importance of fisheries in the assessment of the value of an estate, and in many cases the yield is far too great for home consumption. The rent from the sea fisheries along the coasts is normally expressed in herrings; Southease, Sussex, rendered 38,500, and Dunwich, Suffolk, 60,000. Eels were the most important product of inland fisheries and were caught in great numbers, especially in the fenlands; at Wisbech alone seventeen fishermen paid a rent of 59,260 eels. It is less common to find mention of other kinds of fish, but a fishery belonging to Earl Edwin at Eaton by Chester paid a thousand salmon, Petersham, Surrey, paid a thousand lampreys as well as the same number of eels, and Southease paid four pounds 'for porpoises'. Ælfric is probably describing contemporary conditions when he lets his fisherman say that he sells his catch in the towns and cannot catch as many as he could sell.

There is evidence as far back as heathen times of some trade in luxury articles. Archaeology shows that elaborate jewellery from Kent, glassware from the Rhineland, silver vessels from as far afield as the eastern Mediterranean, found their way gradually into the houses of Anglo-Saxon royal and noble families. Wine was imported also, though it may not have flowed so freely in real life as it appears to do in poetic descriptions of life in royal halls. It was one of the products brought by merchants from Rouen at the end of the tenth century, and in the eleventh an estate of Hyde Abbey was paying as a yearly rent six sesters of wine. It occurs also in the list of imports given by the merchant in Ælfric's *Colloquy*, which runs: 'Purple robes and silk, precious stones and gold, rare apparel and spices, wine and oil, ivory and brass, copper and tin, sulphur and glass, and many such things.' Furs were imported also, and at Chester the king's reeve had a right of pre-emption on any marten pelts brought into the port. A document relating to London in the reign of Ethelred the Unready mentions incidentally the following goods brought in at this port: timber, fish, wine, and blubberfish; it is not said that the first two items came from abroad.

Less can be said about exports; English cloaks are the subject of correspondence between Charles the Great and Offa; wool, cloth, and cheese are mentioned as exports, and the code of about 1000 which deals with the trade of London allowed foreign traders to buy in London wool and fat, besides three live pigs for their ships. They could buy the wool only after it had been unloaded, which I presume to be a regulation to force them to buy from the Londoners, instead of buying the whole cargo direct from a ship bringing it to the city. But the earliest commodity to be mentioned as an export from England is slaves – not necessarily because it was the most important, but because it evoked most interest for other than commercial reasons. In the late sixth century Pope Gregory assumed that boys of English race could be bought in Gaul, and gave instructions for their purchase, that they might be reared in the Christian faith and help to convert their countrymen; Bede and his contemporaries thought it likely that English slaves should be sold in a Roman market in the sixth century; about 679 a Mercian nobleman sold to a Frisian merchant in London a Northumbrian prisoner of war. As late as the eleventh century, an Anglo-Danish great lady was trading English girls to Denmark, according to an accusation levied by William of Malmesbury. We have already seen that attempts to put an end to the overseas traffic in slaves were unavailing, and that it was being carried on at Bristol in the latter part of the eleventh century.

Merovingian coins are found in English deposits of the seventh century, and late in this century coins were struck in England. A few early Kentish coins are in gold, but gold coins are rare in Anglo-Saxon times. Early silver coins, which numismatists call *sceattas*, have no certain king's name, for it is no longer held that a few with PADA or EPA in runes can be assigned to Penda of Mercia or Eorpwold of East Anglia. About 775 two obscure Kentish kings began to issue larger, thinner coins, which numismatists call pennies, on a Frankish model, and from about 785, when Offa of Mercia took over the Canterbury mint, pennies of such excellent workmanship and design were issued in his name that some were imitated on the Continent. In his reign a few pieces have the name and portrait of his wife, Cynethryth, and archbishops of Canterbury begin to issue coins. So do East Anglian kings, and Offa's son-in-law Beorhtric of Wessex, though his successor, Egbert, did not follow his example until after his conquest of Kent in 825. Meanwhile Mercian kings used mints at Rochester and probably at London, while a copper coinage, known as *stycas*, was begun in Northumbria about 830, to be superseded by silver pennies after the Scandinavian settlements.

The good relations between mid-ninth-century kings of Mercia and Wessex are shown by their combining to issue coins, especially when Alfred and Ceolwulf II (whom the Danes allowed to rule in Mercia from 874) each issued a coin with the same reverse. Alfred had coins minted at London when he occupied it in 886. In the reigns of his son and grandsons, as they became rulers of all England, more and more mints were opened all over the country. Towards the end of Edgar's reign (959-75) a great reform produced a type of penny which was to be standard over all England, with dies supplied from one centre, and designs changed at fixed intervals, at first probably of six, then of three years. Current money would then have to be exchanged for the new issue. From this time there were a great number of mints. In its main features this system remained unchanged throughout Saxon times, and it was taken over by the Normans.

*

Trade was certainly not inconsiderable by the eighth century, as can be seen by the care with which kings guarded their rights to receive tolls. The remission of the toll on a single ship for the benefit of a religious house was a matter of enough moment to call forth a royal charter. Æthelbald of Mercia was addicted to gifts of this kind, and charters of his survive which remit the dues on ships at London for the abbess of Minster and the bishops of Rochester, Worcester, and London. Eadberht of Kent freed a ship at Fordwich for the abbot of Reculver and ships at Sarre and Fordwich for the abbess of Minster. In some of these documents it is specified that if the ship is lost or wrecked, it can be replaced by another on the same terms. References in general terms to the payment of toll, or to grant of the right by the king to private persons, are common throughout the period, but it is mainly in Domesday Book that we are given details. It is there that we learn that in the Confessor's time the ferries across the Humber at South Ferriby and Barton-on-Humber were valued at three pounds and four pounds a year respectively; that at Lewes both buyer and seller paid a penny on a horse, and the toll on an ox was a halfpenny, on a man fourpence; that at Southwark no one had any right to toll on the strand or in the water-street except the king. His rights here were valued at £16, but this figure included fines paid by those who committed a crime in these places.

Kings issue trade regulations of various kinds. They may interfere to forbid the export of certain goods, as when King Athelstan forbids the export of horses and various kings prohibit the sale of men across the sea; they establish prices – a wey of wool is not to be sold at more than 120 pence according to Edgar's law; the same code standardizes weights and measures 'as one observes in London and Winchester'; a careful supervision of the mints is maintained; the Church's veto of trading on Sundays and certain festivals is enforced by the secular authorities. Precautions at the ports were necessary to prevent the entry of hostile ships; we know something of the arrangements at Chester, where a ship must await a licence to enter. If a ship arrived or departed without the king's permission, each man on board was liable to a fine of forty shillings to the king and the earl; the ship, crew, and cargo were confiscated if the ship came in in spite of a royal prohibition. But most of all, laws are concerned to see that all trading takes place before proper witnesses, so as to make the sale of stolen goods difficult. Ine's laws, about 700, state the necessity of witnesses, and in the early tenth century Edward the Elder tries to insist that all trading must take place in a town; this innovation was not kept up, but his grandson Edgar enjoined the appointment of a standing body of witnesses in every borough and every hundred, before whom all purchases were to be made.

There was also another problem to be dealt with, namely the possibility of misdemeanours and offences by or against traders as they moved about the country. They must not behave in a suspicious fashion; thus the laws both of Wihtred of Kent and Ine of Wessex contain, by what must have been an agreement between the kingdoms, the clause:

If a man from a distance, or a stranger, journey away from a road, and he then neither shouts nor blows a horn, he is to be assumed to be a thief, to be either slain or redeemed.

An earlier Kentish law made a man who entertained a trader or other stranger more than three days responsible for any injury he might commit, and later King Alfred enjoined that every trader was to bring the men he was taking into the country before the king's reeve at a public meeting, and was to take only such men as he could bring to justice if necessary. Precautions were particularly necessary if trade was to be carried on between men of different kingdoms or different nationalities; already the early laws of Kent protect the Kentishman buying in London, and Alfred's treaty with Guthrum stipulates that hostages must be given as security for peaceful dealings and honest intentions before trading takes place between English and Danes. Similar regulations were necessary for traffic between the English and the Welsh.

Finally, kings might interest themselves in the conditions of trading across the sea. Offa entered into an agreement with Charles the Great by which each undertook to protect the traders of the other country when within their realm, and again, in the eleventh century, Cnut on a pilgrimage to Rome took the opportunity of obtaining from the Emperor and other rulers he met there greater security and reduction of tolls for his subjects, traders and others, travelling in their lands. These instances show that foreign trade was not exclusively in the hands of the foreign traders, and there is other evidence in the same direction. Already in the eighth century an English merchant called Botta was settled at Marseilles, perhaps as an agent for collecting goods to be sold in England. The Viking raids of the late eighth and the ninth centuries disrupted trade on the Continent, but Englishmen may well have taken part in the Baltic trade opened up about this time. At least, there is no reason to deny English nationality to a certain Wulfstan who described to King Alfred a journey taken to the Frisches Haff; he has an English name. In the late tenth century, Ælfric remarks casually that English merchants go to Rome, and Sir Frank Stenton has noted that King Ethelred's treaty with the Danes assumes that English ships will be met with in foreign harbours.

On the other hand, we hear of foreign traders in England from early times. Bede speaks of London as 'the mart of many nations, resorting to it by sea and land', and mentions the purchase of a captive by a Frisian merchant in London. The existence of a Frisian community at York in the eighth century is indicated in the life of a Frisian saint, and at the end of the ninth century Alfred's fleet was partly manned by men of this race. But perhaps the strongest evidence for the amount of sea-traffic in Frisian hands is the assumption of an Anglo-Saxon poet that a seaman is likely to have a Frisian wife:

Dear is the welcome guest to the Frisian woman when the ship comes to land. His ship is come and her husband, her own bread-winner, is at home, and she invites him in, washes his stained raiment and gives him new clothes, grants him on land what his love demands.

Men from other lands came also. At the end of the tenth
century a document dealing with trade in London speaks
of men from Rouen, Flanders, Ponthieu, Normandy,
France, Huy, Liège, Nivelles, and the territories of the
Emperor; from about the same date comes a description
of York as the resort of merchants from all quarters,
especially Danes. Irish traders visited Cambridge about
this time. We learn of this because a certain priest called
Leofstan stole a cloak from them; the incidental nature
of this reference should serve as a reminder of how piece-
meal and fragmentary our evidence is on this subject as
on many others. Nevertheless, the bulk of the internal
trade in England was probably in English hands. It will
be enough to illustrate this by reference to the freedom
from toll over all England claimed by the men of Dover,
or to the incident in 969 when King Edgar took vengeance on the men of Thanet for ill-treating some York
merchants.

The merchant and seaman plied an honoured trade.
The poets speak with appreciation of the seaman 'who
can boldly drive the ship across the salt sea' or 'can steer
the stem on the dark wave, knows the currents, (being)
the pilot of the company over the wide ocean', and it was
at least a current opinion in the early eleventh century
that the merchant who had crossed the sea three times
at his own cost should be entitled to a thane's rank. The
merchant in Ælfric's *Colloquy* stresses the dangers of his
lot:

I go on board my ship with my freight and row over the
regions of the sea, and sell my goods and buy precious things
which are not produced in this land, and I bring it hither to
you with great danger over the sea, and sometimes I suffer shipwreck with the loss of all my goods, barely escaping with my
life.

Towns

The places first mentioned as centres of trade had been towns in the Roman period. Whether or not there was unbroken continuity at such places, it was natural that population should begin to congregate at places conveniently situated for meeting-places, and, throughout the Saxon period and beyond it, new towns spring up on harbours, navigable rivers, at the junction of important roads, or where such roads crossed the greater rivers. For example, at the date of Domesday Book, a Berkshire place called *Ulvritone* is said to have 51 'haws' (townhouses), and it was doubtless this circumstance that caused its old name to be ousted by Newbury, 'the new borough', recorded from about 1080. Or some more accidental circumstance, such as the requirements of an important royal estate, as at Reading, Windsor, or Bedwyn, or of a large monastery, might cause the congregation of a group of tradesmen and artisans. By 1066 there were 46 burgesses at St Albans, 28 at Pershore, while the population of Barton near Abingdon included ten tradesmen dwelling in front of the door of the church. Many other monasteries had towns springing up around them.

Many of the places which are ancient boroughs by the time of Domesday Book may have started from similar small beginnings in a distant past, for which our evidence is woefully scanty. What there is relates mainly to Kent, and Sir Frank Stenton has shown that there was town-life at Rochester and Canterbury by the ninth century. London was an important trading centre already in Bede's time; while it was still under the kings of Essex, the Kentish kings possessed a hall in it; in 857 a bishop of Worcester obtained a house there, not far from the west gate, with certain commercial rights, and a later bishop carried out a similar transaction in 889. It is not likely that this church was the only distant landowner to find it convenient to secure a footing in this city. There is also early evidence for a trading community at York and there were doubtless a number of other places that were something more than agricultural settlements in the period before the Viking invasions.

To combat these invasions, King Alfred inaugurated his 'burghal system', i.e. the provision of fortified centres that could protect a tract of country against enemy attack, a policy continued under his son Edward, from whose reign comes a document known as the *Burghal Hidage*, which gives the names of the boroughs thus formed in the area under West Saxon rule. Some of the boroughs were places which already had some concentration of population and were now supplied with new or improved defences; others, as we are expressly told by Asser, were new, that is were founded at places of little previous importance. Oxford and Wallingford, each founded on eight yardlands of land, seem to belong to this class, and the account in Domesday Book suggests that population had been attracted to them by favourable conditions of tenure. In any case, the security afforded by the new defences of the boroughs would draw traders and craftsmen.

Although by the end of the Saxon period other persons might own property and rights in the boroughs, in general the burgesses held their tenements at a fixed rent from the king, who also had other 'customs', the details of which varied from place to place. The profits arising from the jurisdiction in the borough were usually divided between the king and the earl, two-thirds to the king and one-third to the earl; but there is not complete uniformity, for the king seems to have retained the whole at some places, for example in the Wiltshire and Somerset boroughs, whereas at others he granted some of his rights away: two-thirds of the profits of Fordwich went to the abbey of St Augustine's, the bishop had a third of those at Worcester, the archbishop had all the king's dues in one ward at York. Moreover in most boroughs there were owners who possessed the profits of jurisdiction arising from offences committed on their property or by their men. If there ever was any simple or uniform plan it has been complicated by many private arrangements before the period for which any considerable information is available.

The process by which many landowners acquired property and interests in the boroughs is mainly hidden from our sight. As we have seen, bishops of Worcester were acquiring houses in London at an early date. From the tenth century we get many references to country estates which included among their appurtenances one or more properties, called 'haws', in a neighbouring borough. For example a lease of an estate at Kilmiston, Hampshire, in 961, includes 'the haw in the *port* (market-town) inside the south wall, which belongs to that estate', and similar statements become increasingly common. An eleventh-century bishop of East Anglia disposes by will of a haw in Norwich and another in London. It is no longer usual to connect the ownership of such town-houses by country landowners with the duty of garrison-ing and repairing the borough, laid on the shire. They are always spoken of as sources of profit to their owners. It would obviously be convenient for a landowner to pos-sess a house in a trading centre nearby, and the thanes of North Berkshire tend to possess houses in Oxford, while those of South Oxfordshire regard Wallingford as their centre, thus cutting across the shire system. Many Surrey estates are connected with Southwark, not with Guildford the county-town. But it is obvious that the convenience of a town-house for obtaining supplies for the estates, or as a residence during visits to town, will not explain the number of cases when we find a landowner in possession of a great number of houses in a borough. To take a few by no means extreme instances, the archbishop of Canterbury could not have required six houses in Wallingford, or the bishop of Chester fourteen in Stafford, or the abbess of Barking twenty-eight in London, and it cannot have required ten houses in Bristol to supply the manor of a certain Ælfgar in Bishopsworth. It can hardly be questioned that some landowners have been investing in house-property in the boroughs. A document of 975-8 suggests that land in Winchester had become expensive, for the community at the Old Minster was content to relinquish a country estate of twelve hides which they were holding at an annual food-rent, in order to obtain a plot of only two acres, with the stream adjacent to it, in the city.

According to Tait, there are seventy-one boroughs in Domesday Book, apart from those that had grown up on royal estates, or on those of ecclesiastical or secular lords. It is not easy to estimate the size and population of any of these places, and two of the most important, London and Winchester, as well as some others such as Bristol, Tamworth, Hastings, Romney, Hythe, are not surveyed in this record. A law of King Edgar (959-75) made a rough division of boroughs into two classes; large, which must have a body of thirty-six standing witnesses, and small, with only twelve; King Ethelred, probably between 991 and 1002, divided 'ports', that is trading places, into 'principal', to which he allows three moneyers, and 'others' which are to have only one. The greatest places must lie outside this division, for both before and after they have many more moneyers than this, working at the same time. King Athelstan (924-39) had allowed eight to London, seven to Canterbury, six to Winchester, but towards the end of the Saxon period there were over twenty at London and more than ten at York. The evidence of existing coins and of Domesday Book establishes as front-rank boroughs London, York, and Winchester, Lincoln, Chester, Canterbury, Oxford, Hereford, Thetford, Gloucester, Worcester, Norwich, and Ipswich. Domesday does not state the population, but only the number of burgage tenements, and it is uncertain how many persons inhabited each. The figure five usually taken as a basis for calculating the population is almost certainly too low; it gives not much over eight thousand to York, and though a writer about 1000 may be greatly exaggerating when he says York had a population of thirty thousand adults, would he be quite so wildly out as that? Even retaining this conservative estimate of 5 persons to a tenement, Norwich had a population of 6,600 persons in 1066, Thetford of nearly five thousand; Lincoln seems about the same size as Norwich. All other boroughs are smaller, except, of course, London and Winchester, for which there are no figures.

*

The boroughs and towns possessed arable fields, common pastures, and meadows, but not in a quantity to make them to any degree self-sufficing communities, nor must it be supposed that each burgess cultivated his share; in some places the arable was let out to a few individuals. The majority of the population must have depended for food and other supplies on the produce brought from outside to their markets. One remembers Ælfric's fisherman, who sold his catch in the towns, and we hear also of women who sold butter and cheese in London and of boat-loads of fish, hampers of eggs and of hens, brought to the London market; one of the earliest recorded street-names is that of the vendors of meat. Nevertheless the average Anglo-Saxon town probably presented a some-what rural aspect; there were crofts and gardens within and around the walls, and many citizens possessed cattle which they pastured on the common of the town. There were also several corn mills inside the towns; fourteen are mentioned in the Domesday record of Derby, and the tenth-century boundaries of a small site in Winchester include the west mill, the east mill, and the old mill.

One of the features of a town of the later Saxon period that would have struck a modern observer was the very great number of churches in proportion to the size of the place. Our evidence is incomplete, for Domesday Book mentions them only incidentally; yet we know of about twenty in Norwich and over a dozen in Lincoln. Eight besides the minster are clearly referred to in the Domes-day survey of York, and Derby had at least six. A comparatively small place like Wallingford had three churches of sufficient antiquity for them to be mentioned in the early twelfth century in a charter purporting to come from 948, and five churches at Oxford occur in Domesday. The churches were probably not the only stone-built buildings in the towns in the later period. Royal residences were being built in stone already in Alfred's time, and this material would be most likely to be used for them in towns, where the risk of fire was great. The king's hall is referred to in many towns, and some-times there were halls of other great personages; Queen Emma had one in Winchester, and the Confessor's queen, Edith, in Stamford, Toki, son of Outi, in Lincoln, Thurbert in Colchester, Earl Godwine in Southwark. The majority of the houses were, however, still built of wood, and hence the laws were strict about the responsi-bility for fire. At Chester the man in whose house it started had to pay three ounces of pence, and two shillings to his nearest neighbour.

Mention has been made in an earlier chapter of the voluntary associations, the gilds, into which men were forming themselves in the later Saxon period; a 'knights' gild' at Canterbury occurs as early as the mid ninth century, though it is uncertain what was meant by a knight at that time; it may already have borne its late Old English meaning of an armed retainer of a lord. London had a 'knight's gild' by the eleventh century. Gilds are mentioned at Canterbury and Dover in Domesday Book, and in the reign of Edward the Confessor, according to a survey drawn up in Henry I's reign, there were two 'knights' halls' in Winchester, of one of which we are told that it was 'where they drank their gild and they held it freely under King Edward.' Other Winchester evidence speaks of a chapmen's hall, and later we hear of a hall 'where the good men of Winchester drank their gild.' At a much earlier date, in the reign of Athelstan (924–39), there is a document concerning a 'peace-gild' of the London district, which under the presidency of the bishops and reeves of the area is active for the suppression of theft. Besides its police duties, it has both religious and secular obligations to its members, and it has a somewhat elaborate organization and a common purse. Its officials meet once a month, usually when the butts are being filled, and have their meal together, 'and they shall feed themselves as they themselves think fitting' – an early instance of a civic banquet. The size of London made its organization peculiar; it was divided into wards, each with a ward-moot presided over by an ealdorman, and had a meeting called a husting for settling its civil cases as well as a great open-air folk-moot for maintaining order. Some other towns were divided into wards, but there is no evidence that any had more than one form of assembly, the borough-moot that according to a law of King Edgar was to meet three times a year. The boroughs were under a royal official usually called a port-reeve, and in some of the bigger places, like London and Winchester, there were more than one at a time.

When all is said, it must be admitted that we have inadequate evidence to form a clear picture of how life was lived in an Anglo-Saxon town, but it is worth looking at the so-called Winton Domesday, the text which supplied information about the gilds mentioned above, and which helps to make up for the omission of this city from Domesday Book. In the reign of the Confessor Winchester has a *balchus* of the king where thieves lay in prison. Not only the holders of houses are recorded, but also those who had stalls and shops, some of which had belonged to Queen Edith, and a storehouse which was rented by a reeve from King Edward. The burgesses also possessed storehouses which had since been turned into forges. Among the householders of the town at that time were several priests; a number of moneyers held houses, including a master moneyer, and so did a goldsmith, a shoemaker, a park-keeper, a 'brand-wright', a hosier, a turner, a soap-maker, and some beadles. More than one reeve of Winchester is mentioned. But most of the names occur without any occupations attached. Street-names include tanners' street, shoemakers' street, flesh-mongers' street, and shield-makers' street, showing the tendency of men of the same trade to congregate together. Many of the persons were distinguished by nick-names, which show that the citizens of Winchester were fertile in invention; they include names meaning Clean-hand, Bit-cat, Fresh-friend, Soft-bread, Foul-beard, Money-taker, Penny-purse, and Penny-feather.

CHAPTER VII

THE LAW

THE English tribes came over from their continental homes already possessing an elaborate and developed legal system, whose basic principles were shared by other Germanic nations, though in the course of time modifications made in the various systems caused them to move apart. In England the Christian influence to which the law was exposed from the end of the sixth century caused some alteration, especially in relation to family law, but it left the structure unchanged.

It was owing to the influence of the Church that the law began to be put in writing. The first Christian English king, Ethelbert of Kent, 'established, with the advice of his councillors, judicial decisions, after the Roman model; which are written in the language of the English, and are still kept and observed by them.' What brought this about in the first place was the necessity to add to existing law injunctions relating to the Church. These laws survive, and they begin: 'God's property and the Church's – twelve-fold payment', i.e. what is stolen must be repaid at twelve times its value. They continue, however, to deal with secular matters, among other things putting on record the tariff of compensations to be paid for all types of bodily injury.

After this other kings promulgated laws, when there was occasion either to add new statutes or modify existing ones, or to re-state old law that was being disregarded. Ethelbert's seventh-century successors in Kent issued codes, and so did Ine of Wessex (688–726), probably inspired by his contemporary, Wihtred of Kent. The laws of Offa (757–96), the greatest of Mercian kings, were known to King Alfred, but have not come down to us. Alfred himself issued a long code, with the laws of Ine as an appendix to it, and after his day most of his successors issued codes.

Yet, although the surviving body of written law fills a formidable volume, Anglo-Saxon law was never codified in full in pre-Conquest times. In addition to the enactments of kings we possess a few short private treatises on individual subjects, but a great mass of customary law was handed on orally, and no attempt seems to have been made to codify it until the days of the Norman legists, when much was forgotten or misunderstood. There is no evidence that the English possessed, as did the Scandinavian races, an official law-speaker, whose business it was to keep alive the knowledge of the law by reciting it at public gatherings at regular intervals, but it is worth noting that a poem known as *The Gifts of Men* enumerates among the men whom an all-wise Deity endows with special faculties one who 'knows the laws, when men deliberate' as well as one who 'can in the assembly of wise men determine the custom of the people.' In later times, this expert knowledge was sometimes possessed by the clergy. The aged Æthelric, formerly bishop of Selsey, was brought to the judicial enquiry at Penenden Heath in 1075–6 to answer questions on Anglo-Saxon law, and as late as the reign of William II we find the king recommending that a certain priest called Ælfwig should continue to hold the living of Sutton Courtenay, which he now granted to Abingdon, because he was learned in the law. Something is added to our knowledge of Anglo-Saxon law in the working by the survival of records of law-suits, generally relating to land, and by occasional references in literary sources, and finally, by many statements in Domesday Book on the customs in force in the reign of Edward the Confessor.

These sources reveal variety of custom in various areas. The Norman lawyers recognized three great divisions of Anglo-Saxon law, the law of Wessex, the law of Mercia, and the Danelaw, that is, the law current in those parts of the country ceded to the Danes at the end of the ninth century, including not only Northumbria and East Anglia and the area of the Danish Five Boroughs of Lincoln, Stamford, Nottingham, Derby, and Leicester, but also Northamptonshire, Rutland, Huntingdonshire, Cambridgeshire, Bedfordshire, Hertfordshire, Buckinghamshire, Middlesex, and Essex. When the English kings brought this area back under their rule, they did not greatly interfere with its legal customs. King Edgar states expressly:

> Moreover it is my will that among the Danes such good laws shall be valid as they best appoint; and I always conceded this to them and will concede it as long as my life lasts, on account of your loyalty, which you have always shown to me.

He insists strongly on this right to local differences in general, while imposing a universal measure aimed at the suppression of theft. Some differences between Wessex and that part of Mercia that was never under Danish rule are of older origin, dating from the days when they were separate kingdoms. This threefold division, however, by no means covers all the varieties of local custom revealed in our sources, and we have already noted in previous chapters some instances where the general injunctions laid down in the laws have been modified in individual areas as each of these made special and separate terms with the king.

The king legislates with the advice of his council – in fact, some enactments seem to have gone out in the name of the latter alone. The measures agreed on were put into final form by one of the ecclesiastical members present. In the reigns of Ethelred and Cnut it was Archbishop

Wulfstan of York who framed most of the enactments. Copies were sent to the ealdormen in charge of the various provinces, as is stated at the conclusion of one of Edgar's codes:

Many copies of this are to be written and sent both to the Ealdorman Ælfhere (of Mercia) and Ealdorman Æthelwine (of East Anglia), and they are to send them in all directions, so that this measure be known both to the poor and the rich.

The duty of the Northumbrian earl had been mentioned in a previous chapter of the code. Copies would also be sent to the greater ecclesiastics; the bishop of the diocese, who presided beside the ealdorman at the shire-moot, to deal with cases in which the interests of the Church were involved, would need to keep himself informed of any developments in the law. It is to the Church that we owe the preservation of the laws; the official law-books of the administration have not survived, and our knowledge of Anglo-Saxon law would be poor indeed but for the preservation of the archives of the cathedrals of Rochester, London, and Worcester.

*

Law-suits were brought forward in a public assembly which the early laws call vaguely a folk-moot. There is no suggestion in King Alfred's laws that there was any higher court than this, and an appeal from it was made direct to the king. In the tenth century there appears to have been a reorganization by which the land was divided into areas called 'hundreds' (except in the northern Danish counties, where the term used is 'wapen-take'), which had a court that met every four weeks, while above this there was a shire-moot, which met twice a year. A law of Cnut's suggests that appeal can be made from the hundred to the shire, for it forbids recourse to self-help until justice has been refused three

times in the hundred and once in the shire. The division
into hundreds has a recent and artificial look in the Midlands, for the areas there are often neatly assessed at just
one hundred hides; in the South, however, there is little
sign of such neat assessment, which suggests either that
the name was given to areas that had never consisted of
a hundred hides, or that the division was of a much older
date, so that any original correspondence between the
name and the assessment has been obliterated. Just how
far the organization into hundreds altered pre-existing
conditions it is difficult to say. There is evidence that the
folk-moots met under the presidency of a king's reeve
every four weeks long before any mention is made of the
term hundred in this connexion. The hundreds themselves often bear names of an early form, and met at
places whose names suggest that they have been places of
assembly from early times, occasionally, as at Wye, Kent,
which means 'sanctuary' or Thurstable, Essex, i.e.
'Thunor's pillar', even from heathen days. The later
hundred seems to have taken over the meeting-place as
well as the function of the earlier popular assembly.
The tenth-century reorganization may mainly have
aimed at securing regularity and uniformity over the
country. The meetings took place in the open, often at
some prominent landmark that gave its name to the
hundred; barrows served this purpose at Babergh,
Suffolk, Ploughley and *Cheneward'berge*, Oxfordshire; trees
or stones at Appletree, Derbyshire, Staine, Cambridgeshire, Stone, Somerset and Buckinghamshire, Maidstone,
Kent, etc. The activities of the courts are sometimes mir-
rored in the names, words meaning 'hill of assembly'
as at Modbury, Dorset, or 'hill of speech' as at
Spellow, Norfolk, Spelhoe, Northamptonshire, being
fairly common.

Besides the hundred and the shire courts, references

occur from the tenth century onwards to a borough court which met three times a year. All these assemblies were held for other purposes besides the trial of suits. It was at them the king made known by messenger or writ his will to his people, and many transactions for which it was desirable, or legally essential, to have adequate witnesses were carried out there.

From early times kings were in the habit of granting to private landowners, lay or ecclesiastical, the profits of jurisdiction over their own lands or over their own men, and sometimes over wider areas. This is so already at the date of King Ine's laws. Such a grant came eventually to include the right to hold a private court in the area covered by this immunity. Sir Frank Stenton has pointed out that the existence of some sort of court of this kind is implicit in the terminology of certain ninth-century charters. It may underlie a regulation of King Athelstan (924–39), in which the statement of the penalties incurred by a reeve who takes bribes and allows them to influence his judgement is immediately followed by a chapter beginning: 'If it is a thane who does this.' Moreover, the judge, who according to the laws of Edgar (959–75) is to lose his 'thaneship' if he gives a false judgement is probably to be taken as the holder of a private court; for, if a royal official were all that was meant, one would have expected him to lose his office rather than his thaneship. Several serious offences, such as breach of the peace given by the king's own hand, the harbouring of outlaws, forcible entry into a house, violent obstruction of royal officials when discharging their duty, were almost always reserved for the king's courts when grants of private jurisdiction were made.

*

The procedure in law-suits was strictly formal, and any departure from the common form might cause the loss of a suit. The plaintiff summoned the defendant to appear to answer his charge, and if the defendant failed to appear, after a due number of lawfully given summonses, adequately witnessed, he lost his suit by default; if he, or his kindred for him, did not then pay the fines and compensations involved, he became an outlaw. Henceforward he bore 'a wolf's head', that is to say, anyone could kill him with impunity, and anyone who harboured him, or, worse still, took vengeance for his slaying, became liable to very heavy penalties. The outlaw could recover his rights only by the king's pardon.

If the defendant appeared in court to answer the charge, it was normal for the plaintiff to make a preliminary oath, to prove the honesty of his motives, that he was not acting out of 'hatred or malice or wrongful covetousness.' In most cases the defendant was then allowed to bring forward an oath to prove his innocence, for the law clung to the principle 'denial is always stronger than accusation.' He would do this with the aid of compurgators, or oath-helpers, whose number was conditioned by the nature and severity of the charge involved, and he was allowed a respite, often of thirty days, to get them together, after he had pledged himself to produce the oath. They were not required to supply information of the facts of the case at issue. The defendant swore: 'By the Lord, I am guiltless both of deed and instigation of the crime with which N charges me,' and the compurgators simply swore in support of this: 'By the Lord, the oath is pure and not false which M swore.' In early law, the number of compurgators required for a given charge is somewhat obscurely expressed as 'an oath of so many hides of land', which shows that something like a modern property qualification came into consideration. We are told that a king's 'companion', if a communicant, could swear for sixty hides, and there is evidence that suggests that a churl could swear for five. Sometimes, however, the size of the oath is expressed in terms of money, e.g. 'an oath of a pound in value' and it appears that a churl's oath was valued at five shillings. The size of the oath required was normally related to the amount of the fine involved if the defendant failed to clear himself; for example, a man might have to produce an oath of 120 hides or pay 120 shillings fine. In the later laws, it is more usual for the actual number of compurgators to be stated, as, indeed, had been done from early times in Kent; statements occur such as 'let him deny it with an oath of three twelves.'

If on the appointed day the defendant came to court and performed the oath in full, the suit was ended and he was clear. But there could be circumstances that cut the defendant off from the right to produce an oath. If he were a man of suspicious character who had been frequently accused, or if he had ever been convicted of perjury, he was no longer 'oath-worthy'; or he might have been taken in the act of committing his crime, or in suspicious circumstances, as, for example, in possession of stolen property for which he could not account. In such cases, the court awarded the right of bringing an oath to the plaintiff, who then brought forward his compurgators to swear to the defendant's guilt. Similarly, the plaintiff, instead of the defendant, was awarded the oath if he had witnesses of the crime, who would swear:

In the name of Almighty God, so I stand here by N in true witness, unbidden and unbought, as I saw with my eyes and heard with my ears that which I pronounce with him.

When the plaintiff had in this way produced his oath, or when the oath had been granted to the defendant and he had proved unable to give it, the defendant might then go to the ordeal, the judgement of God. The Church then took control of the proceedings. The ordeal was preceded by a three-days' fast and a mass in which the accused was charged to confess his guilt before receiving the sacrament. This part of the ceremony was in English, and in one version it runs:

I charge you by the Father and the Son and by the Holy Ghost, and by your Christianity which you have received, and by the holy cross on which God suffered, and by the holy gospel and the relics which are in this church, that you should not dare to partake of this sacrament nor to go to the altar if you did this of which you are accused, or know who did it.

In the ordeal of cold water, holy water was given to the accused to drink, and he was then thrown into the water, after the Deity had been adjured to accept the innocent into the water or cast out the guilty. If the accused floated, his guilt was taken to be established. The other forms of ordeal took place within the church itself, and while the preparations were going on each of the parties in the suit was represented by an equal number of members, to ensure that no trickery was attempted. In the ordeal of iron, the accused carried the glowing iron for nine feet, in the ordeal of hot water he plunged his hand into boiling water to take out a stone. The hand was then bound up, and if the wound had healed after three days without festering, the man was cleared of the charge. In serious charges, a man must clear himself by the threefold ordeal, that is to say, the weight of the iron was increased from one to three pounds in the ordeal of iron, the arm must be plunged to the elbow instead of the wrist in the ordeal of hot water. The accuser was allowed to decide between the ordeals of iron and of water.

If the accused were a member of the clergy, the ordeal used was that of the consecrated morsel, which the accused swallowed after pronouncing a prayer that it might

choke him if he were speaking falsely. Elaborate rituals
for use in ordeals of all kinds are contained in the ritual
books of the Anglo-Saxon clergy.

If a man were convicted at the ordeal, he was condemned by the assembled court to the punishment laid
down by the law for that particular crime. In one or two
cases, this was more lenient than if he had been taken in
the act, a circumstance that suggests some uncertainty as
to the infallibility of the 'judgement of God'. Slaying by
witchcraft is punished by death 'if the accused cannot
deny it', i.e. if anyone is taken in circumstances considered so damning as to rob him of the right to an oath,
but by prison and a fine if the accusation is proved by
ordeal after the failure of his oath. A thief caught in the
act 'shall die the death', but a man convicted of theft by
the ordeal alone faces this extreme penalty only if he is a
man frequently accused.

Some crimes – arson, house-breaking, open theft,
obvious murder, treachery to one's lord – are called
'bootless' crimes, for which no compensation can be
offered, but which are punishable by death and forfeiture
of property. In some other cases, a criminal condemned
to death can be redeemed at the price of his own wergild.
The Church favoured the avoidance of the death-penalty,
preferring even the substitution of mutilation, as this gave
the malefactor an opportunity of expiating his crime in
this world and thus saving his soul. This view is strongly
expressed in the laws composed for Ethelred and Cnut by
Archbishop Wulfstan:

Christian men shall not be condemned to death for all too
little; but one shall determine lenient punishments for the benefit of the people, and not destroy for a little matter God's own
handiwork and his own purchase which he bought at a great
price.

This attitude must have had some effect. Elsewhere,

Wulfstan shows that he includes mutilation among the 'lenient' punishments he advocates, and Abbot Ælfric begins the story of a miracle with the words 'A certain thane was mutilated for theft', whereas mutilation is not mentioned in the laws of his time as a punishment for theft. It occurs as the penalty for coining false money, but in general plays little part in the Anglo-Saxon legal system. In spite of Wulfstan's efforts, execution remained the normal fate of a thief; for example, a smith at Hatfield Broad Oak in Essex in the time of Edward the Confessor was put to death for theft and the thirty acres he had held were seized by the king's reeve.

Hanging was the commonest form of execution, and a poem known as *The Fates of Men* gives a gruesome picture of a thief's body left hanging on the gallows. These were often placed on the boundary between settlements, and hence phrases like 'to the gallow tree' or 'to the old place of execution' are not infrequent in lists of boundaries of estates. It is in agreement with native custom that the poet should cause St Juliana to be led out to execution 'near the land-boundary'. Other forms of execution are more rarely mentioned: beheading is one of them, and Ælfric expects his readers to be familiar with it when he says that God will have compassion on the criminal if he call on him 'before the sharp sword descend on his neck.' A woman convicted of encompassing death by witchcraft was drowned at London Bridge in the tenth century, while stoning might be the method of executing a thieving slave if male, burning if female, if we can trust a code of Athelstan which survives only in a later unreliable Latin version.

Some crimes were punished by slavery, and we find lords in possession of penal slaves long after the date of the last reference to this penalty in the laws, in the reign of Athelstan. It must often have resulted from the

offender's inability to meet the fines and compensation
which he had incurred. Occasionally imprisonment, at
the king's estate, is mentioned. By far the commonest
penalty was the payment of compensation and fines, the
former to the injured party, the latter normally to the
king, or to the holder of the private jurisdiction, if such
had been granted. Some fines were divided between the
king and the Church, such as that for perjury, as this involved the breaking of an oath sworn on sacred relics, or
that for incest, as a breach of the marriage law of the
Church. In a suit for homicide, compensation had to be
paid to the kindred, and to the lord of the slain man,
while a fine for fighting was due to the king, and if it took
place in anyone's house, the owner was entitled to a compensation graduated in accordance with his rank, from
the ealdorman who could claim sixty shillings, to the
churl who received six. There were some other circumstances in which private persons other than the injured
could claim a sum for breach of their protection. All fines
and compensations were increased if the crime were
committed in Lent, or certain other Church seasons, or
inside a church or at court, or when the army had been
called out, or against men going to or coming from an
assembly, or in violation of the king's special peace.
More than simple repayment of stolen goods had often
to be made – the laws of Kent demand twelve-fold payment to the Church, nine-fold to the king. Finally, higher
rank, while it entitled men to higher compensations,
made them liable to pay bigger fines for their misdeeds.
Both the fines and the compensations were fixed by the
laws; there was quite a long tariff of the amounts due
for bodily injuries of all kinds, while fines were mainly
fixed at thirty, sixty, or a hundred and twenty shillings,
though other sums occur sometimes. The amount to be
paid for any offence was not left to the discretion of the

court; it was for it to pronounce the sentence in accordance with the law-books.

*

Theft is the crime that occupies the biggest place in the codes, especially cattle-lifting. Many sections are filled with regulations that make it more difficult for the thief to dispose of stolen goods, and easier for the owner to track his property. All goods should be purchased before proper witnesses, so that the buyer can vouch the seller to warranty if the goods are later proved to have been stolen, and from time to time the conditions under which purchase can be made, and the procedure of vouching to warranty, are the subject of careful legislation. It was made incumbent on all men to help their neighbour to track his stolen cattle, and the laws are explicit on the formalities to be observed if the trail should lead into another area of jurisdiction. Athelstan's laws are particularly concerned with the suppression of cattle-stealing, and apparently were effective, for his successor, Edmund, is able to say proudly: 'I thank God and all of you who have supported me for the peace from thefts which we now have.' He was thus able to turn his attention to the limitation of blood-feuds which we considered in a previous chapter. In spite of his determination to suppress theft, Athelstan expressed horror at the execution of young thieves for petty theft, and allowed the death-penalty to be applied only if the thief were over fifteen years of age, instead of twelve years. The freedom from thefts of which King Edmund boasts was short-lived; his son, Edgar, issued elaborate measures in an attempt to make cattle-stealing difficult.

Ethelred the Unready issued at Wantage a code intended to suppress lawlessness and violence in the North. It imposes very heavy fines for a breach of the king's peace, and it employs a method of bringing malefactors to justice that is probably derived from Scandinavian law:

An assembly is to be held in each wapentake, and the twelve leading thanes and with them the reeve are to go out and swear on the relics which are placed in their hands that they will accuse no guiltless man nor conceal any guilty one. And they are to arrest the men frequently accused, who are at issue with the reeve.

Each of these men of ill repute is to pledge that he will stand trial, and to go to the threefold ordeal or pay fourfold payment. If convicted at the ordeal, he is to be beheaded.

These twelve leading thanes are to be compared with the 'lawmen' of whom we hear in later sources at Lincoln, York, Stamford, Chester, and Cambridge, and this measure of Ethelred's, which provides the first instance of a 'jury of presentment', seems called for to meet a situation in which the ordinary machinery of the law has proved inadequate to bring individuals to justice. The weakness of the executive in this reign can be illustrated from events in other parts of the country also, especially in the case of a certain Wulfþold in Kent, who committed many acts of violence and lived unmolested until his death, defying many sentences passed against him in the courts.

*

It may perhaps be of interest to examine one recorded lawsuit and see something of the law in the working. A man called Helmstan had been convicted of stealing a belt. A certain Æthelm then tried to obtain from him an estate by litigation, presumably seizing his opportunity because Helmstan's crime would make him less likely to be allowed to bring forward an oath in defence of his possession. He would normally have been allowed this oath since the law held that 'proof of possession is always

nearer to him who has than to him who claims.' Helmstan asked for help from the man who gives us the account of the case, probably Ealdorman Ordlaf, and because of his intercession King Alfred granted that Helmstan should be entitled to justice, and advised settlement
by arbitration. The arbitrators agreed that Helmstan
should be allowed to produce his title-deeds and make
good his right, the history of the estate was given, and all
thought that Helmstan 'was the nearer (of the parties)
to the oath'; but Æthelm would not accept their decision
without going to the king, who was in his chamber at
Wardour – 'he was washing his hands'. He upheld their
decision and named a day for the oath. Helmstan seems
to have doubted his power to get sufficient compurgators; at any rate, he applied to Ordlaf again, offering
him the estate if he would help him with the oath, and
Ordlaf replied that he would help him to obtain justice,
but not in any false practice, on condition that he granted
him the land. He pledged the estate and the oath was
duly performed.

Then we all said that that was a closed suit when the sentence was fulfilled. And, sire, when shall any suit be ended if
one cannot end it with compensation or with oath? Or if one
wishes to set aside every judgement which King Alfred established, when shall we have finished disputing?

Helmstan handed over his title-deeds to Ordlaf, who
permitted him to use the land while he lived, 'if he would
keep himself out of disgrace.' But a year and a half or
two years later, he stole some cattle and was tracked, and
in his flight he was scratched in the face by a bramble,
and this was brought up against him when he wished to
deny the charge; it provided one of those suspicious circumstances which could cut off a defendant from the
right to bring an oath. The king's reeve seized all his
property because he was a thief and the king's man; but

he could not forfeit the estate which he had given to Ordlaf, for he was only holding it on lease. King Alfred was now dead, and King Edward declared Helmstan an outlaw. He then visited King Alfred's tomb and brought a 'seal' to Ordlaf, who gave it to the king at Chippenham, and he removed the sentence of outlawry. I am indebted to Sir Frank Stenton for the explanation that by 'seal' is probably meant a sealed document certifying that Helmstan had sworn some oath over King Alfred's tomb. Ordlaf exchanged the estate for another with the bishop of Winchester. The very existence of this long letter explaining the whole transaction to the king would seem to imply that it had not gone uncriticized. It contains many features of interest, and it is not the least of them that it brings us face to face with one of those 'often-accused' persons so much mentioned in the laws, and suggests that they were not always dealt with in accordance with the full rigour of the law.

*

Far less information is available on Anglo-Saxon family law. Much of the custom regulating matters like marriage and inheritance was handed on orally, and cannot all be recovered from the scattered references to these topics. It is in this province of the law that the acceptance of Christianity made most difference; the Church had to enforce its rules forbidding divorce and the marriage of persons within the prohibited degrees, and this was not done without a long struggle. Questions relating to marriage were referred to the decision of Pope Gregory by the earliest missionaries; Archbishop Theodore's penitential decrees show that various problems in this connexion were presented to him, and it was one of the subjects discussed at his synod at Hertford in 672; and after the settlement of the northern and eastern districts with heathen Danish immigrants in the ninth century the battle had to be fought afresh in these areas, and as far as Northumbria was concerned, it was fought with indifferent success.

Pope Gregory had been willing to admit marriage within the third and fourth degree of kinship, but the later Church forbade it within the sixth degree, and with the widows or widowers of kinsmen within the same degree, and between co-sponsors. Archbishop Wulfstan's fulminations against incest, rife in the eleventh century, may indicate nothing more than that these strict rules were being disregarded. A very early law-code, of Wihtred of Kent, prohibits illicit marriages, and excludes from the country foreigners who will not conform, and it was found necessary to revive this law well over four centuries later, in the reign of Cnut (1016–35), presumably to apply to the Scandinavians settled in England. One thing that caused grave scandal to the Church was the Germanic practice which allowed a man to marry his stepmother. King Eadbald of Kent did this on the death of his father Ethelbert in 616, but was brought to see the error of his ways by Archbishop Laurentius; his act was repeated in the ninth century, when Æthelbald, the son of the most pious King Æthelwulf, married the Frankish princess Judith, who had been married to Æthelwulf when she was a child; but the cases are not really parallel, for Æthelwulf's marriage had not been consummated.

The earliest Kentish laws suggest that divorce was originally as easy among the English as it was in heathen Scandinavia. They allow the wife who 'wishes to depart with her children' half the goods of the household; but if the husband wishes to keep the children, the wife is to have a share equal to that of a child. The same state of things was re-introduced into the north of England by the Danish settlers, and a Durham writer speaks quite casually of an eleventh-century earl who divorced two wives in succession in order to marry higher in the social scale, and of the re-marriage and second divorce of his first wife. We cannot wonder that Wulfstan, who was archbishop of this northern province, should lament in the pulpit the prevalence of breaches of the marriage laws. One of his predecessors had taken action against a flagrant outrage, and received an estate as payment of a fine by two brothers who had shared one wife, but one gets the impression that the Church had to tolerate easy divorce in this part of the land. One may recall the casual reference in Domesday Book to the separation of Asa from her husband, mentioned in a previous chapter.

The wording of the Kentish laws suggests a crude view of marriage, as the purchase of a wife, as in the injunction:

If a freeman lie with the wife of a freeman, he shall pay his (or her?) wergeld, and get another wife with his own money and bring her to the other man's home.

There are similar implications in the laws of Ine, and in the poem which says: 'A king shall buy a queen with property, with goblets, and bracelets.' Yet the position of women in Anglo-Saxon society was a high one (already Tacitus had been struck by their influential position in the Germanic races), and very soon the bride-price came to be regarded as the property of the bride herself. It is probably what is referred to later on as what the suitor paid 'in order that she might accept his suit.' Before the end of the period the law states categorically:

No woman or maiden shall ever be forced to marry one whom she dislikes, nor be sold for money.

A widow was allowed to decide herself about a second marriage. A woman had also undisputed control of her 'morning-gift', her husband's present to her the day after the consummation of the marriage; if she died childless, her own kinsmen inherited it; she retained it after her husband's death, unless she married again within a year. If she did, the gift became forfeit; Domesday Book tells us that Bishop Æthelmær of Elmham seized an estate at Plumstead, Norfolk, because a woman who held it married within a year of her previous husband's death. A woman had also a right to a proportion of the household goods; the fraction varied in different localities, but was often a third, though in a little legal text called *Concerning the marriage of a woman* the writer says that if it is formally agreed 'it is right that she be entitled to half the property – and all if they have a child together – unless she marry again.' Among the upper classes it would certainly appear that household furnishings were considered the wife's possessions, for it is only women who bequeath such things in their wills. A woman retained her due share of the goods if her husband were convicted of theft and forfeited his property. She was not responsible for stolen property found in her house, unless it were under her own lock and key, for 'she must obey her husband' and could not prevent him bringing what he wished into the house. Among the upper classes marriage agreements were often made about succession to land and goods on the death of either partner of the marriage. The freedom with which women could hold and dispose of land is in striking contrast to post-Conquest conditions.

There were two parts to a marriage: the 'wedding', that is, the pledging or betrothal, when the bride-price was paid and the terms were agreed on; and the 'gift', the bridal itself, when the bride was given to the bridegroom, with feasting and ceremony. Ecclesiastical blessing was not necessary to the legality of the marriage, though the Church advocated it. The Church discouraged second marriages and advised the priests to withhold their blessing from these.

The laws governing inheritance in Anglo-Saxon times are nowhere stated, and all that can be gathered is that it was normal for a man's sons to divide his land between them, and for females to inherit in the absence of male heirs of the same degree of kinship. There was, however, one type of land which the owner was free to bequeath as he liked, and this was known as 'bookland', from the circumstance that this type of holding was created by a title-deed called a 'book' in the vernacular. There can be little doubt that this method of holding land grew up in Christian times, and that the English, like other Germanic tribes, originally regarded land as something which could not easily or arbitrarily be alienated from the family. After the adoption of Christianity it would be necessary to find some means by which the Church could receive some permanent landed endowment. A system developed by which land was freed for religious purposes from the payment of royal dues, which would then go to the upkeep of the religious establishment, and also from the claims of the kindred; by the end of the seventh century, it had become customary to record this act of liberation in writing, and a great number of these 'books' have come down to us. They are an ecclesiastical importation, modelled on the late Roman private deed, and they show us that the consent of the king's council was obtained for the act of creating bookland. Sometimes they mention that money has been paid to the king, and no doubt his rights have been bought out in many cases where no reference to payment is made. They do not say that the consent of kinsmen is necessary, but instances occur where a religious house later had trouble with the donor's descendants, and probably a donor would be well advised to get the consent of his heirs to his gift. The title-deeds were introduced by a religious invocation, and usually by a proem either declaring the advisability of having written record of acts of piety, or advising the purchasing of eternal blessings by the gift of temporal possessions for pious uses; the donation was safeguarded from interference by an anathema calling down the wrath of heaven on any who attempted to set it aside. These religious sections of the deeds increase in length and elaboration as the period advances, although before long it becomes common to make grants of bookland to laymen without there being any intention of its being turned to pious use. The advantage to the receiver of having land which he could alienate at will and which was free from royal dues is obvious, and he was willing to pay for it. Moreover, to the king who made it, a grant of bookland may have afforded a means of rewarding his thanes and others for services rendered, or of raising ready money. The king always retained the jurisdiction over those men who held bookland, which meant that if any of them committed a deed which involved forfeiture, the land came into the king's hands. Litigation about bookland is often brought before Church synods in the eighth and ninth centuries, and later before the king and his council. Land not so freed, land still subject to the king's farm and other charges, and bound by customary rules of descent, is probably what is meant by the rare term 'folkland'. Disputes concerning this were dealt with in the ordinary courts.

CHAPTER VIII

THE CHURCH

AFTER the coming of the English the British Church survived in Wales, Devon and Cornwall, Cumbria, and Strathclyde, and in the little British kingdom of Elmet in the West Riding until its conquest by the Northumbrians in the early seventh century. Bede blames the Britons for making no attempt to convert the hated invader, and regards their subsequent misfortunes as a sign of divine disfavour. Church dedications in Somerset suggest, however, that, unknown to Bede, a certain amount of missionary work was carried on by the Welsh across the Bristol Channel. When the mission sent from Rome by Pope Gregory under the leadership of Augustine arrived in Kent in 597, the king and his court were familiar with some of the outer forms of the Christian religion, for the queen was a Christian Frankish princess and had with her her own bishop to whom had been assigned a church, dedicated to St Martin, which had survived from the days of British Christianity. Men were aware that other buildings had once been Christian churches – Bede speaks of their restoration to this use by the missionaries. Some Englishmen had become acquainted with the new religion abroad; we hear of Saxons with St Columba at Iona a generation before Gregory's mission. Gregory wrote to the Frankish rulers that it had reached him that the English race wished to become Christian, but that the priests in their vicinity were not willing to undertake the task. But King Ethelbert certainly at first regarded the missionaries with suspicion, and there is no doubt that Christianity was a strange and foreign faith to the vast majority of the English when it was preached to them by the missionaries from Rome and Iona.

The process of conversion was a long one, in spite of some early spectacular successes. Ethelbert, king of Kent and overlord of all the lands south of the Humber, accepted the new faith and gave Augustine a see in Canterbury. Gregory wrote to Bishop Eulogius of Alexandria that on Christmas Day, 597, more than ten thousand of the English were reported to have been baptized. Another band of missionaries was sent to join in the work in 601, bearing letters of congratulation and instruction to Augustine, and by this year the conversion had gone far enough to justify the creation of a second bishop for Kent, with his see at Rochester. The king of Essex, King Ethelbert's nephew, had been persuaded to accept Christianity, and one of the new arrivals from Rome, Mellitus, was made bishop in his capital, London. The laws issued by King Ethelbert put the Christian Church in a highly favoured position. Yet it was not until nearly fifty years after Augustine's landing that a Kentish king dared to order the destruction of idols throughout his land and to enforce the Lenten fast, while still another fifty years later the laws of Wihtred of Kent found it necessary to impose penalties for heathen worship. Ethelbert's attempt to convert King Rædwald of East Anglia came to nothing, and on Ethelbert's death in 616 there was a reaction in favour of paganism and for a time the whole fate of Christianity in England hung in the balance. Kent was saved, but not Essex, which remained heathen for some forty years longer, when its permanent conversion came from the North, not from the Kentish Church.

It was not until ten years after Ethelbert's death that the Church made any recorded progress outside the borders of Kent. The marriage of a Kentish princess to

King Edwin of Northumbria caused that king, after some
hesitation and a consultation with his council which Bede
has graphically described, to be baptized. As in Kent, the
spread of the Christian faith appeared to be rapid; all the
nobility of Northumbria and many persons of lower rank
are said to have been converted in the same year as the
king, and we read of baptisms of people in great numbers,
in the river Swale near Catterick, and in the Glen near
Yeavering; Edwin persuaded Eorpwald, king of East
Anglia, to embrace the faith, and it was also accepted in
the province of Lindsey, where an old man who lived
until Bede's time saw as a boy Paulinus baptizing people
in great numbers in the Trent at Littleborough. Churches
were built at York, *Campodonum*, and Lincoln, and Pope
Honorius sent to Paulinus an archiepiscopal pallium in
634, for Gregory had laid down that Britain should be
divided into two provinces, with archbishop's sees at
London and York, and it seemed time to put the latter
part of the plan into effect. But the pope's information
was out of date: more than eighteen months before he
took this action King Edwin had been killed in battle,
Paulinus had escorted the queen back to Kent, the
church at *Campodonum* had been burnt by the pagans, the
building of the stone church at York given up, and there
had been a widespread relapse into heathenism. The results of Paulinus's work were perhaps not entirely
eradicated; his deacon, James, stayed on after the
catastrophe, and Christianity was restored a year later,
but it was mainly from another source, unconnected
with the Kentish Church, that this restoration came
about. In East Anglia, too, Christianity was for the time
being short-lived, for Eorpwald was killed by a heathen
successor very soon after his conversion. Three years
later, however, the permanent conversion of this kingdom
was brought about, for a king ascended the throne who

had become a Christian while an exile in Gaul, and a Burgundian bishop called Felix, who came, intent on missionary work, to Canterbury, was sent by Archbishop Honorius to work in this province.

Gregory had intended that the bishops of Wales and the other territories in British hands should be under Augustine's authority, but the latter's attempt to establish relations with them failed completely. According to the story that reached Bede, this was largely because of his arrogant behaviour, but it was not to be expected that they would welcome subjection to the head of the Church of their hated invaders. Moreover, this invasion had cut them off from intercourse with the rest of the Church, with the result that they were observing an antiquated method of calculating Easter, and had also their own customs in some other matters; they were unwilling to give these up at Augustine's orders, nor did they do so till a long time later. The same peculiarities were shared by the Irish Church, which was an offshoot from British Christianity, but differed from it in the fervour of its missionary zeal in the sixth and seventh centuries. Irish missionaries were active on the Continent towards the end of the sixth century, when one called Columbanus founded the monastery of Luxeuil, preached among the Burgundians and Franks, and eventually crossed into Italy and founded Bobbio. Meanwhile St Columba had crossed from Ireland to the Irish colony in western Scotland, and there he founded the famous monastery of Iona. It was from this centre that most of the remaining districts of England were won to the Christian faith after the breakdown of Edwin's Christian kingdom in 632. The sons of Edwin's predecessor and rival had taken refuge in Iona during his reign and had been converted there, and it was therefore natural that King Oswald should apply to Iona for a missionary bishop once he was established on the Northumbrian throne; and, as Oswald and his successor Oswiu became overlords of southern England also, the Church of Northumbria brought about the conversion of all the Midlands and of Essex. Wessex, however, received a missionary direct from Rome, a certain Birinus, who appears to have had no connexion with the Church at Canterbury. Though he must have taught the Roman, not the Celtic usages, Oswald took no objection to him; as overlord, he joined with the West Saxon king in giving him an endowment for his see at Dorchester-on-Thames. For a time, the English Church was divided, East Anglia and Kent following the practices of Rome, under the authority of the archbishop of Canterbury, Wessex also Roman in usage, but apparently in a position of isolation, and all the rest of the country owing allegiance to the mother church of Iona, except for Sussex and the Isle of Wight, which remained heathen until after the Church had become united under Rome. Yet this picture is over-simplified: in both East Anglia and Wessex Irish ecclesiastics had settled and helped with the work of conversion, Fursey and his brothers at Burgh Castle in Suffolk, Maildubh at Malmesbury, while a band of Irish monks were living at Bosham, Sussex, before this kingdom was converted; on the other hand, James the Deacon continued to teach the practices of the Roman Church in Northumbria for a generation after the arrival of the missionaries from Iona. Roman influence in this kingdom was reinforced when Oswiu married Edwin's daughter, for she had been brought up in Kent and brought her chaplain, Romanus, with her. Oswiu's son, the underking of Deira, learnt to adopt the Roman forms under the influence of his friend King Cenwealh of Wessex, and attracted to him young men who had studied on the Continent or been to Rome, of whom the most important was St Wilfrid, founder of

Ripon and later bishop of Northumbria. The southern Irish had accepted the Roman Easter already in 643 and most of the Irish on the Continent had conformed, including one called Ronan who came to Northumbria. Here, in the autumn of 664, a synod was held in which the Roman party, reinforced by a foreign guest, Agilbert, bishop of Paris, who had formerly held the see of the West Saxons, gained their point. They appealed to the authority of St Peter, and King Oswiu, who had probably decided his line of action beforehand, judged in their favour 'lest, when I come to the gates of the kingdom of heaven, there should be none to open them, he being my adversary who is known to possess the keys.' The extremists of the Irish party returned to Ireland, and founded a monastery on the island of Inishbofin off the coast of Mayo. Because of dissensions, the Englishmen among them were moved to another site, leaving their Irish brethren on the island. English bishops of Mayo are mentioned occasionally in English sources of eighth-century history.

Most of the English clergy who had been reared in the Irish usages remained and conformed on points of observance. They handed on much of the spirit of the Irish Church, its love of simplicity, poverty, and humility, its often exaggerated asceticism, its stress on pilgrimage and voluntary exile for the love of God, its burning missionary zeal. Though the period in which more than half of the English Church looked to Iona for guidance lasted only thirty years, it left permanent results on the ritual, the scholarship, and the penitential system of the English Church. Nor was there any complete cleavage with Iona after the synod of Whitby. One of its later abbots, Adamnan, was a friend of King Aldfrith of Northumbria, and recounts two visits to his court, in 686 and 688, and in the middle of the next century Abbot Slebhine visited

Ripon, where he obtained some information about an historical date he was interested in. Intercourse would become easier after the Englishman Egbert, who lived as a voluntary exile in Ireland, finally prevailed on the monks of Iona to accept the Roman Easter in 716.

*

Much more was involved in the decision at Whitby than the question of usage that was discussed there. The two Churches differed fundamentally in their organization. The Irish Church was purely monastic; a monastery might include among its members or in its daughter houses a number of men in bishop's orders, who were nevertheless under the authority of the abbot. They had no fixed dioceses, but were free to exercise their office wherever they were required. They made long journeys, preaching, baptizing, and confirming wherever they came, and eventually returning to their monastery. They had no personal possessions and they made no attempt to set up permanently-served, non-monastic churches. It was a system well suited to missionary work in a new field; it produced men devoid of all personal ambition, free from any duties of organization that might restrict their preaching work; men who attracted people to the faith by their warm sincerity, their austerity of life, and utter unworldliness. But it was not a system to supply the permanent religious needs of the population when the first stage of the conversion was over, being too haphazard, too dependent on the fervour of the individual preacher. The diocesan system of the Roman Church supplied the necessary stability, and some of the men who opposed the Irish Church realized this.

Some of them had been to Rome, and had been impressed by its magnificence. They came back laden with treasures, books, pictures, and sacred vessels. They imported masons to build churches such as they had seen abroad. They did not admire the poverty of the Irish church buildings, but desired beautiful buildings, services as impressive as gorgeous altar-furnishings, gold and silver plate, and skilful chanting could make them. They wished that bishops should live with dignity, with a retinue befitting their high office. But above all they were alive to the advantage of union with the universal Church, the one society with the experience of government to enable it to supply the organization the English Church so badly needed.

The acceptance of Roman usage now made it possible for the English Church to be organized as a single body, and this was emphasized in 667 when Egbert of Kent and Oswiu of Northumbria together chose an archbishop to succeed Deusdedit at Canterbury 'with the consent of the English people.' Their nominee died in Rome, and Pope Vitalian filled the vacancy by consecrating a Greek monk, a scholar with a great reputation, sending with him another man of learning, Hadrian, an African by origin, who was abbot of a monastery near Naples. As we shall see in a later chapter, these men brought a priceless gift of learning and culture. To Theodore fell the task of organizing the recently united English Church, a task all the more pressing because the great plague of 664 had carried off many of the clergy, and in some areas had caused men to revert to their heathen gods for help.

He made a visitation of the whole country, teaching 'the right rule of life and the canonical rite of celebrating Easter', encouraging ecclesiastical learning, and the Roman method of chanting, consecrating bishops to vacant sees and investigating the validity of previous consecrations. He held at Hertford in 672 the first synod of the whole English Church, in which, among other things, he established the principle of annual synods, passed measures directed against the Irish habit by which bishops did not confine their activities to a fixed diocese, and dealt with questions of Christian marriage. The synod admitted that more bishops ought to be made, but decided to postpone this matter for the present.

Pope Gregory, who may have thought more easily of Britain as a lost Roman province than as a group of distinct kingdoms, had planned its organization as a single Church, divided into two archbishoprics with sees at London and York, each archbishop to have twelve suffragan bishops under him, and, after the death of Augustine, precedence between the archbishops to depend on seniority of appointment. But at the time of the mission, a Kentish king was supreme in southern England and established Augustine in his chief city, Canterbury; before Essex (in which London was situated) was permanently won for Christianity, usage had sanctified the position of Canterbury as the archiepiscopal see. Paulinus had fled from York before he received his pallium, and the North did not receive an archbishop of its own for another hundred years. When it did, he had only three suffragans. Gregory's figure was probably based on the assumption that some sees in the non-English parts of Britain would be under his control, and at a later date York claimed supremacy over the bishops of Scotland, and on occasions consecrated bishops for these sees. South of the Humber at the time of Theodore's arrival there were only five sees besides Canterbury and all were vacant except London. Theodore took every opportunity to divide these great bishoprics, which – except for Rochester – had been conterminous with the kingdoms in which they stood, but he met with much opposition, especially from Wilfrid, bishop of the Northumbrians, whose appeal to Rome on the matter is the first appeal of an English ecclesiastic to Rome. By the time of his death, Theodore had divided East Anglia into the sees of Dunwich and Elmham, Mercia and its dependencies into those of Lichfield, Worcester, and Hereford, Northumbria into the sees of York, Lindisfarne, Hexham, and Abercorn (though this last soon ceased to exist because the Northumbrians lost control of this territory to the Picts), and had also appointed a separate bishop for Lindsey, at that time under Northumbrian control, but soon to be reconquered by the Mercians. The Mercian dependency of Middle Anglia also had bishops of its own in Theodore's time, though the see was not permanently established until 737, Leicester becoming its bishop's seat. After Theodore's death, Wessex was divided, the diocese of Sherborne being carved out of that of Winchester in 705, and the last of the English kingdoms to be converted, Sussex, was given a see of its own, at Selsey, in the time of Theodore's successor. This brought the number of suffragan sees south of the Humber to twelve, for Essex was left undivided, with its see at London, and no changes were made in Kent. A new Northumbrian see was formed at Whithorn in Galloway about 731. The grant of an archiepiscopal pallium to Egbert of York in 735, and the temporary elevation of Lichfield into an archiepiscopal see from 788 to 803, are the only major alterations in this state of things until the disruption caused by the Viking invasions.

*

In Italy dioceses were usually small and could be administered from the episcopal see, where the bishop had his church, his household of clergy, and a school for the training of priests. In England, even after the subdivision effected by Theodore, the dioceses covered far too extensive an area for central administration to be sufficient.

The growth of the parochial system is obscure at many
points of its history. Paulinus seems to have worked from
royal estates, especially places of Roman origin, as at
York, Lincoln, Catterick, and Littleborough; we read of
three churches built or commenced in his time. The
mission from Iona built many churches, perhaps mainly
at royal estates, and Bede speaks more than once of
noblemen who had churches built on their estates. In one
of his commentaries he says:

> When perchance we enter any village or town or any other
> place in which there is a house of prayer dedicated to God, let
> us first turn aside to this.

It is not clear, however, that these places normally received an endowment to support a permanent priest, and
Bede's words to Archbishop Egbert in 734 show that
there was at that time nothing like an organized parochial system in existence. He points out that the archbishop could not visit all the places in his diocese in a
whole year, and therefore advises him to appoint others
to help him 'by ordaining priests and instituting teachers,
who may devote themselves to preaching the word of God
in the individual villages, and to celebrating the celestial
mysteries, and especially to performing the sacred rites of
baptism.'

Some of the injunctions of the Synod of *Clofesho* of 746
relate to the institution of priests to local churches by
bishops, and throughout the Anglo-Saxon period
churches continued to be built in the villages, but there
remained many districts of some size which were served
by 'minsters', that is, small communities of priests supplying the needs of the surrounding countryside from
large churches, some of which still survive. It was necessary to safeguard the financial interests of these minsters
as the habit spread of landowners building churches on

their estates, and so a law of King Edgar (959–75) orders that all tithes and church-scot are to be paid to the old minister to which obedience is due, though it allows a thane to pay one-third of his own tithe to a church on his own land, provided it has a burial-place; if it has not, he must pay his tithe in full to the old church, and endow his private church out of the rest of his income. Soul-scot, that is, burial fee, is always to be paid to the minster that has the right to it, no matter where the body is buried. Ethelred's laws in 1014 graduate churches as regards their right to obtain compensation for the violation of their sanctuary, on the following scale: five pounds is to be paid in English districts to a 'head' minster, 120 shillings to a smaller minster, 60 shillings to one smaller still, where there is nevertheless a burial-place, and 30 shillings to a 'field' church.

The churches had received landed endowment of varying extent, but their main income was drawn from the dues paid to them. By the tenth century these consist of plough-alms, a penny for every working plough-team, to be paid fifteen days after Easter; tithe of young stock, payable at Whitsuntide; tithe of the fruits of the earth, to be rendered by All Saints' Day; Peter's Pence due by St Peter's Day; church-scot, due at Martinmas. By the early eleventh century a payment for lights, due three times a year, was added. Then there was also the burial fee, which was 'best paid at the open grave'. The oldest of these dues, apart from the burial fee, was the church-scot, non-payment of which was punishable by a heavy fine and twelve-fold payment already in Ine's laws about 700, and very similar regulations were in force in Worcestershire at the time of the Domesday Survey. This states, for example:

From every hide of land . . . the bishop ought to have on St Martin's day one load of grain, of the best that is grown there.

But if that day should pass without the grain being rendered, he who has kept it back shall render the grain and shall pay elevenfold; and the bishop moreover shall receive such penalty as he ought to have from his land.

The same amount, one load of grain, had to be paid to the church of Aylesbury, Buckinghamshire, by every 'sokeman' possessing one hide of land or more in any of the surrounding eight hundreds.

Tithe is mentioned as a voluntary payment in Theodore's time, to be devoted to the poor, to pilgrims, and to churches. In the tenth century, however, its payment was enforced by heavy penalties: the king's reeve, the bishop's reeve, and the priest are to go and take one-tenth of the produce of the defaulter, the lord and the bishop are to share eight-tenths, leaving the defaulter only one-tenth of the whole. The same law insists that he who fails to pay Peter's Pence in time must take it himself to Rome and in addition pay a heavy fine to the king. Continued contumacy occasioned still heavier loss. Whether laws of such exaggerated stringency could have been enforced seems doubtful. At any rate an eleventh-century code applying to an area of Danish settlement imposes only reasonable penalties, varying with the rank of the defaulter. About the same time, Archbishop Wulfstan declares that tithe should be divided into three portions, one for the repair of churches, one for the servants of God, one for God's poor, and poor slaves, and that the income that the Church derived from fines should be expended on the provision of prayers, the relief of poor men, the repair of churches, education, the clothing and feeding of those who serve God, books, bells, and church-vestments, and never on vain worldly pomp.

Although the law insisted on the payment of church-scot, soul-scot, and tithe to the old church that originally had the right to them, the churches founded by landowners still might receive enough income for them to be regarded as profitable, and the descendants of the founders treated them as their own property, sometimes in a way that shocked ecclesiastical opinion. Thus Ælfric writes at the end of the tenth century:

> Some men let out churches for hire, just like common mills. The glorious house of God was devoted to the worship of God. . . . It is not fitting that God's house be treated like a mill for wretched toll, and whoever does so, he sins very deeply.

Testators sometimes make arrangements about their churches in their wills – 'my church is to be free and Wulfmær my priest is to sing thereat, he and his issue, as long as they are in holy orders' – and the private ownership of churches, or even of fractions of churches, is frequently recorded in Domesday Book. It is more than a right of patronage that is implied, for the owner could take to his own use a portion of the income, according to whatever bargain he made with the priest he appointed. A striking example of trafficking with a church occurs in the Domesday account of Huntingdon, for the jurors describe how the church of St Mary and the land belonging to it were given by the abbot of Thorney in pledge to the burgesses, and then King Edward gave it to Vitalis and Bernard, his priests, who sold it to King Edward's chamberlain, Hugh, who in his turn sold it to two priests of Huntingdon. At the time of the survey, these priests had been dispossessed, although they had King Edward's sealed writ, and Eustace was holding the church without any evidence of lawful possession, neither livery, writ, nor seisin. But, as Sir Frank Stenton has pointed out, it is the speed with which transaction follows transaction that makes this case remarkable, not the nature of the transactions themselves.

*

The first age of Christianity in England was one of very great monastic fervour. Augustine, himself a monk, began the monastery of St Peter and St Paul, outside the walls of Canterbury, where he and the early archbishops of Canterbury were buried. Seventh-century Kentish monasteries were founded at Reculver and Dover, and nunneries at Folkestone, Lyminge, and Minster in Thanet. To assist in their foundation, at least one continental house, the nunnery at Chelles, had been asked to send disciples. Already before this, Kentish women had entered the religious life at the continental houses such as Chelles and Burgundofara. In the North the first monasteries were of the Celtic type, in which the monks lived in separate cells built close together, with a common church, and the abbot's cell some distance away, the whole surrounded by a wall. The earliest was Lindisfarne, founded by the first missionary, Aidan, himself; it was soon followed by others at Gilling, Melrose, Tynemouth, Gateshead, and Lastingham, and by communities for both sexes at Hartlepool, Whitby, and Coldingham. Many Northumbrians went to Irish monasteries, to add the merit of exile from their native land to their renunciation of the world's pleasures. Some men were searching for a broader, more humane type of monastic life; Wilfrid had spent some time at Lindisfarne in his youth, but after his sojourn in Rome, it was a different form of monasticism that he introduced into Northumbria at his foundations of Ripon and Hexham, based on the Benedictine rule, which he claimed to have first introduced into northern England; Ceolfrith entered the monastery of Gilling, but left it, first going to Ripon and then, in search of an ideal form of monastic life, to study the usages at the abbey of St Peter and St Paul at Canterbury and at the East Anglian monastery of *Icanho*, founded by St Botolph. He finally joined company with

Benedict Biscop. This was a Northumbrian who made several visits to Rome, spent two years at the abbey of Lerins off the south coast of France, escorted Theodore to England on his appointment as archbishop, was for two years abbot of the abbey of St Peter and St Paul, Canterbury, and finally, after another visit to Rome, returned to Northumbria and founded the twin monasteries of St Peter at Monkwearmouth (674) and St Paul at Jarrow (682). In the latter, over which Ceolfrith became abbot, Bede spent most of his life.

Owing to Wilfred's influence, the Benedictine rule was introduced into Mercia, where many small monasteries were placed under his authority. Moreover, the great abbey of Peterborough was founded soon after the middle of the seventh century, and soon had daughter houses in places as widely scattered as Breedon, Leicestershire; Bermondsey and Woking, Surrey; and Hoo, Kent, thus affording a striking illustration of the way in which ecclesiastical arrangements overrode tribal boundaries. Early West Saxon monasteries existed at Nursling and Tisbury, at Glastonbury, and at Malmesbury, originally an Irish foundation, but ruled in the late seventh century by the English scholar Aldhelm, who had studied in Canterbury; in the Thames valley were Abingdon and Chertsey, East Anglia had *Beadricesworth* (later Bury St Edmunds) and *Icanho*, Lindsey had Barrow and Partney, all before the seventh century came to an end. In addition, there were a number of early foundations of whose existence we know from a chance reference here and there, in a charter, a saint's life, or a letter.

The double monasteries of Northumbria have been mentioned above, but this kind of house was not peculiar to that kingdom. Of the same type were the great fenland abbey of Ely, founded by the queen of Ecgfrith of Northumbria, Repton in Mercia, where St Guthlac entered religion, Barking in Essex, to whose nuns Aldhelm dedicated his treatise on chastity, Much Wenlock in the ancient province of the *Magonsæte*, Bardney in Lincolnshire, Minster in Thanet, and Wimborne in Dorset. This type of foundation was primarily a house for nuns, but had alongside it a house of monks, who saw to the external administration and provided the priests to serve the community of women. The whole was under an abbess, often of royal birth, and many of these double monasteries rose to distinction as places of learning and education. Whitby supplied several bishops to the church. Leofgyth, Boniface's chief woman helper in his mission to the Germans, was educated first at Minster, then at Wimborne. Her biographer tells us that at the latter place there were separate monasteries for the monks and the nuns, and the segregation seems to have been more complete than it was, as far as our evidence goes, at other places, for even the abbess spoke to the monks only through a window. Boniface and his fellow-missionaries founded similar establishments in the lands which they converted. After the middle of the eighth century there is no clear reference to them in England, but our evidence is rather scanty, and it would be unsafe to assume that they ceased to exist about this time. Most of the places mentioned above were destroyed in the Danish invasions, and were not refounded as double monasteries.

Like the churches, monasteries were considered the property of the family which had founded them. Alcuin tells us that a small monastery on Spurn Point had descended to him by inheritance, as he was of the kindred of the founder, St Willibrord's father. Such monasteries are mentioned in documents as changing hands by gift, exchange, sale, and bequest. Synods had to interfere to insist that the laity should not be appointed as abbots and abbesses of these houses and that the diocesan bishop must see that proper religious observances were maintained. Bede wrote in 734 complaining that many such foundations were of fraudulent origin, a mere pretext on the part of landowners to get their lands exempted from payment of royal dues as being set apart for religious purposes, with the result that by such frauds the royal resources, which should be available for rewarding the king's followers, were being diminished. He advised Archbishop Egbert to investigate such cases and suppress unworthy houses. The archbishop evidently acted on this advice and it produced papal remonstrance, for Pope Paul I complained to the archbishop's brother, King Eadberht, about the removal of three monasteries from an abbot to give them to one of his nobles. Such suppression of spurious houses did not, however, affect the principle that monasteries were the property of the family that founded and endowed them.

No institution remains for ever in its first fervour, and it is not only in relation to fraudulent foundations that complaints are made of lax behaviour. Bede himself tells how discipline had been relaxed at Coldingham, and Alcuin's letters are full of exhortations to monks to live up to their vows, to avoid luxury in dress, to study the scriptures, and not go fox-hunting, to listen to the voice of the lector in the refectory rather than to the songs of the heathen. The author of a poem on St Guthlac went out of his way to create an opportunity to rail at the slackness in monasteries in respect of vigils and prayers. A calamity such as the sack of Lindisfarne in 793 could not, in contemporary eyes, have occurred unless God were displeased with the monastery. We need not take such admonitions as evidence that corruption was rife in religious houses at this time; but there is Alfred's testimony that, before the destruction of monasteries by the Viking raids, divine studies and Latin scholarship had greatly decayed. When he tried to revive interest in the monastic ideal, he met with little success, and it was not until the middle of the next century that a great and effective monastic revival was carried through.

*

There is no need to doubt the sincerity of the majority of the founders of houses of religion or of the men and women who renounced the world to enter them. These included people of all ranks; kings like Sigeberht of East Anglia, Ethelred of Mercia, Ceolwulf of Northumbria, and that Eadberht whom Pope Paul rebuked for suppressing monasteries, all gave up their thrones to enter monasteries. Royal princesses chose to enter religion, or in some cases were devoted to the service of God from infancy, Oswiu's infant daughter, Ælflæd, whom he devoted to God with a large gift of land in thanksgiving for his victory over Penda in 654, being the most famous instance. Queens often entered nunneries in their widowhood. Other kings gave up their rank to retire to Rome and end their days near the tombs of the Apostles. Cenred of Mercia, Offa of Essex, Ceadwalla and Ine of Wessex all took this course, as at a later date did Burgred of Mercia when the Danes conquered his kingdom. People of other ranks were not behind their rulers in piety. They entered monasteries in great numbers, or became hermits, or chose voluntary exile from their land in Ireland, the Frankish kingdom, or Rome, quoting the example of Abraham and relying on the promise of Matthew xix. 29: 'And every one that hath forsaken houses, or brethren, or sisters, or father, or mother, or wife, or children, or lands, for my name's sake, shall receive an hundredfold, and shall inherit everlasting life.'

The desire for such exile was so strong in some families that the kindred that remained at home was sadly weakened. An abbess writes dolefully to St Boniface of her unprotected condition arising partly from this cause, and the father of the missionaries Willibald and Wynnebald was reluctant to accompany his sons, declaring stoutly that it was shameful to leave one's womenfolk without protection. He gave way in the end, perhaps realizing that he was a dying man. He did not live to reach Rome.

Besides those who went on permanent exile were others who made pilgrimages to pray at foreign shrines. The express statements of contemporaries, and the survival of documents arranging the sale of estates to provide money for the journey, or disposing of property in case of death on the way, and the need to make arrangements for the reception of pilgrims en route and at Rome itself, are all evidence for the prevalence of pilgrimage, especially to Rome. Bede speaks in one place as if he thought that its spiritual benefits could be exaggerated: referring to Bishop Oftfor's resolve to make a journey to Rome, he says: 'which in those days was considered to be of great virtue.' Boniface writes with concern of the moral dangers involved when women pilgrims got stranded; he suggests to Archbishop Cuthbert that it would be a good thing if they were forbidden by a synod to go: 'because for the most part they are lost, few remaining pure. There are indeed few cities in Lombardy, or in France, or in Gaul, in which there is not an adulteress or harlot of the English race.' In the tenth century a Breton pilgrim, living as an anchorite in England, finds it necessary to defend the practice of pilgrimage against those sceptical of its value: 'where the battle is harder, the crown is more glorious.'

His opinion represented the view of the majority, and

pilgrimages remain common throughout the period. The protection of pilgrims was a subject of correspondence between Offa of Mercia and Charles the Great in 796; King Alfred's father journeyed to Rome in 855 taking the child Alfred with him, and Cnut went in 1027, and used the opportunity to secure that English travellers should not be so heavily mulcted in future; it may have been on a pilgrimage to Rome that Bishop Theodred of London (about 926–51) bought at Pavia two chasubles, a white and a yellow, that he valued enough to bequeath them specifically in his will; a Kentish reeve and his wife made the pilgrimage, and so did various West Saxon thanes, and an Anglo-Dane called Ketel with his step-daughter, and Earl Tostig and his wife Judith. The appeal was felt by men of violent temperament like Earl Aldred and Carl, Thurbrand's son, who planned to go to Rome when they had settled their family feud, but were hindered by a storm, with disastrous results. The members of an eleventh-century gild were bound to contribute to the expenses of one of their number going to Rome. In this city there was a quarter known as 'the School of the English', with a church dedicated to St Mary and a hostelry for pilgrims, and hostelries existed at many points on the main routes. There survives an itinerary of Archbishop Siric on his return journey from fetching his pallium in 990, which gives the names of seventy-nine stages from Rome to the Somme.

The journey was no pleasure trip. It was sometimes imposed on men as penance for heavy sins, and those who defended against critics its value as mortification could have listed a number of dangers that beset travellers, whether pilgrims, ecclesiastics, and messengers to the papal curia, or merchants. The first abbot of the monastery of St Peter and St Paul, Canterbury, was drowned crossing the Channel, and St Wilfrid suffered shipwreck

on one of his crossings; an English priest sent by the pope
to King Eardwulf of Northumbria in 809 was captured
by pirates on his return; more than one band of pilgrims
was slaughtered by Saracens in the ninth century; in
the mid tenth century an archbishop of Canterbury was
frozen to death crossing the Alps; in the eleventh century
Archbishop Ealdred of York was robbed by brigands and
had to return to the pope for financial assistance to continue. We know of these incidents when they affected
personages of importance; they were not likely to have
been isolated events. The travellers were often subjected
to exactions on their way, and it is unlikely that it was
only the unhappy women mentioned by Boniface who
found their money giving out before their safe return;
and some people failed to support the physical hardships
of the journey and died on the way, from Abbot Ceolfrith of Jarrow who died at Langres in 716 to the son of
the eleventh-century Earl Ælfgar of Mercia, whose body
was buried by the clergy of Reims, an act which procured for them the grant of two estates in Staffordshire
from the grateful father. It was clearly a wise precaution
for pilgrims to make arrangements before they went for
the disposal of their possessions 'if death befall us on the
way to Rome.'

Yet even the hardships of the journey to Rome did not
content some pilgrims; a few went to Jerusalem. There
survives the life of an eighth-century pilgrim to Syria
written by an Anglo-Saxon nun at the German monastery at Heidenheim from the account received from his
own lips. In the eleventh century the pilgrimage to
Jerusalem is mentioned several times. Earl Godwine's
unruly son Swein undertook it. He had the treacherous
and brutal murder of his cousin on his conscience; but
there is no hint that other persons mentioned are expiating heavy sins. Leofgifu, a London woman, died on

the road to Jerusalem in about 1060, and a Lincolnshire
thane called Ulf set out for this city with his wife just
after the Norman Conquest, making testamentary arrangements before he left 'if I do not come home'. He
was a friend of Archbishop Ealdred, who had himself
been to Jerusalem in 1058. If Ulf did come home, it
would be to find his lands possessed by Norman lords,
and we hear nothing more of him.

*

The voluntary embracing of exile, 'to live as a stranger
for our Lord in order the more easily to enter into the
heavenly kingdom', combined with the desire to spread
the Christian faith among their Germanic kinsmen on
the Continent, sent numbers of English men and women
as missionaries across the sea. The work was begun by
Wilfrid, in 677, three years before he began to convert
the South Saxons, when he delayed on his first journey of
appeal to Rome to convert the Frisians. But his success
was only temporary. The permanent mission to the
Frisians was inspired by an Englishman called Egbert
living as a voluntary exile in Ireland, who wished to go
himself to bring to the faith the nations from which his
people derived their origin. He was prevented by what he
believed to be an expression of the divine will, but it was
at his instigation that Willibrord, the Apostle to the
Frisians, set out in 690, after the failure of a mission sent
two years earlier, and it was from Ireland, too, that two
English priests made an abortive attempt to convert the
Old Saxons, which ended in their martyrdom. Space
does not allow a detailed account of Willibrord's work,
which ended in the conversion of Frankish Frisia and the
creation of the see of Utrecht; nor of that of his even
greater colleague, the West Saxon Wynfrith, who took
the name of Boniface, and who was appointed papal

legate and archbishop to the Germans. He preached for a time in Frisia, but his main missionary work was in Thuringia and Hesse; his other achievements include the introduction of the diocesan organization in Bavaria, and the persuasion of the kings of the Franks to undertake the reform of their church. Both he and Willibrord possessed the veneration for the Papacy that was a mark of the gratitude felt by the English Church for its conversion from Rome. They acted all along in close co-operation with it. The far-reaching effect of this on the relations of the Papacy with the Frankish empire, and on the subsequent history of Western Europe, lies outside the subject of this volume. It is more important for our purpose to stress the great numbers of English helpers that went out to Willibrord and Boniface, whose great achievements would have been impossible without such aid. Englishmen were placed as bishops of newly created sees, and monasteries were founded with English abbots and abbesses at their head. Willibrord consecrated bishops of English race whose names are unknown, but we know more about Boniface's helpers because of the survival of his correspondence. Seven continental prelates of English birth joined with him about 746 in writing to Æthelbald of Mercia, including one archbishop, Abel of Reims. Abbots include Wigbert of Fritzlar, Beornred of Echternach, who became archbishop of Sens (died 797), and Wynnebald of Heidenheim, a double monastery like those they were accustomed to at home, in which he was succeeded by his sister Waldburg. Boniface's chief woman-helper was Leofgyth, abbess of Tauberbischofsheim, mentioned above. Other positions of importance were held by continental pupils of Willibrord and Boniface, for neither neglected to train native clergy from the first.

The work was followed with great interest at home,

for the missionaries wrote home frequently, and received letters from kings, nobles, bishops, abbots, abbesses, and priests – letters of encouragement and of request for their prayers, accompanied by gifts, the most precious being copies of the Scriptures and of theological works. The men abroad did not lose interest in the affairs of their native land, but sent home advice, encouragement, and if need be admonition. Boniface sent to Archbishop Cuthbert the statutes of reform adopted at a Frankish synod, and many of them were accepted in a synod of the English Church. He and his fellow bishops, of English birth, sent a long letter to King Æthelbald of Mercia, urging him to reform his behaviour. In 738, when there seemed a likelihood that the conversion of the Old Saxons might be undertaken, Boniface addressed a letter asking for the support and prayers of all the English nation. When he was martyred at Dokkum in 754, the words that Archbishop Cuthbert wrote to his successor Lul were uttered in the name of the English people; he thanks God that the race of the English 'has deserved to send out from itself before the eyes of all to spiritual agonies and, by the grace of Almighty God, for the safety of many souls, so famous an investigator of divine books and so noble a soldier of Christ, along with many well-trained and excellently instructed disciples.'

English missionary enterprise did not come to an end with the death of Boniface, nor did the interest of people in England flag. A particularly close concern was felt by the Northumbrians in the continuance of the conversion of the Frisians. Young Frisians from the abbey of Utrecht were sent by their abbot, a Frankish pupil of Boniface, to study at York, and one of them, called Liudger, was later called to play a part in the conversion of the Old Saxons, when at last their conquest by Charles the Great made their conversion possible. Meanwhile an

Englishman, Aluberht, was consecrated as bishop for the
Old Saxons at York in 767, and somewhere about the
same time a Northumbrian synod, under King Alhred,
sent out to North Frisia a Northumbrian priest called
Willehad, who operated for a time from Dokkum, but
was later called by Charles the Great to lead the mission
to the Old Saxons. After various set-backs, he was consecrated as the bishop of this people in 787, and he fixed
his see at Bremen. There were other Anglo-Saxon missionaries working at this time, along with men of
Frankish and Frisian birth from the monasteries
founded by the earlier generation of English missionaries,
and English influence left a long-lasting effect on the
German Church. But in the ninth century the Viking
raids depleted the Church in England, and after the
Danish settlement Englishmen must have found enough
to absorb their missionary zeal at home.

*

Lindisfarne was sacked by the Danes in 793 and Jarrow
in the following year, but religious life was resumed after
the raiders had gone, and it was not until the large-scale
invasions in the second half of the next century, which
aimed at the conquest of the country, that churches and
monasteries were destroyed in great number and left deserted. The kingdoms of Northumbria and East Anglia,
and Mercia north-east of the Watling Street, received a
large immigration of heathen Danish settlers, and all the
church organization was dislocated for a time. The remaining monks of Lindisfarne took up St Cuthbert's body
and their other most treasured relics and wandered for
some years before the see was established at Chester-le-
Street, to be removed to Durham in 995; the see of
Hexham ceased to exist, the fate of Whithorn is obscure;
only at York does the continuity seem to have been un-

broken, except for a gap of a year when the archbishop
fled to Mercia. In the Midlands the see of Leicester was
moved for safety to Dorchester-on-Thames and at some
uncertain date joined to that of Lindsey. After the
Norman Conquest, the combined see was moved from
Dorchester to Lincoln. The East Anglian sees of Dunwich and Elmham were both destroyed, and there was
no bishop for this area until about 956, when Elmham
was restored as the see of the whole province. All this area
had been full of important religious houses, but now they
came to an end. One result of this was that little of what
took place in these districts for the next two generations
found anyone to record it, and we know nothing of the
means used to convert the settlers to the Christian religion.

In the eastern counties heathenism seems to have been
fairly quickly eradicated. The Danish king of East
Anglia had agreed to be baptized as part of the terms
he made with King Alfred in 878. Before the end of the
century the cult of St Edmund, the king slain by the
Danes in 869, was well-established, and by 918 the district had been reconquered by the English. Up to the
middle of the century it appears to have been under the
authority of the bishop of London, Theodred 'the Good',
probably a native of the area, and its control in secular
affairs was entrusted to a religiously-minded ealdorman
of West Saxon origin, who was succeeded by equally
pious sons when he retired to end his life in the monastery
of Glastonbury. We cannot tell whether the native
priesthood which had survived the Danish invasion was
adequate to the task of converting the newcomers, or
whether help was forthcoming from the parts of England
outside Danish control. This is probable on general
grounds, for there is evidence that Edward the Elder
encouraged his thanes to settle among 'the pagans'

before he won back the Danelaw, and he may well have directed priests to the area also. It is perhaps worth noting that Bishop Theodred makes bequests in his will to clergy with German names, which makes one wonder whether the continental Churches established by English missionaries sent contingents to their mother-church when it required more clergy to convert the Danes than it could supply, depleted as it was by the Viking ravages. This can only be conjecture. What is clear is that from the middle of the century there are references to small religious communities in the eastern Danelaw, and the foundation of the great fenland abbeys from 970 onwards made this area as advanced as any part of the country in ecclesiastical matters.

It is probable that the Danes of North-East Mercia were converted not much later. They are certainly considered Christians in 942. In 956 and 958 large estates in Nottinghamshire were granted by the king to the archbishop of York, on one of which, Southwell, an important minster, was subsequently founded. Soon after the middle of the tenth century the see of Lindsey seems to have been temporarily revived, but possibly only as a subordinate see to that of Dorchester, with which it merged again later. In Northumbria there was a Christian Danish king reigning some years before the close of the ninth century, and there was hardly a break in continuity at the see of York. But Northumbria was conquered in the early tenth century by a fresh heathen invasion, that of the Irish Norsemen from Dublin, and it is probably on this account that more is heard of heathen worship here. The name *Othenesberg*, 'Othin's hill', was given to Roseberry Topping and a tenth-century encroacher on the lands of St Cuthbert swore by Thor and Othin. The Scandinavians took oath to suppress paganism at their treaty with King Athelstan in 927, but the English chronicler regards the

Norsemen of York as heathen in 942. Northumbria passed permanently under the English crown in 954. We hear no more of heathen gods; but heathen customs were not so easily eradicated, and they are still being preached against and legislated against in the early eleventh century. As we have seen, the laws of the Church relating to marriage and divorce were often ignored. The monasteries destroyed by the invaders were not restored in the North. Yet Northumbria was not cut off from the ecclesiastical movements of the South. Even before the last Scandinavian king was driven out in 954, it had been ruled by the English kings for several periods of some years, and during these the archbishop of York normally attended the meetings of the English council, sometimes in Athelstan's reign accompanied by the bishop of Chester-le-Street (to which place the see of Lindisfarne had been removed) and by at least one other suffragan, of some unknown see. From 956 the archbishops of York were not chosen from the Northumbrian clergy, perhaps because the last holder of the see under the Scandinavian kings had been suspected of favouring these kings rather than the West Saxon royal house. Men of southern education were appointed, and usually men from the eastern counties, who would be familiar with the Anglo-Scandinavian speech and customs; and, because the northern province had been impoverished by the Danish invasions, it became customary to allow the see of York to be held in plurality with that of Worcester. The benefits of this arrangement would not be material only, for Worcester had an ancient tradition of learning and belonged to the one part of England that had escaped serious ravaging. It meant, however, that the archbishops might spend much of their time outside their northern diocese, but for all we know the kings may have considered that they thus kept a closer control over the primates of a part of the kingdom whose loyalty to the West Saxon rulers was suspect.

*

The long drawn-out Viking wars had brought about a decline in the Church also in the parts of England that were not ceded to the Danes. Only the Severn valley had suffered little from the raiding armies, and even its churches had not escaped impoverishment caused by the general dislocation of affairs and the taxation imposed to pay tribute to the Danes. King Alfred's labours brought about some degree of recovery in Wessex, with outside aid from Mercia, Wales, and the Continent, and his successor subdivided the great diocese of western Wessex by creating three new sees, Ramsbury, Wells, and Crediton, which must have resulted in more effective episcopal control. Alfred also founded a monastery at Athelney and a nunnery at Shaftesbury, and his son completed the church of Newminster, Winchester, which his father had planned. But there was little monastic zeal in the country at that time; many places that had once been monasteries were possessed by bodies of secular clerks, often married, and though many of them may have been sincere and religious men – for we need not accept all that their enemies and supplanters tell us at a later date – before the middle of the tenth century there was a widespread feeling that the situation was unsatisfactory and that reform was desirable.

Meanwhile there had been a great Benedictine revival on the Continent and it profoundly influenced the reform in England. Of the main English movers in this matter, Dunstan had spent two years at the reformed house of Blandinium in Ghent, and he continued to keep up a correspondence with his hosts after he returned to England, where he was made archbishop of Canterbury in

960; one of his predecessors, Oda, a Dane by birth and an effective reforming prelate, sent his nephew Oswald to study the new monasticism at the great abbey of Fleury-sur-Loire, and this Oswald became bishop of Worcester and archbishop of York. He placed a fellow student from Fleury over his foundation at Winchcombe, and when later he founded at the request of the East Anglian ealdorman a large monastery at Ramsey in Huntingdonshire he invited from Fleury a distinguished continental scholar, Abbo, to instruct his novices. The most energetic of all the reformers, Athelwold, abbot of Abingdon and later bishop of Winchester, had wished to go to Fleury; when prevented, he sent a monk from Abingdon to learn the practice of the rule there. The reform was strongly supported by King Edgar, who earned the epithet 'father of the monks'; the secular clerics were replaced by monks in many existing houses and new houses were founded, especially at places where former abbeys had been destroyed by the Danes, the most important being the fenland abbeys of Peterborough, Ely, and Thorney, which Athelwold restored. A common form of usage was drawn up, and monks from Ghent and Fleury came over to assist in its preparation.

The influence of this movement on art, learning, and literature will be considered in a later chapter. A reaction, on the death of Edgar in 975, especially in Mercia, had only a temporary success; the monks were supported by most of the great nobles, and the founding of Benedictine houses continued. A great West Saxon family, Ælfric's patrons, founded Cerne Abbas, Dorset, and Eynsham, Oxfordshire, and, more important, a very wealthy and influential Mercian thane, Wulfric Spott, endowed in the North-East Midlands, an area otherwise lacking such houses, the great abbey of Burton-on-Trent. The movement made no headway in the North, though most archbishops there were men trained in houses founded by it. It probably proved impossible to interest sufficient Anglo-Danish nobles in the endowment of monasteries.

Great effort was made in the late tenth and early eleventh centuries to improve the quality of the parish clergy. Abbot Ælfric produced a pastoral letter for Bishop Wulfsige of Sherborne to circulate to his clergy, setting out what the canons demanded of men in their office, and Archbishop Wulfstan, himself a man very learned in the ecclesiastical canons, obtained from Ælfric two such letters for the clergy of his own diocese. He had himself composed an address of exhortation to 'all the thanes, lay and ecclesiastical, entrusted to his direction in spiritual concerns' and a set of ecclesiastical injunctions known as *The Canons of Edgar*. Ælfric's books of homilies for the whole Christian year were aimed at improving the preaching of the clergy, and Byrhtferth of Ramsey wrote in 1011 a treatise on computation to help priests 'to relax their dice-playing and obtain a knowledge of this art.' Secular canons are enjoined to live a communal life and two of the best-known Frankish works regulating this manner of life, the rule of Chrodegang of Metz and that of Amalarius of Metz, were translated into Old English. Complaints of the shortcomings of the clergy are not lacking; some men seek orders because of the greater dignity of station; bishops should examine carefully the qualifications of candidates for ordination; tirades against ignorance, neglect of duty, and drunkenness occur. Many village priests were supporting existence in a position little better than a poor peasant, and it would be too much to expect high standards of scholarship everywhere. But the episcopate cannot be accused of neglecting their duty of supervision. All these pastoral letters try to impress on the clergy the principle of celibacy, but in this they failed. Frequently references to married priests occur; a testator can leave a church to a priest and his issue, and it is not uncommon for a son to follow his father in his clerical office. It is definitely accepted in the eleventh-century law issued for the priests of the diocese of York that they are likely to be married.

Reform in the Church seems to have gone on steadily in spite of the resumption of Danish invasions in the reign of Ethelred the Unready, but churchmen must have had an anxious time when the kingdom passed to Cnut at the end of 1016. However, the young king came under the influence of the English bishops, especially the veteran Archbishop Wulfstan of York, who drew up his laws for him and may well have been instrumental in inspiring him with the ambition to reign like his Christian predecessors. The agreement reached between English and Danes at Oxford in 1018 decided: 'that above all other things they would ever honour one God and steadfastly hold one Christian faith.' Cnut showed himself a defender of the rights of the Church, and a generous donor to religious houses. His laws include statutes against heathen practices. During the rest of the Anglo-Saxon period most sees were occupied by men of learning and integrity, and as Professor Darlington has shown, the English Church was neither decadent nor corrupt when the Normans came.

Moreover, it had the vitality in the tenth and eleventh centuries to be active again in missionary work. If only we had as good evidence, the story of the English missions to Scandinavia might be little less interesting than that of the conversion of Germany. But no correspondence relating to it has survived. There are references to English priests working for Hakon the Good and Olaf Tryggvason in tenth-century Norway, to an English bishop who was given an estate in Skåne in the reign of Swein Forkbeard, which he used as a base for work in Sweden and Norway, and to bishops and priests from England in attendance on St Olaf in the eleventh century. In general, however, the part played by the English Church has to be surmised from the undoubted influence it had on the organization and ritual of the Churches of Scandinavia, especially that of Norway.

CHAPTER IX

EDUCATION AND LATIN SCHOLARSHIP

Since under the Roman system a bishop was bound to have at his see a school for educating suitable persons for the ministry, Augustine at Canterbury and his suffragan at Rochester would establish such schools. Afterwards, when East Anglia was converted, King Sigeberht, who had been converted in Gaul and 'was eager to imitate the things which he saw well ordered there', set up a school in his own land, 'Bishop Felix helping him and furnishing him with masters and teachers according to the custom of the people of Kent.' These early schools probably attracted pupils from beyond the frontiers of the kingdom in which they were situated; already before the middle of the seventh century men of Anglo-Saxon race were equipped to become bishops, and two of them, Deusdedit the West Saxon who was made archbishop in 654, and Damian the South Saxon who became a bishop in the next year, were from areas where no education was obtainable at that early date. Similarly, the Irish missionaries at once commenced the education of a native clergy. Aidan was given twelve boys to train for this purpose, and one of them, Eata, was abbot of Melrose by 651. About the middle of the century, education could also be acquired from the Irish community settled at Malmesbury, and it was here that Aldhelm was introduced to learning.

In these early schools attention was first concentrated on the knowledge essential for the priestly office – the Latin language, the Scriptures, the computation of the

Church seasons, the music necessary for the services. How far beyond this studies went before the days of Theodore and Hadrian is uncertain, but Ogilvy has drawn attention to the citation of Rufinus's Latin translation of the Greek *Ecclesiastical History* of Eusebius at the synod of Whitby in 664, and to the familiarity with Latin authors revealed by Aldhelm very early in his literary career.

Northumbrians flocked to the monasteries of Ireland in the second half of the seventh century. Aldfrith, later king of Northumbria, went 'to acquire celestial wisdom', and Cynefrith, brother of Abbot Ceolfrith, 'to study the Scriptures'. Theology held first place in the curriculum, but as the Irish schools had lain far from the path of the barbarian invasions, they had not shared in the general decline, and continued to study grammar and rhetoric, which included some attention to secular Latin literature. By the end of the century Aldhelm is claiming that as good an education is obtainable in England, though many unnecessarily go to Ireland. We have already seen that before this several young Northumbrians looked towards Canterbury and the Continent, even as far as Rome, and a new era set in for scholarship in England with the arrival of Archbishop Theodore, whom Bede calls 'a man deep in all secular and ecclesiastical learning, whether Greek or Latin', and Abbot Hadrian, a man of similar attainments. Benedict Biscop stayed two years with them in Canterbury, and his foundations of Monkwearmouth and Jarrow doubtless benefited by their teaching.

Bede, who spent his life in these foundations, and his older contemporary Aldhelm, who was educated at Malmesbury and then at Canterbury and who became bishop of Sherborne in 705, were both men of great erudition and must have had access to libraries well equipped with the works of Latin authors. They were, of course, familiar with the Bible and the writings of the Christian Fathers, and with the Christian poets, Juvencus, Prudentius, Sedulius, Prosper, Fortunatus, Lactantius, and Arator. Bede makes use of a number of historical writings, of Josephus, Eusebius (in Latin translation from the Greek), Orosius, Cassiodorus, Gregory of Tours, etc., and of saints' lives such as Paulinus's *Life of Ambrose*, Possidius's *Life of Augustine*, Constantius's *Life of Germanus*. Of classical authors, both Bede and Aldhelm knew Virgil and Pliny at first hand, and Aldhelm used Lucan, Ovid, Cicero, and Sallust. Citations of other authors occur, but could have been taken from the works of Isidore of Seville, or from the Latin grammarians, of whom a really remarkable number were available in England already in the seventh century. Some very rare works had already found their way to England, and one, the grammar of Julian of Toledo, owes its preservation to this circumstance, for all surviving manuscripts go back to an English copy. The apocryphal literature of the early Church also was known in England, and works like *The Gospel of Nicodemus*, *The Vision of St Paul*, various legends of the Apostles, and rarer works like *The Pseudo-gospel of St Matthew*, and the legend of Jamnes and Mambres, influenced both Anglo-Latin and vernacular literature.

Books must have been imported in great numbers soon after the conversion for such learning to have been possible. King Alfred believed that Augustine's equipment included Pope Gregory's *Pastoral Care*, which is probable enough. Theodore and Hadrian may have come provided with some Greek books as well as Latin works, for Bede testifies to the proficiency of their disciples in the Greek language, but it is difficult to discover direct influence of Greek writings in Anglo-Saxon authors, though some Greek influence on liturgical manuscripts can be demonstrated. We read also of the book-collecting activities of Benedict Biscop, Acca, and Bishop Cuthwine of Dunwich (716–31), who collected illuminated manuscripts, and of the dispatch to England of many books from a monastery in Gaul in the seventh century. William of Malmesbury has preserved a tradition of Aldhelm looking among the merchandise landed at Dover for valuable books, and it is likely enough that traders were quick to realize that there was a market for books in England.

The books that were introduced were not left to lie fallow. They were industriously copied in the scriptoria of English monasteries. Already by 678 Wilfrid ordered for his church of Ripon the four gospels 'in letters of purest gold on purpled parchment and illuminated'; the first abbot of Jarrow, Ceolfrith, ordered three whole bibles, of the 'new' translation by Jerome, to be transcribed in his monastery. One which he had meant to present to the Pope, if death had not overtaken him on his way to Rome, still survives to witness to the skill of this recently founded house, and fragments of another are in the British Museum and Durham. The famous Lindisfarne Gospels were produced about this time. Other biblical manuscripts and copies of other works were produced in England in considerable number in the eighth century. The missionaries on the Continent frequently write home to ask for books to be written, both elaborate, impressive copies of the Scriptures for ceremonial use, and also plainer texts, and it is of interest to note that women practised this art, not men alone. Boniface asked the Abbess Eadburh to copy the Epistles of St Peter in gold. Meanwhile the import of books from abroad did not cease and by the time of Alcuin York had an excellent library, of which he gives some account in his poem on the saints of York, and for which he sighed after he left England in 782 to help Charles the Great in his educational schemes. As late as the mid ninth century, an abbot of Ferrières applies to it for the loan of some rare books. Well could Alfred say in about 890: 'I remembered how I saw, before everything was ravaged and burnt, that the churches throughout all England were filled with treasures and books.'

*

It was not very long after the conversion to Christianity that the English were producing original works themselves, in the Latin language. Aldhelm's major works, his poem and prose treatise on virginity, are alien to modern taste both in subject and style, but the number of surviving manuscripts witnesses to their great popularity in the Middle Ages. His style was ornate and artificial, fond of rare words and elaborate similes, and full of alliteration. It was admired in his own day, and imitated by many later writers, though fortunately others preferred the simple straightforward style of Bede. Aldhelm's letters and shorter poems have more interest for us; he describes in detail a contemporary church, and tells us something of Theodore's teaching at Canterbury; a long letter addressed to King Aldfrith of Northumbria includes a hundred metrical riddles, the first examples in this country of a type of intellectual activity that proved popular among men of scholarship in their lighter moments. It had classical authority in the work of the fifth-century poet Symphosius, and the example was followed by Hwætberht, abbot of Monkwearmouth in succession to Ceolfrith, and by Tatwine, archbishop of Canterbury from 731 to 734. Boniface and his fellows also amused themselves with riddles and acrostics, and the metrical riddle was adopted by vernacular poets. While the riddles vary greatly in literary quality, they often show the authors' acute observation of the things around them, and are of assistance to the historian who desires a picture of everyday things. As far as we know, Aldhelm was the first Englishman to compose Latin verse.

Meanwhile Northumbria was producing a crop of biographies. Prior to the work of Bede are anonymous lives of St Cuthbert and of Ceolfrith, abbot of Jarrow, the life of St Gregory by an anonymous monk of Whitby, and Eddius's interesting life of St Wilfrid. These were all known and used by Bede, who also had access to a lost life of St Æthelburh of Barking, the nunnery for which Aldhelm wrote his prose work on virginity; the writing of saints' lives was therefore not confined to Northumbria. Bede was in communication with learned men from all over the country. It was Albinus, abbot of the monastery of St Peter and St Paul at Canterbury, who encouraged him to write his *Ecclesiastical History*, and supplied him with material from Kent, and Nothhelm, a priest of London, searched the papal archives in Rome to find for Bede the letters relating to the English mission. Bishop Daniel of Winchester, the writer later on of shrewd advice to Boniface on the conversion of the heathen, corresponded with Bede about the history of the conversion of Wessex and Sussex, and an East Anglian abbot Esius and Cyneberht, bishop of Lindsey, were consulted on matters in their provinces. We have seen that Aldhelm was in correspondence with the learned king, Aldfrith of Northumbria, and Bede speaks with appreciation of Tobias, bishop of Rochester, and Tatwine, who was a Mercian. It is clear that political boundaries formed no obstacle to scholarly intercourse. Aldhelm was also in correspondence with a continental abbot, Cellan of Péronne.

Bede was not, first and foremost, a historian in contemporary eyes, and his most famous work, his *Ecclesiastical History of the English Nation*, belongs to the end of his literary career, which began with the writing of text-books, on metrics, orthography, science, and chronology. In connexion with the latter subject, he included a short chronicle of world history, and his verse *Life of St Cuthbert* was written early in his career, but between these works and his major historical works must be placed volume after volume of commentaries on various books of the Bible, and it was as a theologian rather than a historian that the Middle Ages honoured him most. In 721 he wrote his prose *Life of St Cuthbert*, followed a few years later by his *Lives of the Abbots*. His longer chronicle can be dated 725, and he finished his *Ecclesiastical History* in 731. Between this and his death in 735 can be placed a commentary on the Acts, and a long letter on Church organization addressed to his pupil Egbert, archbishop of York, and there survive also a number of theological treatises, homilies, hymns, etc., whose date is uncertain. In contrast to the writings of Aldhelm, there has never been a period in which Bede's work was entirely neglected; manuscripts were multiplied throughout the Middle Ages, and it has always formed the basis of modern historical studies of the early Saxon period. One cannot sum up better the reason for this than to quote Sir Frank Stenton's words: 'But the quality which makes his work great is not his scholarship, nor the faculty of narrative which he shared with many contemporaries, but his astonishing power of co-ordinating the fragments of information which came to him through tradition, the relation of friends, or documentary evidence. In an age when little was attempted beyond the registration of fact, he had reached the conception of history.'

During Bede's lifetime a work of a different kind was

compiled by a man who called himself 'a disciple of the Humbrians'. It consists of a collection of the answers and decisions given by Archbishop Theodore on matters of penance and canon law, and goes under the name of *Theodore's Penitential*. Bede's pupil Cuthbert wrote an account of the last days of his master, and to the pen of another pupil, Archbishop Egbert, there is ascribed a penitential and a dialogue concerning ecclesiastical government. This last work illustrates the system of teaching used in the school of York, a school which under Egbert and his kinsman Ethelbert became one of the most famous centres of learning in Europe. It was here that Alcuin was educated, and he speaks with great reverence of his master Ethelbert, the founder of the great library there, and Egbert's successor in the see. From the work of Alcuin and his biographer we find that pupils were instructed both by exposition and by disputation, and the purpose of the dialogue was to give practice in discourse in the Latin tongue, and at the same time impart necessary information on an important subject. Alcuin carried the method with him to the Continent, and some of his own work is couched in dialogue form. He had himself succeeded Ethelbert as master of the school of York, and acquired a reputation that brought foreigners to study there, before he was invited to take charge of Charles the Great's palace school, and left Northumbria in 782 to spend most of the rest of his life abroad, assisting the revival of learning in the Carolingian empire. Latin poems, sent to him by his students at York, on the miracles of St Ninian, are extant, and much work from his own pen, treatises, letters, poems, etc. He saw himself divinely called to the Continent to combat the Adoptionist heresy, and much of his writing is on religious polemic. Of greater general interest are his poem on York, and his life of the Anglo-

Saxon missionary St Willibrord. He was not an original scholar, but his work was influential out of all proportion to its literary merits, and Dr Levison has pointed out that his methods opened the way for later thinkers of greater independence. His work as a liturgical and biblical scholar had very far-reaching results, and he left behind a number of men, some of them of English nationality, to carry on his work in the ninth-century Frankish empire. He lived to see and be overwhelmed with grief by the first of the Viking raids, the sack of Lindisfarne in 793, but not to know that this was but the beginning of a catastrophe destined within a century totally to destroy Northumbrian scholarship. It was on the Continent, not at home, that his work had permanent results.

From the lands south of the Humber few original works have been preserved, though the letters of St Boniface reveal a powerful intellect that might have been productive of distinguished literary work if the writer's energies had not been so completely occupied in other affairs. As it is, there are only these letters and a grammar from his pen. There were many men and women throughout England of adequate education to write good Latin letters to him and his successor Lul, and an English nun at Heidenheim, one of the monasteries founded in Germany by the missionaries, by name Hygeburh, has left us a most interesting work, the *Lives of St Willibald and St Wynnebald*, in the third quarter of the eighth century. It includes a fascinating account of a pilgrimage undertaken by Willibald to the Holy Land, written from his recollections. From the Midlands a generation earlier comes Felix's *Life of St Guthlac of Crowland*, a work which throws some welcome light on a period and locality for which evidence is hard to come by. In spite of scanty evidence, one gets the impression that in almost all parts of England during the eighth century there were centres where a liberal education could be obtained, and it was not confined to the male sex. Aldhelm's writings for the nuns of Barking and Rudolf's *Life of St Leofgyth*, Boniface's helper in his missionary work, who was educated at Minster and at Wimborne, show that women, like men, studied the scriptures and their fourfold interpretation, the works of the Fathers, chronography, grammar, and metrics.

*

Already Bede's *Ecclesiastical History* includes several examples of a type of literature that attained a great vogue, the accounts of visions of heaven and hell revealed to various individuals to whom it is permitted to return to earth to relate what they have seen for the benefit of others. The visions of the Irish hermit Fursey and of the Northumbrian Dryhthelm became particularly renowned, and often survive as separate extracts in our manuscripts. One of Boniface's letters describes at length a similar vision seen by a man at the abbey of Wenlock, in which he saw prophetically King Ceolred of Mercia among the damned, and this letter was later translated into English. The terror of the Danish invasions in the ninth century caused men to see more visions, and in 839 envoys sent by King Æthelwulf of Wessex to the Emperor Louis warned him of the vision revealed to a certain religious priest, which threatened famine and pagan attack if men did not amend their ways and, in particular, keep religiously the proper observance of Sunday. This seems like a reference to the work of a priest Pehtred, who wrote in the province of York (though not in that diocese or that of Lindisfarne) before 837 a book which has been lost, but whose contents are known in part from the horror its heresy roused in the breasts of the archbishop and of his suffragan at Lindisfarne. It told of a deacon Nial who came to life after being dead for seven weeks, and never partook of food afterwards; of a letter of gold written by the hand of God, dealing with the due observance of Sunday, and found on St Peter's altar in the days of Pope Florentius. This tale had been condemned by a Frankish capitulary already in the eighth century, and the bishop of Lindisfarne is urgent that effective steps be taken to suppress this heresy. With a historical sense proper to a countryman of Bede he had consulted lists of popes and failed to find any trace of a Pope Florentius. Yet the fact that no fewer than six vernacular homilies are to be found in tenth- and eleventh-century manuscripts which accept the authenticity of this letter from heaven indicates how unsuccessful were the efforts of the saner element of the population to prevent the spread of such wild tales.

However, Northumbria was not only producing heresy in the ninth century. A certain Æthilwulf wrote a long Latin poem on the abbots of an unidentified Northumbrian monastery, as well as a work on the English saints which has not survived; and the monks of Lindisfarne wrote in letters of silver and gold their 'Book of Life', containing the names of those for whom they were bound to pray. York was still in touch with at least one continental monastery. Wessex, too, had its continental connexions: King Æthelwulf at one time employed a Frankish secretary, and was a benefactor to continental houses. The knowledge shown of the lives of Frankish saints in the ninth-century Old English *Martyrology* is further evidence of intercourse across the Channel. Book-production had not entirely ceased. Yet already Alcuin had complained of a decline in the zeal for study in England, and this can only have been hastened by the constant threat of Viking raids. King Alfred's impression was that before the monasteries were destroyed by these raids

the monks in them did not know Latin and could make
no use of their richly equipped libraries.

*

Alfred's educational reforms, which he found time to put
into force during the latter part of his reign, aimed at
spreading the ability to read English and at supplying
suitable books in English – a subject which belongs to the
next chapter. Men destined for the Church are, however,
to study Latin, and it is clear that Alfred regrets that the
decay of Latin scholarship should have made translation
necessary. The half-century following his death is not
prolific in signs of intellectual activity, and it may well be
that men's energies were largely absorbed in the re-
conquest and re-conversion of the areas ceded to the
Danes; yet it was not as utterly devoid of such signs as
the mid tenth-century reformers and their pupils were
ready to believe. Oda, who became archbishop of Canterbury in 942, and who is the author of a short series of
Latin canons, had been able to obtain an education in a
thane's household. King Athelstan was generous in gifts
of books to religious houses, obtaining some from abroad.
The copy of Bede's *Life of St Cuthbert*, in prose and verse,
which he gave to the church of that saint at Chester-le-
Street, was however an English production, probably
from Glastonbury; and there survive manuscripts of
works of Bede and Aldhelm which are assigned to this
period. The influence of Aldhelm's style is visible in the
highly flamboyant Latinity of the charters of this period.
There is evidence of the production in England of a
version of the *History of the Britons* of Nennius during the
reign of King Edmund (939–46), and a Latin poem on
the life of St Wilfrid by a certain Frithegod was dedicated
to Archbishop Oda. Parts of a Latin verse panegyric on

King Athelstan are quoted by William of Malmesbury. Manuscripts of vernacular prose were being copied. Nevertheless the best minds of the time thought that in scholarship as in monastic usage England was behind the Continent, and the reform movement drew its inspiration from abroad.

The monastic reformers devoted great care to the teaching of Latin in their monasteries. Works meant solely for use there are in Latin. Athelwold translated the Benedictine Rule into English, but there is a possibility that he did so for the use of communities of women. At any rate, it was at the special request of the king and queen that he undertook this task, receiving an estate in recompense. His own compilation for securing uniformity of observance in the monasteries of England, the *Regularis Concordia*, he wrote in Latin, and similarly his pupil Ælfric, master of Old English prose though he was, used Latin for his letter to his monks at Eynsham which is based on this *Concordia*, and for the Life of St Athelwold which he meant for monastic reading. This life contains a brief comment on Athelwold as a teacher:

> It was always a pleasure to him to teach young men and boys, and to explain books to them in English, and with kindly exhortations to encourage them to better things.

Archbishop Oswald brought over from Fleury a distinguished continental scholar, Abbo, to teach his monks at Ramsey, and Abbo wrote a grammar for their use and a Latin *Life of St Edmund*. It was a monk of Ramsey who wrote a Latin biography of St Oswald. When Ælfric and Byrhtferth of Ramsey write works in English, they are thinking of a wider public than those trained in monasteries. Byrhtferth shows his belief that the education of the average priest would be below that obtainable in the cloister, when he says:

But because we know that these things seem complex enough to clerks and rustic priests, we will now address our words to the young monks who have occupied their childhood with scientific books. I mention a few such, out of many; they have investigated Sergius and Priscian, and gone slowly through the *Distichs* of the bald fellow Cato, and the narratives of Bede, the venerable scholar.

To assist in the teaching of Latin, Ælfric wrote a Latin grammar, a Latin-English glossary, and a colloquy to exercise his pupils in Latin conversation. The characters are a master, a novice, and representatives of the various crafts. This work has been drawn on in previous chapters for the evidence it affords of contemporary conditions.

It is clear both from extant manuscripts and also from the knowledge revealed by writers of the period, chiefly by Ælfric and Wulfstan, that the monastic revival led to the introduction into England of many Latin works of the Carolingian revival and later, especially canonistic writings, some of which were translated into English. Scholars of this age knew, in addition to the works of the Fathers and classical writers, those of the more recent authors Alcuin, Hrabanus Maurus, Amalarius of Metz, Atto of Vercelli, Smaragdus, Haymo of Halberstadt, and so on. And Abbo was not the only foreigner to write in England; one of the earliest lives of St Dunstan was the work of a foreigner, and an account of the miracles of St Swithin was written at Winchester by someone whom Ælfric calls 'Landferth, the man from across the sea.' Winchester possessed also a writer of Latin verse, an Englishman called Wulfstan the precentor, whose poem on St Swithin is extant, and to whom William of Malmesbury attributes a life of St Athelwold.

One Latin work is written by a layman, Ealdorman Æthelweard, a patron of Ælfric. He was a descendant of King Alfred's elder brother, and he wrote, for the benefit of his kinswoman, Matilda, abbess of Essen, a descendant of Alfred, a Latin chronicle, based in general on the Anglo-Saxon Chronicle, of which he seems to have possessed a manuscript better in some respects than any that have survived. If the printed text of his work, which, except for a few badly scorched and illegible fragments of the burnt manuscript, is all that we possess, fairly represents him, he wrote a strange and at times incomprehensible Latin; but it is remarkable that a layman should attempt such a task at all.

Another result of the revival was an enormous activity in manuscript production, which continued for the rest of the Saxon period. There poured out elaborate illuminated manuscripts and plainer utilitarian ones; manuscripts in Latin and in English; gospels, psalters, service books of all kinds; works of earlier Latin writers, including the English scholars Aldhelm and Bede, Felix's Life of St Guthlac, and the Life of King Alfred by the Welshman Asser; collections of canons; books of extracts from various sources; calendars, almanacs, etc. Before 1066 the libraries must have again become as full as ever they were in the days before the Viking ravages.

CHAPTER X

VERNACULAR LITERATURE

FAR back in heathen days the Germanic races had their songs. Tacitus speaks of these as the only type of memorial and chronicle they possessed, mentioning specifically that the former leader Arminius was celebrated in song; and the historians of the individual Germanic nations, Jordanes who wrote of the Goths, Paul, the historian of the Lombards, the anonymous Frank who wrote of the acts of Charlemagne, could draw information from poems which have not survived. The English tribes brought over with them traditions in verse form, relating to the heroes of their homeland, and naturally they would continue to compose such poems in their new settlements. Some of the statements in Bede's works and in the Anglo-Saxon Chronicle are probably derived from such sources. Though historical writers, from Tacitus onwards, are mainly interested in poems celebrating the heroes of the past, it is probable that poems of other kinds existed from early times – dirges for the dead, hymns in honour of heathen gods, and mnemonic poems, by which the wisdom of the past could be handed on in easily remembered form; but in England pre-Christian poems had little chance of being written down, and only a few fragments survive, embedded in the work of later Christian writers. Thus a poem of Christian date, *Widsith*, which purports to be a minstrel's account of the races and courts he has visited, includes catalogues of kings and peoples which express the point of view of the age of national migration rather than that of England in Christian times; and the gnomic poetry, which seems to be a collection of the more memorable utterances of wise men, added to from age to age, includes a passage accepting cremation as the normal burial-rite –

The holly shall be kindled; the inheritance of the dead man divided; fame is best –

side by side with passages of Christian date, such as:

Feud first came to mankind when the earth swallowed Abel's blood. That was no enmity of a single day, from which sprang for men, for many peoples far and wide, bloodshed from strife, great crime, pernicious hatred.

The poet of *Beowulf*, who was undoubtedly a Christian, knows that his audience will be familiar with tales of family feuds among the races who were neighbours of the English on the Continent, and it is probable that he drew his descriptions of long-discontinued funeral rites from poems with their roots in a distant past. In the charms one even gets an occasional remembrance of a heathen deity as a protective power.

The survival into Christian times of the older poetry was aided by the interest which the Anglo-Saxon royal and noble families took in the traditions of the deeds of their ancestors. Bede sent his *Ecclesiastical History* to King Ceolwulf of Northumbria for his criticism because he was well versed in the ancient traditions of his race, and it may be that heroic verse was included among the Saxon songs which King Alfred made his children learn. Aldhelm, bishop of Sherborne from 705 to 709, sang and composed vernacular songs, and his contemporary St Guthlac was in his youth inspired to the profession of arms by remembering the deeds of the heroes of old; both these men were related to royal houses. So also was St Dunstan, whom we know to have been interested in native poetry, while the chronicler Æthelweard, who betrays in his work a knowledge of the old traditions, was descended from King Alfred's elder brother. Men such as these could see to it that what they were interested in should be written down, and it is to them or others like them that we owe the preservation of works that are without ecclesiastical interest; but we need not assume that their tastes were not shared by the lesser folk who could not employ the services of scribes. It was not by the scribe, but by the minstrel, whether professional or amateur, whether king's thane or humble singer in taverns, that this poetry was normally transmitted, and the bulk of it has not come down to us.

*

According to Bede, it was a man of the peasant class who first had the inspiration to employ the diction and metre of native verse for Christian themes; it was while he was taking his turn at guarding the cattle of the abbey of Whitby that Cædmon saw one night in a vision a man who told him to sing of the Creation. The lines which he composed in his sleep and repeated next morning constitute the earliest datable English poetry, for they survive in a manuscript written two or three years after Bede's death. It may therefore be of interest to quote them in the original as well as in translation. They are as follows:

> Nu scylun hergan hefænricaes uard,
> metudæs maecti end his modgidanc,
> uerc uuldurfadur, sue he uundra gihuaes,
> eci dryctin, or astelidæ;
> he ærist scop aelda barnum
> heben til hrofe, haleg scepen.
> Tha middungeard moncynnæs uard,
> eci dryctin, æfter tiadæ
> firum foldu, frea allmectig.

(Now we must praise the guardian of the heavenly kingdom, the powers of the Creator and his thoughts, the works of the Father of glory, as he, the eternal Lord, appointed the beginning of every wondrous thing; he, the holy Lord, the Guardian of mankind, first created for the children of men the heaven as a roof. Then the eternal Lord, Ruler Almighty, afterwards adorned the world, the earth, for men.)

The metre of Old English verse is sufficiently akin to that of Old Norse, Old Saxon, and Old High German to prove that it descends from the same Germanic verse-form. Rhyme is rarely used, and then only as an additional ornament; it is alliteration that binds together the two halves of the line, which is divided into more or less equal parts by a caesura; either one or two strongly stressed syllables of the first half-line alliterate with the first stress of the second half-line (any vowel being able to alliterate with any other). Each half-line belongs to one of a limited number of rhythmical types, the most widely acknowledged system of scansion recognizing five main types with various subdivisions; the number of syllables is not fixed, and it is generally held that the normal half-line consisted of two stressed portions, known as lifts, and a varying number of unstressed syllables. This is not the place to go into technical detail – nor, in fact, is there complete agreement on the subject; but it should be noted that rhythm and alliteration follow the natural logical emphasis of the lines, and that the sentences are often long and may be stopped at the caesura as well as at the end of the line. The length of the sentence arises not so much from elaborate periodic structure as from 'parallelism', the restatement in fresh words of significant elements in the sentence – as for example the expressions for God in Cædmon's hymn – or even of whole clauses. In the best Old English poetry this is not empty repetition; the concept is given a fresh significance by each new reference to it: Hrothgar's 'hall-troop' becomes his 'war-band', the vague 'land' is particularized as 'steep hills' and 'broad sea-headlands' in the succeeding lines, 'famine' is personified as a 'pale guest at table'.

What was carried over into the service of the Christian religion was far more than the metre. Poetry had its own diction. The requirements of alliteration had already brought into being a large vocabulary of synonyms, many of which are not found in prose. To some extent this is a question of date: some words had become archaic when we begin to get vernacular prose, but others may have been poetic from the beginning. This applies especially to the poetic compounds and kennings (brief descriptive expressions used instead of the name of the thing itself, such as 'gannet's bath' for the sea, 'candle of the heavens' for the sun, etc.), which made it possible for an Old English poet to pack into a few words great richness of description and association. By the time of Cædmon many stereotyped expressions were in use and were taken over by the religious poetry; words such as 'battlemen', 'warriors', brave leaders', were applied to the disciples, and the Christian God was spoken of in the various terms used of the chieftains of heroic poetry. How far this terminology retained its original martial connotation is a moot point, but it came easy to the Anglo-Saxon to conceive the relationship between God and his angels, or Christ and his disciples, in terms of the Teutonic code of loyalty between man and lord, and it required little modification to turn pre-Christian lines advocating liberality into praises of the Christian virtue of almsgiving, or to give a Christian emphasis to the Germanic insistence on the acquisition of a good reputation. The mnemonic poetry could enlarge its compass to include the Christian account of the origin of all things, as one poet puts it (in W. S. Mackie's translation):

It is, thinking man, an obvious example to every one who can by wisdom comprehend in his mind all the world, that long ago men, well-advised people, could often utter and say the truth in the art of song, by means of lays, so that most of mankind, by always asking and repeating and remembering, gained knowledge of the web of mysteries. So let him who is zealous, the studious man, inquire about the secrets of Creation, inscribe in his understanding the art of narrating them, fix his mind on them, ponder over them well. An earnest man must not become weary of wisely completing his knowledge of the world.

And thus we have poems that illustrate the workings of divine providence in the distribution of gifts and fortunes to men by a series of cameo-like descriptions of men's various occupations – minstrelsy, seamanship, the gold-smith's craft, hunting and hawking – and of the ways by which men meet their end; and poems of practical mnemonics, on the festivals of the Church and the fasting seasons. There are also poems of direct religious and moral exhortation, such as *An Admonition to Christian Living* and *The Advice of a Father to his Son*. An address of a sinful soul to the body it has just left is one of the few poems to survive in more than one version, and there are poems that deal dramatically with the Last Judgement.

Of the many poems on religious themes which Bede tells us Cædmon composed, nothing has come down that can with certainty be ascribed to him except the few lines quoted above. He had many, in Bede's opinion inferior, imitators before 731, and some surviving poems may date from this time. During the eighth century the English missionaries to the Continent probably spread the habit of composing biblical paraphrases in alliterative verse, for the extant Old Saxon poetry betrays English influence. The extant Anglo-Saxon religious verse is varied in range and style. Besides the works already mentioned, it includes close paraphrases of the Old Testament, as in *Genesis* and *Daniel*; a heroic poem on how Moses led the

Israelites across the Red Sea; poems on Christ's descent into Hell and his Second Coming; and saints' lives, of Andrew, Helena, Juliana, Guthlac, all based on Latin originals and none earlier than the second half of the eighth century. Two of these are the work of a poet called Cynewulf, of the late eighth or the ninth century, whose work is distinguished by a graceful mastery of technique and by a logical clarity and smoothness of syntax that owes something to his classical scholarship. Two other poems, one on the Ascension, and one a brief summary of the deaths of the Apostles, are known to be his. Of learned origin also are some fragments of a *Physiologus*, and a poem on the Phoenix based on the Latin poem ascribed to Lactantius, and Latin inspiration lies behind the verse riddles. Much more original is the well-known poem called *The Dream of the Rood*, of which some lines were carved in runes on the stone cross at Ruthwell; in this a poet with deep religious feeling, imaginative insight and an amazing restraint and economy of expression, allows the cross to tell its own story of the crucifixion and of its metamorphosis from forest tree to instrument of death and then to a glorious and venerated symbol of redemption.

It is not true, as is sometimes maintained, that all Anglo-Saxon poetry is gloomy. Another type of religious poetry deals poignantly with the transitory nature of all earthly joy, but it is only for those who dismiss as mere empty convention the final conclusion of *The Wanderer:* 'Well will it be with him who seeks mercy and consolation from the Father in heaven, where for us all that security stands', or the claim of *The Seafarer:* 'for my heart warms more to the joys of the Lord than to this dead life', that these poems sound a despairing note. Moreover, these poems would move us little if their authors were less conscious of the beauty of the world around them and of the human relationships that will not last for ever. Anglo-Saxon poets excel at painting nature in its stormy and forbidding moods, but they did not see it exclusively like this; it was the Christian's duty to esteem the works of the Creator, and any impression of the poetry is one-sided that leaves out of count passages such as the following:

Full often, O King of Glory, thou sendest through the air the soft morning rain for the benefit of men. Many a plant shall then awaken, and the groves of the forest teem with branches.

or again:

Groves begin to blossom, the courts become fair, the plains grow beautiful, the world quickens.

The poet of the longest extant poem, *Beowulf*, is similarly alive to the beauty of nature and of some of the works of men's hands; of shining headlands, of the sailing ship driven by the wind 'most like a bird', of the flash of the sun on the gold-adorned helmets of a marching band of men. Like most Old English poetry, this poem cannot be dated exactly. Most scholars place it between 650 and 750; to me the extent of Christian education it assumes in its audience suggests a date late in this period, or even during the following half-century. It tells how a strong and valiant hero, trusting in the help of God, saves first the Danish royal hall, and later his own people, from the ravages of evil monsters, the descendants of the first murderer, Cain. By subtle reminders to an audience steeped in stories of the past, the poet supplies a realistic background to this theme, and a foil to it, putting it in a setting of human strife, of civil or foreign warfare; and he seems to point a moral that there are intangible and permanent values that remain untouched by the vicissitudes of fortunes in this life, where all is transitory. Both

the races the hero delivers have a tragic history ahead of
them, and the hero slays the dragon only at the cost of
his own life; but, dying, he is not afraid to face 'the Ruler
of men', and the poem closes with the building of a
barrow to his memory, that it may, as he wished:

tower high on *Hronesnæs*, so that in after days seafarers, who
urge their tall ships from afar over the mists of the ocean, may
call it Beowulf's barrow.

Another poet, using the stories of old heroes to impart
a moral, has left us the little lyric *Deor*, which purports
to be the utterance of a minstrel who has been supplanted
by a rival, and who comforts himself in a series of
strophes each referring to the sorrows of a character of
heroic legend, and concluding with the refrain: 'That
was surmounted, so can this be.' In other so-called lyrics
the speaker is anonymous. In one, a woman laments her
unhappy situation, due to the machinations of her husband's kinsfolk and his alienation from her; some would
connect with this poem another in which a man who has
gone into exile across the sea sends for his wife to join him
in his new-found prosperity. It is probable that such
poems are concerned with the sentiments of people in
typical situations, not with personages of specific story.
Neither conveys any religious message, whereas a poem
known as *The Wanderer* poignantly describes the desola-
tion of a lordless man and of a ruined city in order to
contrast it with the security of trust in the eternal Lord,
and another, known as *The Seafarer*, shows how a man's
yearning for 'the joys of the Lord' impels him to undertake afresh a journey across the sea in spite of his suffer-
ings, most graphically recounted, on former voyages.
Both poems, and also a fragment called *The Ruin*, contain
laments for the splendour of earlier and greater civiliza-
tions. Only fragments remain of direct heroic narrative,

two of a poem on Waldere, the Walter of continental story, and one of a highly dramatic account of a fight at Finn's hall, which was also the theme of a lay sung by a minstrel in *Beowulf*.

*

The vast bulk of Old English poetry has come down to us in four codices compiled towards the end of the tenth century or early in the eleventh; it is mostly of much earlier date than these manuscripts, which must owe their existence to a desire to preserve the work of the past. Little survives from the second half of the ninth century or later, but it would be unsafe to assume that this means that little was being produced, for the chances of survival, at any rate for secular verse, were not high. Somewhat prosaic verse renderings of the *Metra* of Boethius and of the Psalms have been preserved, and the latter part of a vigorous poem on *Judith*. A manuscript containing a long Old Saxon poetic paraphrase of parts of the Bible reached England some time towards the end of the ninth century or in the first half of the tenth, and the English were sufficiently interested in the productions of a daughter church on the Continent to make an illuminated manuscript of one of these poems, the *Héliand*, and a translation of part, at least, of the other, the *Genesis*. Several hundred lines of this were inserted into the Old English poems on this subject. It stands out from this not only by differences in language and metre, but also by its spirit, for it is a vigorous, dramatic, and unorthodox treatment of the story of the Fall of the Angels and the Fall of Man. Some historical poems are entered into the Anglo-Saxon Chronicle of the tenth and eleventh centuries, and show that the conventional expressions of the old heroic poetry were still in use. By far the best poem of the later Saxon period, that on the battle of

Maldon fought in 991, has been preserved by the accidental circumstance that the leader in this battle was also a great benefactor of monasteries. There may have been many poems of a like nature which were never entered in manuscripts at all. *The Battle of Maldon* employs very few of the clichés of the older poems, but it inherits their spirit, dealing as it does with men whose loyalty forbids them to return from a fight in which their lord has fallen. As in *Beowulf* it is not success that matters, but a living up to a code of honour even when it leads to certain death.

*

Vernacular prose for utilitarian purposes began early. Laws were from the first written in English, beginning with those of Ethelbert of Kent, and interlinear glosses in the vernacular were written in Latin texts in the seventh century, and had begun to be collected into glossaries by the end of the century. Bede was engaged in translating into consecutive prose the Gospel of St John when he died. This has not survived, and except for laws and a few charters, the history of English prose has to begin with the reign of Alfred. It is probably accident that this is so; as we know that pre-Alfredian manuscripts of verse existed and have been lost, the same may have happened with prose works. Alfred declares that many in his day could read what was written in English, which may suggest that there were things for them to read which have not survived. It is likely that there were homilies in the vernacular, for preaching was done in the native tongue, and it is improbable that every preacher composed his own sermons. The spread of the heretical matter from Pehtred's book, mentioned above, would presumably be among the less learned, since it was frowned on by the higher clergy, and it may well have been facilitated by English versions. Some of the materials available to the compiler of the Anglo-Saxon Chronicle in Alfred's day may have been in English. An Old English martyrology, of which fragments survive in manuscripts of Alfred's reign, may date from before the Alfredian revival. The works of Bede, Aldhelm, Adamnan, Eddius, Felix, as well as of older Latin writers like Gregory and Jerome, were used for this compilation, and also lives of Frankish saints and apocryphal matter such as the *Passions of the Apostles*.

King Alfred grew up in a court with Frankish affinities. He was almost certainly aware of what Charles the Great had done to improve the standard of learning among his people, and the measures he employed in his distress at the decline occasioned by the Danish invasions may owe something to this example. Like Charles, he invited learned men from abroad; he asked assistance from Fulk, archbishop of Reims, who sent him a Frankish scholar called Grimbald, and he invited Asser from Wales and John from the Old Saxons. Other helpers, Plegmund, later archbishop of Canterbury, and Werferth, bishop of Worcester, and two priests came from Mercia. Probably in, or soon after, 890, Alfred sent to each of his bishops a letter accompanying a gift of his translation of *The Pastoral Care* of Gregory the Great, and in it he outlined his plan by which all free-born youths of adequate means were to be taught to read English, and the books 'which are most necessary for all men to know' translated into English. The books chosen were *The Pastoral Care*, which had always been a book much used by the English clergy; the *Dialogues* of the same author; two history books, the *Universal History against the Pagans* of Orosius and Bede's *Ecclesiastical History of the English Nation*; Boethius' *On the Consolation of Philosophy*, the book which handed down to the Middle Ages some of the ideas of the Greek philosophers; and part of St Augustine's *Soliloquies*, to which was added material from other writers on similar topics, the heavenly wisdom and the relation to God of the human soul. Gregory's *Dialogues*, which treat of the lives of the early saints of Italy, and Bede's *Ecclesiastical History* were translated by Mercian scholars, and there is great doubt whether Alfred himself translated Orosius; but the other works are his own, with the help of his assistants. As translations, they do not rank very high; at times the rendering is clumsy and the meaning, especially in the philosophical works, misrepresented. Yet it is these works which have the greatest interest, for in them Alfred, who had no slavish attitude of literal fidelity to the texts, often adds passages from other sources and from his own experience and ponderings on such matters; sometimes he gives a concrete simile to make clear the abstract reasoning of his author, as when he compares God's foreknowledge to the steersman's anticipation of a great wind at sea before it comes, and occasionally he inserts a whole chapter, like that on the art of government quoted in Chapter IV above. The *Orosius* also has additions to the source, including an account of the geography of Northern Europe with two seamen's accounts of voyages in these regions. In such passages one has a chance to judge what Old English prose could be when unshackled by the need to render Latin, and though the balance and smoothness of an Ælfric is lacking, it is a workmanlike medium enough. Early post-Conquest authors attributed to Alfred a translation of the Psalms, part of which may well be preserved in the *Paris Psalter*, and even of the whole Bible, but it is natural that the thought of a king translating for his people's good should fire men's imaginations and cause works not his to be attributed to him. We see something of the impression his work made already in his lifetime, in a Latin acrostic on him in a Cornish (or perhaps Welsh) manuscript, which ends (in W. M. Lindsay's translation):

Rightly do you teach, hastening from the false sweetness of the world. Behold you are ever fit to turn shining talents to profit. Learnedly run through the fields of foreign lore.

The author is much hampered by his need to begin and end his lines with the letters of Alfred's name, but through his stilted language we glimpse genuine admiration of a king who turns from temporal pleasures to the discipline of scholarship.

There is manuscript evidence that the Old English *Orosius*, *Bede*, *Boethius*, and *The Pastoral Care* were being copied in, or soon after, the first half of the tenth century, and so was the *Martyrology*. Copies of all the Alfredian works survive from the time after the monastic revival, and we have Ælfric's evidence that they were obtainable in his day a century after they were composed. Moreover Æthelweard about the same period speaks of his translations with admiration, especially the *Boethius*, and his words imply that this work was read aloud to those unskilled in reading. Alfred's labours had more than a temporary effect.

*

Modern, like medieval, scholars have been ready to attribute works to Alfred. There is no clear evidence that he was responsible for the compilation of the Anglo-Saxon Chronicle, though it is possible that the rather rapid multiplication of manuscripts of this work owes something to royal encouragement. The Chronicle was based on older records, on Bede and regnal lists, on some epitome of world history, and on various sets of brief early annals, in Latin and perhaps sometimes in English; these materials were put together in Alfred's reign, the annals becoming much fuller as the period within living memory was reached. Round about 890 copies began to be disseminated. The oldest extant copy is written up to 891 in a single handwriting, and it is already two stages removed from the original work; this version was at Winchester in the tenth century and may have been originally copied for this house. All other surviving manuscripts are later, and represent copies of versions kept at different religious establishments. Three of the manuscripts go back to a text which had been at some northern centre, probably York, and had there had dove-tailed into it a large amount of northern material, from Bede and from some sets of local annals, and one of these manuscripts reached Peterborough by the early twelfth century, where it was kept up until the early days of 1155, all the other versions having come to a close at various earlier dates. Each version contains passages peculiar to it, usually of local interest, but over long stretches several versions – and sometimes all – are in agreement. The problems of relationship and transmission of the various versions are too complicated to be dealt with in a para-graph. More independence is shown from the reign of the Confessor on. The extent to which the Chronicle is kept up varies at different periods; the later campaigns of Alfred, and the re-conquest of the Danelaw by his son, are recorded in minute detail, though the latter account reached only one of our extant manuscripts. There is a full and excellently written record of the reign of Ethelred the Unready, possibly written at Abingdon, which achieved wide circulation. In the intervening period the Chronicle was neglected, and the gap filled later with scrappy entries, poems, and notices of events of mere domestic interest. But unequal though it is, the Chronicle is a remarkable achievement, a historical source of the first importance over centuries, which allows us to study the development of prose writing, not based on Latin originals, over a long period. From a brief record of outstanding events it develops at times into a moving and vivid narrative, letting us see the contemporary attitude to events as well as the events themselves.

*

Our materials suggest that the period of more than half a century between Alfred's death and the revival due to the Benedictine reform of the mid tenth century was somewhat barren of literature. It was prolific in lawcodes, following Alfred's example, for he had issued a long code, moved by the example of the early Kentish kings, his predecessor Ine, and Offa of Mercia, whose laws are lost. The Chronicle was kept up fully until the end of his son's reign, and a short set of annals known as the *Mercian Register* was written in Mercia. The works of Alfred's reign continued to be copied, and the period was not altogether devoid of Latin culture, but we cannot assign with certainty much original work to this age. It is possible that some of the homilies collected in the Blickling and Vercelli manuscripts may belong to the first half of the tenth century; they are little touched by the standards of the post-revival writers. There may have been writings that have perished, for Ælfric complains in 990–1 of the currency of many English books that contained error, and works frowned on as unorthodox by the monastic party would have small chance of survival. We know of conditions in the religious houses prior to the revival only from the writings of the reformers themselves, and the picture given of the sloth and ignorance of their predecessors may well be overdrawn.

The first vernacular work to result from the tenth-century monastic revival was Bishop Athelwold's translation of the *Benedictine Rule*, about 960, but the real harvest of post-revival literature begins with the generation of students taught by the first reformers. The homi-list Ælfric, a pupil of Athelwold, issues his first work about 990, Wulfstan's datable work begins in the next decade, while Abbo's pupil, Byrhtferth of Ramsey, wrote his scientific manual in 1011. Works of about the same period have come down from many writers whose names we do not know. The range is varied. There are direct translations of continental canonistic and penitential books, of Chrodegang and Amalarius of Metz, Theodulf of Orleans, Halitgar of Cambrai, and Benedict of Aniane; Ælfric and Byrhtferth both wrote works on scientific matters, based largely on Bede, but using later work, like that of Hrabanus Maurus, as well; the Gospels and a part of the book of Genesis were translated by anony-mous writers, while Ælfric is responsible for renderings of parts of the Hexateuch, of Judges, Job, Esther, and Judith, and he wrote a treatise on the Old and New Testaments. All these translators show a competence above that of the Alfredian writers, and an ability to write a smooth and often a distinguished prose style. The more exacting standards of this age in the matter of style can be seen by comparing the revision made at this time of Werferth's translation of the *Dialogues* of Gregory with Werferth's own work. Ælfric prefers to translate afresh passages from Bede instead of using the existing English version.

Great variety exists in the subject matter of the very extensive homiletic literature of this date. There are sermons of plain moral instruction, perhaps diversified with *exempla*, and of straightforward teaching on the out-lines of the Christian faith; there are impassioned de-nunciations of society and appeals for repentance, and semi-poetical descriptions of the Last Judgement and the torments of the damned; there are homilies of exegesis, explaining the symbolism of the gospel for the day, and numbers of saints' lives and apocryphal legends. These are mostly of a length suitable for preaching, for it was the aim of writers like Ælfric to raise the level of morality by providing the priesthood with material for sermons, but Felix's *Life of St Guthlac* is translated in full. There are great differences in style as in theme. Ælfric holds the first place in this, as he does also by the sheer bulk of his work; he developed, under the influence of his classical training, a restrained and balanced style which carries his argument to its conclusion so inevitably that the reader is almost unaware of the artistry by which this marvellous lucidity has been obtained – of the carefully chosen rhythms, accentuated by alliteration, of the use of antithesis, rhetorical question, and other devices. We know that much of his work is based on Latin originals, on the Latin Fathers, historians, and canonistic writers, but we should not have guessed this from his style. The stilted translation prose is a thing of the past.

But Ælfric is not the only stylist of distinction. Equally remarkable is the fiery eloquence of Archbishop Wulfstan, who like him wrote a deliberately rhythmical prose, but with a vehemence and intensity as suited to his denunciatory sermons as Ælfric's calm reasonableness is to his logical expositions. One is surprised to find that Wulfstan's utterances are often translated from Latin canonists, most carefully selected and translated with attention to a felicitous and forcible rendering. And there are anonymous homilists capable of writing a highly rhetorical prose, heightened by poetic diction, simile, and metaphor; and at the other end of the scale, there is the stylist who added to the Chronicle the account of the reign of Ethelred, in comparatively straightforward narrative, with an economy of artistic device, which he can yet use effectively to convey his emotions at what he has to relate – exasperation, contempt, and occasionally pride. He is a master of ironic understatement. The general high level of English writing is truly remarkable, and Chambers has demonstrated that its influence never died out, but was handed on to modern times through a line of Middle English authors.

Apart from the Chronicle and legal documents, the amount of extant prose that was written for non-religious ends is small; naturally so, for such is less likely to survive. Yet we have a few small pieces to indicate a taste in the literature of the marvellous, which descends ultimately from Greek texts of the early Christian era. Of this genre are the two texts immediately preceding *Beowulf* in our only manuscript, the so-called *Letter of Alexander to Aristotle* and the *Marvels of the East*, which survives in another manuscript as well. Both deal with the strange creatures men were willing to believe lived in remote lands, such, for example, as the men with such enormous ears that they could sleep on one and cover themselves up with the other. Here, surely, we have the prose of entertainment rather than instruction, and so also one must regard the fragment of a Greek romance *Apollonius of Tyre*. More didactic in purpose are dialogues in prose and verse such as that of *Salomon and Saturn*, a collection of strange lore from many sources, especially the Orient, and finally must be mentioned manuscripts with collections of medical recipes of various origin, presumably for practical use – though one hopes that some were left untested –, and lunar almanacs, which Förster has shown hand on, practically unchanged, material that ultimately goes back to ancient Babylon.

CHAPTER XI

ANGLO-SAXON ART

THE artistic ability of the Anglo-Saxons can be studied to some extent in the actual remains which date from this period, in the churches and parts of churches, in the stone crosses and tombstones, in the jewellery and weapons, the church-plate and ivories, the coins, and the illuminated manuscripts. All such things give us some insight into the taste, the technical skill, and the various influences to which the art of our forefathers was exposed. Nevertheless, information so gathered is incomplete. Objects of secular use have rarely survived except from the heathen period, when they were buried with the dead; some types of work, such as wood-carving and embroidery, are little represented because of the perishable nature of the material; while few of the more valuable objects, of gold, silver, and gems, escaped the rapacity of later generations. The larger church ornaments, great crosses covered with gold and silver, crucifixion scenes, with figures of St Mary and St John, which were given by various donors to churches in the late tenth and eleventh centuries, were carried off by plunderers or sold to pay the debts of the church. The cathedrals and greater monastic churches have been replaced by later buildings. It is necessary in considering Anglo-Saxon art to make use of documentary evidence as well as that of surviving works; thus, while the St Cuthbert stole and the Bayeux tapestry let us understand why English needlework was so prized on the Continent, it is the constant reference to precious objects – a cloak of remarkable purple, interwoven throughout with gold in the manner of a corselet, which was turned into a chasuble; robes of silk interwoven with precious work of gold and gems; a beautiful chasuble that shone like gold when worn in the house of the Lord; a chalice of gold flashing with gems 'as the heavens glow with blazing stars'; great candelabra, all of gold; images of the saints, covered with gold and silver and precious stones; and countless other treasures – vestments, altar-cloths, tapestries, dorsals, shrines, croziers, bells, etc. – which explains the great impression made on the Norman conquerors by the richness of the equipment of the English churches. We should never have guessed this without the aid of literary records.

*

Poetry shows that the Anglo-Saxons were alive to the beauty of metal-work and to the impressive splendour of the warrior in his grey steel mail with its glittering appliqués, his sword-hilt adorned with gold plates or filigree, his boar-crested helmet and polished spear-tip glancing in the sun. Remains show that skilled weapon-smiths and jewellers existed even in the heathen age, and some of their products, such as their garnet-inlaid brooches and buckles, their drinking-horns mounted with chased gold bands, arouse general admiration. Many of the objects of this time, however, are covered all over with vigorous design, full of vitality and energy, which is unrestrained and often misdirected. The commonest decoration is the Germanic zoomorphic style, which, long before the Anglo-Saxons used it, had lost all naturalistic intention and become a mere pattern formed by distorted animal or bird forms, or even by detached parts of such forms, heads or limbs arranged as mere elements in a design. This motif is sometimes combined with another, the interlace, and a space may be adorned with a pattern of beasts or birds with intertwined necks or legs. Other types of decoration go to make up the advanced decorative art of the Anglo-Saxon period, seen at its best in manuscript illumination of the late seventh and early eighth centuries; there is a purely abstract, curvilinear style derived eventually from late Celtic art, transmitted to the Saxon invaders by some obscure, or at least disputed, means; and geometric patterns of a simple nature are used also.

To these motifs others of Mediterranean origin were added in Christian times. This was to be expected. Our sources refer frequently to the introduction from the Continent both of objects of art and foreign workmen. Augustine probably introduced Italian masons, whereas Benedict Biscop brought his from Gaul, and there is a corresponding difference in style between the southern group of early churches, with their wide nave, their eastern apse, almost as wide as the nave, from which it was separated by a triple arch, their several porticos, and the narrower northern type of church with very high walls and a small rectangular chancel. Wilfrid brought masons from Rome for his ambitious buildings at Ripon and Hexham. From descriptions we know that these churches had side-aisles and columns, spiral staircases and passages – but nothing is left but the crypts. From Gaul Benedict Biscop brought glaziers, and they taught their art to the English; perhaps not all branches of it, however, for in 764 a later abbot of his monastery asked the missionary Lul to send him from Germany a man who could make vessels of glass well. Wilfrid had the windows of the church of York glazed, and he also brought across from the Continent 'artisans of every kind'.

Mention has been made in a previous chapter of the great influx of books from abroad. Some of them were illuminated. Pictures also were brought from Rome, so that in Bede's day the church at Monkwearmouth had its walls surrounded with paintings of the Virgin and the twelve Apostles, of scenes from the Gospels and the Book of Revelation, while the church of Jarrow had pictures to illustrate the connexion between the Old and the New Testaments, and the Lady Chapel a series depicting the life of our Lord. Pictures of the Virgin were brought back from Rome by three unnamed pilgrims, along with books and with silk vestments of brilliant colours. Two cloaks, all of silk and of incomparable workmanship, which Benedict Biscop brought back, were considered so valuable that King Aldfrith gave him an estate of three hides in exchange for them.

Men such as Benedict, Wilfrid, and Aldhelm spared nothing that would make the worship of the Christian God impressive and beautiful, and a contrast to the sacrifices to heathen deities. Wilfrid had a case of the purest gold set with most precious gems made for his magnificent gospel-book, and the altar at Ripon was vested in purple woven with gold; Aldhelm describes a church with an altar-frontal of gold filament, and a chalice of gold and paten of wrought silver; it had twelve lesser altars dedicated to the twelve apostles, and its windows were glazed; Acca filled Hexham with ornaments of gold, silver, and precious stones. We are not told that all these things were imported, and it is likely that native craftsmen, skilled in metal work as we know them to have been, learnt to turn their talents to the service of the Church, and to copy the treasures from abroad. It is easy to see how foreign styles and motifs could be introduced into native art.

The most important of the new decorative motifs is the vine scroll, whether with birds and animals in the volutions of the scroll or not. Its closest parallels seem to be with the eastern Mediterranean, and its appearance in England must be attributed to foreign craftsmen or objects. But foreign influence was not confined to the importation of new patterns; it introduced the English to a representational art, to pictures of human beings and the scenes of biblical and other narrative, and it taught them to restrain the over-exuberance of their decoration and to impose some feeling for order over the whole. A combination of native and foreign influences is seen in the manuscript illumination; Italian representations of figures are imitated in the pictures of the Evangelists, or of David, while the pages of ornament are filled with the motifs of the earlier native art, greatly advanced in grandeur and sumptuousness, and, in the best examples, such as the famous Lindisfarne Gospels of about 700, arranged in panels so that the rich and elaborate detail is subordinated to a clear and dignified main theme. The use of bright contrasting colours adds to the general effect of magnificence. More and more, however, the native love of decoration triumphed over the classical art of natural representation, and even the figures of the Evangelists were not immune from a decorative treatment; they become less realistic, and are schematized as if they are merely part of a pattern. Manuscripts illuminated in this style, though with less restraint, are also produced in Ireland, and hence the style is known as Hiberno-Saxon, but scholars are not agreed as to which country originated this manner of illumination.

Remarkable though it is to get so soon after the conversion to Christianity the production in England of a decorative art of the high standard of the illuminated manuscripts, a still more striking phenomenon is the appearance about the same time of a school of Christian sculptors which has no parallel anywhere in Europe at that date. The excellence of some of the figure sculptures on the great Anglian crosses at Bewcastle in Cumberland and Ruthwell in Dumfriesshire led some scholars to believe that they could not be earlier than the twelfth century, but the art-motifs, the form of the inscribed runes, and the language of the inscriptions show that they belong to the earlier period of Northumbrian art. It has been suggested that it was the sculptured remains of the Romano-British period that gave the Anglo-Saxons the idea of erecting large monuments in stone, into which medium they could translate figures, scenes, and decorative motifs introduced into England on small objects such as ivories. The belief that the Bewcastle cross bears the names of Alhfrith, sub-king of southern Northumbria until soon after 664, and his wife Cyneburh, which would suggest a date when he was still remembered, has been strongly questioned.

There is also literary evidence for the existence of such crosses, and one reference is of particular interest in showing that they were not confined to Northumbria, and in indicating the purpose for which they might be raised. We are told in the *Life of St Willibald*, a West Saxon who left England in 720 and later became bishop of Eichstadt, that he was taken as a child in the hope that he might be cured of an illness to the cross of the Saviour, it being the custom of the Saxon people to erect a cross for the daily service of prayer on the estates of noble and good men, where there was no church. Such a purpose would be well served by the Bewcastle and Ruthwell crosses, for, as it has been recently emphasized, the subjects sculptured on them were chosen to 'convey to the faithful the essential ideas of Christianity.' Both crosses give central place to the majestic figure of Christ as judge, trampling on the beasts; the Bewcastle has above this a representation of St John the Baptist, below it one of St John the Evangelist, and the other three sides of the cross have decorative motifs only, vine scrolls, plaits, and chequer patterns. At Ruthwell two faces have figures sub-

jects, the Magdalen at the feet of Christ, the healing of
the blind man, the Visitation, the Annunciation, the
Flight into Egypt, St John the Baptist, the hermits Paul
and Anthony in the desert, breaking bread, an allusion
to the Mass. The cross-head is mutilated, but probably
originally had the symbols of the four Evangelists; the
narrower faces of the shaft have ornamental scrolls. All
over the north of England crosses or cross fragments are
common, though few can have attained the grandeur and
dignity of these two; but we have seen that in Wessex
also it was apparently a common thing for a cross to be
erected, and this is supported by William of Malmesbury,
who describes two stone pyramids with sculptured figures
which he saw at Glastonbury, one of which bore names
of persons living at the end of the seventh century and
the very beginning of the eighth. It seems likely, in view
of the rarity of remains from the south of England,
that the elaborately sculptured stone cross never had the
vogue there which it had in Northumbria, where it continued, with modifications in style by natural development and by Scandinavian influence, into the eleventh
century. From Northumbria it spread into Mercia in the
ninth century. Crosses in wood were set up also, as for
example that raised at Oundle over the place where St
Wilfrid's body was washed, but naturally these have not
survived.

Some surviving crosses have inscriptions that say they
were set up in memory of a particular person or persons.
This would not prevent them from serving the purpose
mentioned above, but sometimes they were simply
funeral monuments, set up in the graveyard of a church.
Æthelwold, who was bishop of Lindisfarne from 724 to 740,
had a stone cross made of skilful workmanship, and inscribed with his name in memory of him. It can hardly
have been on a large scale, for the monks of Lindisfarne

carried it with them when they wandered with St Cuthbert's body. It was eventually erected in the cemetery of Durham and was there in Symeon's day. The grave of Bishop Acca of Hexham, we are told, had two carved crosses, one at its head and the other at its foot, and it is generally assumed that the remains of a beautiful cross now restored to the church of Hexham are from one of these. They have no figure subjects, but are ornamented solely by vine scrolls, without any bird or animal figures in the scrolls. The purpose of another cross mentioned in our records is uncertain. A Northumbrian nobleman founded a monastery at an unidentified place in the early eighth century, and later the fifth abbot of the house was buried by the high cross which the 'prince' set up. Perhaps the founder set it up as a memorial to himself, or as a place from which the Gospel could be preached. At a much later date Bishop Oswald of Worcester (961–92) was in the habit of preaching by a cross set up as a sepulchral monument when his congregation was greater than his church could hold.

*

Throughout the eighth century sculpture and illuminated manuscripts continued to be produced in the same style in Northumbria. The name of an early eighth-century illuminator has come down to us, an inmate of the unnamed monastery just mentioned, called Ultan. He was a priest of Irish race, and a ninth-century writer considered that his work surpassed anything which his own age could produce. Contact with the Continent was maintained, and in fact probably increased, during this period. Pilgrimages and visits to Rome continued, and gifts and letters were exchanged with the English missionaries in Frisia and Germany. Foreign works of art reached the North. We are not told what the royal gifts sent by Pippin, king of the Franks, to King Eadberht (737–58) consisted of. Archbishop Lul sent to Jarrow a robe all of silk for the relics of Bede, and a multicoloured coverlet to protect Abbot Cuthberht from the cold; this must have been considered too good for such a use, for the abbot gave it to clothe the altar in the church of St Paul. Alcuin also sent home to Northumbria silk robes, and Charles the Great sent dalmatics and palls to all the episcopal sees in Northumbria and Mercia. When Alcuin was at home, his demands on his continental friends are for simpler things, garments and hoods of goat-hair and wool, and linen; his most interesting request is for pigments of colours good for painting. But the Northumbrians could give as well as receive; their illuminated manuscripts went abroad and were much copied in continental scriptoria, and Abbot Cuthberht sent to Lul in return for his gifts 'two palls of subtle workmanship, one white, the other coloured', along with books which had been asked for.

As a result of the intercourse with the Frankish kingdom, the effects of the Carolingian revival reached Northumbria. The vine-scroll becomes more natural, with recognizable leaves and delicate tendrils as in Carolingian ivories, and there is a return to a more realistic representation of figures. The Easby and Rothbury crosses have crowded figure scenes which in general arrangement and in some of their detail resemble those of Carolingian illuminations and ivory carvings. Dr Kendrick thinks that the North would have developed further in a classical direction if the Danish settlement in the latter part of the ninth century had not taken place.

*

It is now necessary to turn back to consider what was going on meanwhile in the South and Midlands. From the days of the first missionaries onwards these areas received art treasures from abroad, just as Northumbria did. An illuminated copy of the Gospels, now at Corpus Christi College, Cambridge, may well have been brought to Canterbury by Augustine himself, and churches in Wessex could be richly equipped already in Aldhem's time. The letters of St Boniface show that elaborately illuminated manuscripts were being produced at southern monasteries in the early eighth century. The earliest surviving Christian works of art from the lands south of the Humber seem to be the Golden Gospels, now in Stockholm, and the Vespasian Psalter, which probably were produced at Canterbury about 750, or a little later, though they have been claimed for Lichfield. There now seems to be some doubt whether a carved column at Reculver, which used to be assigned to the seventh century, belongs to anything like so early a date. In these manuscripts the decoration is mainly of the Hiberno-Saxon type, but, as might be expected from the close contact with the lands across the Channel, foreign influence is visible also, in the use of the acanthus leaf and the rosette in the decorative portions, and in the greater naturalness and solidity of the figure subjects.

Though one cannot with certainty assign manuscripts to East Anglia or the Midlands during this period, it must not be supposed that the monasteries and churches in this area were necessarily unproductive. Among the many Anglo-Saxon illuminated manuscripts which were taken to the Continent by the missionaries, one was a copy of an Italian manuscript of Sedulius's *Carmen Paschale* which had been owned by Cuthwine, bishop of Dunwich; while it was from Worcester that Lul tried to obtain the work of Porphyrius on metre. Some of the manuscripts of mixed continental and Hiberno-Saxon styles may have been executed in Mercia. The most spacious and impressive of surviving pre-Viking Age churches is a Mercian one, Brixworth in Northampton-shire, an aisled basilica which, like the early Kentish churches, had originally a triple arcade at the east end, opening into a square presbytery with an apse beyond it. Towards the end of the eighth century and during the early part of the ninth, stone carving was being produced in Mercia. In Derbyshire there are crosses imitating Northumbrian work, but the best Mercian work is on friezes and other architectural ornaments, as at Breedon-on-the-Hill, Leicestershire, and Fletton, Huntingdon-shire, and shows some influence from Frankish art, hav-ing features which occur in Merovingian illumination. In the early ninth century there is evidence for book-production at Lichfield, and one of its results is the *Book of Cerne*; some of its contents – it is a book of prayers – are of Northumbrian origin, and Dr Kendrick con-siders some features of its illumination to be closer to contemporary work in the North than that in the South. Some of the manuscripts of the late eighth century, and early ninth, which art historians designate vaguely 'southern' may come from West Saxon scriptoria; but we cannot be certain. There are also a few pieces of sculpture and minor objects of metal from early ninth-century Wessex which reveal Frankish influence.

*

The Viking Age was naturally not a period of great pro-ductiveness in the arts, though King Alfred encouraged them, as he did literature. Asser tells us of his building of halls and chambers wondrously constructed in wood or stone. He even speaks of buildings in gold and silver, which cannot be dismissed altogether as empty rhetoric, for the *Beowulf* poet conceives a royal hall as 'gold-adorned', 'treasure-adorned', 'adorned with (gold-)

plating'. Alfred invited craftsmen from all nations, in great numbers. The description of the church of his foundation at Athelney shows that he followed Carolingian models. It has been suggested that the angel-panel at Deerhurst dates from Alfred's reign, and as a representative of minor works there remains the famous Alfred Jewel. Each of the copies of the *Pastoral Care* which the king gave to his bishops' sees was to be accompanied by a precious object, perhaps a pointer, of fifty mancuses, i.e. about 3,500 grains, of gold.

In the reigns of Alfred's immediate successors one reads of the continued exchange of gifts with foreign royalties, by which foreign works of art reached this country, and King Athelstan gave to Christ Church, Canterbury, a gospel-book which contains the names of Otto the Great and his mother, and which was probably a gift from this German prince. Athelstan gave to other religious houses illuminated manuscripts which had been produced in France, and one from Ireland. One of the books which he gave to St Cuthbert's was, however, an illuminated copy of Bede's *Life of St Cuthbert*, of southern English origin, perhaps made at Glastonbury, and English illuminations were added to a psalter obtained from France. The beautiful stole, woven with figures of saints and prophets, which was found in St Cuthbert's coffin, is English work of the second decade of the tenth century. It is not, however, until after the monastic revival of the mid tenth century, and as a result of it, that the second 'golden age' of English art begins. The centre of this is as definitely in the south of England as that of the earlier 'golden age' had been in the north, and it is often, for convenience, called the 'Winchester School'. This place took an important part in the revival of art and learning, and some works of art can be located there; but the name is used to cover works in the new style, many of which were not from Winchester, but from all over the area where the monastic revival was effective.

The monastic revival owed much of its inspiration to the Frankish Empire, and it is from there that the art styles come also. To some extent it was the repayment of a debt, for the art of the Carolingian revival, which exercised such a strong influence in England at this time, was in itself partly based on the earlier Anglo-Saxon manuscripts taken over in the eighth century by the English missionaries. It drew from this source its fondness for covering whole pages with ornament, and the arrangement of this in panels filled with minute patterns. The interlace survives, but the commonest decorative pattern is not one derived from insular art, but the acanthus of classical art. Far more important than any new decorative motif, however, was the return to a representational art. The Caroligian schools of illuminators went back to late antique models of the fifth and sixth centuries and produced illustrated psalters, bibles, sacramentaries, etc., and these in their turn were imitated in England. There are numbers of such manuscripts, for this is the period of tremendous activity in many English scriptoria. Early in the series is the *Benedictional of St Athelwold*, written about 980 by Godemann, later abbot of Thorney, a beautiful manuscript of gorgeous colours and rich in gold, with the figure paintings in architectural settings and heavily framed in borders of acanthus. Later examples in this style show greater mastery and grace in figure drawing. Outline drawing is also common on the manuscripts of this period, and it is often both dignified and expressive. All manner of subjects are represented, and the artists are skilful in suggesting swift action and deep emotion. There is a breakaway from the older, static representation; the figures are clothed in fluttering draperies, which

give a restless quality. This is especially present in manuscripts affected by the mannerisms of a continental school
of outline-drawing best known from the Utrecht Psalter,
a work of the early ninth century, from near Reims,
which was much copied. The figures have shrugging
shoulders, necks poked forward, exaggerated fluttering
garments; yet the drawings are full of vitality and vigour,
they depict crowded scenes and other difficult subjects,
and are drawn with swift clear strokes. They attempt
both architectural and landscape backgrounds to the
figure scenes. Illumination in these styles continued
throughout the rest of the Saxon period, and before very
long English manuscripts were being taken across the
Channel, and some still survive in French libraries. A
benedictional from Fleury, now in Paris, may be the one
given to that house by the abbey of Ramsey between 1004
and 1029, and another was given by Queen Emma to
Archbishop Robert of Rouen, and remains in the library
there. Judith, wife of Earl Tostig, gave to Weingarten an
illuminated gospel-book, which is now in the Pierpont
Morgan Library in New York.

The artistic revival produced also a 'Winchester'
school of sculptors, who carved naturalistic figures in low
relief, such as the angels at Bradford-on-Avon and
Winterborne Steepleton, the Harrowing of Hell in Bristol
Cathedral, the Virgin and Child at Inglesham. It is disputed whether the Romsey Rood and the Chichester
panels, depicting Christ coming to Mary's house and the
raising of Lazarus, are of this period or poet-Conquest.
As there are no examples of stone sculpture on the Continent at this time, it is probable that the figures were
copied from ivories.

*

Only little of the 'Winchester' art reached the North, as
far as we can judge. Some illuminated manuscripts

reached Durham, and some of the treasures given by the archbishops of York, who were all men from south of the Humber, may have been of southern or continental provenance. Aldred's great pulpit and crucifix at Beverley was 'of German work'. But it has not survived, nor has the shrine of gold and silver and precious stones 'of incomparable workmanship', made at Beverley in the time of his predecessor. When the Normans burnt the church of York, its ornaments and books perished. Earl Tostig and his wife gave to Durham a great crucifix flanked by images of St Mary and St John, such as we hear of in southern churches, and it is possible that the equipment of the major churches of the North did not represent a very different taste from that in vogue elsewhere; but the unhappy years after the Norman Conquest were not favourable to the survival of works of art. The North did not share in the great activity in book production, for this was mainly carried on in monasteries, and there were none north of the Humber.

The very beautiful, though mutilated, carved stone slab of the Virgin and Child in York Minster is sometimes claimed as pre-Conquest work, though some would date it twelfth-century. It is in any case exceptional; the stone carving of the North is abundant, but is influenced by Scandinavian, not continental, taste. Stone crosses and grave-slabs in the Hiberno-Saxon style continue to be set up, with its animal-ornament influenced more or less by what Dr Kendrick has called 'a Scandinavian wildness and evenly distributed heaviness.' The main type of decoration goes by the name of Jellinge, after a seat of the Danish kings in Jutland where work in this style is found, and it is a barbaric interpretation of the Anglian beast motif of the Northumbrian crosses. Vine-scrolls are retained but in a flattened and stylized form. There are also some crosses put up by the Irish-Norse settlers, with

Celtic designs, and subjects from Scandinavian legend take their place beside Christian themes on some monuments. The most spectacular is the cross at Gosforth, Cumberland, with tiny figure subjects more like those on Manx crosses than the monumental figures of earlier Anglian crosses. This is a round shafted cross, and there is a group of these mainly in Derbyshire and Staffordshire and in that area of South Yorkshire which from documentary evidence we know was being penetrated by Mercian thanes in the tenth century. It is probable therefore that the round-shafted cross represents Mercian taste, and it appears to be a survival of pre-Viking art represented by remains at Dewsbury and Collingham. Remnants of Hiberno-Saxon art, untouched by Viking devices, are also to be found on grave slabs in East Anglia, Lincolnshire, and Cambridgeshire.

When the Danish invasions culminated in the conquest of England by Cnut, another form of Scandinavian art became influential in England. This, known as the Ringerike style, is a development in Scandinavian hands of the acanthus pattern of English illumination and ivories, etc., and it is found, not in the areas of Scandinavian settlement, but in the south of England. It presumably indicates a vogue for Scandinavian motifs during the reigns of the Danish kings. As one might expect, various types of art met in London; several examples of Viking art occur, whereas recent fragments discovered at All-Hallows-by-the-Tower are in the style of the Anglian panelled crosses, although apparently of eleventh-century date.

*

Most of our surviving Saxon churches date from the tenth or eleventh centuries, and in the sources for this late period, such as the *Life of St Wulfstan*, one not infre-

quently reads of the bishop being called to dedicate a
new church. Churches of this later Saxon period are
often easy to distinguish; they have 'long and short work',
that is stones set alternately upright and horizontal, at
the quoins, walls decorated by pilaster strips and rounded
or triangular arcading, double-splayed windows and
mid-wall shafts, west-end towers sometimes divided into
stages by horizontal strips. Doorways are occasionally
triangular-headed, but arches always rounded. The
greater number of Saxon churches still standing, whether
in part or complete, are small, but there are a few of
impressive size, such as Bosham in Sussex and Great
Paxton in Huntingdonshire, which were 'minsters', that
is churches served by a body of priests and acting as the
mother-church of a considerable area. This style of architecture seems to have drawn its inspiration from the
Rhineland, and it is in the Carolingian empire also that
one gets parallels to the great cathedral and monastic
churches. None of these survives, but enough can be
gathered from literary sources and uncovered foundations to show the influence of the Carolingian buildings.
Like these, many English buildings had altars at both
ends of the church, the western one being placed either
in a gallery, or a western transept, or a western apse.
They had towers at the west end and over the central
crossing, as well as minor circular towers containing
spiral staircases. The major towers were sometimes a
series of receding stages of open arcading, built in timber.
The churches built by Bishop Athelwold for his cathedral
at Winchester and his foundations of Ely, Peterborough,
and Thorney, and Archbishop Oswald's church at Ramsey all had some of these features, but Athelwold's
earliest building, the church of Abingdon, was a round
church. Sporadic examples of centrally-planned churches
occurred elsewhere, in the eighth century in Hexham,

in the ninth at Athelney, in the tenth at Bury St Edmunds, and in the eleventh at St Augustine's, Canterbury, where, however, the great rotunda begun by Abbot Wulfric was never finished. Extensive building was going on in the later Anglo-Saxon period; St Oswald built a new church at his see of Worcester, St Dunstan extended Glastonbury, Bishop Aldhun built a cathedral at Durham 995–9, the last three Saxon archbishops of York made great additions to Beverley, Exeter was restored in the time of Cnut, and all the time new religious houses were being built. We cannot judge Anglo-Saxon architecture from its minor monuments, which are all that are left. Sir Alfred Clapham has well summed up the position: 'In the major art of architecture it is not unreasonable to suppose that, left to themselves, the Saxons would have travelled along the same road as their Rhineland kinsmen and, given peace and prosperity, would have produced an architecture not unlike the Carolingian Romanesque of the great cathedrals and abbey churches of that province. . . . As it was, the greater Saxon churches of the tenth and eleventh centuries, though lacking the scale of their continental contemporaries, were probably not unworthy to survive, and in every other direction were quite up to the standards of the age.'

CHAPTER XII

CONCLUSION

A MILLENNIUM and a half separates us from 'the Coming of the English' and close on nine hundred years from the last persons mentioned in these chapters. We still call most of our towns and villages by the names the Anglo-Saxons gave them, often after the man or woman who settled there in this distant past. Sometimes we know a little about the persons who thus left their names: about Pega, St Guthlac's saintly sister, whose name survives in Peakirk; Wulfrun, a noble Mercian lady, who possessed Wolverhampton; or Esgar, an official of Edward the Confessor, the name of whose 'town' has been corrupted to East Garston; or Tola, of Tolpuddle, a Danish lady who was a benefactor of Abbotsbury. More often they were lesser folk whose doings history does not record.

Tangible remains of Anglo-Saxon civilization are not lacking. It is true that the great Saxon churches have vanished, superseded by the grander buildings of a later age. Only the crypts survive of Wilfrid's buildings which contemporaries thought to be unsurpassed on this side of the Alps. But many smaller churches – whole or in part – have continued in use until to-day, and several of them, Brixworth, Great Paxton, Deerhurst, Earls Barton, are not unimpressive, nor to be venerated on grounds of antiquity alone. Beautiful carved crosses have come down to us, some still *in situ*, others preserved inside churches and museums. The latter are full of specimens of Anglo-Saxon handicrafts, the garnet inlays of Kent and Sutton Hoo, the elaborate gold filigree work, the ivory caskets and diptychs, and other objects, including some, like the Alfred Jewel and the St Cuthbert stole, which add to their intrinsic interest the more sentimental appeal of their connexion with historic figures.

Our older libraries are full of their manuscripts, many with a beauty of script and illumination that has never been surpassed. Some bring us very near to the people of whom we read. Among the treasures of the Bodleian Library are the Italian copy of the Acts of the Apostles which Bede used when writing his commentary; the copy of King Alfred's translation of Gregory's *Pastoral Care* which the king himself sent as a gift to his friend and helper Bishop Werferth of Worcester; and a book of tropes and sequences, with musical notation, in which the litany prays: 'that thou wilt deign to preserve King Ethelred and the army of the English.' The Lindisfarne Gospels, now in the British Museum, accompanied St Cuthbert's body as its guardians bore it from place to place in search of safety in the chaotic years that followed the Danish invasion. The medieval monks of Canterbury were very ready to claim that books in their possession had been brought over by St Augustine, and they were usually wrong, but a Canterbury book of Gospels at Corpus Christi College, Cambridge, is old enough to have been brought by the first missionaries, as the monks of St Augustine's Abbey, to whom it once belonged, believed. Continental libraries have numbers of manuscripts produced in England in pre-Conquest times. Among the most interesting are the great bible codex at Florence, which Abbot Ceolfrith of Jarrow, with pardonable pride, intended to present to the pope in 716, as a specimen of what was being produced in this northern outpost of Christendom; and the calendar at Paris which belonged to St Willibrord, the missionary to the Frisians, in which the saint has entered in his own hand his consecration by Pope Sergius in 695, adding the words 'although unworthy'.

And in the books and documents that survive are many passages that bring us nearer still to these remote ancestors of ours. One reads the tactful remark with which King Alfred disarmed criticism as he sent to his bishops an English version of a Latin work: 'It is uncertain how long there may be such learned bishops as now, by the grace of God, are almost everywhere'; or the angry reply of a litigant, whose brother will pay a fine for him if he will relinquish an estate, that 'he would rather that fire or flood had it'; or the noble letter of condolence written by the archbishop of Canterbury to Boniface's followers after his martyrdom; and as one reads, the Anglo-Saxons come alive as individuals whose mental processes we can follow and whose aspirations and sorrows rouse our sympathy.

Subsequent volumes in this series will doubtless show how the society here depicted changed gradually by natural growth or more violently by external influence. The time is past when historians regarded the Norman Conquest as a complete break in the continuity of our history. Quite apart, however, from any question of what they handed on to us, the people who in the eighth century led the scholarship of Western Europe, who were mainly responsible for the conversion to Christianity of the German and Scandinavian peoples, and who, alone of the Germanic races, have left behind from so early a date a noble literature in verse and prose, are worthy of respect and study for their own sake.

SELECT BIBLIOGRAPHY

The following list of suggestions is confined to works written in English. It only exceptionally includes articles in periodicals and journals. The reader who wishes to pursue any subject more deeply should consult the bibliographies given below, and also W. Bonser, *An Anglo-Saxon and Celtic Bibliography* (Blackwell, Oxford, 1957) and the new periodical, *Anglo-Saxon England* (Cambridge, 1972–), which deals with all aspects of the period. Valuable articles on many topics are in *England before the Conquest: Studies in primary sources presented to Dorothy Whitelock*, ed. P. Clemoes and K. Hughes (Cambridge, 1971).

A. *General and Political History*

F. M. Stenton's *Anglo-Saxon England* (Oxford History of England, II, 3rd edn, 1971) has largely superseded previous general histories. It has an excellent bibliography. His collected papers are published as *Preparatory to Anglo-Saxon England* (ed. D. M. Stenton, Oxford, 1970). See also P. Hunter Blair, *An Introduction to Anglo-Saxon England* (Cambridge, 1956); H. R. Loyn, *Anglo-Saxon England and the Norman Conquest* (2nd edn, London, 1968). For special periods, see R. G. Collingwood and J. N. L. Myres, *Roman Britain and the English Settlements* (Oxford History of England, I, 2nd edn, 1937); P. Hunter Blair, *Roman Britain and Early England 55 B.C.–A.D. 871* (Edinburgh, 1963); R. H. Hodgkin, *A History of the Anglo-Saxons* (3rd edn, Oxford, 1952); E. S. Duckett, *Alfred the Great and his England* (London, 1957); H. R. Loyn, *Alfred the Great* (The Clarendon Biographies, O.U.P., 1967); L. M. Larson, *Canute the Great* (New York, 1912); F. Barlow, *Edward the Confessor* (London, 1970); D. C. Douglas, *William the Conqueror: The Norman Impact upon England* (London, 1964); R. R. Darlington, *The Norman Conquest* (The Creighton Lecture in History, London, 1963); H. R. Loyn, *The Norman Conquest* (Hutchinson University Library, London, 1965); and D. Whitelock and others, *The Norman Conquest: Its Setting and Impact* (ed. C. T. Chevallier, London, 1966). Many books on the Vikings include T. D. Kendrick, *A History of the Vikings* (London, 1930); J. Brøndsted, *The Vikings* (Pelican Books, 1960); Gwyn Jones, *A History of the Vikings* (London, 1968); D. M. Wilson, *The Vikings and their Origins* (London, 1970); and P. H. Sawyer, *The Age of the Vikings* (2nd edn, London, 1971).

B. *Institutions, Social and Economic History*

For early Germanic society, see H. M. Chadwick, *The Heroic Age* (Cambridge, 1912). For Anglo-Saxon society, see R. I. Page, *Life in Anglo-Saxon England* (London, 1970). On agrarian matters, see C. S. and C. S. Orwin, *The Open Fields* (3rd edn, Oxford, 1967); and H. P. R. Finberg, *The Agrarian History of England and Wales, I, Part II, A.D. 43–1042* (Cambridge, 1972). F. M. Stenton, *The Latin Charters of the Anglo-Saxon Period* (Oxford, 1955) is important for land tenure and other matters. For geographical factors, see S. W. Woodbridge and E. Ekwall, in *A Historical Geography of England before A.D. 1800* (Cambridge, 1936). On towns, see J. Tait, *The Medieval English Borough* (Manchester, 1936) and J. W. Benton, *Town Origins: the Evidence for Medieval England* (Boston, 1968). Principles of law are dealt with in F. Pollock and F. W. Maitland, *The History of English Law* (2nd edn, Cambridge, 1898) and T. F. T. Plucknett, *A Concise History of the Common Law* (London, 5th edn, 1956).

C. Ecclesiastical History

General accounts are given by W. Hunt, *History of the English Church* (ed. W. W. Stephens and W. Hunt, London, 1907), Vol. I; and J. Godfrey, *The Church in Anglo-Saxon England* (Cambridge, 1962). For the early period see P. Hunter Blair, *The World of Bede* (London, 1970); S. J. Crawford, *Anglo-Saxon Influence on Western Christendom* (Oxford, 1933); and W. Levison, *England and the Continent in the Eighth Century* (Oxford, 1946). For the later period see J. Armitage Robinson, *The Times of St Dunstan* (Oxford, 1923); Dom David Knowles, *The Monastic Order in England* (2nd edn, Cambridge, 1961); R. R. Darlington, 'Ecclesiastical Reform in the Late Old English Period' (*English Historical Review*, li, 1936); F. Barlow, *The English Church, 1000–1066: A Constitutional History* (London, 1963).

D. Literature and Learning

On Anglo-Latin scholarship, see M. L. W. Laistner, *Thought and Letters in Western Europe* (revised edn, London, 1957) and J. D. A. Ogilvy, *Books known to the English, 597–1066* (Cambridge, Mass., 1967). On vernacular literature, see S. B. Greenfield, *A Critical History of Old English Literature* (New York, 1965); *Continuations and Beginnings* (ed. E. G. Stanley, London and Edinburgh, 1966), which contains seven studies by experts on important authors or aspects; and K. Sisam, *Studies in the History of Old English Literature* (Oxford, 1953). The following works on *Beowulf* are most illuminating to the general reader: C. W. Kennedy, *The Earliest English Poetry* (O.U.P., 1943); W. W. Lawrence, *Beowulf and Epic Tradition* (Cambridge, Mass., 1928); K. Sisam, *The Structure of Beowulf* (Oxford, 1965); and D. Whitelock, *The Audience of Beowulf* (Oxford, 1951). On Wulfstan see the introductions to D. Bethurum, *The Homilies of Wulfstan* (Oxford, 1957) and D. Whitelock, *Sermo Lupi ad Anglos* (3rd edn, London, 1963). For further bibliography see *The Cambridge Bibliography of English Literature* (Vol. I, ed. F. W. Bateson, 1940, Supplement, ed. G. Watson, 1957) and the annual issues of the *Year's Work in English Studies* (English Association, from 1921) and of the periodical *Anglo-Saxon England*.

E. Art and Archaeology

Only a small selection of works on these subjects can be mentioned. General works: G. Baldwin Brown, *The Arts in Early England* (London, 1903–37); T. D. Kendrick, *Anglo-Saxon Art to A.D. 900* (London,

1938) and *Late Saxon and Viking Art* (London, 1948); *Dark Age Britain: Studies presented to E. T. Leeds* (ed. D. B. Harden, London, 1956); and D. M. Wilson, *The Anglo-Saxons* (London, 1960). The periodical, *Medieval Archaeology*, begun in 1957, is valuable. For evidence relating to the Saxon settlements, see works cited in A above, and also J. N. L. Myres, *Anglo-Saxon Pottery and the Settlement of England* (Oxford, 1969). Rupert Bruce-Mitford, *The Sutton-Hoo Ship Burial: A Handbook* (British Museum, 2nd edn, 1972), largely supersedes earlier works on this subject, and has a good bibliography. Sir Cyril Fox, *Offa's Dyke* (London, 1955) is a definitive study. On Viking antiquities, see works cited under A above, and also H. Shetelig and H. Falk, *Scandinavian Archaeology* (English translation by E. V. Gordon, Oxford, 1937). On architecture, see A. W. Clapham, *English Romanesque Architecture before the Norman Conquest* (Oxford, 1930) and H. M. Taylor and Joan Taylor, *Anglo-Saxon Architecture* (2 vols, Cambridge, 1965). On illumination, see O. E. Saunders, *English Illumination* (I, Florence and Paris, 1928); E. G. Millar, *English Illuminated Manuscripts from Xth to XII Century* (Paris and Brussels, 1926); W. Oakeshott, *The Sequence of English Medieval Art* (London, 1950); F. Wormald, *English Drawings of the Tenth and Eleventh Centuries* (London, 1952); and R. L. S. Bruce Mitford, *The Art of Codex Amiatinus* (Jarrow Lecture, 1967). Expensive facsimiles of illuminated manuscripts can be consulted in our major libraries, e.g. those published by the Palaeographical Society (1873–94) and the New Palaeographical Society (1903–30); the British Museum publication, *Schools of Illumination*, Part I: *Hiberno-Saxon and Early English Schools, 700–1000* (1914); Sir E. M. Thompson, *English Illuminated Manuscripts* (London, 1895); E. T. De-Wald, *The Utrecht Psalter* (Princeton, 1933); *The Cædmon Manuscript of Anglo-Saxon Biblical Poetry*, with introduction by Sir Israel Gollancz (O.U.P., 1927); *Evangeliorum quattuor Codex Lindisfarnensis* (ed. T. D. Kendrick and others, Oltun and Lausanne, 1956–60); and F. Wormald, *The Benedictional of St Ethelwold* (London, 1959). Other specialist studies include W. G. Collingwood, *Northumbrian Crosses* (London, 1927); M. H. Longhurst, *English Ivories* (London, 1926); R. Jessop, *Anglo-Saxon Jewellery* (London, 1950); D. M. Wilson, *Anglo-Saxon Ornamental Metal Work 700–1100 in the British Museum* (Catalogue of Antiquities of the Late Saxon Period, vol. I, 1964); *The Relics of St Cuthbert* (ed. C. F. Battiscombe, O.U.P., 1956); and *The Bayeux Tapestry* (ed. Sir Frank Stenton, London, 1957).

F. *Main sources available in Modern English Translation*

A large selection, with studies and bibliographies, is contained in *English Historical Documents* (general editor D. C. Douglas), Vol. I, *c.* 500–1042 (ed. D. Whitelock, 1955), Vol. II, 1042–1189 (ed. D. C. Douglas and G. W. Greenaway, 1953). Latin sources: Bede, *Ecclesiastical History*, translated by L. Sherley-Price (Penguin Classics,

revised edn by R. E. Latham, 1968) and in the edition by B. Colgrave
and R. A. B. Mynors (Oxford, 1969); B. Colgrave, *The Life of Bishop
Wilfrid by Eddius Stephanus* (Cambridge, 1927), *Two Lives of St
Cuthbert* (Cambridge, 1940), *Felix's Life of Saint Guthlac* (Cambridge,
1956), and *The Earliest Life of Gregory the Great* (University of Kansas
Press, 1968); E. Kylie, *The English Correspondence of St Boniface* (London,
1911); C. H. Talbot, *The Anglo-Saxon Missionaries in Germany* (London
and New York, 1954); L. C. Jane, *Asser's Life of King Alfred* (London,
1926); A. Campbell, *Æthelwulf, De Abbatibus* (Oxford, 1967) and
The Chronicle of Æthelweard (Nelson's Medieval Texts, 1962); Dom
Thomas Symons, *The Regularis Concordia: The Monastic Agreement*
(ibid., 1953); A. Campbell, *Encomium Emmae Reginae* (Camden 3rd
Series, lxxii, 1949); and F. Barlow, *The Life of King Edward the Confessor* (Nelson's Medieval Texts, 1962). Of Anglo-Norman historians
who used lost pre-Conquest sources, William of Malmesbury and
Florence of Worcester are translated in *Bohn's Antiquarian Library*,
and Symeon of Durham in *The Church Historians of England*, Vol. III,
Part II. Domesday Book for most counties is translated in the *Victoria
County Histories*; see also C. W. Foster and T. Longley, *The Lincolnshire Domesday and the Lindsey Survey* (Lincoln Record Society, 1924)
and J. Tait, *The Domesday Survey of Cheshire* (Chetham Society,
Manchester, 1916).

Vernacular sources: *The Anglo-Saxon Chronicle* is translated by
G. N. Garmonsway for Everyman's Library (revised edn, 1960) and
by D. Whitelock, with D. C. Douglas and S. I. Tucker (London,
corrected impression, 1965); the laws by F. L. Attenborough, *The
Laws of the Earliest English Kings* (Cambridge, 1922) and by A. J.
Robertson, *The Laws of the Kings of England from Edmund to Henry I*
(Cambridge, 1925); the charters by F. E. Harmer, *Select English
Historical Documents of the Ninth and Tenth Centuries* (Cambridge, 1914)
and *Anglo-Saxon Writs* (Manchester, 1953), by D. Whitelock, *Anglo-
Saxon Wills* (Cambridge, 1930), and by A. J. Robertson, *Anglo-Saxon
Charters* (2nd edn, Cambridge, 1956). The best prose translation of
Beowulf is by E. Talbot Donaldson (New York, 1966) and among
verse renderings may be mentioned those by A. T. Strong (London,
1925) and C. W. Kennedy (O.U.P., 1940). For other poems, see
R. K. Gordon, *Anglo-Saxon Poetry* (Everyman's Library, revised edn,
1956); C. W. Kennedy, *The Cædmon Poems* (London, 1916), *The Poems
of Cynewulf* (London, 1910) and *Early English Christian Poetry* (London,
1952); *The Exeter Book* (E.E.T.S., Part I, ed. Sir Israel Gollancz,
1895, Part II, ed. W. S. Mackie, 1934); A. Campbell, *The Battle of
Brunnanburh* (London, 1938). Standard editions of prose works with
translations are *King Alfred's West Saxon Version of Gregory's Pastoral
Care* (ed. H. Sweet, E.E.T.S., 1871), *The Homilies of Ælfric* (ed. B.
Thorpe, London, 1844–6), *Ælfric's Lives of Saints* (ed. W. W. Skeat,
E.E.T.S., 1881–1900) and *Byrhtferth's Manual* (ed. S. J. Crawford,

E.E.T.S., 1929). Alfred's version of *The Soliloquies of St Augustine* is translated by H. L. Hargrove (Yale Studies in English, 22, New York, 1904) and Alfred's *Boethius* by W. J. Sedgfield (Oxford, 1900).

G. *Ancilliary Sources*

Place-names should be studied in the publications of the English Place-Name Society and in E. Ekwall, *The Concise Oxford Dictionary of English Place-Names* (4th edn, 1960). For general accounts, see P. H. Reaney, *The Origin of English Place-Names* (London, 1961) and K. Cameron, *English Place-Names* (London, 1961). Very important is F. M. Stenton, 'The Historical Bearing of Place-Name Studies', delivered to the Royal Historical Society, 1939–43, now reprinted in his collected papers (see A above), pp. 253–324.

Collections of Anglo-Saxon coins are being published in *Sylloge of Coins of the British Isles*; twenty vols. (O.U.P., 1958–73) have appeared. See also Michael Dolley, *Anglo-Saxon Pennies* (British Museum, 1964); C. E. Blunt, 'The Anglo-Saxon Coinage and the Historian' (*Medieval Archaeology*, iv, 1960); and *Anglo-Saxon Coins: Studies presented to F. M. Stenton* (ed. R. H. M. Dolley, London, 1961).

An important contribution to Anglo-Saxon studies is the *Map of Britain in the Dark Ages* (Ordnance Survey, 2nd edn, 1966.

SELECT INDEX

Abbo of Fleury, 185, 201 f., 220
Abercorn, 164
Abingdon, 61, 67, 126, 135, 170, 185, 218, 239
Acca, Bishop, 192, 226; cross of, 230
Adamnan, 62, 160, 215
Ælfgar, Earl, 176
Ælfheah, Archbishop 69
Ælfhere, Ealdorman, 137
Ælfric the Homilist, 23, 27, 51, *et passim*
Æthelbald, King of Mercia, 31, 33, 49, 115, 121, 178 f.
Æthelbald, King of Wessex, 150
Æthelflæd, Lady of the Mercians, 76
Æthelweard, Ealdorman, 78, 93, 202, 205, 217; Chronicle of, 93, 102
Æthelwulf, King of Wessex, 58, 60, 150, 198
Æthilwulf, Northumbrian poet, 199
Agilbert, Bishop, 160
agriculture, 14, 18, 98–104
Aidan, St, 169, 189
Alcuin, 37, 43, 171 f., 192 f., 196 f., 199, 202, 231
Aldfrith, King of Northumbria, 62, 160, 190, 193 f., 226
Aldhelm, St, 12, 31, 91, 107, 170 f., 189–95, 198, 200, 205, 215, 226, 232
Aldred, Earl, 44 f., 175
Aldwulf, King of East Anglia, 24
Alfred, King of Wessex, 7, 12, *et passim;* Cornish poem on, 216 f., laws of, 38, 40, 43, 81, 109, 137; life of, *see* Asser; tomb of, 149; works of, 59, 66, 215–17, 234
Alfred Jewel, 234, 241
Alhred, King of Northumbria, 53, 179
amusements, 90–2, 107 f.
Angles, 11 f., 13, 19, 48
Anglo-Saxon Chronicle, 16, 32, 72, 74, 81, 88, 202, 204, 213 f., 217–22

apocryphal literature, 191, 215, 220
archaeological remains, 17, 49, 108, 118 f., 223 f.
architecture; domestic, 88 f., 108, 131 f., 233 f.; church, 161, 225, 233 f., 239 f.
army, 64, 66, 72–5, 145; desertion from, 30, 72, 74
art motifs, 224–38
Asser, 55, 60, 66 f., 70, 76, 88, 105, 127, 203, 215, 253
assessment, 68, 76, 137 f.
Athelstan, King, 46 f., 55, etc.; laws of, 55, 74 f., 76, 110, 139, 144, 146; panegyric on, 200
Athelstan, Half-King, Ealdorman 78
Athelwold, St, 185, 201, 219, 239; benedictional of, 235; lives of, 201 f.
Augustine, St, of Canterbury, 155 f., 158, etc.

Bath, 17, 50, 53, 62, 81, 89, 113
Bayeux tapestry, 88 f., 223
bear-baiting, 66
Bede, 11–16, 21, *et passim;* translation of, 215
Bedwyn, Wilts, 46, 98, 113, 126
Benedict Biscop, 36, 170, 190, 192, 225 f.
Benedictine Rule, 169 f., 201, 219
Beorhtric, King of Wessex, 120
Beorhtwulf, King of Mercia, 77
Beowulf, 21, 25, 27, 29–31, 39–42, 59, 89, 91 f., 94, 205, 211–13, 222, 233
Berhtwald, Archbishop, 111
Bewcastle cross, 227 f.
Bible, translation of, 215, 220
Birinus, St, 159
blood-feud, *see* vengeance
boar-emblem, 21
Boethius, translation of, 66, 213, 215, 217
Boniface, St, 12, 171, 173–9, 192–8, 232, 242
bookland, 153 f.

books: export of, 179, 192 f., 231; import of, 161, 191 f., 200, 225 f.; production of, 192, 199 f., 203, 232 f., 235–7
bootless crimes, 143
borough-moot, 133, 139
boroughs, 58, 75 f., 79 f., 126–33
Bretwalda, 48
bridge-repair, 64 f., 76 f., 85
Brihtnoth, Ealdorman, 34 f., 87, 89–91
Bristol, 112, 120, 129, 236
British Church, 155, 158, 163
Britons 15, 17 f., 111, 155
bull-baiting, 107
Burghal Hidage, 76, 127
Burgred, King of Mercia, 173
Burton-on-Trent, Staffs, 86, 185
Byrtferth of Ramsey, 89, 93, 186, 201, 219 f.

Cædmon, 107, 206–9
Cambridge, 15, 46, 117, 125, 147
Canterbury, 24, 31, *et passim*; archbishops of, Ælfheah, Augustine, Berhtwald, Cuthbert, Deusdedit, Dunstan, Honorius, Laurentius, Oda, Plegmund, Siric, Tatwine, Theodore; St Augustine's at, 113, 128, 169 f., 175, 194, 240, 242, *see also* Abbots, Benedict Biscop, Hadrian; St Martin's at, 155; St Pancras at, 24
Carolingian influence, 231, 234, 238–40
Carolingian revival, 196, 202, 215, 231, 235
cattle-stealing, 47, 92, 108, 146, 148
Ceadwalla, King of Wessex, 173
Celtic art, 225, 238
Cenred, King of Mercia, 173
Cenwealh, King of Wessex, 159
Ceolfrith, Abbot, 169, 176, 190, 192, 242; life of, 193
Ceolred, King of Mercia, 198
Ceolwulf, King of Northumbria, 173, 205
Ceolwulf II, King of Mercia, 121
chancery, 58

Charles the Great, 31, 33, 37, 60 f., 95, 119, 123, 175, 179 f., 193, 196, 204, 215
charms, 21–3, 25 f.
Cheddar, 88
Chelsea, council of, 112
Chester, 60, 70, 76, 119, 122, 129 f., 131, 147
Chester-le-Street, Durham, 56, 60, 180, 183, 200, 234
children, upbringing of, 45, 94
Christianity: conversion to, 7, 16, 24 f., 55, 58, 119, 155–64, 194; influence of, 19, 22 f., *et passim*
church, 155–88; income of, 153 f., 165–7; legal position of, 134, 137, 142 f, 145, 166; private ownership of, 165–8
churl, 73, 83–6
Clofesho, synod of, 165
Cnut, King, 8, 44, 54 f., etc.: laws of, 36, 38, 46, 55, 99, 137, 143, 150, 187
coinage, 120 f.; *see also* mint
Columba, St, 155, 158
compensations, 33, 41–4, 80, 84, 92, 98, 109, 112, 134, 143–5, 147; *see also* wergild
continental influence, 199–201, 232, 234, 237–9
coronation, 50, 53, 113
cotsetlan, 101 f.
Crediton, 71, 93, 184
Cuthbert, Archbishop, 174, 179
Cuthbert, St, 56, 180, 182, 230, 234, 242; lives of, 16, 194 f., 200, 234; stole of, 223, 234, 241
Cuthwine, Bishop of Dunwich, 192, 232
Cynthryth, Queen of Mercia, 120
Cynewulf, King of Wessex, 32, 38, 88, 115
Cynewulf, poems of, 210

Danegeld, 68, 70
Danelaw, 49, 52, 136, 167, 183; conversion of, 181–3, 202; reconquest of, 218
Danes, 7, 59, etc.; treaties with, 98, 110, 122 f., 187

Danish boroughs, 79; *see* Five Boroughs

Danish invasions, 48 f., 54, *et passim*

Danish settlement, 44, 68 f., 76 f., 99, 120, 137, 150 f., 167, 180, 231

Daniel, Bishop, 194

death-penalty, 51, 75, 109, 143 f., 146 f.

Deusdedit, Archbishop, 162, 189

dicing, 91, 186

dioceses, division into, 161–4, 180, 182–4

divorce, 95, 148–51, 183

dogs, 65 f., 92

Domesday Book, 65, 67, *et passim*

Dorchester - on - Thames, 159, 180–2

dress, 95 f., 172

Dunstan, St, 34, 53, etc.: lives of, 202

Dunwich, Suffolk, 118, 164, 181, 192, 232

Durham, 56, 113, 151, 180, 192, 230, 237, 240

Eadbald, King of Kent, 150

Eadberht, King of Kent, 121

Eadberht, King of Northumbria, 60, 172 f., 231

Eadred, King, 52, 56 f., 69

ealdorman, *passim, especially*, 77–82

Ealdred, Archbishop, 176, 237

Eardwulf, King of Northumbria, 175

earl, 77, 80 f., 83, 86, 116, 122, 127, 151

Easby cross, 231

East Anglia, 9 f., 35, *et passim*; Kings of, Aldwulf, Edmund, Eorpwald, Guthrum, Rædwald, Sigeberht

Easter, calculation of, 158, 160–2; name of, 21

Ecgfrith, King of Northumbria, 32, 43, 56, 70, 170

Eddius's *Life of Wilfrid*, 194, 215

Edgar, King, 50, 52 f., *et passim*; laws of, 122, 129, 133, 137, 139, 165

Edith, Queen, 101, 133

Edmund, King of East Anglia, 59; cult of, 181, life of, 34

Edmund I, King, 43 f., 51, 62, 92, 146, 200; laws of, 43, 53, 55

Edmund II, King, 55

Edward the Confessor, King, 8, 52, *et passim*

Edward the Elder, King, 70, 74, 76, 127, 149, 181; laws of, 122

Edward the Martyr, King, 54

Edwin, Earl, 118

Edwin, King of Northumbria, 24, 32–4, 49, 59, 70, 157–9

Egbert, Archbishop, 36, 164 f., 172, 194, 196; *Dialogue* of, 43

Egbert, King of Kent, 162

Egbert, King of Wessex, 120

Elmham, Norfolk, 90, 152, 164, 181

Ely, 89 f., 104, 117, 170, 185, 239

Emma, Queen, 67, 131, 236

Eorpwald, King of East Anglia, 120, 157

Essex, 8, 22, *et passim*; Kings of, Offa, Sigeberht

Ethelbert, Archbishop of York, 196

Ethelbert, King of Kent, 24, 59, 134, 150, 155 f.; laws of, 150, 156, 214

Ethelred the Unready, King, 8, 34, *et passim*; laws of, 42, 129, 143, 146 f., 166

Ethelred, King of Mercia, 173

Ethelred, King of Northumbria, 33, 37

Exeter, 46, 55, 67, 73, 82, 113, 240

exile, voluntary, 31–3, 160, 173 f., 177

Falconers, 65, 105

famine, 69, 103, 112, 198

Felix, St, 158, 189

Felix, Frankish secretary, 58, 199

Felix's *Life of St Guthlac*, 197, 203, 215

fertility cults, 19–21

fighting, penalty for, 51, 80, 84, 98, 145

fines, 51 f., 64, 75, 77, 80 f., 84, 109, 112, 141, 144 f., 151, 166
fisheries, 100, 103, 118
Five Boroughs, 136
five-hides unit, 18, 72, 84 f., 98
Fleury-sur-Loire, 62, 185, 201, 236
folkland, 154
folk-moot, 81, 137 f.
forcible entry into houses, 51, 80, 84, 98, 139
foreign craftsmen, 50, 66, 70, 225, 227, 234
foreigners: harbouring of, 122; inheritance after, 64, 114
foreign masons, 16, 161, 225
foreign scholars, 62, 184 f., 201 f., 215
foreign visitors, 58–63, 66
forfeiture, 51, 64, 81 f., 87, 143, 149, 152, 154
fortress building, 64, 75 f., 85
fox-hunting, 91, 172
Frankish influence, 66, 215, 232, 235
Frisian merchants, 120, 124
Frisians, 60, 70, 111, 177, 179 f., 231
furniture, 89 f., 152
Fursey, St, 16, 159, 198

Gebur, 98, 100, 102
geburland, 98
geneat, 98 f., 102
gesith, 29, 83 f., 94
gilds, 46, 132, 175
Glastonbury, 111, 117, 170, 181, 200, 229, 234, 240
Godwine, Earl, 80, 87, 131, 176
Golden Gospels of Stockholm, 232
goldsmiths, 105 f., 133, 208
Greek, 162, 190 f., 192, 222
Gregory the Great, 24, 119, etc.; *Dialogues* of, 215; life of, 194; *Pastoral Care* of, 191, 215, 234, 242
Grim's Ditches, 22
Guthlac, St, 25, 170, 241; life of, 197, 203, 220; poem on, 172, 210

Guthrum, King, 60, 122

Hadrian, Abbot, 162, 190 f.
harbouring of outlaws, 46, 50, 84, 123, 139 f.
Harold, Cnut's son, King, 54
Harold, Earl, 88
Harold Fairhaired of Norway, 62
Harthacnut, King, 52, 54, 69
haw, *see* town-houses
hawking, 65 f., 91 f., 105, 208
hearg, 23
heathen burial customs, 26, 49, 88, 205
heathen religion, 19–28, 48, 138, 156 f., 162, 182 f., 187, 203–5, 223 f.
heriot, 35 f., 97
Hertford, synod of, 149, 162 f.
Hexham, 164, 169, 180, 225 f., 230, 240
hide, 68, 71, 73, 76, 84, 97 f., 140 f., 167
Honorius, Archbishop, 158
horse-racing, 92
hospitality, duty of, 56, 62, 79
hostages, 32, 34, 123
house-carls, 57 f., 69 f., 73
hundred, 24, 69, 71, 116, 123, 137–9, 167
hunting, 91, 103, 208; duties of, 65, 85, 91, 99
huntsmen, 65, 91, 105
Hwætberht, Abbot, 193
Hwicce, 8
Hygeburh, nun of Heidenheim, 197

Icanho, 169 f.
illuminated MSS, 192, 223, 225–7, 232–8, 242; export of, 231 f., 236; import of, 232, 234
incest, 145, 148
Ine, King of Wessex, 50, 172; laws of, 103, 122 f., 134 f., 139, 151, 166, 219
inheritance, 64, 100, 114, 148–54
Irish Church, 158–62, 169 f., 189
iron industry, 116 f.
ivories, 223, 228, 231, 236, 238, 241

James the Deacon, 157, 159
Jarrow, 36, 170, 180, 190, 192, 226, 231
Jellinge style, 237
jewellery, 95 f., 118, 224 f.
John of Beverley, St, 94
John the Old Saxon, 215
jurisdiction, private, 61, 122, 128, 139, 145
Jutes, 11 f., 13, 19

Kenneth, King of Scotland, 56, 60
Kent, 8 f., 13 f., *et passim*; Kings of, Eadbald, Eadberht, Egbert, Ethelbert, Wihtred; laws of, 83, 123, 145, 150 f.
kindred, 37–47, 94, 111 f., 145, 149–53, 173
king, deposition of, 53; election of, 53–5
king's council, 54–6, 136, 153 f., 157, 186
king's farm, 64, 68, 80, 154
king's peace, 51 f., 56, 139, 145, 151
king's priests, 54, 58, 65
king's reeve, *see* reeves
king's writ, 65, 81 f., 139, 168
knights' gild, 132

Lǽt, 97
land, grants of, 30, 34, 76, etc.; held by title-deed, 85, 153 f.; lease of, 100, 149; services on, 92
Latin scholarship, 172, 200, 219
Laurentius, Archbishop, 150
law, courts of, 137–9, 145; districts of, 136; promulgation of, 137
lawmen, 147
lead-mining, 117
Leofgyth, St, 171, 178; life of, 198
Leofric, Earl, 78, 80
libraries, 191–3, 200
Lichfield, 113, 164, 232 f.
Lincoln, 15, 130–1, 136, 147, 157, 165, 181

Lindisfarne, 164, 169, etc.; bishops of, Aidan, Cuthbert; gospels of, 192, 227, 242
Lindsey, 157, 164, 170, 180, 182, 194
London, 8, 15, *et passim*; bishops of, Mellitus, Theodred; bridge at, 144; councils at, 55, 194; St Pauls at, 72
Lothian, 60
Louis, Emperor, 198
Lul, St, 179, 197, 225, 231 f.

Magonsǽte, 8, 171
Maldon, poem on battle of, 34 f., 87, 213
manumission, 82, 86, 94, 107, 112–14
maritime guard, 65, 85
marriage, 42, 45, 59–61, 111 f. 145, 148–53, 162, 183; of clergy, 168, 184, 186
Mayo, English see in, 160
Mellitus, Bishop, 156
merchants, 63, 86, 105, 119, 124 f.; *see also* traders
Mercia, 8 f., 49, *et passim*; ealdormen of, Ælfgar, Ælfhere, Edwin, Leofric; Kings of, Æthelbald, Beorhtwulf, Burgred, Cenred, Ceolred, Ceolwulf, Ethelred, Offa, Penda, Wulfhere; law of, 50, 136
Mercian Register, 21
Middle Angles, 8, 164
minsters, 165 f., 182, 239
minstrelry, 59, 91, 107, 204 f., 209
mints, 82, 120 f., 129 f.
missions: to the continent, 12, 158, 171, 173, 177–80, 187, 192, 197, 209, 230–2, 235, 243; to Scandinavia, 187 f., 243
monasteries, 43, 62, 161, 169–73, 178–81, 184 f., 199, 232; double –, 169 f.; Irish –, 161; private ownership of, 171 f.; reform of, 8, 62, 173, 184 f., 201–3, 217, 219, 234; spurious –, 172 f.

money, purchasing power of, 9, 96, 146
moneyers, 129, 133
Monkwearmouth, 36, 170, 190, 193, 221, 226
Morcar, Earl, 87
morning-gift, 152
murder, 33, 41, 52, 143, 176
mutilation, 143 f.

Northumbria, 7 f., 18, *et passim;* Earls of, Aldred, Morcar, Uhtred, Waltheof; Kings of, Aldfrith, Alhred, Ceolwulf, Eadberht, Eardwulf, Ecgfrith, Edwin, Ethelred, Oswald, Oswiu, Oswulf
Norwich, 66, 128, 130 f.

Oath-helpers, 41, 46, 140 f., 148
oaths, 27, 33, 41, 46, 50, 53, 84, 86, 140 f., 145, 147–9; expressed in hides, 140 f.; in shillings, 141; preliminary – , 140
occupations, 90–5, 132 f.
Oda, Archbishop, 185, 200
Offa, King of the Angles, 48
Offa, King of Essex, 173
Offa, King of Mercia, 31, 48 f., etc.; dyke of, 75
Oftfor, Bishop, 174
Ohthere, voyage of, 13, 59, 63
ordeal, 142 f., 147
Orosius, 59, 191, 215–17
Oswald, Archbishop, 184 f., 201, 239, 241 f.; life of, 201
Oswald, King of Northumbria, 31, 158 f.
Oswiu, King of Northumbria, 36, 68, 159 f., 162, 173
Oswulf, King of Northumbria, 33
outlawry, 46, 140, 149
outlaws, harbouring of, 46, 50, 84, 159 f.
overlordship, 48 f., 55, 59–61, 156, 159, 163
oxen, price of, 9, 51, 96, 100 f., 103, 108

Oxford, 73, 75, 82, 127, 128–31, 187

Parish churches, 164–7
Paulinus, St, 157, 163
Pehtred, book by, 198, 214
penal slavery, 112 f., 144
Penda, King of Mercia, 69, 120, 173
penny, 9, 84, 120
perjury, 141, 145
Peterborough, 170, 185, 218, 239
pilgrimage, 44, 62, 123, 160, 173 f., 176 f., 197, 230
Pippin, King of the Franks, 59, 231
Plegmund, Archbishop, 215
ploughland, 68, 97
poetry, 12, 17 f., *et passim;* aristocratic interest in, 205 f.; diction and metre of, 206–8; MSS. of, 213; nature in, 210 f.
pound, value of the, 9, 75, 108
precious objects, 17, 49, 61, *et passim;* export of, 231; import of, 129, 225–32, 234
prison, 81, 132, 141 f.
prose, vernacular 214–22
protection, breach of, 51, 80, 84, 145

Queen, income of, 67

Rædwald, King of East Anglia, 24, 33, 156
radcniht, 99, 102
Ramsey Abbey, 185, 201, 236, 239
Reculver, 16, 121, 169, 232
reeves, 52, 76, 81 f., etc.; king's – , 64, 80–2, etc.; *see also* town-reeve, sheriff
relics, 58, 61 f., 113, 145, 147
Rhineland, 13, 118, 239 f.
riddles, 111, 193 f., 210
Ringerike style, 238
Rochester, 77, 120 f., 126, 137, 156, 163, 189, 194
Roman Britain, 11–19, 125, 162, 165, 228

Roman Church, usages of, 159–62

Roman influence, 13, 17, 134, 153, 190, 228

Rome, 120, 123 f., 162, 194, 225 f., 241; appeal to, 163, 177; English 'School' at, 175; missionaries from, 155 f., 159, 178; *see also* pilgrimage

Romsey rood, 236

Rothbury cross, 231

royal estates, 64, 67, 80, 145, 165

royal officials, 67, 77–82, 139; *see also* ealdorman, earl, reeve, sheriff

runes, 20, 25

Ruthwell cross, 210, 228 f.

Salt, 115 f.

Saxons, 11–13, 19, 78

Saxons, Old or Continental, 12, 48, 177–9, 215; poetry of, 209, 212

Scandinavian influence, 7, 44, 60, 77, 150 f., 229, 237 f.

Scandinavian law, 135, 147

Scandinavian literature, 19, 57

Scandinavian religion, 20–3, 26

schools, 164, 180–91, 196–8, 200–2

sculpture, 17, 227 f., 233 f., 236–8

sculptured crosses, 223, 228–30, 233, 237 f., 241

Selsey, 135, 164

sheep, price of, 9, 96, 100, 146

Sherborne, Dorset, 111, 115, 164

sheriff, 65, 80 f., 106

shilling, value of, 9, 51, 77, 83 f., 97

ships, 62, 69–72, 81, 85 f., 120–2

shipwreck, 121, 125, 175

shire, 78–80

shire-moot, 63, 81, 137–9

Sigeberht, King of East Anglia, 173, 189

Sigeberht, King of Essex, 42

Siric, Archbishop, 175

slaves, 18, 82, 86, 94, 96 f., 99, 101 f., 106, 108–14, 119–21, 144, 167

slave-trade, 111 f., 119 f., 122

smiths, 106, 117

soulscot, 166 f.

Stamford, 136, 147

stepmother, marriage with, 150

stone-quarrying, 117

Streonwald, 35

sulungs, 68

Sunday observance, 121, 198 f.

Sussex, 8, 22 f., 51, etc.

Sutton Hoo, 49, 241

Swein Forkbeard, King, 69, 187

Tacitus, 19 f., 22 f., 27, 29 f., 34, 40, 57, 151, 204

tapestry, 49, 88 f., 223

Tatwine, Archbishop, 193 f.

thanes, 36 f., 43, *et passim*; twelve leading thanes, 148; gild of, 46

theft, 41, 82, 107, 122, 124, 131–4, 141–9, 152

Theodore, Archbishop, 43, 162–4, 167, 169, 190–2, 196; penitential of, 37, 42, 111 f., 149 f., 196

Theodred, Bishop, 175, 181 f.

three public charges, the, 64 f., 75, 77, 85

tithe, 166 f.

tithing, 46

title-deeds, 85, 148, 153 f.

tolls, 64, 82, 108, 116, 121 f., 123 f., 168

Tostig, Earl, 175, 236 f.

town-houses, 88, 126, 128–9

town-reeve, 81 f.

towns, 81 f., 122, 126–33; *see also* boroughs

trade, 13, 63, 81 f., 108, 111, 115–26, 128 f.

traders, 81 f., 118–25, 192; *see also* merchants

treachery to a lord, 30, 33, 38, 50, 53, 143

treasure-giving, 29–31, 35 f., 93

treasury, 58, 66

Uhtred, Earl, 44, 89

Ulfcytel of East Anglia, 35

Ultan, illuminator, 230

Utrecht Psalter, 236

Vengeance, 31–3, 36–43, 45–7, 51, 125, 140, 146, 205
Vespasian Psalter, 232
Viking raid', 7 f., 75, *et passim*
vouching to warranty, 108, 146

Waltheof, Earl, 45
Wansdyke, 22
Wapentake, 137, 147
Watling Street, 180
weapon-smith, 21, 106, 117, 224
Welsh, 8, 18, 32, etc.; 'Welsh expedition', 65
weoh, 23
Werferth, Bishop, 215 f., 220, 252; Gregory's *Dialogues* translated by, 220
wergild, 39–47, 50f., 75, 80, 83–6, 97 f., 108, 112, 114, 143, 151
Wessex, 8 f., 49 f., *et passim;* Kings of, Æthelbald, Æthelwulf, Alfred, Beorhtric, Caedwalla, Genwealh, Cynewulf, Egbert, Ine
Whitby, 107, 169, 171, 190, 194, 206; Synod at, 160, 190
Whithorn, Galloway, 164, 180
widows, 150–2
Wihtred, King of Kent, 123, 134; laws of, 156
Wilfrid, St, 31 f., 90, 159, 163, 169 f., 175, 177, 192, 225 f., 229, 241; Life of, 194; Latin poem on, 200
Willehad, St, 180
William of Malmesbury, 107, 120, 192, 229
Willibald, St, 173; Life of, 197, 228

Willibrord, St, 171, 177; Calendar of, 242; Life of, 196 f.
Winchester, 55, 67, 81, etc.; bishops of, Athelwold, Daniel, Swithin; Newminster (Hyde Abbey) at, 184; Old Minister at, 90, 129
'Winchester School' of art, 234, 236 f.
Winton Domesday, 133
witchcraft, 23, 41, 143
witnesses, 82, 108, 122, 129, 139, 143, 146
women: education of, 192, 198, 201, occupations of, 93 f., 96, 106; position of, 45, 87, 93–5, 150–3
wool, 118 f., 121
Worcester, 65, 69, 75, etc.; bishops of, Oftfor, Oswald, Werferth, Wulfstan
Wulfhere, King of Mercia, 49
Wulfric Spott, 86, 185
Wulfrun, foundress of Wolverhampton, 241
Wulfsige, Bishop of Sherborne, 186
Wulfstan, Archbishop of York, 38, 53, 99, etc.
Wulfstan, St, Bishop of Worcester, 45, 112; Life of, 239
Wulfstan, precentor, 202
Wulfstan, traveller to the Baltic, 59, 124
Wynnebald, St, 173, 178; Life of, 197

Yeavering, 88
York, 15, 24, 52 *et passim;* (Arch)bishops of, Ealdred, Egbert, Ethelbert, John, Oswald, Paulinus, Wilfrid, Wulfstan